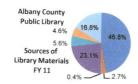

Sendero Gringo

Sendero Gringo

(Gringo Trail)

James Lannan

Library of Congress Control Number: 2011962239
ISBN: Hardcover   978-1-4691-3382-9
                   Softcover   978-1-4691-3381-2
                   Ebook   978-1-4691-3383-6

Cover illustration by Eumir Carlo Fernandez
Author photo by Nate Lannan

This book was printed in the United States of America.

To order additional copies of this book, contact:
Xlibris Corporation
1-888-795-4274
www.Xlibris.com
Orders@Xlibris.com
108437

To loves unrequited and exploits past

.

Pronto pronto

(Pretty Soon)

An incoming tide brought five-foot swells that leapt skyward when they hit backwash from shore. The waves tumbled into a white froth then heaved twice more before sliding up the grainy carpet of the beach. Between the roaring birth and hissing demise of one such rank, Albert Sharp rolled a cigarette, struck a match, and ducked his head to shield the flame from a chill wind that blew in off the brine.

Some distance up the beach, diminutive figures barely visible in afternoon haze cast their nets among troughs between the waves. A three-member pelican wing glided above the turbulence. Where Albert came from, there would have been no pelicans or fishermen to mark the winter day, and the gray overcast would have smelled of snow and ice rather than salt and seaweed.

He guessed an hour had passed since he'd plopped down on the sand, wedged a copy of *El Comercio* under his bootheel, and gazed out upon the horizon. He could have checked his pocket watch to be certain, but he forced himself to finish smoking first. In four and a half days, he'd be on a flight headed north. There was no one expecting him at home, no job he had to get back to, no business interests that required his attention; but once he'd decided to wrap up the South American trip, time had put on the brakes.

Albert snuffed his cigarette in the sand, split the butt end with his thumbnail, and consigned the tobacco remnants to the wind. There was nothing to do afterward but consult the dreaded timepiece.

Surprisingly, an hour and twenty minutes had gone by since he'd last looked. Twenty bonus minutes had been awarded him in recognition of his patience.

He got to his feet, slapped sand off the newspaper, carefully rerolled it, and tucked it into his hip pocket. Took fifteen seconds maybe. Without wishing to, he counted his steps as he headed back toward town. At his tenth stride, he questioned what the spatial interval translated into clockwise. At least another quarter of a minute had gone by without notice, and he also hadn't noticed how long it took for him to make the calculation. No contradiction there at all. He wondered how long it would take for him to go stupid-crazy while he contrived to steal a march on time.

Ocean waves to his right continued to form long, uncouth ranks that charged to shore like a hoard of suicidal rats. To calm the scene, Sharp recalled what the Pacific shore looked like from the window of a commercial jet. From high above, ocean surf appeared unmoving. Maybe that meant time lost its power to agitate all and sundry the farther you got away from it. If so, what he needed to do right now was get away from time for the next four days.

Right.

Three hundred yards up the beach lay a dead sea lion that had been rotting above the tide line for the past two days. Pink gouges scarred its coarse brown hide, side flippers were wedged under the thousand-pound inert bulk, the dead female's split tail lay flattened on sand behind swollen genitals. It seemed to Albert that instead of being left to rot on the beach with eyes bulging out of its head and tongue curled under its chin, the carcass ought to be disposed of. A turkey buzzard perched on the dead creature's back spread ratty wings and lumbered into the air as he approached. Sharp walked quickly past the decomposing mass, regretting that he'd disturbed the vulture's attempt to speed up nature's reclamation project.

On the far side of the sidewalk that led into Huanchaco ran a dirt road that met pavement as it reached town. Hostels, hotels, and restaurants lined the road; a couple of disco joints and a few residences were located also in the mix. The beachfront buildings, most no higher than two stories, were constructed of brick and stucco with many walls left unpainted and roofs unfinished. Large red blossoms grew in raised concrete beds for a short stretch above the beach, a few trees survived within village environs, and fields of reed plants cultivated for construction of banana-shaped *caballitos* had been planted well above the shoreline. On the flat top of a hillock at the backside of the pueblo loomed a behemoth church with an arched roof, suggesting more of a disaster refuge than a worship hall. On the left side of the church extended the concrete wall of a cemetery wherein family crypts, iron fences, and wooden crosses sprawled across a dirt and gravel yard. This gray time of year, the whole village had a drab and damaged look.

Sharp slogged across loose sand to the sidewalk. He planned to continue past the town's municipal building and mount a pier that jutted a hundred yards out into the sea from the midpoint along the front edge of the village. Last Sunday, the locals had celebrated the feast of Saint Peter with a procession and a boat race, and there had been quite a crowd gathered on the dock's wooden planks. Today was Wednesday though, and the platform was attended by no more than a handful of idlers as empty-headed and unmotivated as he was.

Near the pier, he heard someone call his name. Across the street, a man seated at a table in front of an open-air café waved at him. Albert had met Roger D. two weeks before in Huaras. Over lunch, they had caught up on sport and political news from gringo land.

"*¿Qué pasa? amigo,*" Albert said, as he shook the Englishman's hand. Peruvians hardly ever said "*¿Qué pasa?*" but Sharp's Spanish was of Mexican origin.

"Will you join us?" Roger D. asked.

Four other men were seated at the Brit's table, along with a woman who seemed to be partnered up with one of the guys. They ranged in ages from early twenties to mid-thirties, the woman and her friend being the oldest of the group. The youngest among them wore his blond hair in a buzz-cut that didn't suit him. He had small gray eyes and a hooknose and came off looking like a vagrant. Roger D. also wore his hair cropped close, but with his athletic build and sharp features, he affected dash. The Englishman had come to *Sudamerica* to climb Andes peaks, surf the coastlines of Peru and Ecuador, and hike in Patagonia.

"What ya got going, Roger D.?"

"We're having a drinking game."

Indeed. With half a dozen 600 ml beer bottles arrayed on their table, the group appeared outfitted for a lengthy competition.

"Too early for me."

"Come along, guv, have a seat."

"Naw, man, you guys would bury me."

"Where are you from?" the woman asked from across the table. She wore her brown hair jaw-length with an under flip. Accent possibly Dutch.

"Bet you can guess."

She smiled. "How long have you been traveling?"

"Better than ten months."

The woman nodded as though impressed. "How much longer do you plan to stay?"

"I'm flying out of Lima in four and a half days."

"Back to the USA?"

"Right on your first guess."

"Are you sad to be leaving?"

"Nope. I'm ready to pack it in."

"Really?"

"Really."

"I think I will be sad at the end of my holiday."

Albert smiled to be polite. "Some are like that," he said. "Some people never want to go home." It bothered him to be reminded how eager he was to bring an end to his trip. He felt guilty and inadequate, as though he'd squandered the past ten months of his life.

"Where have you been?"

"Started in Caracas, got down to Punta Arenas, and then as far north as Cuenca."

"Around the entire continent then."

"Almost," Albert agreed.

Roger D. broke in, which suited Sharp fine. He turned from the Dutch woman and listened as the Brit explained the rules of the game he was organizing. Each player, instead of a name, would identify himself with a gesture. To illustrate, the Brit demonstrated his own moniker. When called upon, he would stand, lift two fingers of his right hand, and say, "Hey, babe." After that, he would call upon another player, by means of his chosen gesture, who would then repeat the routine. Failure to perform a turn correctly would result in a penalty: two inches of beer down the hatch.

After the game commenced, Sharp hung by for a while. The seedy-looking kid was first to screw up, and then the Dutch woman botched her name. In about an hour, Albert reckoned, everyone seated at the table would be falling off his chair. Or her chair, as the case may be.

Before the players started slurring their words, Albert slipped off. He was on his way to the pier again when he spotted a couple of other people he knew. The two women sat on a bench alongside the walk near the municipal building. He angled in their direction.

Roger D. had introduced him the day before to the ladies. One was Swiss, the other Australian. The Swiss had a round, pretty face and thick, curly bright-red hair that blew every which way in the wind. Her body was of a pliant, pleasing shape. The Aussie was a strapping gal with rope-colored hair and rough-and-tumble outback features. He'd actually met the Aussie about a month before Roger D. had made introductions, but it wasn't surprising that she failed to recognize him from their first encounter. Her breasts had been bare back then and painted green.

The two women were engrossed in a conversation when he walked up, so rather than interrupt them, he sat down on the bench next the Swiss and waited to be acknowledged. He was attracted to the redhead in a shameful way; she had good looks and acted as if she'd just come from a carnival where she'd won a teddy bear. Because Nadine was so distinctly girlish, he took care not to let on how he felt about her. A fifty-year-old balding man moving among young women was advised to best keep romantic notions to himself. It required no effort on his part to hide his feelings about the Aussie though; they were guarded from the get-go.

"What do you think, Albert?" Martha asked without warning.

Sharp raised his eyes.

"About what?"

Nadine's ankles had distracted him. On the basis of the little skin exposed, he had been trying to imagine what Nadine's legs looked like when she shrugged out of her loose-fitting khaki slacks.

"About hiking to the ruins."

"You mean by way of the beach?"

"Right."

"Yeah," Albert said, "why not?" He wasn't sure what the Aussie was getting at.

"Two women were robbed in Cuzco last week," Nadine put in, and then he understood why his opinion was being sought.

11

"That's Cuzco," he said. "It's safer around here than in Cuzco." Nadine had blue eyes to go with her red hair and a complexion as inviting to the touch as a basket of flower petals. He liked it when she looked at him, not only for her eyes, but also for the scattered bits of halo hovering about the outer fringes of her hair.

"How long's it take to get to the ruins on foot?" Martha wanted to know.

"I'm not sure. I took a *colectivo* myself. But I've heard you can get to *Chan chan* in two hours by following the coastline."

"There's nothing out there but sand, is there?"

"Fishermen, a few huts, not much else. It'd be a nice walk."

"Over open country."

"Pretty much."

"So there'd be no place to run, say, if we met a robber."

"At least you'd see him coming."

Both women broke up when he said that. He hadn't intended to make a joke, but they seemed to think he'd let loose a real knee slapper.

"Do you imagine that I run faster than a man?" Nadine prodded. Again they were face to face.

"Faster than me, I'll bet," Albert answered, to amuse her further.

She threw her head back when she laughed, and not a single blemish was visible along the sweep of her pale skin from chin to bosom.

"She'd have to make a break for it every time a rotter approached," Martha put in, and by her tone accused him of taking lightly a serious matter.

"Probably better for her to take a *colectivo* then," he advised.

"It isn't fair," Martha countered.

"Right. Thieves are definitely unjust."

"I mean, it isn't fair that you can walk along the beach by yourself and Nadine can't."

"Sorry. Would you like me to escort you, Nadine?" He had little desire to see the ruins a second time, but the idea of hiking along the seashore with lovely Nadine at his side tempted him to reconsider.

Nadine drew breath, sufficiently large to lift and expand her chest and might have invited him to join her on the hike had not Martha intervened again.

"That's not the point."

"Right," Sharp said, careful to maintain a bland expression.

"They prey on women."

The Aussie ticked him off. He could have pointed out that men got mugged too, but decided there was nothing to be gained by adding fuel to Martha's smolder.

"A woman can't even walk through the market without some creep stalking her."

Albert wouldn't have uttered a word then, had the Aussie pointed a pistol at his head. In a way, she had trained a gun on him. One wrong word and, kerpow! There had been a time when he'd objected vehemently to veiled and not-so-veiled condemnation of his gender, but arguments that resulted usually ended with him getting blown away.

"Oh, it is such a pain," Nadine lamented. "That's what Americans say, such a pain?" She'd turned her sweet visage on him again, so what could he do but meet her eyes and nod sympathetically? "Last week, in Pisco," she went on, to illustrate her experience with creeps, "I was sitting by myself in the plaza—"

Martha cut her off. "Two women were raped on the road to Pisac last week." The Aussie had fired up a full head of indignation and was dead set on venting it. "As they were walking along the road out of Cuzco, a man pulled up on a moped and offered to give them a ride to the next site up the Sacred Valley. Naturally, he'd have to take them one at a time because there wasn't room for both of them on the bike. The first woman climbed on, the man drove a ways up the road, and then turned into the forest where he threw her down and raped her. Then he came back for the second woman."

For just a second, Sharp let down his guard. He thought the story apocryphal on the one hand and, on the other, could not at the moment imagine the alleged rapist dashing back and forth between his victims without recollecting also bumbling pratfalls by Keystone cops.

"What are you laughing at?" Martha demanded when she heard him giggle.

"Nothing," Sharp responded immediately, painfully aware that he'd screwed up. "Sorry," he quickly added and glanced in Nadine's direction, hoping to be forgiven for his indiscretion.

"How'd you like your daughter to be raped?" Martha demanded.

"I don't have a daughter," Sharp answered, though he knew this was no excuse for his insensitive behavior.

"The aboriginal people in my country know how to deal with rapists."

"How do they?" Nadine asked on cue.

"When they catch a rapist," Martha gladly informed her, "they split his penis in two with a knife. After that, the blighter will never commit rape again."

"Because he can't get it up anymore," Sharp put in, pretending to endorse Martha's right opinion.

"No, not that. Whenever he drops his pants in front of a woman, she'll know what he is. She'll see two halves of his wank waggling away down there." Martha laughed heartily then, and Nadine joined her, though at a lesser level of enthusiasm.

It occurred to Sharp that their derision was less righteous as they thought. Seemed to him the pair was at least partly wrong in celebrating misery willfully inflicted upon another human being.

As if she could read his mind, Martha clarified the moral principle that applied. "A rapist deserves to have his cock split in half."

Albert tittered again in spite of himself. He was picturing a sex fiend in possession of not one but two cranks to turn on. Martha glared at him.

No one spoke for about a minute. Sharp hoped that if the silence lasted long enough, their conversation would shift to a different topic.

"Would you like to come with us?" Nadine asked.

Tempting, and if it were just he and Nadine on the outing, he would have accepted the invitation gladly. But Martha had long since laid claim to the chippie. The Aussie had been a pain in the ass the first time he met her too.

"When?" he asked amiably and as if seriously considering the proposal.

"Soon. We must return before nightfall."

He almost smirked. Rapists lurking in the dark, you know. No telling what manner of boogeyman came out at night. Or what manner of rotter accompanied you into the obscurity. "Sorry," he said and pulled a long face. "Probably be better if you went without me."

"What other plans do you have?" Nadine pouted. He studied her expression for a moment and concluded she wasn't all that disappointed.

"I'd rather not say."

"Oh."

A couple minutes later, he bid the women farewell. One lucky aspect of being *en camino* was the opportunity to part company easily from someone you never wanted to see again. Not Nadine of course, but every benefit came with a drawback.

In his room at the hostel (small quarters but tidy and free of vermin), Albert retrieved a notebook from his travel bag and sat down on the single bed. Time to add the day's events to his journal. 23 July 00, Huanchaco. Out of place and stuck in time, he wrote, and then went on about little men standing in chill surf and casting nets among the waves. He described the dead sea lion lying on the beach. Roger D.'s drinking game figured into his account along with the discussion he'd had with Nadine and Martha concerning the plight of defenseless women. Then he composed a poem because he thought it'd take a while. This was what he came up with:

> Peal,
> nascent waves,
> wind-charged jumbled rank upon reeling rank
> stripped from riptide,
> launched to bejesus.
> Roar, mad curls risen,
> fallen,
> risen yet again.
> Beat into froth and smear upon
> mealy sand fore-slickened.
> Join the reaper's fest,
> ancient waves,
> sound an endless harvest knell.

After he wrote the final word of his entry, Albert closed his notebook. He forced himself not to peek at his watch, afraid that the little time he'd killed since leaving the beach would depress him. A block and a half down from the hostel, he ate dinner at a small restaurant where he knew the cook. Over beefsteak, eggs, and fried potatoes, he read about *futbol* in the sports section of *El Comercio*. The Peruvian national selection had fallen into turmoil because the team had recently lost crucial games against Brazil and Ecuador. Being a fan of Chile's national team himself, the articles questioning the courage of Peruvian players failed to alarm him.

After the waiter took away his plate, he ordered a second beer and perused articles concerning preparations for a national march organized by a man named Toledo who had pulled out of presidential elections the month before, charging fraud. The march was scheduled to begin the day after Sharp's plane left Lima, but activists from outlying districts planned to set out for the capital one to three days in advance. This information made Albert worry that the highway from Trujillo might be jammed the night he planned to board the bus to Lima.

He quit the restaurant in darkness. At a table just outside the door, half a dozen newcomers to town had settled and ordered drinks. Albert nodded politely to the group as he walked past. Last week he might have stopped for a chat, but last week he still considered himself a citizen of the traveler nation.

Across the road that fronted the beach, he turned left and angled toward the water. Children played near the waves, as they played every night at the edge of yellow glow cast from town. As his pace slowed, raucous phosphorescent heavings pounded the side of his head. The rhythmic blows soothed him; the smell of kelp and salty ocean put him at ease. Another day had come and gone; it'd soon be time for sleep.

But he was not alone. He sensed movement behind him, turned about, and beheld the figure of a man rendered dark and indistinct against the backlight. The man approached steadily, and Albert awaited his arrival.

"Dollars," said the man, when he pulled up. His tone was agitated, and he spoke at a volume above the crash of surf. Close up, Albert made out the fellow was not a man at all but a boy in his late teens. The kid clasped his hands together and raised them to the level of his head.

"Good evening," Albert answered cautiously in Spanish, knowing his response was inappropriate.

"Dollars," the boy repeated, no louder than before, but with an emphatic outthrust of his hands.

"I speak your language," Sharp said.

"Dollars" was all the boy had to say.

So Albert shook his head. "No."

The other hesitated for a moment, frozen in his awkward stance, unsure what to do next. Then he moved his doubled hands slightly toward the distant light. "I have a pistol."

"I see you have a pistol," Albert answered evenly. "The answer is still no."

"I will shoot you," said the boy, but he sounded unsure of himself.

"Why?"

"What?"

"Why will you shoot me?"

"Because you won't give me dollars."

"That's not a good reason."

"What?"

"You have no good reason to shoot me."

"I don't need a reason. I have a pistol."

"That makes no sense, and you know it."

"Shut up. Give me dollars."

"They're my dollars, not yours."

"I'm going to kill you."

"You already said that."

"You don't believe I will shoot you?"

"I don't believe you won't."

Again the interloper paused, presumably to ponder what he had just been told. Possibly Albert had made a mistake in grammar.

"That is to say, I don't believe you won't kill me. I don't believe you will kill me either. That is to say, I haven't formed an opinion on the matter."

"Stop talking," the boy demanded through clenched teeth.

"Very well."

Albert waited. The boy waited too, but he ran out of patience first.

"Give me dollars."

"No."

"Are you crazy?"

"No, I'm not crazy."

"Don't you want to live?"

"Yes, of course I want to live."

"Then give me dollars."

"No. The answer is still no."

"I'm going to shoot you and take your dollars."

Albert didn't answer. He surmised that spoken words under the circumstance accomplished nothing.

"What did you say?"

When Albert still didn't answer, the robber took one cautious step forward and thrust the pistol out farther from his chest. Then he took another step and another until the muzzle of the pistol stopped an inch in front of Albert's forehead. There it remained for several seconds. Sharp stared cross-eyed at the gun muzzle.

"Do you want to pray before I kill you?"

"Sure. I'll pray for your mother. She must be disappointed."

"Dollars will make my mother happy."

"Take me to your mama's house, and I will give her money."

"You are lying."

"Certainly I am lying."

The boy finally realized Albert wasn't going to give in. "Stick it to yourself," he said at last, dropped his arms, and thrust the pistol into the waistband of his trousers.

After blinking to refocus, Albert directed his gaze on the assailant. He had curly bangs that fell nearly to his eyebrows. His face was shaped like half an American football turned on end. He squinted at Albert and pursed his lips.

"Pig," the boy said and spat in the sand. Then he about-faced and began marching up the beach.

Albert watched him walk away. He kept his eye on the mugger as he slipped into a shadow, reemerged in light, shrunk in size, and finally disappeared around a distant building.

Turning back toward the waves, Albert felt empty and untouched by anything around him. He wondered why he'd been unafraid when the boy stuck a gun in his face and threatened to rub him out. What had possessed him to speak the way he had to the robber? Why did he not feel relieved to have survived the assault?

By and by, he set upon the path the boy had taken. To what purpose, he couldn't say. He wondered how many minutes had elapsed since the boy's departure. Was it okay now to check his watch?

Flor y fuego

(Flower and Fire)

A Mozart recording played softly from the open doorway of the hostel's tiny kitchen while Reynaldo washed his clothes by hand in a sequestered corner of the garden. Now and then, he heard the maids exchange comments as they tidied rooms. His own voice joined timidly with the general rumor of fruit and flower and with blue sky shining through abundant foliage. When he became engrossed yet again in remonstrations with his former spouse, other murmurs regressed.

"What's that?"

He stopped rubbing soiled trousers against the corrugated concrete of the *lavadora* board and turned his head slowly toward the speaker.

"Hey, Ian, you're back," he answered, glad to see his friend again. On the other hand, the Scot could have shown up at a more opportune time.

"You were talking to yourself."

"No, I was chatting with Dorotea," Reynaldo said and pretended to search the immediate area for the maid. "Where'd she get off to?"

"You were alone," Ian had the temerity to insist.

The Scot was one of those *fulanos* who never engaged in soliloquy, or if he did, never got caught at it. He was a fit young man with alert blue eyes, a rough complexion, and laid-back ears. A three-day growth of whiskers ruddied his chin and jaw just now, making him appear somewhat the worst for wear.

"So?"

"Where I come from, only deranged people talk to themselves."

"You're a long way from home," Reynaldo countered.

His friend lifted the brim of a battered straw hat off his brow with the tip of his walking stick. Reynaldo could smell the sweat on Ian's shirtfront, a musty odor only slightly less pungent than soapsuds. He could smell the sweet perfume of limes and oranges that hung from trees throughout the garden too. Tattered banana leaves drooped across the short dirt path Ian had followed into the laundry nook. He had come from the central open rectangle of the hostel where most the flowers grew: poinsettias, roses, lilies, and other varieties of bloom Reynaldo had never seen before arriving in Ecuador.

"So what were you talking about with Dorotea?"

"When you walked up?"

"No, when I fell out of a tree."

"I was listing the many errors I have committed during my misspent life."

"Sounded like a man with a guilty conscience. What'd you do, commit murder?"

"Hardly. I've never done anything worse than screw myself over."

"I'll still feel sorry for you, if you like."

"No need. There's no one better to screw over than the one doing the screwing."

"You lost me."

"That's why I was talking to myself."

Reynaldo dropped fairly clean trousers into the blue plastic bucket of rinse water he'd set on a knee-high shelf next the stone sink. Ian stepped back to avoid being splashed.

"How was the hike?" Reynaldo asked to change the subject.

His friend answered with a slump of his shoulders. "A lot more work than I thought it'd be."

"Where'd you go?"

"We followed the river trail more or less, but I couldn't say where we camped. The girls wanted to tramp through brush and raid cornfields."

"You guys start the fire?"

This morning, when he'd stepped into the street outside his digs, Reynaldo had been surprised to discover conflagration on a mountain just outside town. He'd been alarmed by the runaway blaze, but few of the locals had seemed all that concerned about it.

Ian laughed at his accusation. "I've got an alibi. How about you?"

"Yeah, right. Man goes off into the forest with a couple of robust Israeli women, and when he returns, the trees are on fire. What am I supposed to think?"

"That maybe those two started the fire. I couldn't keep my eye on them all the time."

"Or off them most the time."

Ian snorted to show what he thought of Reynaldo's innuendo. "Next time, you go with them."

"What makes you think they'd have me?"

"What makes you think they had me?"

"Are you being honest?"

"No chance they'd ever sleep with me."

"And yet you slept with them."

"I did not."

"Well, where did you sleep if not with them?"

"You know what I mean."

"I'm going to rat on you to your Brazilian sweetheart."

This is in reference to a woman the Scot had met in Manaus a couple of months before. By Ian's account, the two had fallen in love and pledged themselves to one another. In that Ian journeyed now in Ecuador while his intended remained behind in Brazil, Reynaldo judged their arrangement farfetched.

"She's going to be upset I haven't called her for the past three days," Ian said and heaved a sigh.

Reynaldo went to work on a T-shirt. "No wonder."

"I don't know what else I can say to convince her she has nothing to worry about."

"Those phone calls cost what, a dollar a minute? True love if ever there was."

"Too bad she doesn't think so."

"Maybe it's the language barrier."

"We manage to communicate all right."

"Then how can there be any misunderstanding?"

"It's because she lives in South America that she can't understand my dream. I've wanted to explore the continent all my life."

"Could take the rest of your life to complete the trek," Reynaldo observed tongue-in-cheek. He suspected the Scot's true love feared the geography of South America might give a man cause to procrastinate indefinitely.

"I'll marry her when the time is right," Ian said.

"Go ahead. But never say I didn't warn you."

"Not all marriages end in divorce, you know."

"So I've been told, so maybe it's true. Still, you should be grateful for the preview I'm giving of your next dream."

Ian had a sudden inspiration. "Is divorce what you were talking to yourself about?"

"Man, you look like you could use a nap."

"If I leave, will you start talking to yourself again?"

"I haven't decided."

Ian watched Reynaldo rinse his clothes. He hung a pair of trousers, three shirts, and three changes of underwear on a nylon line that stretched between the trunks of a couple of trees that grew behind the *lavadora*. To signal completion of the laundry chore, Reynaldo buttoned a wrinkled khaki shirt over his flabby midsection.

"Will your girls be joining us for cocktails?"

"They're at the spa," Ian answered. "Michelle said they needed a massage."

"Vilcabamba suits them."

"Naturally. Haven't you heard that people around here live to be a hundred?"

"Good God. I'm leaving as soon as my clothes are dry."

Ian went to clean up in one of the hostel's communal showers, and Reynaldo returned to his room. A single bed, a small desk, and a chair summed up the furniture inside. Dim yellow light entered the room through a lowered bamboo window shade. At night, the bare bulb hanging from the ceiling at the end of a twisted pair of wires provided harsher illumination.

He'd traded with an *Aleman* he'd met in Peru for a survey copy of the pre-Socratics. The deal had cost him Camus's story of *The Plague*, which at the time struck him as an unbalanced exchange, but then he'd started to read cryptic fragments of Heraclitean philosophy and found the principle of eternal strife encouraging. The famous aphorism about the impossibility of stepping twice into the same river currently caught his attention. Bemusedly, he pictured the old

Greek standing on a riverbank watching green water flow by and listening to a gurgling echo. In Reynaldo's fantasy, when Heraclitus lowered his robe and attempted to enter the stream, the river shied away from his wrinkled body.

Setting the book aside for the moment, he leaned back on the headrest of his bed and closed his eyes. As he knew would happen, the vision of another nude materialized. The second naked form was more alluring, one the river took to itself and caressed. What motivating *nalgas* the nymph displayed and what admirable palm-sized *tetas* she had. Reynaldo wondered if he'd ever again make it through a day without obsessing about the woman who had ceased to be his wife.

A knock on the door sundered his reverie. He jumped up fumbling with his zipper.

"*¿Quién está?*"

"We're going for a beer, mate. Would you care to join us?"

Opening the door, he found Martha the Australian and Mary the Englishwoman standing just outside. Martha was a thick woman with mannish features; wide-hipped Mary had the plain round face of a schoolmarm. The Aussie was prone to pouty moods, the Brit kept an even keel.

"Sure," Reynaldo said. "Let me grab my hat."

"That's new," Mary observed once he stood on the tiled walkway outside his room.

"Thanks for noticing. I bought it factory-direct on my run to Cuenca. Genuine Panama."

"Except this isn't Panama," Martha pointed out.

"It's a little known fact that Panama hats are woven in Ecuador and Colombia. Lord knows why they're called Panama hats."

"That's interesting," Mary said.

Martha harrumphed.

Reynaldo followed the girls outside the hostel and across the street to a *tienda* next to an adventure shop. Besides renting horses and booking camping trips, travelers could log onto the Internet at the shop.

The *tienda* entrance was situated beneath a second-story wooden balcony. Inside the cramped store were stocked bagged, boxed, canned, and plastic-wrapped *alimentos*, all manners of household necessities and, more to the point, large bottles of cold beer. Foreign customers were encouraged to serve themselves from the cooler tucked beneath a rack of shelves in the back.

After making their purchases, the trio returned to the hostel's large porch. The girls settled in a pair of wicker chairs beneath the overhang, and Reynaldo sat down on the stoop. He cocked a leg on a lower step in order to face the women.

"Do you think it will reach us?" Mary asked, worried about the blaze on the mountain. A cloud of smoke hung above the fire, and they could hear the sporadic crackle of flames.

"Not bloody likely," Martha said.

"Why not?"

"It's on the other side of the river."

Without looking at the Aussie, Mary pondered the pertinent geographical feature pointed out to her. "I imagine you're right," she admitted.

Reynaldo suspected it wouldn't be long before these two parted ways. They bickered a good deal and seemed to share little common interest. Mary was a vegetarian; Martha ate her steak rare. The Brit hung around the garden most days while her partner tramped about the countryside.

"Here comes that man," Mary said.

"Bloody rotter," Martha scoffed.

The fellow mentioned approached astride a horse from the direction of the fire. His mount's hooves clomped upon bricks that paved the road leading by the hostel. The horse was short of stature and had a gait that seemed awkward to Reynaldo. Rich, the man on the horse, had explained to him previously that an outward flip in stride was characteristic of the Peruvian breed and made for a smooth ride. With sunken cheeks, heavy eyebrows, and stalky frame, Rich reminded Reynaldo of Chester on *Gunsmoke*. Seemed to him that the man was slated to be somebody's sidekick.

During the same conversation whereby Rich had instructed him about horses, he'd also given a garrulous rundown on his history. He'd come to Ecuador seventeen years before from New Zealand, married a Vilcabamba woman, and fathered a son by her. For a while, he'd worked for a local rancher, then as a tour guide, and finally started his own guide business. Rich was proud of the fact that over the years, he had become a pretty good drunk.

"I just came from the fire," Rich said when he pulled up before the trio on the porch. He expected the tourists to be impressed by his scouting expedition.

"How'd it start?" Reynaldo asked, truly interested.

"Pablo was burning brush, and the fire got away from him." Rich had a habit of dropping local names to demonstrate his long establish residence in the area. "If the flames reach Pablo's cornfield, they'll really take off." The rider's basso voice grated. Rich always sounded as if he had an ax to grind.

"Too late. Looks to me like the fire has already taken off." This appraisal came from Martha.

"It'll be out by nightfall," Rich patronized. "Enrique and his cousins are up there helping Pablo snuff the blaze. Their cane field's on the other side of the hill."

"How they fighting it?" Reynaldo wished to know. In the States, someone would have phoned the fire department by now.

"They beat the flames out with tree branches."

"Why aren't you helping fight the fire?" Martha asked pointedly.

"Why aren't you?" Rich countered as he dismounted.

"I'm having a beer," Martha said as if he had no right to ask.

The New Zealander tied his horse to one of the square pillars that supported the porch's overhang. "So am I," he said then turned and crossed the street to the *tienda*.

"Bloody rotter," Martha iterated when he'd gone.

"I think he's rather dashing," Mary opined.

"I think so too."

Ian had come out of the hostel in time to add his jovial comment to the conversation. Two other guests accompanied him. Jan, the livelier of the pair, was a tall blonde with blue eyes, a long thin nose, and muscular forearms. Jon, her husband, had a fleshy build and an affable demeanor. He was a practical, accepting sort who didn't speak unless he had something worthwhile to say.

The Swedish couple had brought chairs with them and placed them now at the side of the door opposite Martha and Mary. Ian parked himself on the stoop next to Reynaldo. His light-red hair was still damp from a shower.

"*Dashing* is the last word I'd use to describe that arrogant no-account," Martha said. "Unless the law was after him. What do you think, Reynaldo? That's not your real name, is it?"

Ian chuckled. Just now, in the late afternoon, his freshly shaven face assured Reynaldo that all was right with the world.

"No, but I've gone native, don't you see? And as for Rich, he's okay, though I will admit he comes off as a somewhat seedy fucker."

"Seedy fucker," Jan squealed, pronouncing the phrase oddly. "I've just learned a new American expression."

It occurred to Reynaldo that she'd misheard what he'd said. "Not *CD* like the music discs," he corrected Jan pleasantly. "*Seedy*, like what vegetables in your garden become if you don't harvest them in time."

"CD fucker," Jan repeated the phrase in the way she'd pronounced it the first time. "I'm going to say CD fucker from now on."

Reynaldo and Ian glanced at each other and grinned.

"Here he comes again," Mary said.

The CD fucker stepped from the *tienda* with a bottle of beer in his fist. Jan put a hand to her mouth in an attempt to stifle a giggle. Rich failed to notice. He leaned nonchalantly against the pillar his horse was tied to on the far side of Ian. Then he shifted his brown felt cowboy hat to the back of his head so that the front brim would not interfere with his drinking.

"Ah, that tastes good," he said when he lowered the amber bottle from his lips. "I've already drunk a bottle of gin today."

"A bottle of gin, huh," Reynaldo commented as if there were a good reason for Rich to inform the company about his rate of alcohol consumption.

"If I were a drunk, I wouldn't brag about it," Martha said.

"Too bad," Rich answered, toasting her. "You'll never be famous."

Martha muttered something only Mary could hear. The Brit frowned at her and then shifted her gaze to Rich. She smiled at him meekly.

"Do you know where I could buy CDs in this town?" Jan asked as innocently as you please.

Reynaldo rolled his eyes.

"Not here," Rich answered. "Loja maybe, but I don't know. I never buy CDs."

"That's funny," Jan told him. "You look like the CD type."

Rich shrugged disdainfully and took another pull on his beer. Then, in surveying the constricted expressions on the faces around him, he caught on that he was being made an object of ridicule.

"I came to South America to get away from modern technology," Ian put in, and Reynaldo was grateful for his friend's attempt to save the tour guide embarrassment. He was ashamed of himself for what he'd said about the New Zealander before.

Unfortunately, Rich wasn't of a mind to be mollified. He was confused by the conspiracy directed against him and, as often happens with a man put upon, lashed out at the first target that caught his attention. In this case, the recipient of his ire happened to be the very fellow who had expressed sympathy for his cause.

"What else you running from?" he challenged the Scot to make clear in the first place that he did not appreciate tongues wagging behind his back and, in the second, that he accepted no man's pity.

"I didn't say I was running from anything," Ian answered brightly. "I'm following a dream."

"That Brazilian *señorita* part of your dream?"

"I'm going to marry her when the time is right."

"Sure you will."

"Yes, I will," Ian asserted.

The group on the porch sensed mounting unease. Reynaldo regretted again calling Rich a seedy fucker; he had done so merely to placate Martha. Neither had Jan intended harm in poking fun at Rich, but her joke had fallen flat.

"What the heck, let's be friends," Reynaldo suggested to clear the air.

"I don't make friends with liars," Rich returned darkly.

"Who you calling a liar?" Ian demanded, hackles rising.

The horseman jerked himself off the pillar and stepped up to the Scot. Ah hell, Reynaldo thought and hung his head.

"How about the deal we made?" Rich growled.

"There was no deal, and you know it."

"We had a deal."

"No, we didn't."

"What happened out there between you and those Israeli girls? I'll bet your *señorita* would like to know."

"Leave her out of this," Ian said, reddening. He placed his hands carefully on his knees, preparing to get up quickly if need be.

"She should know you're a liar," Rich mouthed at a low volume as he bent over the Scot.

Ian gave not an inch. "I didn't rent from you because you don't own any horses. If I wanted a tour, I'd make a deal with the *señor* you rent from yourself. Cheaper that way."

Without warning, Rich lashed out. He struck Ian on the jaw with a blow that sounded more like a slap than a punch. Ian lurched forward and drove his shoulder into Rich's midsection. Both men fell to the paving stones. Ian ended up on top of the New Zealander with his arms wrapped around the man's hips. The back of the New Zealander's head struck the fitted bricks in the street when he went down, and his hat lifted off his crown. The beer bottle he'd been holding shattered.

Jon charged off the porch and straddled the pair. He clutched the back of Ian's shirt with both hands and attempted to pull the man off his adversary. Because Ian wouldn't let go of Rich, Jon ended up lifting both men a foot off the ground. Then he lost his grip and fell over backward. When the scufflers dropped to the ground again, Ian's forehead thunked against Rich's chin, and the man's teeth clacked together.

Jon got back to his feet and took hold of one of the Scot's shoulders. "Could you help me?" he called to Reynaldo.

If Reynaldo hadn't responded, Martha, who by now was also off the porch, would have thrown her own self into the dustup. Luckily, he managed to intercept her before she reached the fray, or there was no telling what punishment she would have inflicted upon the New Zealander. He felt foolish, but what else could he do? Martha tried to shove him aside. He brushed her arms off him. She grabbed at his wrists, and then they started slapping their hands away from each other. When Mary approached to calm Martha down, the Aussie accidentally smacked her in the nose. Mary gave a startled cry and doubled over with splayed fingers covering her face. Martha quit thrashing as soon as she saw that her partner was hurt. Jan came off the porch to put her arm around Mary's shoulders. Reynaldo figured then that the Aussie would behave herself and headed for the other mess.

Jon had managed to separate Ian from Rich by then, so all Reynaldo had to do when he arrived at the original fracas was help Rich to his feet. The man wobbled when he stood upright.

"Let go of me," Ian shouted. "I want to smack him."

"You already did," Jon pointed out.

"Not with my fist."

"What'd be the point?" Reynaldo said, trying to make Ian see reason. "The fight's over, and you won."

Ian quit struggling then and took a good look at his opponent. "Had enough?" he barked at Rich. The man appeared too dazed to register the Scot's question.

"See what I mean?" said Reynaldo.

Ian turned to him. "Yeah, okay," he admitted.

Jon dropped his hands but stood ready to grab Ian if he tried to go after Rich again. Fortunately, the Scot decided to let the matter stand. He returned to the porch and sat back down.

While Jon checked on how the women were faring, Reynaldo attended the New Zealander. Still discombobulated, Rich struggled to keep his feet and shook his head to regain his bearings. His hat tumbled off the back of his head and landed on the ground. Reynaldo picked it up, returned the headgear to Rich's rattled noggin, and coaxed him to a seat on the porch step.

The New Zealander kept quiet while Jon returned to his chair, and Jan guided Mary into the hostel. Martha followed the pair as far as the doorway but then let them go inside without her. "She needs a cold cloth for her bloody nose," the Aussie commented matter-of-factly. Nobody said anything else for a bit. Now that the scuffle was over, Reynaldo took stock. He imagined he'd just participated in a comedy routine. Glancing Jon's way, he concluded by the suppressed grin that met his gaze that the Swede thought so too.

It was Rich who broke the silence. "Somebody owes me a beer," he complained without looking up from his boots. One leg of his tight-fitting jeans had been soaked with beer when the bottle he'd clung to exploded. It was all Reynaldo could do to keep from cracking up.

"Cheeky rotter," Martha mumbled.

"Somebody owes me a beer," Rich repeated, ignoring her. He still hadn't looked up from the ground, and his hat hung cockeyed on the back of his head.

"I'll get you one," Reynaldo volunteered.

"Somebody better," Rich threatened.

"I'll go," Ian said, standing. "I need a beer too."

"Hey, man, I spoke first," Reynaldo called out, but the Scot had already mounted the steps to the *tienda*.

Nobody had anything to say while they waited for Ian to return. Reynaldo lowered himself to the spot on the stoop his friend had vacated. He tried to come up with a witty remark to lighten the mood. "Well, that sure beats sitting around and having a friendly conversation" might have served or "Now that we're through kicking the shit out of each other, let's go watch Enrique and his cousins fight a forest fire." In the end, he chose to keep clever quips to himself.

Rich's wife walked up then, at first oblivious of anything obnoxious having taken place, but she became aware soon enough that she had entered upon the aftermath of calamity. When her questioning eyes fell on Reynaldo, he looked away, reckoning it wasn't his business to bring her up-to-date.

The wife wore a cowboy hat, same as her husband, and black jeans that pinched her crotch and hips. She approached Rich uncertainly, laid a hand on his shoulder, and bent at the waist to whisper in his ear. She'd been pretty once, Reynaldo adjudged, before the last few of her thirty-five or so years had done a number on her face.

"No," Rich shouted and jerked his head up. "I'm not leaving till somebody buys me a beer."

The wife tried to ease him to his feet, but Rich shook her off. "I'm staying here till I get my beer."

"It's on the way," Reynaldo explained to the wife.

She stepped back and waited. She wanted to tow her husband off the premises, but there was no getting him to cooperate. Reynaldo wanted to tell her not to feel bad, that what had happened was not her fault.

Ian emerged from the *tienda* soon after with a load of amber bottles in his arms.

"You bring my beer?" Rich barked at him when he'd crossed the street.

"I didn't know you wanted one," Ian answered. He had been about to hand Rich one of the bottles, but the guy's crappy attitude changed his mind. Instead, Ian stepped onto the porch, gave Martha a beer, then Jon, and finally handed one to Reynaldo. "Two left," he said as if surprised. "Suppose I could give you one of these," he proposed to Rich.

The guide snatched the peace offering from Ian's hand. He slammed back a long draught and lowered the bottle petulantly. Possibly, he was trying to think of the perfect insult to fling at his tormentor. In that the words he sought failed to reveal themselves, he pushed himself to his feet, adjusted his hat, and untied his horse. Reins in hand, he started up the street toward the square. His wife fell into step beside him.

Reynaldo watched them go, the wife a head and a half shorter than her husband. He thought the two of them made an apt picture of shared dejection. Tenderness welled in his breast. For a brief moment, he envied Rich.

"CD fucker," Ian mouthed quietly. Martha guffawed.

Jan came back out of the hostel to report that Mary had decided to lie down for a while. Ian asked if she was going to be all right. Jan assured him that Mary would be fine. The Scot then apologized to everyone for losing his cool. Martha said to hell with that; she just wished she'd been given a clear shot at the rotter.

"You had your shot," Reynaldo said. "But your aim was off."

"How'd you like me to take another one?" Martha retorted, and Reynaldo thought for a second she was serious. But then the Aussie laughed, and he decided she wasn't such a badass she couldn't take a joke.

"Lady," he answered, "you'd kick my ass without breaking a sweat."

"Believe it, Yank," she said, "you and me have unfinished business." Reynaldo sensed a message, which he'd just as soon not decipher.

His attention shifted to the fire on the mountain, and he was about to point out that the flames did appear to be subsiding, just as Rich had predicted they would, when Jon began telling the group about a walk he and his wife had taken to the white cross on the hill other side of town. He remarked upon a rock face they'd spotted across the canyon, which reminded him of the prow of a ship. There was a tree out there with red-flowered cactus clinging to its lower branches. Matted rows of thick, greasy grass grew layer upon layer up the side of the hill they'd climbed. "Beautiful country, Ecuador," Jon mused. Jan nodded in agreement as she sipped the beer her husband had offered to share.

At twilight, the group agreed to go to dinner together. Reynaldo suggested that Mary might like to accompany them and, when Martha failed to make the appropriate move, went to fetch their injured comrade himself. He found that Mary was reluctant to leave her room. She said she didn't want anyone to see her swollen nose. "Doesn't look that bad," he confided honestly to the teary-eyed Brit, but she refused to believe him. "I doubt it's broken," he went on when she let him touch her face. The vibes he got from Mary while he probed gently for cracked cartilage unsettled him. Mary expressed more gratitude for his attention than was warranted.

"I'll come if you escort me," she at last allowed.

To make conversation at the restaurant on the town square where they caught up with the rest of the crew, Reynaldo described an art exhibit he had happened upon during his visit to Cuenca. He had wandered into a room off the spacious lobby of a bank and discovered therein a considerable collection of Old-World-style crosses. No paintings or sculptures, just crosses. Many hung on walls around the room; the most valuable among them were kept in glass cases positioned about the linoleum display floor. At first, the sheer variety of the icons fascinated him: Roman Catholic glorification of suffering proclaimed in rich dark wood, burnished silver and gold, and precious jewels. After a while, though, repetition of the holy-unto-death theme depressed him. He had asked himself how many crosses a man could bear before succumbing to overkill.

Mary, seated so closely next to him that their shoulders touch, listened raptly to his description of the exhibit and said she simply must go see it. Reynaldo thought that odd; he'd just given her ample reason not to bother. Martha reminded Mary of their plans to swing back through Peru when they left Vilcabamba. Mary pretended not to hear. She urged Reynaldo to tell her more about Cuenca. The Aussie let on then that she didn't care whether Mary accompanied her to Peru or not. She turned her attention to the conversation going on between Ian and the Swedes.

Actually, the side trip to the museum took an upswing, Reynaldo continued for Mary's benefit. Leaving the bank lobby, he had inadvertently caught sight of an unsigned poem taped to a wall near the entrance. He'd memorized the poem; would Mary like to hear it? Why yes, she would.

> Cuando veo a la negrita
> Bien vestida y peinadita
> Me dan ganas de abrazarla
> Y besarle esa boquita.

"Oh, I do wish I understood Spanish," Mary gushed when he'd finished the recitation.

"Just another rotter pining after a sheila," Martha jumped in.

Reynaldo smiled. The Aussie was right of course, but she gave the author no credit for the glad spirit of his verse. The poet granted respite from the oppressive sanctity of a room full of crosses.

After the meal, he took a stroll around the square with the mismatched pair. Not the way he would have preferred to spend the remainder of the evening, but Jan and Jon had drawn him onto the walk and then wandered off by themselves. Ian returned to the hostel to phone his beloved.

He and the girls passed a few times around a blue mosaic fountain located at the center of the square. Lamps mounted atop wrought-iron poles on the perimeter of the small plaza graced trees, bushes, and flowers with a tender glow. Mary kept to Reynaldo's side during their amble while Martha wandered out ahead. After the third or fourth circle around the fountain, the Aussie steered onto a road that led toward the river. They dropped down a hill to a bridge at the edge of town. It was dark on the bridge and a scatter of stars shone brightly overhead. Reynaldo had no difficulty locating the Southern Cross, for he had kept track of the constellation's position in the night sky ever since a German pilot had pointed out the famous formation to him in Bolivia. He made it a habit to view the Southern Cross every night after that.

After hoisting himself upon the waist-high concrete wall that ran along the side of the bridge, he swung his legs out over the river. While he continued to look at the stars, Mary scooted up next to him, and Martha leaned her elbows on the abutment at his opposite shoulder.

"What's it look like to you?" Mary asked, tracing his line of sight.

"Like a box," he answered flippantly, meaning to discourage the intimacy Mary suggested by her breathy question.

"What's in the box?"

"Secret stuff."

"Fascinating," she answered in all seriousness, which made him want to tip her into the drink. "Whose secrets, do you think?"

"I was kidding," he told her and rolled his eyes at Martha, which was a mistake. The Aussie grinned at him mischievously.

"Still, it fits," Mary said.

"They might be your secrets in the box then," Reynaldo granted.

"Oh my, aren't we being profound," Martha broke in.

"What's it look like to you?" Mary challenged her.

"Like a kite."

"That's hardly original. Everybody says the Southern Cross looks like a kite."

"Because it does."

"Reynaldo's description is more inspiring."

"I don't know about that," Reynaldo interrupted to head off a squabble.

Mary laid a hand gently on his shoulder. "It was a lovely thing you said just now. I'd like to think my secrets are locked away in the sky."

Good thing Martha was there, or he might have felt duty bound to give the Englishwoman's hand a sympathetic pat.

"I still say it looks like a kite," Martha grumbled.

When they returned to the hostel, Reynaldo bade the girls goodnight and ducked into his room. He wasn't ready for sleep but had had enough of their company. Maybe after a while he'd go look for Ian or sneak back out onto the bridge to take a longer gander at the Southern Cross by himself. The woman who was no longer his wife entered his thoughts, and he admitted yet again how much he missed her. Pretty sappy, he decided. He wished he could relegate his former spouse to a box of secrets and only trot her out to make common cause with other men obsessed with the women they'd lost.

There came a knock on his door. It'd be good now to go have a beer with the Scot and discuss the latest episode in his long-distance affair with the Brazilian. Then he realized there was no possibility whatsoever that his friend had stopped by. Why? Because it had to be one of the girls out there. The only question was which one. Since Mary would be easiest to send away, he guessed Martha had come calling, and he was right.

The Aussie stood at the entrance to his room wearing nothing other than a T-shirt that fell barely to the top of her thighs. "You wanna know my secret, Yank?" she tossed off superciliously as soon as he opened the door.

"I'm tired, Martha," he answered. "Maybe another time."

"No, you're not," she contradicted, stepped into the room, and closed the door behind her.

"Oh please," he complained as she crossed her arms in front of her and lifted the T-shirt over her head. A good-sized hunk of naked woman stood before him then, a woman endowed with thick muscles and surprisingly firm breasts. Hempen hair was exposed at four locales on her body; connect the dots and what you got was a blurry sketch of the Southern Cross. To his regret, he was developing a hard-on.

Martha pushed him back onto the bed, unfastened his belt buckle, and yanked his trousers down to his ankles. Then she slipped up his shirtfront and cupped her palms on his breasts. When she straddled him, snugged his johnson into that warm cavity beyond her nether lips, his hands grasped automatically her grinding buttocks.

"I want you to know I'm bisexual," she stated, keeping her back straight. Her steady brown eyes examined him from a raised perspective.

"Couldn't have guessed," he answered brusquely as excitement mounted in his groin. Good God, it felt good to be inside a woman again, even if it had to be one who did not altogether epitomize her gender. He groaned and shuddered and stared at Martha's face. Her expression conveyed victory.

"Now you know my secret," she said as if giving the solution to a difficult puzzle.

"Thanks for unburdening," he answered as offhandedly as he was able.

Abruptly, she climbed off him, scooped her shirt off the floor, tossed it over her head, and was out the door without looking back. "That was quick," Reynaldo noted in the emptiness she left behind. He rose, pulled up his pants, and sat back down on the mattress. He expected to start remonstrating with his former spouse again, but instead, he drew a blank. Felt like it was just him in the room.

No more than five minutes later, there came another knock at the door. What'd the crazy Aussie want now? he wondered. But no, he knew Martha hadn't returned. He divined the identity of his second caller well before admitting her to his chamber. The knock sounded timid after all. He shook his head, not quite believing what was happening to him. He had expected fanfare at release from his obsession. If not bright light and trumpets, at least a glimmer of dawn and the twitter of little birds. But the world didn't work like that. It was the unheralded goofiness of life that saved a man from ruin.

To show his appreciation for Mary's company, once he admitted her to his room, he thought he might offer to translate the rotter song. She'd be pleased, no doubt. He'd be pleased as well to recall the poet.

> When I see the silly Limey girl
> Decked out and combed so pretty
> I want to fling my arms around her
> And kiss her blameless face.

"Okay, *mano*," Reynaldo soliloquized as he headed for the door. "I'll admit I've taken liberties with your verse. But surly, you, of all people, will grant me license at this my hour of deliverance."

No te vayas

(Don't Leave)

Atop the bluff at the north end of Huanchaco, he asked Ricky about the rules of cricket.

"What I don't understand is how a player gets put out."

Before their climb from the beach below, the two of them had been swatting a pink rubber ball back and forth with Day-Glo paddle rackets. Ricky had become impatient with the cooperative aspect of the exercise and suggested they have a go at British sport. So they'd constructed a wicket out of sticks they'd found jutting from the sand and taken turns trying to bounce the ball past each other.

"If the bowler hurls the ball at the batsman's head, he'll turn a bit prickly, I expect."

It took Albert a moment to make out that his playing partner misunderstood the question.

"No, I don't mean get pissed off. I mean how does the batsman make an out?"

"Right." Ricky's full lips parted, giving ironic exposure to his pearly canines. His brown eyes smiled too. Curly black locks that fell from the lower fold of his dark woolen stocking cap ruffled in a chill wind. Brownish fuzz grew at the corners of his mouth, and a sparse patch of whiskers darkened the underside of his pointed chin.

"Someone bowls over the wicket, mind."

British speech never failed to tickle Albert. To him, the accent always sounded as if the English were pulling his leg. Since Ricky was an immigrant to London and didn't look at all like your typical Brit, the effect in his case came off as particularly comic.

"Of course. I suppose it was perfectly silly of me to inquire. After the batsman puts the ball in play, what else might the fielders do but bowl over the bloody wicket?"

"Now you have it, mate."

"So how many outs in an inning?"

At that moment, Ricky's almond-shaped eyes swelled, and his jaw dropped. Albert couldn't imagine what gaffe he'd now committed to cause such a shocked reaction.

"I mean, how many wickets fall before the team at bat takes the field?"

Evidently, he still failed to clarify what he was after because the Londoner's olive complexion paled. "What the bloody hell?" Ricky mouthed.

And then, Albert realized his friend wasn't looking at him anymore; instead, his eyes were fixed on what was going on behind his American pal.

He craned his head about and was startled to see that two Peruvian soldiers in rumpled olive drab had materialized out of nowhere and presently charged in their direction. In their haste to close the gap between themselves and the foreigners, their heavy boots scattered gravel before them. One of the soldiers struggled with the awkward burden of his rifle.

Albert leapt to his feet. The clay and gravel bluff Ricky and he had climbed after their go at cricket fell off precipitously to their rear. Just then, he couldn't remember how they'd managed to climb the cliff.

"*Alto,*" cried the soldier whose arms were free. He packed a sidearm at his waist and outstripped his partner by several paces.

"What's that chap on about?" Ricky blurted from next to Albert's ear.

"He said halt," Albert answered, still unable to make sense of what was happening.

"Better we tear out I think."

"Where to?"

Indeed, given that the men at arms had advanced to within thirty yards of them by now, it would have been futile to flee.

"What'd we do?" Ricky squawked.

"How should I know?"

The lead uniform rushed up, and the one carrying the rifle followed hard upon his heels. The first let loose a burst of indignation.

"What's he say?"

"He's talking too fast for me to understand. But I think we're trespassing."

"Trespassing? Where?"

Albert had no idea, but this was hardly a time to ponder mysteries. "We don't know," he answered their accuser in Spanish, realizing then that a flood of adrenaline had muddled the language circuitry in his brain. "Where are the news?" he added stupidly.

The pistol packer barked again, his strained expression alarming.

"What's he on about?"

"We're supposed to accompany him somewhere."

Albert glanced back at his cricket partner and met eyes grown big as walnuts.

"You fancy that a good idea?"

"No, I think the idea sucks."

"Tell him we prefer to be on our way."

Albert opened his mouth to speak, but at this juncture, the one with the rifle slammed back the bolt and chambered a round.

"I don't think they're inclined to negotiate."

Without further ado, the soldiers flanked their prisoners. The one with the pistol gave Albert a shove, and he stumbled forward, smacking himself in the knee with his paddle racket. Then all four men commenced to quick march abreast toward a squat of colorless one-story buildings that rose about a half-mile distant on the dun mesa. Dread took charge of Albert's guts.

"Sonofabitch," he bellowed suddenly. "I don't believe this shit."

"They going to execute us?"

"Oh Jesus, man," he hollered at his partner. "You think we're watching the evening news?"

Albert knew he shouldn't shout, but he wanted the clowns providing escort to appreciate his high level of disgust with the whole rotten situation. On second thought, if they figured out he meant to insult them, woe be unto the defenseless idiots they had in their power. Sharp sucked in breath and clenched his teeth. "They'll probably lock us up," he said, willing himself to sound calm. It was a difficult acting job, given the rapid pace of their forced march. "Oh, shit fire anyway."

"For how long?" Ricky cried in despair.

"For as long as they goddamn well please." Only for the sake of argument did Albert add, "Maybe we could offer a bribe."

"How much would it take, you think?"

"Who cares? Damn, if I'm going to let these yahoos fleece me."

"Just as well for you, mate. I don't fancy spending holiday in Borstal."

"Fuck 'em."

Albert hardly felt as bold as he sounded. Years before, during a vacation trip to Jalapa, Mexico, he'd caught another unlucky card, one of forty-three issued during a midnight street riot. Of the three to four thousand participants, he had been one of the chosen few who had ended up crammed into a holding tank on an early Sunday morning. His week in the filthy den had provided ample material for entertaining stories to tell back home, but this new threat to his freedom struck him as insidious to high heaven. He couldn't decide whether to curse the concoctor of his bad luck or sink to his knees and weep.

An unforeseen turn of events occurred when the marchers reached their objective. The guards halted their captives fifty feet away from a company of about a hundred uniforms formed in ranks upon a parade ground bordered on three sides by military barracks. Upon arrival, the guards broke off. The one with the pistol steered toward a hut on the far side of the formation while the other propped his rifle against the wall of a nearer building and commenced to engage in a slap fight with a fellow who loitered apart from the assembly.

At sight of the horseplay, Albert experienced a tease of hope. He began cautiously to suppose that trespass in the bad dream he was having was not so dire an offense as he feared. The slap fight continued to his right. The men in rank to his front had no captain standing before them barking orders and therefore exhibited no compelling reason for their muster. Slouching in mass and casting sideways glances in the direction of the prisoners, they appeared to be on less than full alert. In truth, they too seemed to be living a bad dream, only they had become resigned to it.

Sadly, in the dream, it wasn't the prerogative of unmotivated extras to decide what was to be done with the prisoners. For this reason, Albert remained anxious. He could hope his situation was not as dire as he had at first assumed, but only time would tell whether hope prevailed.

The man with the pistol returned, but rather than inform Albert and Ricky what was in store for them, he joined his partner in the slap fight, making the contest a three-way affair. Albert gazed in the direction the *soldado* had come from and spotted a gent who leaned his elbow upon the windowsill of a hut at the far end of the base. A conference took place between this man and another inside the building.

Following an excruciating interval, the man at the window straightened and made his way nonchalantly toward the intruders. He was taller than the other soldiers and, unlike them, wore no baseball cap on his head. Stopping before the detainees, he addressed Albert.

"You speak Spanish?" A reasonable question at the outset. The speaker comported himself with the assurance of a loan officer in a bank.

"*Sí,*" Albert admitted.

"This area is prohibited to civilians."

"I'm sorry. We didn't know." Albert gave thanks he had calmed sufficiently to speak *español* correctly.

"What are you doing here?"

He was tempted to answer that he had no business whatsoever in this place and that it was the last locale on earth where he wanted to be. But he figured sarcasm wouldn't square with present company.

"We're tourists is all. We had no idea there was a military base up here. We didn't notice any signs."

"This area is prohibited to civilians," the officer repeated, ignoring Albert's implied argument in his defense. "Training of military personnel must not be interrupted."

"Clearly you are right," Albert was quick to allow, though he couldn't see any training taking place. "We're sorry we . . ." The Spanish word for *violated* escaped him. "It's your territory," he added quickly. "Sorry, but we didn't see any signs."

"What does he say then?" Ricky put in anxiously.

"We're not supposed to be here."

"Have you told him we didn't know?"

"I have, as a matter of fact."

"But they're going to lock us up anyway."

"It's not clear yet what they're planning to do."

"You said they were going to lock us up."

"Would you be disappointed if they didn't?"

The tall *señor*, having waited patiently for the exchange between Albert and Ricky to conclude, deigned then to deliver his verdict.

"You must leave."

Glory be, and no kidding, Albert thought, but continued speaking with utmost respect. "We have great urges not to stay here."

"If you come again, we will detain you."

"Is that to say, we may go?"

"*Ida sin vuelta.*"

The officer pointed to a road Albert had not noticed before. It consisted of nothing other than tire tracks that barely scarred the flat surface of the mesa. There were no vehicles around to account for the tracks.

"Follow the road and do not deviate. The road leads to the edge of the mesa and then drops down into the *pueblo. Ándale ahora mismo.*"

"*Gracias, señor,*" Albert thanked the man effusively, having yet to become wholly convinced that he and Ricky had been granted a reprieve. "*Muchíssimas gracias, señor.*"

Their savior then allowed a sly grin to crease his lips. "*Qué le vaya bien, señor.*"

Albert wanted to tell the officer he was one funny *fulano*. Instead, he contented himself with a nod to Ricky, and the two of them set out briskly in the direction indicated. They had advanced barely ten yards, however, when one of the men who had captured them rushed up from behind.

"*¿A dónde vas, amigo?*" inquired the *pistolero*.

"The *señor* gave us permission to leave," Albert answered apprehensively.

"*Claro.* But where are you going?"

"Far away."

"*¿Qué cosa? compadre.* Stay a little while longer with us."

"*Lo siento, pero no podemos.* We have an appointment below."

"*Aí carajo. No te vayas.*" The soldier's round face turned playful when he laughed. Seemed like lately everybody wanted to pull Albert's leg.

A command from the officer yanked the guard up short. Ricky made to turn about.

"Not on your life, bud," Albert warned him. "Face front and keep walking."

About a quarter mile from the parade ground, for no discernible reason, the road wound to their right, and they followed the turn. They could see that the tire tracks swerved left up ahead, but rather than cut across the switchback, the two of them followed the road exactly as instructed.

"They'll be watching us now," Ricky warned.

"They are watching us."

"I mean they'll spy on us till we leave Huanchaco."

Albert weighed the possibility and reached a tenuous conclusion. "I doubt it," he said, but he didn't breathe easy until they'd hiked off the hill. Checking rearward finally, he took some consolation in verifying for himself that no notice of a military base had been posted anywhere in the area. How the hell could innocent folk passing though town be expected to know where not to go without proper signage?

Ocean waves pounded the beach to their right. Wind-blown, briny air blew in off the water. When he and Ricky reached the outskirts of town, they cut left, seeking cover among block dwellings that butted narrow side streets. Best to be out of the wind and out of sight of anyone keeping watch from above.

Hardly a soul stirred in the neighborhood they entered, and the close arrangement of its buildings muffled the roar of the sea. They continued walking for a time in the soothing quiet. Then, around one corner, Ricky let out a boisterous yelp. He'd spotted a familiar figure.

The young man he marked stood with his back turned in their direction a block and a half up the street. He wore padded clothing fit for the gray winter weather, but it was not the apparel one expected to see on a surfing instructor. As the foreigners approached, Ricky's pal faced about.

"*Hola,*" Ricky greeted the *muchacho* brightly. Albert envied his partner's easy change in mood. Mere minutes before the Brit had been convinced the two of them were going to be shot, and now he was positively jocular. It would take Albert a good while longer to forget the crisis they'd left behind.

Ricky had become acquainted with the surfer a couple of days before while he asked around town about where to rent a board. Fancied learning to surf while in Peru, he'd told Albert. Being an impetuous, trusting, and likeable bloke, Ricky had had little trouble making good business with Antonio, which actually turned out to be not so surprising, given that it was the off season in Huanchaco. The *muchacho* had rented Ricky a board, a wetsuit, and thrown in five surf lessons for less than it cost to bed three days at the Hotel Suiza. In addition, Ricky was granted the freezing cold waters of the Pacific for his singular use.

Albert had done a little business with Antonio too, or rather, he'd provided the surfing instructor with financial counsel. It so happened that Antonio needed help cashing a hundred-dollar money order, which he'd received through the mail from a Belgian girl who had taken lessons from him the previous summer. Probably, the lessons included extracurricular activities, Sharp conjectured. Why Antonio requested his company to the post office did not come clear until after they arrived in Trujillo. Once there, the woman behind the desk in the government building fired a dozen questions at the surfer, insinuating that he'd come by the money order by some nefarious means. Albert caught on quickly that the woman judged Antonio undeserving of the windfall. Too bad. Her countryman presented a legal document, and she had to pay up. To fortify his claim, Antonio had brought along an American expert to vouch for his right to the cash. After Antonio signed for the hundred-dollar bill surrendered him, he told Albert that it was the first time in his life he'd applied his name to an official document.

Now, when Antonio invited the gringos to his home, Albert suspected he'd be asked to grant another favor. He didn't mind being the surfer's occasional patron but didn't want the practice to become a habit. Halfway up the block, Antonio stopped before the door of his apartment, one among contiguous single-story dwellings that butted either side of the street. They entered a dimly lit room where several surfboards in varied states of construction and repair leaned against the walls. On the walls as well hung wrinkled posters of Latin American film talent.

"You fancy we tell him about our escape?" Ricky suggested.

Albert grimaced. Seemed to him the word *farce* more accurately described their recent adventure. But if it were a serious matter they had become involved in, why spread the news around?

"Bit of a story is all," Ricky demurred. "But maybe best not to tell."

"That's my thinking."

Antonio lit a candle and rolled a joint. Albert sat on Antonio's metal cot; Ricky settled on one of two wooden folding chairs in the room. The surf instructor switched on a tape player that had seen better days, and Peruvian pop music crackled from the speakers. Without being prompted, the surfer started talking about how rotten business was. Albert saw where Antonio's complaint was headed and steered the conversation to another subject. He asked the beachcomber's opinion concerning the recent election. Was he a supporter of Toledo or Fujimori? Antonio declined to discuss politics; he was more concerned about raising enough *plata* to buy a better tape player.

After the joint was lit, Ricky wanted to talk about another ambition he hoped to realize while in Peru. Did Antonio know where he could score San Pedro? Albert hadn't heard of the drug before. Ricky informed him that tea brewed from the cactus provided a powerful hallucinogen.

"You know, San Pedro is legal in Peru," Ricky said.

"Brilliant," Albert returned.

Antonio gave directions to a market in Trujillo where San Pedro was sold. Sharp assumed that when Ricky visited the market, he'd want a Spanish speaker along to seal the deal. Again, he would be granted the honor of participating in another lively adventure. Never a dull moment when Ricky was around.

"It surprises me we've become such good mates," Ricky put in.

"Why's that?"

"Most older blokes aren't so patient."

"Some older blokes don't know any better," Albert replied.

Just before they left, Antonio tapped Sharp for ten bucks. Initially he asked for fifty—the electric bill had come due and he needed supplies for his repair business—but he settled for ten when Albert reminded him of the money order. Ricky pocketed a bag of weed on their way out the door.

Back in the street, the gringos set off walking toward the Suiza and arrived back at the hotel without taking any more side trips.

Albert left Ricky in the room they shared and climbed to the hotel roof. Up top of the Suiza was an open space outfitted with a round table, several chairs, and a small *baño*. He stepped to the hip-high abutment that ran along two sides of the second-story observation deck. Windows in the houses below gaped like the mouths of tombs. A few palm trees, their shaggy fronds pitched sideways in the wind, grew near the distant beach. Immeasurably farther out, beyond furrows of white water, a flat blue ocean extended to a wan horizon.

He was sitting with one haunch and thigh propped atop the abutment when a woman emerged from the stairwell. She too was a guest at the hotel; he had passed her on the stairs the day before. Early twenties, wavy brown hair, handsome features. Far as he could tell, she traveled alone. She wore a light-green sweater under a bright red windbreaker, loose-fitting trousers, and waffle-soled hiking boots.

"I'm Albert," he said, taking a chair at the table across from the woman.

"I know," the woman answered. She had brought a spiral notebook with her, which she opened on her lap.

"How do you know my name?"

She smiled at him. "We have a mutual friend."

He hadn't run into many American women along the gringo trail, and those he had met were accompanied by male friends. "Let me guess," he suggested, returning her smile. "You know Ricky."

"I met him on the *micro* from Trujillo, yesterday afternoon. When the bus collided with a donkey cart, Ricky became upset and got into an argument with the driver. It was an odd debate they had, in that Ricky doesn't speak a word of Spanish."

"Your story captures the very essence of my *compadre*."

"I think the driver would have eighty-sixed your friend if I hadn't intervened."

Albert laughed. "I had a similar first encounter with Ricky."

"Yeah?"

"I was waiting for the bus in Huaras, the night bus of course—you ever wonder why down here all the buses leave at god-awful hours? Well, not all, just the ones you want to take. I'm rambling, aren't I. Never mind. I was sitting in a claustrophobic waiting room, fighting brain fever, when in whirls, this will-o'-the-wisp who insists that I am bound with him for Huanchaco. Actually, I was bound for Trujillo and from there to Ecuador, but Ricky had other plans for me."

"Pure serendipity," the woman said and laughed.

"I guess. But doesn't serendipity connote a fortunate occurrence?"

"Is this another story about a wreck with a donkey cart?"

"Oh no, I didn't mean my story was similar in a literal sense."

"Hum. Can a similar event ever be literal?"

Albert liked the girl. Not only was she young and pretty (thank you, God, for your blessings), but she also liked word games. Given half a chance, the two of them might hit it off.

But then, Ricky showed up again.

"Here you are, Jill," he opened, as if he'd been searching high and low for the woman. He pulled a chair from the table and sat down.

"Here I am," Jill agreed.

"Are you getting on with my mate?"

"Famously."

"He's patient for an old bloke, wouldn't you say?"

"A paragon of patience. And for an old bloke, he's hardly wrinkled."

What the hell? Albert thought.

"Has he told you about our escape?"

"Why, no. Where did you escape from?"

"From the Peruvian army. Did you know about the military base atop the hill?"

"What military base?"

Albert wanted to commend Jill for her astute nonobservation, but Ricky was on a roll.

"There's a fort up there, mind, where several hundred crack troops are having a bit of training. They got snooty when we arrived unannounced. If not for my mate, they would have tossed us in Borstal and tortured us, I expect, or stood us before a firing squad. I was terrified, but my mate here, calm as a sword swallower."

"Sounds dicey," Jill said, mimicking British speech, "especially the bit about torture."

"You take my meaning. Those blokes were anxious to start tearing off bits of flesh."

"My goodness. How did you escape?"

"Albert spoke in confidence with their commander, naturally. He let on that we were CIA agents acting at command of the American president. The officer had no choice but to release us straightaway."

"Good thinking, Albert."

Albert didn't mind in the least having his leg pulled by Jill.

"One thing I don't understand," she continued though, dividing her attention equally between her admirers, "is why you were at the fort in the first place."

In that Ricky hesitated, Albert answered, having no trouble whatsoever remembering the reason they had detoured to the encampment.

"'Fancy a climb,' you said."

"Right," Ricky allowed, "my idea, wasn't it?"

"I believe it was," Albert answered, pretending he still might not be sure. After another couple of seconds, he added, "Yes, I'm certain it was your idea to scamper up the bluff and assault the Peruvian army."

"I didn't go that far, mate."

"No, I suppose you simply suggested we scamper up the bluff, but once on top, I decided to proceed on our secret mission."

"It's a gripping story the way you tell it."

Jill looked at Albert with a gleam in her eye. He began to consider astounding possibilities.

"What's that you're writing?" Ricky asked then, indicating with a nod the notebook in Jill's lap.

Albert feared the question embarrassed the woman. Probably her writing was none of Ricky's business.

"I'm writing a poem."

"Brilliant," Ricky gushed. "What's it about?"

"Why don't I read it to you?"

"Splendid," Ricky said.

Albert cringed and hoped with all his might that it was not a bad poem.

"You must understand it's a work in progress," Jill warned.

Albert pursed his lips apprehensively.

"Oh, have a go," Ricky said and leaned back to hear her recite. Jill read:

In the forest,
a bleating lamb hops about rock and brush,
and I ask,
what troubles you, my lamb?
Bleat answers bleat
and the little one
scampers back to a familiar woolly body.
Such is the wisdom of the lamb,
the meaning of its life.
I am not wise,
nor does my life make sense.
For reasons forgotten,
I hop anxiously about rock and brush,
bleating over and over,
despite the certainty
that for me there will come no answer.

Albert breathed relief. He thanked the evasive gods of written words for treating Jill decently. Not that the poem was terrific, but the gods had refrained at least from humiliating her.

"Why is it you birds write about lambs?" Ricky asked and then caught the look of consternation on Jill's face. "Well, not entirely," he qualified. "But I know a chippie in London who goes on about puppies and kittens."

Jill closed her notebook. "Have you read Sylvia Plath?" she asked airily.

"I must say I haven't."

Albert butted in. "The poem's not about lambs," he informed Ricky.

"You're mistaken, mate. I distinctly heard about a bleating lamb."

"But may I ask why the lamb was bleating?"

"That's what lambs do. Ewe's bleat as well, so I've heard."

"Does your mother bleat?"

"Can't say I've ever heard her bleat."

"There you have it."

"There I have what?"

"What the poem is about."

Ricky frowned. "You're not being clear, are you, mate?"

Generally I find
twenty ways to say anything but
what I want to say—
twenty-one,
if you count this way.

"I believe you're having me on," Ricky decided.
"I believe you're right, and I apologized."
"No harm. Fancy a ride to Trujillo?"
"Not now. Maybe later."
"I'll go," Jill said, rising. "Sure you won't join us?" she asked Albert.

Seemed an abrupt transition to him, but he reconsidered the offer when Jill made it. Love to, he could have answered, and Ricky wouldn't have cared that he'd refused his invitation while accepting Jill's. But he wasn't in the mood for a bus ride just now: the jostle of passengers at multiple stops, a trudge through the crowded streets of Trujillo, hanging back while Ricky did his happy dance with other tourists. Wasn't his scene at the moment. He'd rather go to his room and be alone for a while. Maybe hike down to Mama Mia's in an hour or so and order a burger.

"You guys go ahead," he said. "We'll meet up later."

"I'm counting on it," Jill answered and, before descending into the stairwell, winked at him. "*Ciao*, for now."

She must be partial to older blokes, Albert thought, once she'd gone.

In the quarters he shared with Ricky—a fairly large room with a pair of double beds and thin, dusty curtains covering its bank of windows—he pondered Jill's poem. Really he thought about Jill by way of her poem. She sounded lonely, which stretched his credulity. After all, with her good looks, all the woman had to do was snap her fingers to get over loneliness. At her signal, any man within a hundred yards would come a makin' jolly. So the question was, why did Jill complain of loneliness? Well, let's say she hadn't met the right guy yet. And if this were so, one wondered what she was looking for in a companion. What'd a man have to do to pique her interest? Did a middle-aged man with a large nose, hazel eyes starting to sink into his skull, square chin, and ears that stuck out—a man who looked like somebody's inconspicuous uncle, have a shot at Jill? Don't be ridiculous. What'd Albert Sharp have to offer? Hell, he was so inconspicuous and ineffectual that he wasn't even an uncle. True, he could talk some; he could tell a joke once in a while, but that hardly constituted stuff that dazzled. Ricky said he was patient. Okay, but what'd that signify besides stultifying reluctance to take any initiative? Even if patience tallied as a virtue, in romantic endeavors, it cut no ice. So he could forget about Jill. She'd be crazy to entertain serious notions about a man whose major asset had to do with him keeping to himself.

Later on, Albert left the hotel and made his way by the backstreets of town to Mama Mia's. Most foreign visitors to Huanchaco dropped by Mama Mia's sooner or later. The restaurant had but two tables inside and two on the porch outside, and yet its many customers made do with the spare space provided. They came because Lucas and his wife served up a taste of home.

When Albert showed up at the restaurant an hour before the usual evening rush, Lucas sat on the porch by himself reading a newspaper. He was a light-skinned man in his mid-thirties, fairly fit, somewhat aloof in bearing. Albert invited himself to the proprietor's table, which was okay by Lucas. The owner's wife, a fine-featured woman with luxuriant hair that fell to her shoulders, emerged from the kitchen to take Sharp's order.

"What do you think about the march?" he asked Lucas after his wife departed.

"Certainly, the election was a fraud," the restaurant owner answered him in an even tone, his brown eyes steady. There could be . little dispute about the rigged election, but such was the exercise of power in Peru. As to the candidates, Fujimori had done good things for the country. He'd stabilized the government; built schools, roads, and hospitals; put down a revolt. But corruption riddled his cabinet, unemployment ran high, and the schools he erected were shoddily built. That said, Lucas doubted Toledo could do better.

"Will he pull off the march?" was what Albert mainly wanted to know.

There might be a march, Lucas opined, but Fujimori had the army on his side, and so there was little chance the uprising, even if it did happen, would bring about a recall.

His wife brought Albert a burger and a beer and stood by to hear what he and her husband were talking about. Sharp voiced his opinion that the march would prove historically significant and that a majority of Peruvians rightly took it seriously. The woman listened politely and then exchanged an inscrutable glance with her husband. "We will see what happens," Lucas said, and Albert then realized that the Peruvians thought he understood little of what was happening in their country. Of course they were right.

It was late when he caught up with Ricky and Jill again. Daytime wind had weakened to breezy gusts, which blew in from pitch-black darkness beyond the breakers like homebound ghosts. A string of lights running the length of the Huanchaco peer marked their landing strip.

Up the beach, in a double-sized lot between a pair of stucco buildings, stood a *papa-rellena* stand. Under its rickety wooden awning, two women cooked spuds and fry bread on charcoal braziers set up at either end of planks nailed together in the shape of a large rectangle. Albert found his pals slouched on a long bench that fronted the planks on one side of the stall. The only other customer, a white guy he had not seen in town before, sat at the long table on the other side of the stand. The stranger looked to be in his forties. He had black hair and thick shoulders. He nodded genially to Albert.

Jill caught hold of his right biceps and rested her head on his shoulder when he sat down. Her display of affection was unexpected.

"I'm so stoned," she said, looking up into his eyes. In the soft light of the potato stand, her strong features enchanted him.

"Nice ride, I take it," he answered, unsure what she wanted at the moment. The man seated across the stall watched them without being conspicuous about it.

"What ride?" Jill said and giggled.

"To Trujillo. You went to Trujillo with Ricky." If not, where had they spent the afternoon? Had the Brit made a move on her?

"We found San Pedro," Ricky broke in as if it were the most amazing accomplishment. "Had to ask around and follow directions from one bloody market to the next, but at last we found San Pedro."

"So that's where we were," Jill concluded stupidly and pulled away from Albert.

"How much?" he asked Ricky out of curiosity.

"Didn't buy any, did we?"

"Why not?"

"Everywhere we went, piggies were there first."

Albert chuckled; easy to imagine his friend wandering about a crowded market, rubber necking at every turn. Ricky's mode of life in London, which brought him in frequent contact with keepers of the English peace, accounted for the paranoia he brought to Peru. "San Pedro's legal here, didn't you say?" he teased.

"Couldn't take the chance, mate. We were being watched."

"Were you now?"

"But we know where to score San Pedro, Albert. That's the thing."

"I suppose so," Sharp granted. It was apropos, given his so-called patience, that he be volunteered to make the buy. "How about you, Jill, will you come along?"

"Let me finish. I haven't eaten anything all day."

She thought he intended to depart immediately. "Do you like your *papa*?" he asked rather than correct the misunderstanding.

"The most delicious potato I've ever eaten."

When the man across the way tittered, Albert looked at him.

"I'm Reynaldo," the fellow said. Neatly trimmed lank locks topped his round head and harmonized with full lips, shapely nose, and star bright eyes. His torso was muscular beneath soft outer flesh.

"Albert. And this is Jill. Over there's Ricky."

"*Mucho gusto,*" said Reynaldo with a nonchalant wave.

"*Gusto* to you," said Ricky.

Jill rose up. "Are you stoned?" she asked the guy across the stand.

"Me? Not really."

"You look stoned."

"I get that all the time," Reynaldo answered her.

"You're pretty, you know."

"I get that too."

Jill squinted. "The prettiest man around. Sure you're not stoned?"

"Not to my knowledge."

"Well, I'm so stoned I don't know who I am."

"I don't know who I am either. So maybe I'm stoned."

"Please don't mess with my head."

"Wouldn't think of it."

"I'm serious. I really don't know who I am at the moment. I feel like I've been changed into a lizard."

"You're one up on me then. I don't feel real at all."

"What are you chaps going on about?" Ricky interrupted. "I can't make it out."

"We're talking about not knowing who we are," said Reynaldo. "It's a common dilemma."

"Philosophy, isn't it?" Ricky said. "My mate's a philosopher."

"I am not," Albert protested.

"Certainly you are. The way you go on."

"What's reality?" Jill asked. Albert thought the question silly, but she was asking Reynaldo, not him.

"Search me."

"I can tell who you are, mate," said Ricky. "You're a Yank."

Good guess, Albert surmised. Tonight, this town was fair infested with Yanks.

"You're a Limey," Reynaldo responded.

"I'm East Indian, actually."

"Does being East Indian tell me who you are?"

"I'm not East Indian," Jill said.

"I'm not either," Reynaldo answered her.

Interesting way to flirt, Albert commented to himself. It hadn't occurred to him that absurdity might be what Jill was after. He was curious to find out if Reynaldo's way of hitting on her worked.

"May I explain?" Reynaldo asked.

"Only if you clear up this conversation," Albert interjected.

"Can't promise that."

"Come along now. Give it a go," Ricky urged with enthusiasm.

"Happy to oblige," said the stranger, smiling good-naturedly, and since none of the three across from him objected, he continued. "I'm nothing other than a figment of my imagination. In the past, I thought I was someone real, but that idea turned out to be false. I can still imagine who I am, but I can't figure out who's doing the imagining."

"You're a Yank," Ricky put in. "That's what I imagine."

"Which might establish who I am once and for all. That is, if you stick around to remind me."

"You want my e-mail address," Ricky offered.

"Pardon?"

"Send a message when you're perplexed. I'll send back that you're a Yank."

"Maybe that's what I'll do."

"You don't get it," Jill accused Ricky. "I know what he's talking about."

"Thank you," Reynaldo said.

"You mean down deep none of us knows who we are," Jill continued.

"Can't speak for everyone."

"Exactly."

"Why aren't you real?" Albert interrupted, because he was damned if he was going to let an interloper monopolize Jill's attention.

"Because there's nothing left of me," Reynaldo replied. "I spent all my reality on someone else."

"That's sad," Jill said so mournfully Albert shook his head.

"Not really," Reynaldo answered. "I'm getting used to being nothing."

Oh brother, Albert thought.

"Would you like to go for a walk on the beach?" Jill asked the nonentity.

"I don't know. Maybe."

"Com'on, answer."

"How can he decide if he's not real?" Albert pointed out without much hope of intercepting the inevitable.

"That's my problem all right," Reynaldo agreed.

Jill rose from her chair and made her way around one end of the potato stand. Reaching Reynaldo, she patted him on the back. "Com'on, take a walk with me."

Reluctantly, the man pushed to his feet. He allowed Jill to take his arm and lead him off into the night. Once the couple disappeared, Albert smiled to himself. Fair work for a man who didn't exist.

"Blimey," Ricky commented from next to him.

"*Buen dicho,*" Albert answered.

"You sorry to see them go?"

"Not so much."

"You fancy Jill, I expect."

"A little."

"We could tear after them, if you've a mind to."

But the woman who ran their end of the spud stand walked up then and asked who was going to pay the bill. Albert fished into his jacket pocket for his wallet. He hadn't eaten anything at the stall, but in Peru, he could afford to act generously toward his friends.

The two pals set out at a slow pace, steering back toward the Suiza. The side street they followed put them directly in line with an open-air café just down from the hotel. Ricky suggested they stop by for a couple of beers before turning in. It turned out they had three apiece before bedding down.

As Albert was nodding off, there came a knock on their door. Ricky stirred but didn't wake up so Albert pulled on his pants to answer the call. Jill stood in the hallway outside, glaring at him.

"Why did you let me traipse off with that fool?" she demanded.

He shrugged. How do you answer such a question?

"Aren't you going to invite me in?"

He stepped back to let her pass. She entered in a huff and sat on the edge of his bed.

"Why so glum?" Albert asked, still standing.

"Can you believe it? I offered to sleep with him."

"Uh-huh."

"You know what he said?"

"No, I guess not."

"He said he wasn't ready to be real again."

Ricky giggled from the shadows.

"So am I crazy, or is he?" Jill complained with her focus on Albert.

He groped for an answer. Tough part was she asked a loaded question.

"Why don't you shag my mate?" Ricky suggested. "He'd like that."

The woman sighed, a bit melodramatically in Albert's view. "Would you like that?" she asked.

"I suppose I would."

"And would you?"

"Would I what?"

"Shag me."

"I suppose."

Jill rose from the mattress. "I suppose that's all I wanted to know." Then she marched out of the room.

After she left, Albert stood for a minute staring at his bed. He didn't know what to make of Jill. He was still wondering what to make of her when he pulled off his pants and climbed back between the sheets.

"Fancy that," Ricky commented from the darkness.

And the next day, they would go to market to buy San Pedro. Or rather, Albert would make the deal for the drug while Ricky waited in the street, hidden from the cops. Then Ricky would burn himself on the ankle while brewing cactus tea, scream and hop around like a scarecrow set afire, and it would be up to Albert to calm him down and apply salve to the wound and wrap it in a bandage from his first-aid kit.

They never would run into Jill or Reynaldo again. And in three more days, Ricky would be down the road too. Albert would take a bus to Ecuador alone and come back to Huanchaco after a while to find a dead sea lion rotting on the beach.

Sobre el terreno

(On the Spot)

We're finally here, Marci thought, and yet she couldn't quite believe it. She recognized the site from numerous sunny pictures she'd seen in magazines and travel guides, but examining photographs was one thing and encounter with the lost city a whole other experience.

This morning, heavy clots of fog clinging to the daughter peak obscured large portions of the famous lithic maze. The ruin's multiple grassy tiers shone through breaks in grounded vapor. Chilly air filled Marci's nostrils, and humidity dampened her face.

We're finally here, she repeated to herself as incredulity persisted. Now all will be well, she added, but she didn't quite believe that either.

Neither she nor her husband spoke as they descended from the visitors' center to a humble trapezoidal gate that gave entrance to the acclaimed ancient city. At the end of the first packed-earth path within, three woolly llamas emerged from morning haze and pulled up when they spied intruders. With parenthetical ears erect, the *camelitos* appeared apprehensive.

"They want to walk by," Jerry said and motioned Marci to step back. The llamas trotted past them and out the gate.

Already several other two-legged visitors assembled on the rise where the administrative building was located and, in proximate hours of daylight, many more would arrive. The llamas preferred to absent themselves from a mounting hubbub that had nothing to do with them.

Marci followed Jerry through a jog in the entrance alley, stepped over a flat-topped rock that jutted from the path and turned with him around the corner of a wall whose blocks were lichen-mottled and chinked with leafy creeper. They descended a long flight of rude steps and passed through a door without a lintel. Crossing the threshold of another opening in the walls, they arrived at a nook Marci could identify on the basis of what she'd read about the ruin.

"Wings of the condor," she said, her voice sounding crisp. "I so wanted to see them."

"You mean those two boulders?" Jerry answered with a flip of his head.

One of the oblong stones he so offhandedly dismissed stood straight up; the other leaned to the right. Smaller rocks had been fitted to the topside of the canted wing. "I don't see boulders," Jerry said. "I see feathers."

"You've got a vivid imagination."

Her husband's first impulse in nearly every conversation he engaged in was to compete head-on for his hard-nosed point of view. His insistent style of address served him well in business, but he wasn't inspecting one of his chain stores now. Instead, he stood with his wife on holy ground, which was no place for him to be obstinate even if he didn't feel blessed.

"I suppose if we were at a Greek or Roman ruin," Marci ventured, "it would be easy to make out divinities carved in marble. That's because classic Old World masters gave the gods human form. Here . something else is going on. Something prior to ideals."

"You mean the Incas weren't very good sculptors."

"No, I don't mean that at all. For them, granite and limestone rocks had lives of their own. In other words, the Incas devoted themselves to presence rather than contrivance."

"Whatever," Jerry commented dryly. "One of the rocks around here has what, twenty-two right angle cuts? I'll grant you the people who built this city had a knack for masonry."

"Once again, you're missing the point entirely. The stone you refer to has twenty-two cuts, maybe more, because some rocks need help fitting in with their neighbors. Condor wings require adjustment before taking flight. A sundial must be polished to disclose secrets of the seasons. But these were mere arrangements descendents of the sun god made to accommodate sacred inhabitants of the forest."

Someone spoke above them and someone else answered. The exchange between the unseen man and woman took place in a language neither of the Americans understood. When the voices trailed off, Jerry looked up at her. He had lowered himself onto one of the stump-sized stones jumbled before the funeral grotto.

Though a buff intramural athlete in college, at forty-two, his torso exhibited pudgy girth. Large shoulders, barrel chest, thick thighs, Jerry cut yet a formidable figure. A receding, red-tinted hairline gave way to his pronounced forehead, knobbed nose, and square chin. Over time, his cheeks had expanded, but his brown-green eyes maintained narrow focus.

"You want your picture taken?"

"If you like."

"I asked first, dear. What would you like?"

"Sure, take my picture. That'd be nice."

Her spouse retrieved a digital camera from a side pocket in his hikers' tunic, pressed the power button, and framed a shot on the display screen. "Marci at Machu Picchu," he jested and started to put the camera away. "You've just made history."

"Let me see."

She moved forward, intending to sidle around behind her husband and lean on his shoulder. At arm's length, however, Jerry handed over the camera, letting Marci know he wasn't feeling affectionate at the moment.

"Who designed the site?" he asked while she appraised the electronic image. There she was standing in front of the condor chamber. To the left of her image, at thigh level, could be seen a sand-colored upward extension of the room's base stone carved in the three-tier shape of the Inca cross. Behind her slanted the rough-cut edge of a ten-ton mantle that served as roof and brace above the entrance. To step inside the hollow, Marci would have had to bend at the waist and duck her head.

"I doubt there ever was a master plan," she answered, which brought to mind her own lack of a master plan. The Cuzco vacation was supposed to provide an opportunity for her and Jerry to spend some time together without the kids. Their children had been sent off on other summer excursions: Tom to baseball camp, Sasha to an actor's workshop. That left Mom and Dad free to explore Inca land undistracted. But Marci had formulated no master plan to guide her enterprise; she had consigned herself to hope.

"Someone platted this town," Jerry countered. "Otherwise, there'd be evidence of sprawl."

"No place to sprawl to here. This is a make-it-or-break-it kind of space."

Jerry missed the innuendo. "Someone with a blueprint built this town," he insisted.

"Incas weren't builders in the way you mean. They fitted stones together as if arranging flowers. The city happened over time. Some pursuits are destined to turn out well, others are sure to fail." Thus, she offered him a second chance to read the subtext in their talk.

"More than one generation then," he went on, oblivious. "The first engineer passed on his plan for a city to his progeny."

"No, Machu Picchu in essence was always here. The Incas were first to notice is all, and being first, they made the most of what they found. Centuries later, Bingham chanced upon the site, though by then the gods had retreated."

Jerry's wide smile encouraged her. It seemed, if nothing else, she still amused him. When he spoke, however, her chest deflated.

"Careful, dear, you're starting to sound like a convert to paganism."

She handed back the camera, and he put it away. For a moment, the picture had pleased her. The salon tan she'd developed specifically for the trip suited her choice of hair color and authenticated her big brown eyes. She had put on a friendly smile for the lens. If her nose was a bit too pointed and her jawline a bit too angular, the visage in the photo was still attractive. But at Jerry's veiled reproach, she had switched focus to her rounding shoulders and widening hips. He had meant to say that she sounded like an airhead, but the end result was he made her feel frumpy.

"Not to worry. Folk who founded this city were guided by a vision far beyond my capacity to comprehend."

That said, Marci spun on her heel and walked out of the condor's nook. If Jerry had any sense, he'd have chased after her immediately and apologize for his patronizing remark. But he seemed to have no idea what was at stake between them. He believed that he'd fulfilled his husbandly duty just by agreeing to accompany her to Peru.

After making her way through more twists and turns in rock walls, she emerged upon an open field at the center of the ruin where several other tourists occupied the grass. Some consulted guidebooks, others strode forth with a purpose. Morning fog had begun to lift, portending a sunny day. Marci wandered to the middle of the field and tried to feel cheery. After a minute or two, Jerry made his way to her side. Nice of him to take the trouble, Marci thought, but said nothing.

"Isn't that the peak you wanted to climb?" he asked, pointing toward a rounded hump on the far side of the ruin.

"Huayna Picchu, eldest son in the Picchu family," Marci answered without looking at him.

"Let's go then. We could use some exercise."

By which he meant his buggy wife needed to walk off her snit.

"Don't you want to explore the ruin first?"

"It'll be here when we get back."

True enough. She could count on Jerry to come up with a right response to any objection she might make to his ever-ready action plans. A hike was an excellent idea from his perspective, in that the walk would likely put Marci in a forgiving frame of mind. Fine, let's go, she allowed mentally, but first, the clever husband owed his annoyed wife an apology.

"Look, if I said something wrong—"

"Yes?"

"If I said something wrong, I'm sorry."

And that, she knew, was the fullest extent of contrition Jerry would offer. To be fair, he had just proved that he did care about how she felt, but it bothered her how often she had to remind him that he did. How she'd got the job of emotional overseer to their union had puzzled her ever since she'd found out hope and forgiveness were her assigned fields of expertise.

At a registration booth, they jotted their names, nationalities, and time of departure in a ledger, which made for a sensible precaution. Their entries joined a list of twenty or so other hikers thus far signed up for the ascent of Huayna Picchu. Beyond the overseer's hut, a dirt trail ascended to a ridge that gave a backside view of the ruin.

In sunny disposition, Machu Picchu reminded Marci of a dollhouse, which recalled as well a longing that had gripped her often in childhood. Back then, a fascination for dwellings in miniature inspired her to take up cardboard and strips of fabric to construct several dollhouses of her own design. For hours, she had arranged and rearranged the lives of tiny figurines within the walls of her creations. It was the desire to step inside a doll's world that drew her later to work in theatrical scene design. Now, as those first cardboard dwellings had done, Machu Picchu beckoned her, and she was sorry she had not lingered within the lost city's cozy rooms before embarking on a side trip. The ruin seemed to chide her for not staying longer.

Turning from the site, she watched Jerry trudge upward without her. He moved at a steady pace, no doubt expecting her to catch up. Yanking on the straps of her daypack, she set out with a purpose, meaning to reach her husband quickly, but the trail up the mountain was too beautiful to be passed over at a glance. Wild strawberries and clover, fern and grass, clumps of cactus with hooked spines caught her eye and slowed her step. Moist rich soil nourished a forest that smelled of Eden. Trees with long pointed leaves abounded, and from the open side of the climb, a fecund canyon loomed. When she hurried forward again, she discovered that despite hours spent on the stair-stepper back home, she lacked the stamina to match Jerry's gait.

Never mind. Sooner or later he would realize they had become separated and be obliged to stop and wait. He might resent her dalliance, but a pause would do him good. The essential aim of their trip would be served when the forest cast its spell on him. Take a break, Jerry, look around you. Once distracted from the urgency of your every project, you can't help but be entranced by the marvel that attends you. Hanging back requires less effort than you think. In fact, once at rest, you will wonder what you were in such a hurry for. And then I will rise to meet you, and you will be glad.

Hard-soled boots scraping dirt and rock to her rear underscored wilderness murmur. She could distinguish the strides of two hikers, their combined tread tatting a thematic riff. From around a corner of dark wet stone, two young men in brightly colored shorts and caps appeared, sleek calf muscles flexing with each step they took. Heads bent to their work, the pair failed to notice Marci at first. Then the men caught sight of her boots and both raised their chins. The first barely acknowledged her; the second muttered something in French as he swept by. They both swept by, and in their wake,

Marci experience a brush with vigor. As the two disappeared around a bend, she appraised the lively bounce of their haunches.

Feeling compelled to pick up her pace, she ducked her head and strode out with greater determination. At one curve, the trail reached within a rocky indent where black stone steps had been carved along a ledge. Here the path became wet and slippery, which required that she grip a cable bolted at waist level to the rock face. A chasm slid off precipitously to her left, and she willed herself to be brave as she negotiated the traverse. But there was no lessening of danger around the next turn in the trail, and a short ways ahead plodded yet another hiker. The two she pursued must have passed him by and raced out of sight. Perhaps the slower climber deplored being outstripped by the hard-charging duo, for the way he bent at the waist, clasped and yanked on the next section of steel cable fastened to the mountain side, bespoke grim resolve. Approaching to within ten yards of the man, Marci became aware of his panting breath.

Evidence that she was not the least fit explorer on Huayna Picchu that morning both consoled and emboldened her. Though her legs had begun to ache and her arms had weakened, she planned to hustle by the rotund straggler without giving any sign of fatigue. Nearing the man, she suppressed heavings in her chest. Unfortunately, the trail narrowed at this stretch so there was no safe way around him, and so they ended up plugging on together and panting in unison. Marci tittered at their pitiful display.

"What you laughing at?" the man demanded without turning around.

She couldn't think how to answer but truthfully. "At us."

"What about us?"

Marci laughed again, and the expulsion of air burned her lungs. She coughed, sucked in more air, and pulled up hacking. The man stopped and faced about.

"It's just that," Marci began, coughed, and bent at the waist. She eyed the portly climber with her hand cupped over her mouth. Sweat glistened on his shallow forehead and moon cheeks. He drew himself erect and, as another of firmer physique might have swelled his chest, puffed out his belly. "It's just that, here we are"—gasp—"busting our humps"—cough—"risking a fall that would surly kill us"—gasp—"and in all likelihood, we won't even reach our objective."

The fellow regarded her evenly. His skin was of a mestizo cast, and his brown eyes fixed upon her a penetrating look. He wore a red T-shirt and over it a dark plaid flannel blouse left unbuttoned. Sleeves rolled to his elbows exposed meaty forearms. "Stick with me," he asserted at rapid-fire rate. "You'll make it to the top."

"Of course we will," Marci answered contritely. "I was being silly."

"Well, get serious. I'm in training for the US Marine Corps."

By the severity of his expression, the man dared her to doubt him. His voice sounded remarkably deep, too deep for his years. Marci now saw that the other hiker was still young enough to take himself seriously in even trifling situations. His abrupt manner caused concern. Jerry should have been with her then.

"You ought to go on without me. I doubt I'll be able to keep up."

"You were doing okay just now."

"But no way can I compete with a marine."

"I'm not a marine yet," he corrected. "I'm in training."

Just her luck to be abandoned in a Peruvian rain forest and happen upon an aggressive ape who entertained self-aggrandizing delusions. Don't laugh, Marci told herself, and whatever you do, don't look the brute in the eye.

To communicate submission, she stared down the long drop that began at the toes of her boots. Way down there, the Urubamba River at one visible bend on its course winked up at her. Across the canyon rose a cliff scalped granite gray and slashed with streaks of white. Let this beauty not be the last I see, she prattled inanely to herself.

"You're afraid," said the overgrown youngster. He had lowered the volume of his voice so that his words sounded threatening.

"Yes," Marci admitted and prayed the ape be merciful.

"You're feeling defenseless."

"Yes, I am."

He hesitated; she listened to him breathe.

"Sorry," he finally allowed, "you don't need to be scared of me. You're a good person, and I never hurt good people."

How reassuring. "I'm glad you think I'm a good person."

"You are, I can tell. My name's Simon."

"I'm Marci."

"Relax, Marci."

She raised her head and nodded. Simon continued to study her for a time. "Let's go," he said after he finished sizing her up.

When he took to the hike again, she followed. It seemed they had struck a truce, which Marci would do nothing to jeopardize. To humor her unsought companion, she asked, "Why here?"

"What you mean?"

"Why train here?"

"The fort. Warriors train here."

At risk of irritating the boy, she dared to correct him.

"Machu Picchu was never a fort. Eighty percent of human remains found at the site are female. There's a good chance the city served peaceful purposes."

"Conquistadors razed the place."

"Hardly. Spanish explorers knew nothing of Machu Picchu's existence. It was abandoned before they arrived on the continent."

"Nobody fought here?" Simon questioned, clearly put out.

"No battles of record," Marci answered apologetically.

"Well, what the fuck am I doing here?" He stopped and turned. For a large man, his movements were surprisingly quick and agile. Marci pulled up in alarm.

"You know for a fact nobody ever attacked the fort?" he questioned.

"Not for a fact," she responded meekly.

"So there could have been battles."

"Maybe, but not likely."

"What's the point of a fort if nobody fought over it?"

"Likely no fighting, and therefore no fort."

Simon shook his head in disgust. He thought about arguing with her further but then decided to resume the march. After a few steps, however, with his back to her, he gave way to his first impulse.

"What were women doing at the fort?" he groused as if female inhabitants could be blamed for his disappointment.

"No one knows for sure. They might have been priestesses."

"You saying Machu Picchu's a church?"

"What appear to be temples are located on site. Beneath the wings of the condor is a chamber where the dead were prepared for afterlife."

Simon continued up the trail, giving due consideration to the information passed onto him. "Do you believe in God?" he asked suddenly.

Though unforeseen, his query struck her as apropos. Precarious ground underfoot, sheer drop-off to her left, wannabe warrior two steps ahead; it seemed exactly right that she consider at just this moment who was in charge of her life.

"In the sun god, you mean?" she asked, feeling giddy.

"You don't believe in God," Simon retorted without the slightest shred of doubt.

"I didn't say that."

"Sounded like it."

"In any case, I don't believe faith or lack thereof matters much to an Almighty Being."

"'In any case,' huh?"

"Think about it. God's supposed to know everything and be able to do anything, so what's he care whether I believe in him?"

Simon wheezed. "You're one of those intellectuals, aren't you?" After another labored breath, he added, "College graduate, I'll bet."

"What's wrong with that?"

"You going to tell me now what's right and wrong?"

"As if I couldn't possibly be qualified?"

"How about my dad abusing me? Was that wrong?"

Had to say something like that, didn't he? Just as she had started to believe that if she plunged to her death off Huayna Picchu it wouldn't be because she was pushed, the crazy ape alluded to a violent personal history. Goddamnitall, where was Jerry?

"That was wrong," Marci admitted.

"Hit me in the back of the head with a baseball bat."

It was hard to tell whether Simon was telling the truth or improvising a tale to impress her. She could only hope that he exaggerated whatever trauma had accompanied his upbringing. "I'm glad your father isn't with us then."

"He's in jail. When he gets out I'm gonna kill him."

What else? True or not the boy's account jived perfectly with dread that now occupied her guts. Her legs felt shaky, and her arms seemed at the moment to belong to someone else.

"You're afraid of me again, aren't you."

Surely not, Marci almost said, but even an idiot would have seen through the lie. One thing she'd figured out about her companion, he was no idiot.

"Violence terrifies me," she confessed.

"Think I'm going to turn on you?" Simon asked smugly.

"Does it matter what I think?"

For half a minute, he held her in suspense. He continued trudging up the path, but she could tell he also listened intently to her trailing footsteps. She sensed his attention as a doe must sense a hunter when the hunter closes upon its hiding place.

"Nope," Simon vouchsafed, "I'm gonna lead you to the top of the mountain. Never thought of doing anything else."

"That's good news," Marci answered, unconvinced.

"Had ya goin' for a minute though, didn't I."

"Well, put yourself in my place."

"Sorry."

"It was a bad joke."

"You the sort of person who holds a grudge?"

"Sometimes."

"Like now?"

"Maybe."

"I don't hold grudges."

Given his stated intent to commit patricide, Simon's latest avowal could not be understood as other than absurd.

"Right. And what about your dad?"

"That's not a grudge. He's good as dead."

"I see," Marci mumbled though she didn't see at all.

Simon brooded while they scraped on and unseen birds chirped and chittered cries of warning. "Let's say you fall," he suggested out of the blue, and Marci nearly freaked.

"But I'm not going to fall," she sputtered, struggling to maintain emotional equilibrium.

"Well, if you did," he continued. "Haven't you ever heard about people falling off a cliff before?"

"Sure I have. But you wouldn't want me to fall, would you?"

"Are you crazy? Why would I want that?"

Indeed. She must have taken leave of her senses for a second there.

"What I'm saying is, if you did fall, I'd stay till help came."

"Glad to hear it," Marci answered.

"Only right. Would you do the same for me?"

"Sure I would."

"You promise?"

What'd he want from her? She couldn't understand what Simon was getting at. Was he trying to establish a bond between them? Oh my, what other betrayals, besides his father's brutality, had the kid suffered?

"You promise?"

How sad. Her hiking partner was not a savage ape after all but a confused adolescent who could use a little sympathy.

"Okay, Simon," she said. "If you were to fall, which I don't believe for a second will happen, I'd stay till help came."

"Thanks," he answered, "I knew you were a good person."

As they neared the top of the mountain, their path became more dry dirt and gravel than mud and slippery stone. The sky expanded overhead. By now, Marci was plenty ready to be reunited with her husband. When she met up with Jerry again, the boy might just as well wander off by himself. He was okay for a mixed-up kid, but time had come for them to part company.

Three figures stood on a boulder wedged among other boulders that jutted above a break in vegetation. It was thus against a backdrop of clear sky that Jerry reappeared in company with the two hikers she had attempted to keep pace with before. The three watched her and Simon work their way up the trail.

"Tell me you're standing at the top of Huayna Picchu," she called to her spouse.

"You're never wrong," he called back.

"At last you admit it."

Jerry turned to one of his companions and spoke using hand gestures. The other answered also with gestures. Marci couldn't make out what either of them said, but the familiar resonance of her husband's voice filled her with relief. She wanted to rush to his side at once, and would have, had not Simon blocked the way.

When she stood below Jerry at last, she extended her arms. He smiled and stepped forward on the slanted rock from which he looked down upon her. Before their hands touched, his boots shot from under him, and he fell over backward. The two men behind him lurched in unison and grabbed his shoulders. Marci gasped.

But Jerry slid only a short way down the boulder, his boots halting at the level of her head. Grateful that he remained unhurt, she patted one of his ankles.

"Be careful," she admonished him.

"I'm always careful," he returned. "You're always right, and I'm always careful. Did you enjoy the climb?"

Aware that Simon stood close by, she merely nodded. "I missed you though."

"Missed you too. Sorry I went on ahead, but it couldn't be helped." With a wag of his noggin, he indicated the two climbers who had straightened behind him.

"A race to the top, right?"

"I was obliged to prove the mettle of American manhood."

"Oh man, can't you ever just relax?"

"Sure I can. For the past twenty minutes, I've been resting up."

"Good. Now that I'm here, you can give me a tour."

Jerry puckered his lips. She knew the expression; he was about to tell her something she didn't want to hear.

"What?" she croaked.

"Beautiful view of the cloud forest from up top."

"But what?"

"The challenge is still on, I'm afraid." Again he bent his head toward his associates.

"Jerry."

"Hundred bucks says I can beat 'em down the mountain."

She turned away briefly in exasperation then faced back before he had a chance to say anything else. "You've just lost a bet," she stated flatly.

"Let's not quarrel in front of strangers."

"To hell with that. Your pals can do whatever, but you're staying behind with your wife."

At that moment, one of the Frenchmen hopped nimbly off his perch and took to the trail. The second followed his example.

"They're getting a head start," Jerry complained as he slid from the rock.

"Jeeerry."

But he had made a decision, and it was non-negotiable. "See you at the bottom," he called, hurrying after the competition. "We'll do lunch," he added before he slipped from sight around the first downward bend in the trail.

"Come back, you dork," she cried to no avail. It was unbelievable that he had run off again. She leaned back heavily against the rock her husband had vacated. Oh hell, now what? Was it so terribly much to ask that he spend a little quality time with his wife? Damn him. That's right, damn him.

"Sometimes love feels like loathing," Marci mouthed aloud. She had no idea where the words came from, though they served precisely to express her dejection. The words held forth as if they sprang from the inside wall of her skull. Sometimes love—yes, goddamnit love. Heaven help her.

"So what?" said the young man standing in front of her.

She hadn't been paying much attention to Simon, and when he spoke, she wished he'd go away.

"Com'on," he urged. "Let's check it out."

Meaning the view from above, the very view she had wanted to experience in Jerry's company. No chance of that happening now. Her husband had gone tripping down the mountain as if she were of no more concern to him than any other adoring member of his fan club.

"Go ahead. Sorry, but I'm upset."

"You going to let him ruin your day?"

"Sometimes I could throttle him."

"No you couldn't. You're not the type."

No, she wasn't. She was more the type to smother in a poisonous cloud of frustration and choke on resentment.

"This was supposed to be our time," she groaned. "You know? We were supposed to be together, just the two of us. But he couldn't care less."

Simon withheld comment.

"You go along thinking things are going to get better. For years, you go along. Someday the children will be on their own, and then the two of you can pick up where you left off when they were born. But your husband has developed interests in the meantime that don't include you. He knows his marriage is unraveling, but so what. He figures it's up to his wife to knot it back together. When she tries, he doesn't lift a finger to help."

Simon stood across the trail grimacing. Strange that he turned out to be her confidante.

"Ah, screw it," Marci told the boy. "If he doesn't care, to hell with him."

"I don't think you mean that."

She studied Simon's face and detected thereupon a species of remorse that stopped her cold. So striking was his look of sorrow that it made her forget her own misery for a moment. How had a person of his young age come to know despair? Then Simon changed faces. He didn't want her to see inside him.

"I guess I'll meet up with him later and try again," she admitted.

"What else?" the boy answered.

They took the last several steps to the summit in tandem. As seen from below, the peak had appeared round as a fingertip on top, but at its top, it turned out to be not so round. Instead, the crest comprised boulder shards pinned one against the other to form a jagged cluster that obliterated the footpath up to them. Their slanted sides gave slippery purchase, and with a dozen or so climbers already occupying the rocks, the top of Huayna Picchu was a crowded place.

But Simon led the way, and his bulk coupled with brash comportment obliged other occupants of the summit to make room for them. He commandeered a spot at the raised edge of one chunk of rock that hung like a toppling shelf above a severe drop-off that swooped into a tributary of the Urubamba. The perch was better suited to the clawed talons of a raptor or a carrion bird than to Marci's tender butt, but neither was she winged and therefore had to make do. When she sat down, Simon stood by protectively.

Across the wide canyon to the fore, tucked within tight folds of rain forest flickered a waterfall. The same bright sunlight that shone on its distant cascade also fell upon and warmed her face. Looking down into the canyon, she began to relax. Her churlish mood gave way to marvel. By and by, an event occurred that made her forget all about Jerry.

Gray water vapor, gathering above a sea of green, congealed to form a cloud, which in its birthing rose to the level of her head and from there into bright blue sky. Once ventured from the custody of trees, the puffy nimbus suffered an assault of whizzing solar ions and was torn apart. Marci had never witnessed conception and death of a cloud before. The drama astounded her; the dynamics of sun and forest transfixed her. Opposing forces at work in the Eden theatre powered also the beating of her heart. She knew now why the Incas identified this land as the navel of creation.

She sensed movement from Simon before she actually saw him step out upon their slant of rock. Her head wrenched in his direction. She reached out instinctively to grab hold of his shin as she might have tried to grab the arm or leg of one of her wayward children. On family outings, both Tom and Sasha had a habit of venturing impulsively beyond her care. In this case, mother's instinct failed by half a second.

As the young man's feet jetted from under him, he twisted around and fell hard upon his belly. His palms slapped the pitted surface of the rock he'd been standing on and his fingers flexed in an attempt to halt his slide. The effort accomplished nothing. He disappeared over the edge of the precipice in an instant. One second he was there within reach; the next, he was gone. The last Marci saw of Simon, his eyes were fixed on hers and his mouth gaped in amazement. A millisecond before he was lost, one corner of his lips curled upward. She would remember the expression ever after. It looked as though the boy wished to convey an unworried mix of irony and affection before he disappeared.

As if a nerve viper drove its fangs into Marci's cranium, her body locked up. The arm she'd extended toward the boy froze in midair and her head felt as if it were stuck in a vice. In another instant, her mouth dropped open, and she heard a scream and believed for a moment that the freight-train bellow in her ears erupted from her throat. Then she realized the cry couldn't have come from her. It was spewed across a blinding sheen of sunlight in words understandable only had she been conversant in at least three foreign languages. Her hand dropped to her side; her shoulders bowed. When her lips rejoined, she stared at the faraway blink of waterfall. Over there, a mesh of trees surrendered wisps of mist. Another cloud was about to form, but something more riveting had transpired. A catastrophe so banal and decisive as never to be rescinded.

Hands grasped her shoulders, first one muscle shelf then the other. Faces were thrust before her face, and voices babbled behind her. Shouts and moans added to the tumult. Tears burned her eyelids, but weeping was beside the fact. Beside the fact shouts and groans, fingers tightening on her shoulders, all the hurly-burley. What was the fact? Simon had been irrevocably wrenched from the world.

"Breathe," said one of the faces before her face. "You must breathe."

German accent, thin visage, lank chestnut hair the tips of which teased bony clavicles. The twenty-some-year-old looked frightened, which also struck Marci as beside the fact. She tried to speak and realized then that indeed she wasn't breathing.

Beyond the pair that held her tight, a broad-shouldered man in a denim cap crept to the edge of the cliff and peered down. She watched for a change in the scout's expression, one that might convey hope. But the hatted man examined only the tragedy of hope betrayed. In time too brief, he straightened and sidestepped cautiously up the slant of rock upon which Marci's legs lay limp. Others on the mountaintop begged him to be careful.

"He your son?" the scout murmured, drawing near.

"What?" Marci returned with a start. "Can't be. Tom stayed home."

"He your friend then?"

She shook her head to clear it, which didn't help at all. "My friend?"

The man in the denim hat shook his head too as if the gesture dismissed a fact as yet comprehended by no one.

"His name was Simon," she added evenly. "That's all I know about him."

The two who had taken hold of her shoulders helped her rise and gave support while blood rushed back to her feet. They offered water from a blue plastic bottle, which she accepted without thinking. The water tasted synthetic.

"What did you see?" she entreated the scout.

"You don't want to know," he answered and turned away. Several of the hikers to the summit had bunched at the apex of the slanted rock and presently stretched their necks to catch a glimpse of Simon's body over its bottom edge. "Step back," the scout cried and waved a hand at them.

Two among the curious dropped onto their hands and knees and edged forward. "Watch out," the scout yelled, anxiety straining his voice.

"Maybe he's not dead," Marci whimpered.

"You'll fall, you fools," the scout shouted at the men creeping out on the rock.

"Maybe he's not dead," Marci repeated.

The scout ripped his hat off his head and spun toward her. "His spine's twisted as a piece of taffy and his skull's split open. It's not possible he's still alive."

Vision of what the scout described produced havoc in Marci's mind. Her hands trembled as they rose to shield her eyes from the horror she beheld and then collapsed with the rest of her body.

Next thing Marci would remember ever after was her descent from the mountain. The youth who had commanded her to breathe following Simon's fall walked in front of her and his partner trailed behind, each offering a hand when she needed one, which was often now that her legs buckled without warning and every glance she cast in the direction of a right-side drop-off met an uprush of terror. Others who had borne witness to the tragedy struck out ahead to spread news of the accident. She dreaded the account she would be obliged to give at the bottom of Huayna Picchu, and the visions reignited in the telling. She was therefore grateful for not being required to speak during the descent.

A soft weight settled upon her shoulders and pressed round her head. It was an exhausted kind of grief that enveloped her, seemingly endorsed by her helpers. Seemingly they sought relief from their own remorse by doting on Marci.

During the retreat from Huayna Picchu, Marci pleaded with herself to stop asking what she could have done to avert disaster. She might have been more watchful, she might have reached out more quickly, she might have conversed more energetically with the boy prior to his witless foray upon the rock. In this way, she might have forestalled his stumble. Vain speculation, though, in the aftermath; the moment of Simon's eradication stood inviolate, an event unalterable, a reality implacable. She considered whether it was cowardly to claim impotence. "One thing happens, then another" droned in her head, implying a causal chain not of her making. She imagined a line of dominoes falling one after another. In their mad tumble, the dominoes branched off and initiated other topplings. A whole world of cascading dominoes invested her imagination, and their clattering cacophony prodded a desperate query. Wherein events set in motion resides the specificity of herself? To what end does she admit authorship for one rank of happenings and not another? On this day, blind chance had placed her at the center of catastrophe. Prior to its occurrence, where the stamp to her affect?

Such was the near exoneration she accomplished during her descent or was compelled to arrive at step-by-step as she distanced herself from Simon's fall. The defense she concocted was justified, as far as she could tell, though even as reason guided her thoughts, it failed to dispel her anguish. Guarding yet rational convictions, she achieved near reverence for the testimony she could give, but when delivered to her spouse at Machu Picchu proper, Marci sensed anger encroach upon her state of mind. Jerry had not been present at the death; he knew nothing of its horror nor of its bewilderment. The strife that cross-stitched their marriage, as much a part of the patchwork of their union as love and loyalty were parts, as consideration and pity were as well, brought a surge of jealous ownership for her rare elevated status. Once life with Jerry resumed, she feared the mystery befallen her would never again exist as revelation in itself.

On the central plaza where she joined her husband, the German boys gave a brief account of the accident. His eyes shifted nervously from them to her, and grasping at straws, he questioned whether the boy might have survived the fall. The German boys shook their heads in defeat. Marci's look obliterated the last possible vestige of denial. His shoulders slumped as belatedly he took on his share of the burden she had borne from the mountaintop.

"It wasn't my fault," she told him after the German boys walked off.

"Of course not," he answered and tightened his lips. His eyes shifted toward the dreadful peak.

Marci glanced in the same direction. Half a dozen Peruvian rescuers, two of them with coils of rope draped diagonally across their torsos, set off at quick-time march up the Huayna Picchu trail. Their effort came too late, Marci adjudged bitterly. They could fly to the top of the mountain and alter salient facts not one iota.

"Everything's changed, and it's not my fault."

"Marci—"

She stepped back to avoid embrace. "You don't understand."

"Easy. Take it easy."

"That's what I mean," she said and set her jaw. "You don't understand."

He lowered his arms and slipped his hands into his trouser pockets. He studied the ground at his feet. She watched him fret and allowed him an opportunity to give the right response to her challenge. What form the response should take she made no attempt to contrive. He was aware of a test presented him and discerned as well that there was little chance he'd pass the test.

People moved about the plaza, some crossing it, some pausing to study one or another aspect of the stone constructions surrounding them. Some were joined in conversation, some paused between remarks, but all remained oblivious of any cause to be dour, mournful, angry, or dejected. Marci begrudged the complacency of each and every one of these bystanders.

"We better get away from here," Jerry said.

"Why?"

"Because everything has changed."

Marci laughed mirthlessly at his attempt to placate her.

"That's what you said," he protested.

"You don't understand, do you?"

"How could I? I wasn't there."

That answer came close to being correct, but she held firm.

"I'm sorry I wasn't there," he added, which only underscored his betrayal.

"Better you weren't," she stated meanly. "You wouldn't have been amused."

Jerry looked up, met her gaze, and frowned.

"Nothing I say will get me off the hook."

"Don't even try."

"Look," he commanded then shook his head violently back and forth with his jaw gone slack. "Look, let's get out of here. Let's go anywhere you want, but away from here. This place is bad. Bad for both of us."

"I know," she answered. "You and I can never be happy again."

They took a tour bus down to Aguas Calientes. It had been Marci's plan to visit the ruin, hike the footpath back to town, and spend the night at one of the hotels. But when the bus let them off, all she wanted to do was board the train back to Cuzco. Unfortunately, the conveyance would not arrive until late in the afternoon. Thus, she faced, in the company of her disgraced husband, the remainder of a horrible day. Neither of them nurtured hope for consolation.

For a while, they traipsed along a row of craft stalls that fronted two sets of railroad tracks. Jerry held himself erect. Woolen blankets and wraps put up for sale mocked Marci's desperation. In an attempt to put the best face on their dreadful plight, Jerry stopped at one of the stalls and asked sheepishly if there was anything on display she wished to buy.

"As a memento?" she questioned vindictively.

He gave no rejoinder.

Later, they mounted a paved walkway that climbed toward the *pueblo*'s hot springs. Jerry's rigid bearing made her feel guilty for punishing him. At the mid-afternoon hour, she could have suggested they stop by one of the restaurants for a meal. Taking food together might have eased their standoff, but she gave no sign that it was time to reconcile.

Since her barbed comment at the stalls, Jerry had determined that silence was the only tactic available to him in the war of nerves he fought with his sullen wife. He climbed with her between buildings that appeared recently constructed, ready to suffer whatever accusation she flung at him. His taciturn behavior only aggravated Marci's guilt and, as a result, consigned her to a cauldron of resentment. She knew she exploited Jerry's belated commitment to her service but concluded he had brought retribution upon himself. She wanted him to feel as guilty as she did. Too bad for him he chose to be at her side only when she could no longer abide his presence.

An hour before the train arrived, nearly at the end of their strained wits, the two collapsed into plastic shell chairs at one of the cafés situated along the railroad platform. By then, the Machu Picchu crowd had returned from the ruins, and those not wandering among the stalls mobbed the eateries. While bodies pressed upon them, Jerry cautiously ordered the day's special and a beer. At his urging, Marci also asked for food: rice, a piece of fried beef, sliced tomato and bread, *mate* to drink. Their waiter was a young man with dark wavy hair who took a particular interest in the withdrawn foreign woman seated at his station.

Jerry noticed first, which wasn't like him. Usually when they went out together, he became engrossed in his own agenda. At dinner parties, Marci's mate required only that she confirm entertaining stories he told, and second the motions he made to further his commercial interests. Because he could count on her support without asking, he focused on those in their company who needed to be stroked. It was odd, therefore, that he cited a milieu in which she starred.

"You have an admirer," he said.

"Not in this weather," she answered, misunderstanding him completely.

His chuckle startled her, and she frowned in response. "The waiter," he added apologetically. "He thinks you're a peach."

Reluctantly, Marci turned her attention on the young man he referred to. He was a skinny boy with bent posture. His nose protruded sharply from a slim face with high cheekbones and a delicate jawline. Small eyes sunken beneath thick eyebrows darted in her direction.

"Not on your life," Marci contradicted.

"You just watch," Jerry said.

When the waiter returned, he delivered their plates with a flourish, took one step back from the table, and stared at Marci.

"Drinks," her husband put in snidely.

The waiter spun about and hurried off.

"Jeeze," Marci mumbled, following the boy's retreat.

"What'd I tell ya?" Jerry muttered.

The waiter returned with a bottle of beer and cup of coca tea on his tray.

Marci's dropped her eyes. "Knock it off," she commanded her spouse.

A thin-fingered hand set the cup and saucer before her and lingered on the gloss-white tabletop. Looking up, Marci met calf eyes.

"You go to Machu Picchu?" the boy asked shyly.

So that was it. Their waiter had heard about the accident on the mountain and learned somehow of Marci's involvement. He felt sorry for her.

"Why do you ask?"

"Stay in Aguas Calientes?"

Did he mean investigators expected her to remain in town for questioning? But not a one had approached thus far.

"No, we're leaving for Cuzco as soon as possible."

"You dance?"

She shot a questioning look at Jerry. He was about to bust a gut.

"What's that got to do with anything?"

"Stay," the boy pursued. "Dance in Aguas Calientes."

Marci smiled then in spite of herself. Jerry was right after all; she had an admirer. He couldn't have been much older than her son.

"If you're asking me to a dance, I'm flattered."

The youngster straightened, puzzling over what she'd said. Then he caught on that his invitation was suffering rebuff. "You go," he concluded.

"'Fraid so," Marci answered gently.

Offering his hand, the boy made a parting. "*Mucho gusto*, missus."

"Me too," she answered, accepting his hand.

"Lucky, mister," he told Jerry.

"Better believe it, pal."

When the waiter left, Marci rebuked her spouse. "You needn't have sounded so smug."

"No problem. He didn't understand a word I said. Anyway, my comment was meant for your benefit."

Marci appraised his timid smile. When he wanted to, Jerry could be charming, even sweet. Could this be the sort of moment she had hoped for in setting up the trip to Peru? Without thinking, she reached for her husband's hand. Maybe her hope had not been in vain after all; maybe reconciliation came at a price she could not have reckoned on. Big hope, high price. Simon had picked up the tab.

"You know, we could stay the night," Jerry suggested with admirable discretion.

She was still thinking about Simon. "I couldn't," she answered, closing her eyes and tightening her grip. "I just couldn't. Let's get out of here."

The train pulled into the station and nearly all café clientele boarded. Passenger cars were painted orange with broad yellow stripes running their lengths. Inside, straight-backed benches, thinly padded in black vinyl, faced one another in pairs. Marci and Jerry took seats near the front of one car with their backs to the direction of travel. By chance, no one sat across from them.

Lush forest rising up the side of a hill passed nearly at her shoulder as the train set out. Gaining speed, their coach swayed widely. Marci caught glimpses of the Urubamba's white water out the windows across the aisle. About half the train's passengers were foreign tourists. The other half, Peruvians, all wore sweaters and jackets.

At a village stop, several vendors boarded the train to offer *choclo*, pastries, ham and cheese sandwiches, and flashlight batteries for sale. The train resumed travel while they hawked their wares. Several of the vendors were of grade-school age and yet they crossed over exposed couplings between oscillating cars with ease.

After passing through a series of tunnels that blanked ambient light for as long as a minute at a stretch, the train coasted onto open land. Red and white carnations, large yellow flowers on tubular stalks, and prickly pear cactus grew next the tracks. In the middle distance rose blue and green fir trees and stately eucalyptus. A pink and white canyon wall, lifting toward gauzy white swaths of cloud, backdropped the landscape. Day gave way to twilight as they passed through pastureland where cows and pigs were tethered to stakes. The train rolled by fields of cereal crop. The temperature in their car dropped precipitously with oncoming darkness.

Marci pressed her knees together and crossed her arms against the cold. Jerry retrieved their jackets from the overhead rack. When he sat back down, he scooted close to her and wrapped an arm about her shoulders.

"Better?" he asked.

"I can't stop thinking about—"

"Must have been terrible."

"Not your fault."

He hesitated, no doubt considering an argument in defense of his conduct on Huayna Picchu. Wisely, he chose to refrain from justifying his selfish actions. In any case, what he'd done or failed to do on the trail before Simon's fall had lost significance for Marci. The last look on the boy's face was what she clung to. That look, when she remembered it, made her shudder.

"What's on the agenda for tomorrow?" Jerry asked.

Marci felt a stab of remorse for the young man who had lost all his tomorrows. One moment he had been with her. Next moment . . .

She realized it was unfair to expect Jerry to participate in her grief. Unfair too to resent him for not being nearby at that terrible moment when everything had changed. This moment, he was with her. She should be grateful. This moment, he made an effort to alleviate the awful sting of her remorse. Next moment, he too could be lost.

"I don't know," Marci said, and then to show appreciation for her husband's attention, "maybe Pisac."

"What's in Pisac?"

"More ruins. It's the first stop up the Sacred Valley."

Why hadn't Simon gone to Pisac instead of Machu Picchu? He could have done his marine training on a different mountain. She wouldn't have met him, and he'd still be alive.

"Sounds like a plan."

"Not a plan, an idea."

"The town has hotels?"

Marci shook herself. "I don't know. On Sunday, people come from all around to attend a market fair."

"Well, this is Friday, isn't it? I think we should go to Pisac tomorrow and spend the night. After dinner make excellent use of a quaint little room."

Maybe her hope would be fulfilled. Was that so terrible? Was it so awful that she wanted to put the poor boy's death behind her?

"What's wrong with making excellent use of the room we have in Cuzco?"

He drew her nearer. "I didn't think you were ready to bother with me again."

"I've never stopped wanting to bother with you."

He nodded, which encouraged her to go on.

"I want you to be with me, Jerry. That's all I've ever asked."

"I'm here now."

"I know. You can't imagine how grateful I am."

"Yes I can."

Could he? Marci wondered. If he could, he must sense now how much she needed him. She wanted him to hold her close. One moment you could be with a person, the next he might be gone forever.

"Nothing you have ever, ever done has lessened my love for you." If he understood what she felt for him, there was no need to explain. Turned out she shouldn't have tried to explain. His body tightened next to hers.

"Believe me, Marci, I wish I could change the past."

She realized then that a reminder of transgressions having nothing to do with Machu Picchu had arisen. Old, nasty, ugly stuff. Oh please, not now.

"I'm telling you I love you is all. I love you no matter what. Be with me, Jerry. That's all I ask."

His arm lifted from her shoulders. He turned away and clasped his hands between his knees.

No matter her intent, a most painful aspect of their life together had come under review. Self-reproach followed on both sides; it was so unfair. It was worse than unfair that the taboo subject cropped up now.

"They don't matter," Marci hastened to explain. "I've come to understand that they never had the power to ruin our life together."

"I don't know you at all," he whispered. "Why do we have to go over all that again?"

The lights in the car flickered; the engine rumble, which Marci had ceased to notice for many miles, changed to a shrill whine that sounded like a huge balloon deflating. As the sound died, so did the train's momentum abate, and the lights in the car went out.

A stir among passengers commenced. Several pressed their faces against windows on both sides of the car to peer into darkness outside. Other than a few stars, there were no lights to be seen anywhere. The engine had quit mid-route between village stops. Jerry shot out of his seat and set off down the aisle.

The conductor, with flashlight in hand, entered their car and gave a report in Spanish. Though understanding not a word the man said, Marci concluded his news was bad. The Peruvian passengers acted upset. The conductor suffered their protests in silence as he continued on to the next car.

After he left, Jerry returned to his seat and told her a guy who spoke both Spanish and English, seated toward the back of the car, had translated the conductor's message. Seemed there'd be a delay of at least an hour and a half.

If it weren't so cold, Marci wouldn't have minded at all. She even welcomed the unscheduled stop. It ended the nasty talk she and Jerry had been engaged in. There had come about an excellent excuse to forego the taboo subject. She and Jerry were together on the train—that was the important thing. Peru was the sort of place where trains broke down and where travelers should be prepared to meet travails. The two of them would face the hardship together. So what if it was cold. Together they could handle anything.

"I hope the crew includes a good mechanic," Jerry joked.

"No chance of phoning triple-A, is there?" Marci said to encourage his comic impulse.

"Better take off for the nearest farmhouse. Rent a burro before prices skyrocket."

"I concur. Panic now and avoid the rush."

For an hour, they sat huddled together in discomfort, but assuredly, this couldn't have been the first time a train had broken down on the return trip to Cuzco. Surely, folks who ran the railroad had formulated contingency plans. And yet the Peruvian passengers continued to stew and grumble.

When the engine restarted and the lights came back on, an emphatic sigh of relief was joined all around. Grateful cheers rose not only from their car but also from cars front and rear as well. The general mood brightened. It seemed safe to suppose the train would reach Cuzco after all.

"That just goes to show," Marci said when other riders had settled down.

"Show what?"

"If we stick together, everything will turn out all right."

"Can't help but be okay when we stick together," Jerry buoyantly agreed.

Marci kissed him because that's what he wanted. Then she kissed him a second time because he kept his lips close to hers. When he started lowering the zipper on her jacket, however, she balked.

"Easy, cowboy. Wait till we get to the barn."

"No time to be coy, cowgirl," he answered and laughed. He gave her breast a squeeze before backing off.

Half an hour later, the engine whined, and the lights went out again. They were detained on this second occasion of engine failure for forty-five minutes, during which time, Peruvian ire notched up a level. When the motor restarted and the train crept forward, the mood in the car was one of apprehension rather than relief.

They pulled at last to a scheduled stop. At this juncture, it became clear that most of the foreign travelers had lost confidence in their current mode of transport. Half the passengers in the car got to their feet, gathered their bags, and headed for the doors. From her window, Marci watched the mob descend upon a dimly lit shack that stood at the edge of a *pueblito* sprouted beside the tracks.

"What are they thinking?" she wondered aloud.

"They're going to take a bus," Jerry answered, leaning across her so he could see out the window too.

"What bus. Do you see a bus?"

"No. But maybe one will come along."

"And maybe not."

Her husband sank back in his seat, mulling options. The last of the line of passengers abandoning the train from their car dropped out its rear door. He made a decision.

"Let's go," he said, rising to his feet.

As he reached for their daypacks in the overhead rack, she turned from the window. Just then, it did not sit well with her that he acted unilaterally.

"Com'on," he said, noting her hesitation.

"I'm staying with the train," she answered.

"Marci, com'on."

"Go ahead if you want."

The last thing she wanted now was to test his loyalty, but when their eyes met, it came clear that's exactly what was happening.

"This train will be lucky to limp into Cuzco tonight," he argued.

"What's the difference? Wait for a bus that may or may not show up, or wait for a train that did show up but may not run."

"Those people can't all be wrong."

"Not in everything they're thinking, only in the one thing they're thinking alike."

Jerry saw then it was no use trading speculations with his wife. If there was any sure thing he could bank on at the moment, it was that his commitment to her had come under scrutiny. He chose rightly to confirm their alliance, but the decision cost him effort.

"What the hell," he said, plopping down beside her. "Might as well stay with the old bucket."

"The word *bucket* refers to a boat, I think."

He grimaced. "Well, at least we won't drown."

Marci felt vindicated when the train left the station. Following an affirmative lurch, the engine revved to a deep-throated rumble and sped forward unhampered by the drag of its swaying cars. In less than half an hour, a distant lake of lights twinkled into view. Had to be Cuzco. Hot tea and warm beds in the offing. Marci turned to her husband, ready to celebrate their deliverance.

"Seems you made a good choice," Jerry admitted.

"So did you."

"You left me none but the right one."

"That's not true."

Or was it? Would he have remained on the train had she not insisted? What if she had acted more dismissively when she told him to go ahead and take the bus? Or made a game of his decision rather than a test? You take the bus; I'll ride the train. We'll see who's waiting for whom at the end of the line. What choice would he have made then?

It bothered her to think that Jerry had remained behind only to fulfill an obligation. Truth to be told, she had coerced him into taking this trip to Peru, too. She had complained that the usual plan for a family vacation no longer excited her. Two weeks at a condo that included access to a swimming pool and golf course had lost allure. Prospect of another holiday spent mostly with the children rather than her husband turned Marci off.

At least consider the challenge, she'd pleaded. The two of us embarked upon a rugged road absent itinerary and with few amenities. Let's see if we still have the stuff to improvise, see if we can have a good time on our own. Eventually he had granted her request, though more for the sake of fairness than in the spirit of hope.

"Jerry, do you love me?" she asked as the train clacked and rattled through the cold darkness.

"You know I do," he answered and gave her shoulder a perfunctory squeeze.

"How do you love me?" she pursued, aware that she risked guttering their allegiance candle.

"I love you as a flower loves the rain." Her serious tone put him on the defensive.

"Would you ever leave me?"

"Of course not. Absolutely out of the question."

"Why?"

He paused before answering, having ascertained that this was one of those times when he was called upon to appease his wife. Complete assurance was not in his power, but to put the question of commitment to rest—at least for the moment to rest—he would be thorough in his response. She could see wheels turning in his head.

"Companionship first off. I'm not the solitary sort, and over the years, I've grown to appreciate your company. We can talk to one another, for instance, without any need to be germane. Just prattle on sometimes, and so what."

Marci nodded.

"Then there are the children, naturally. They're not your kids or my kids, but our kids. And I think they count on our staying together."

Point taken. What was next?

"Finances? To be practical, and somewhere along the line we have to get practical, our resources are so enmeshed that if we ever did split up, it'd take a platoon of lawyers and accountants to ax out shares."

He waited for the scenario of a court battle to sink in.

"And sex goes without mention. At the end of the day, we're pretty good lovers. I once asked one of my employees, a dowdy woman who'd been divorced for years, if she had a boyfriend. She said there was a fellow who dropped by now and again. I asked how the relationship worked. She said they were comfortable together, and that's all I needed to know. And she was right, that's all I did need to know. I'm not about to shine on the one woman I'm comfortable with."

Marci waited to hear if there was anything else.

"So what's it all come down to?" Jerry summarized. "Simple, I think. It wouldn't be my choice to dissolve an established partnership."

As he waited for a response, Marci reviewed his presentation. The first two bullets on the white board he no doubt conjured in his head she agreed to without reservation. The third was right but understated in that he was by far the greater contributor to their wealth. Her work in theater would not be possible were it not for Jerry's success in business. The fourth bullet marked the beginning of disquiet. A certain taboo subject left unstated. Jerry's flings with those pert little packages. He might be faithful now only because she had laid down the law.

What it all came to was as he said; they had become contractual partners. She hated Jerry's summation. Was their marriage no more than a solid business relationship?

"I would never leave you," she murmured in a tone that was supposed to express conviction. She wanted to believe that their marriage went beyond a win-win deal.

"I know. We're partners all right."

Oh, Christ. "I mean, I'd never leave," she cried desperately. "During your last affair, I realized there was no way I'd ever leave. My ultimatum at the time was complete bluster."

"Marci, please, lower your voice. And don't hold past mistakes over my head. To be honest," he added, "you weren't completely faithful either."

"We were dating then. We weren't married yet."

"Still counts."

"I'm not keeping score. Please don't think I'm keeping score."

"Then what?"

She didn't know what, other than there was a *what*, a huge *what* that got bigger and bigger the nearer she crept up to it and the more cunningly its meaning evaded her grasp. The w*hat* was a prickly force that pushed her and Jerry apart even while it prevented their separation. She could no longer abide the *what* without his help. He must sneak up on the *what* from his side so that with arms outstretched the two of them could close on the meaning of the *what* together. But Jerry hadn't spotted the *what*, or so he claimed. He did not want to deal with the wicked wondrous *what*, and that's why he pretended to be unaware of any need to join her struggle.

When the train engine whined and the lights in the car died a third time, she gave up. Jerry swore angrily; the Peruvians griped among themselves. But Marci felt no hostility; she thought only of the day's collapse. Despair clung to her like a crippled appendage. She knew for sure the train engine had quit for good this time, that its exhausted crew had given up the fight. The conductor wouldn't bother to come round to their dark car again. At culmination of the day's collapse, another *what* emerged, or really the same wicked wondrous *what* manifest in all instances of hopelessness.

For several minutes, Marci and Jerry sat without moving in the stalled car. The night's humid cold penetrated their wraps and assaulted their bones. At the moment of truth, they hung by each other like sides of beef left to age in a freezer locker.

Then a local man who sat across the aisle from them quit scowling at the ceiling and rose to his feet. He issued an order. His wife pushed upright, roused their three drowsy children, and began to assemble the family's possessions. With one hand, the man caught up two satchels and with the other lifted their youngest child to his shoulder. Once organized, he led his charges to the front of the car and ushered them into the darkness outside.

Jerry glanced at Marci; she had nothing to say. He shrugged and crossed to the window the Peruvian had abandoned.

"See anything?" she asked, still hugging herself on the bench.

"Just our *compadre* standing next to a dirt road with his wife and kids. Bag and baggage gathered at their feet. Think refugees."

Sluggish minutes passed, while Jerry, with one arm propped on the narrow windowsill, awaited developments. Marci sank into herself and eased toward lethargy.

"More *compadres* have joined them," Jerry observed by and by.

His voice parted the curtain Marci had lowered before her mind.

"I'll be damned," he added.

"What?"

"A cab just pulled up. The driver's loading luggage."

She straightened.

"You wouldn't believe how many people you can fit in a taxi," Jerry said.

"Room for two more?"

"Nope. They're gone."

"Maybe the driver will come back."

"Of course he will. He's hit the mother lode."

Without further delay, Jerry stepped back across the aisle and reached for their bags. Marci scooted by him to see for herself what was happening outside. As she watched, one, two, three sets of headlights, four, five—a veritable fleet of automobiles wound out of the darkness and closed upon the becalmed train.

"We're saved," she quipped in the rising commotion.

"Let's get in line," Jerry returned brusquely. "Unless you're still dead set on staying with the old bucket."

If not near the end of her rope, Marci might have bristled at his latest dig.

Taxis pulled up as close to the train as the agitated throng next the tracks allowed. Headlights swept the melee briefly before drivers parked with beams aimed every which way. Passengers mobbed the taxi nearest them or, if that cab filled before they arrived, scrambled to the next closest. For the sake of order, Marci would have been willing to wait her rightful turn to be picked up, but Jerry, ever the competitor, joined the fracas. He jerked her away from a last look at the crippled train engine, now dark as a tomb. Pulling her this way and that, he hollered at one driver and another, offering to pay whatever exorbitant rate the market required. He soon discovered, however, that offers of money received no notice. Opting then for a more aggressive tactic, he forced his bulk into the open door of the forth cab he encountered and thrust Marci into the last cramped space available within. After she was wedged into the taxi, he crammed her backpack in on top of her.

"Jerry, don't leave me," she cried through a closed window.

"It's all right," he shouted back at her. "There's another cab over there. I'll meet you back at the hostel."

And then, the overloaded car took off, or edged into motion rather, the weight it bore having flattened its worn springs and ballooned its bald tires. Within the close quarters of the vehicle, Marci could barely move, so that before the driver completed a turnabout, she had lost sight of Jerry. Again they had become separated, which state of affairs was beginning to feel routine. "Why fight it?" was her reaction to Jerry's latest betrayal. She was on her own again.

As the taxi reached cruising speed, Marci faced bravely forward and surrendered to discomfort. The door handle at her side dug into her ribs, and there was no chance of shifting position to alleviate the hurt. An infant in the front seat of the packed crate screamed defiance. Marci wanted to howl too, but what good would that do?

Her door had to be opened from outside, once the cab pulled up at Cuzco's main square. Sudden release from confinement toppled her into the street where she landed on hands and knees. Her backpack tumbled after and fell against her arm, causing it to buckle. A man exiting next stepped on her calf. He hadn't meant to, hastened to apologize, and even took the time to help her up. Then, once she stood erect, he went about his business. Well and good, Marci needed nothing more from him. She paid her fare, shouldered her pack, and stepped off the street, trusting that Jerry would be along soon.

But as other taxis pulled up to the curb to disgorge their loads, he failed to turn up. At first, the cabs arrived in a steady stream, and she eyed expectantly each fanning out of fares. When the line of cars began to peter out, she set to pacing in the cold and wondered what had detained her husband. She considered returning to their room and waiting for him there but was afraid that if she left her post, he wouldn't know what had happened to her.

To gain a wider view of the square, Marci made her way to its central fountain, sloughed off her pack, and stood hugging herself. Water spilled from the horns of stone sea nymphs and over the edges of stacked urns. The town's main cathedral was bathed in orange light, looking more like a fantasy castle than a divine residence. Few other people occupied the plaza. At its north end, restaurant hucksters, standing beneath a block-long run of arched facades, looked like they were ready to call it a night.

It was the postdinner hour, when most tourists still awake had settled in side-street bars. According to guidebooks, Cuzco's taverns offered cocktails and live music. In Marci's state of anxious loneliness, it struck her as blasphemous that the city's contemporary guise gave so little reminder of past empire.

She finally caught sight of Jerry as he rounded a corner near the lesser cathedral at the south end of the plaza. He was in company with three other people—the two French boys he had raced off Huayna Picchu and a woman with blond hair feathered onto the back of a green, insulated jacket. Her husband disappeared around a corner as she called to him. She called his name louder, grabbed her pack, and charged off in the direction he'd taken.

By the time she reached the corner, he was nowhere to be seen. Hurrying along a narrow sidewalk beyond, she discerned that he could have taken any of several tight arteries that angled upward into blocks of abutted two- and three-story buildings. She stopped and called his name again; the silence returned her was enervating. Cuzco was known to be a rough town at night, the neighborhoods teeming with thieves who preyed on unwary travelers. She didn't know whether she should turn back toward the plaza, whose light shown behind her, or soldier on into dark and forbidding territory. Pack straps dug into her shoulders; her legs felt leaden. She stood alone for several minutes unable to decide what to do, turning her head up the street and down, recounting in self-pity how often on this cursed day she had been forsaken.

A cab pulled up soon after she returned to the square. Its driver helped load her pack onto the backseat and then held the front door open. She gave the name of her hostel as they pulled away from the curb. They passed under an arch that gated the street leading to the address. Along the way, they ran by sidewalk food stands, whose owners were shutting down for the night, and then entered dark environs she and Jerry had been ferried though two nights before. Small groups of sinister-looking men lurked in the gloom of eroding buildings. The cabby waited while she knocked at the wooden door of the hostel named Providence. Jimmy, the night watchman, answered. Key in hand, he led her to her room. Inside, she reset the lock, disrobed, and climbed into bed.

In dead of night, fumbling hands woke her from a dreamless sleep. She blinked at Jerry's dark form hovering above, unable to make out his features. He leaned over the edge of the bed and stroked her breast though the blankets. He reeked of alcohol. When his cold fingers slipped to bare skin beneath the covers, she cringed. "You've got to be out of your fucking mind."

"Make excellent use of the room," he answered as his hand slipped to her belly.

By the slow, careful way he spoke, she knew he was profoundly drunk. When intoxicated, Jerry took extreme care not to slur his words.

"Where the hell have you been?"

She wanted to relate details of her most recent torments, but he answered before she could formulate a narrative.

"Came here first. Told you I would."

"When did you say that?"

"Last thing before you drove off."

Possibly he had said they would meet back at their room, but that didn't exonerate him from forcing her into a taxicab against her will.

"I wanted to ride with you," she reproached him.

"Wanted to stay with the train too," he pointed out.

"If you must know," she countered, ire rising, "I took my cue from the Peruvians. I figured they understood better than the rest of us what was up."

"Stayed with the train because they're poor. Already bought one ticket to town."

"Why'd you keep that insight to yourself?"

"Seemed you wanted me agreeable."

"How chivalrous."

It was unfair and a mistake to mock him. She felt his hand stiffen.

"Chivalrous," he repeated slowly. "Trip your idea, as I recall. Went along. Wanted to accommodate—"

She cut him short.

"You should have spoken up. Instead, you preferred to pout."

"Pout?" he repeated with a pretense of disbelief. "Pouting is your department."

"That's right, I forgot. Stern silence is more your style."

He backed away and shuffled to his side of the room. The other mattress creaked as he lowered himself upon it. Rather than point out that his behavior verified her complaint, she turned toward the wall.

"I wonder why we stay together," she muttered. "You ever wonder why, Jerry?"

One of his boots dropped to the floor. She waited, but evidently, his other boot was too much trouble for him to deal with just now. Bedsprings creaked again.

"Don't be ridiculous," he answered, and she knew it was his parting shot for the night. No matter what she added, he would say nothing else. He would fall asleep, willfully ignorant of her fury.

She'd like to have possessed his power of forgetfulness, for then she could have slept too. But she didn't, and as a consequence, she couldn't. No, Marci lay in bed listening to her husband breathe. Her mind raced over images uncalled for and too insistent to be dreams. If they were at home, she would have gotten out of bed and gone downstairs to read. She'd have fallen asleep in her favorite recliner.

But Simon's disembodied head entered upon the scene, and stone condor wings rising out of forest greenery gutted a newborn cloud. Jerry's snores toppled dollhouse walls that had been erected at the epicenter of an earthquake. "Sometimes love feels like loathing," she murmured while her heart banged against her ribcage. Trembling bones, shuddering trees, and toppling rocks resounded. Collapse of her world went on and on, but the pounding failed to grind consciousness to dust.

When love feels like loathing, you don't get to sleep; you face the morning instead with your head aching from exhaustion. If you didn't know better, you'd say you'd tied one on the night before. But it was your business partner—his summation of the relationship, remember—who attended last night's party and left you to confront the hangover.

With morning already attended to by people outside the room, Marci permitted herself to be drawn to the toilet. The shower spigot's tepid outrush revived her somewhat, and toweling off, she stared at her faded image in a mirror above the sink. Her blank expression registered no reaction to affront. Out of habit, she brushed her teeth and combed her hair.

Once dressed, she sat at the foot of her bed and contemplated hairline cracks spread like a thicket on a dirty yellow wall next the bathroom door. Notion of a program for the day seeped out of the branching fissure and made reference to an identical notion, which had revealed itself sometime yesterday. Jerry had endorsed the notion as she recalled, but whether before or after the boy had fallen off Huayna Picchu she couldn't say. It required too much concentration to relive yesterday's chronology, easier to blow off spent events and face a temporal unraveling yet in the making.

Her husband lay on his back in his boxer shorts (hadn't he gone to bed last night fully clothed?) with pale light streaming dust motes, crinkly as pubic shavings, upon his midsection. Though his head remained in shadow, his open mouth and hairy nostrils were in evidence. The knuckles of one hand, fingers curled, touched upon a grungy linoleum square beneath his bed.

"Time to get up," she said with no conviction.

He barely stirred.

"Time to face the music," she added to herself.

It could be that remonstrations would again ensue when he woke up, but that was tough luck. The next act in their absurdity play had already started. She no longer felt like the lead in their ridiculous drama, and if ever the director, she'd resigned the flop. And yet the show must go on. With a weary nod to inevitability, Marci forced herself to rise, step to the edge of Jerry's bed, press her hand to his solar plexus, and work his pump.

"Yeah?" he groaned without opening his eyes, breath smelling of unnamable rot.

"We're off to Pisac," she said, taking consolation in the disruption she caused his sleep.

"A piece of sack? Christ, Marci, what do we want with piece of sack?"

"Pisac," she repeated curtly, then giggled in spite of herself. "It's a place, not a thing."

"We taking a train to this place?"

"We're taking a bus."

His lashes fluttered and his pupils peeked out from between a pair of slits in his head. "Hate to break the news, babe."

"Go ahead. I'll be brave."

"It's a little known fact, but a fact nonetheless, that buses break down more often than trains."

If this sort of banter continued between them, the coming day might be tolerable.

"The bus to Pisac never breaks down. According to an article published in *National Geographic*, the bus we're taking is the most reliable ever built."

"Sure as hell then, it's toast."

"No, they change it out every week with an even more dependable bus."

Jerry closed his eyes again, and Marci despaired. A certain policy, lately indemnified by the most reliable of insurers, was about to be put in force. She could deny the policy's relevance to current circumstance but would only be going through the motions.

"You're not coming with me, are you?"

His hesitation bespoke regret—she had to give him that.

"Really sorry, but I'm too beat up to move. I just can't, babe. Maybe in an hour or two. Better yet, this afternoon."

Irritation registered in her belly, but the emotion lacked staying power.

"Reckon it's my never mind then."

He turned away from her, definitely in pain. "Wait till I'm better," he pleaded, and a few shallow breaths later added, "But suit yourself. I wouldn't blame you for taking off without me."

Challenging his wheedling excuse would have produced about as effective a result as kicking a sick horse. Better to walk away from Old Paint before the nag made her cry.

"You're sure."

"I'm not sure of anything."

"Just so you know I'm leaving."

"Okay."

"I don't know when I'll be back."

"Well, be careful."

"I will. Sure you don't mind?"

"Not your fault I'm incapacitated."

"Right. Just so you know."

"I'm fine, Marci, with whatever you decide. Really."

So that was that; the day's program did not include Jerry's participation. After dropping a half-empty bottle of filtered water into her daypack, she left the room.

Outside, map-blue sky glanced though shifting gaps in an itinerant mass of ash-colored cloud. In anticipation of cool weather, she had put on a tweed vest and nylon pullover before setting out. A rumpled olive drab fedora covered her head. Thus she sallied forth more or less in local costume, for hereabouts women often wore felt fedoras in public. Their men folk, by contrast, either sported baseball caps or eschewed headgear altogether.

On the cobbled street outside Providence at mid-morning hour, Cuzco's residents steered toward the city center. A few blocks down the byway, three stone arches loomed above an awkward rank of portable stalls that spilled off a sidewalk curb in front of small bakeries and closet-sized *curio* shops. The other side of the street sprawled a neighborhood market where heaps of citrus fruit and salad vegetables were made available to the Indio public. For breakfast, Marci could have selected from a hearty fare: chunks of beef heart spitted on a wooden stick with a whole potato stuck on top, grilled chicken parts served on a paper plate, or an ear of corn freshly roasted. She could have sat on a squat stool in front of a charcoal brazier while she ate, and while a cacophony of taxicabs and minibuses assaulted her ears. Children roamed freely about the market and women looking too old to be bearing babies yet stood by with infants slung in shawl hammocks on their backs. Stray mongrels scrounged for and fought over choice bits of refuse. At the end of the street stood newsstands, where knots of middle-aged men perused headlines of various national dailies tacked to and overlapped upon display poles. It occurred to Marci as she made her way through the noisy crowd, and as she inhaled a current of vegetable odors and unwashed socks, that Peruvians faced their days with glum expressions. They maintained dour demeanors even when they smiled, which wasn't often.

Windy spray, blown from the Plaza de Armas fountain, caught her in the face as she emerged from the walkway tunnel to the left of a greater arch that served motor traffic. At the apex of the structure, either Jesus or one of his faithful saints stood on a flat pedestal with arms uplifted and with a pair of condors perched either side of him. She stopped at a sweets stand on the sidewalk adjacent the plaza to buy two small cellophane bags of roasted *habas* (browned lima beans, heavily salted) whose nutty flavor appealed to her taste.

This morning, the bus that ran the Sacred Valley route wasn't crowded. During the half-hour ride to Pisac, she nodded off then woke groggy and disoriented and fumbled with her daypack while the driver waited patiently for her to disembark. A short walk uphill to the village cleared her head. Off-center of the *pueblo's* three-step cobbled square grew a single palm tree. At the back of its shaggy fronds rose a church with tall blue double doors and three arched bell mounts. Green hills (or perhaps they were tall enough to be called mountains) backdropped the town.

She crossed its square to a combination café-grocery store, and took a seat at one of two folding tables set up inside. The Dutch owner, a fiftyish gent with a full head of salt and pepper hair, poured her a cup of *mate*. The two of them struck up a friendly conversation during which Marci learned that the trailhead she sought was located behind the village church. Her host asked if she'd visited Machu Picchu yet, and Marci made mention of Simon's fall the day before. The proprietor hadn't heard about the accident. It surprised Marci how calmly she filled him in on the details. Either time had ameliorated the horror, or she was too brain-dead at the moment to recall grief.

It didn't take long for her to recognize that the verdant hills at the back of town were considerably steeper than they appeared from the square. Coca tea had given her a boost, but by the first crosscut in the trail leading to the ruins, she was bent at the waist and breathing hard. Lack of sleep had done her in. According to her guidebook, the hike would take two hours, which, in her weakened state, seemed an interminable length of time. No way was she going to endure a two-hour climb.

A short ways above town, she happened upon a stripped tree branch some previous hiker had cast aside. Hefted, the stick measured the right height to serve as a staff. By short and steady steps after taking up the prop, she managed to negotiate a number of switchbacks before stopping for a blow. Tan roofs checkered a placid street grid below. Farm terraces laddered neighboring hills across the wide, gentle flow of the Urubamba. The Sacred Valley made stark contrast to the wild dynamics of rain forest at Machu Picchu. Marci took comfort in the view. Here, she thought, domestic Inca spirits had provided means for an ancient people to grow their crops and raise their children.

Grass and shrub covered the steep slope above her; pink and dark-gray rocks dotted the incline. Clusters of cacti with long-bladed leaves sprung up throughout. In a short while, both town and terraces disappeared from rearward view and Marci drew deeply on paltry reserves of vigor. When it came to her that she had met no living soul since leaving the village, she worried she might be lost. Being alone on the mountain, she feared she might miss a critical turn in the track. The guidebook she'd left behind at the hostel included no photographs of the site she made for, nor were there public notices along the trail to direct her. She plodded on searching in vain for some sort of landmark until fatigue engendered a fantasy in which she imagined herself an aimless wayfarer. There was a sense in the fantasy of wandering beyond clues even to her identity.

At one particularly steep pitch on the slope, she stopped, heaved a sigh, and raised her head. It was here that she spotted a change in the landscape. Rows of cut and fitted stones, mottled with light aqua, gray, and black lichen, jutted to a height of twenty feet or so from a mountaintop. It wasn't surprising that she hadn't noticed the construction earlier, for its colors blended perfectly with the hues of surrounding terrain. Marci leaned forward on her stick and studied the redoubt. Crosswise, the wall had been built in a trapezoidal shape, which recurred in its turret apertures and the zigzag layout of its base. She trudged the last fifty yards to the near corner of the construct and followed a path that led to a circular flat within a squat tower. Straw and grass matted the enclosed ground; three rock windows set in the turret's curved front gave a panoramic view of the valley. Were Simon with her, he might have pointed out that soldiers keeping watch from the tower could spot an enemy's approach long before the invading army bivouacked and prepared for assault.

In memory of the boy, she lingered for several minutes before the fortress vista. Poor Simon. He had wanted in the worst way to don a uniform, shoulder a rifle, and enter battle. Who knew what her accidental cohort might have achieved had his life not been cut short, had she intervened at that crucial instant when his future hung in the balance? There was nothing she could do now but submit to pity, and as if responding to pity's call, his face appeared out the middle turret opening.

Simon had the same gleam in his eye that she had glimpsed just before he fell, and the same ironic grimace creased his lips. Marci gasped. The apparition made to speak, but before it did, she spun away from the tower window, stumbled onto the path outside, and rushed up a shallow slope to the mountain's crest. She ran along a ridge toward fallen walls and roofless buildings, hoping that scattered stone and dilapidated edifice would provide refuge, which was a crazy way to think, though no more insane than the panic that churned her feet. When clamor erupted from a hump of earth to the left, she thought Simon's ghost had circled round and sprung an ambush.

Snarling, barking dogs rushed upon her with bared fangs ready to pierce and rend tender flesh. So sudden was the attack that Marci had time only to react instinctively. She gripped her staff with both hands and pointed its blunt end at the charging animals. They pulled up at her show of resistance, coiled back on their haunches, lunged at her, recoiled, lunged again, raged at her like a pair of murder-bent psychopaths. The slightly smaller of the two, a brown and caramel-spotted longhair, skittered left of the stick, while the larger, a black-and-white shepherd mix, closed from the right. "Help me," Marci whimpered as she retreated, but there was no other human being around to hear her plea.

The brown dog lowered its head and sprang at her legs. Marci jerked up on the stick. Miraculously, the tip caught the critter squarely under its muzzle, slamming shut its jaws and snapping together its teeth. The cur let out a yelp and scooted rearward, half a dozen paces.

For an instant, her lucky shot seemed to have ended the onslaught. But then, the black dog redoubled its berserkery; it lunged forward and caught the end of the staff in its jaws. Marci held on tightly as the beast shook the stick violently back and forth. A sob broke from her throat. With her defenses neutralized, Marci braced for pain.

A fist-sized rock whizzed by and struck the brown mutt's ribcage. It grunted and stumbled sideways. Another stone zipped by its head. Both dogs turned away from Marci and directed their outrage at a woman crouched up the path with another missile raised to the level of her ear. Letting fly, she barely missed the shepherd mix. In response to the counter attack, the dogs gave ground.

Striding forward, the stranger made to hurl another rock. For several seconds, the dogs answered with threats of their own. In that the stone-slinger continued her advance, however, they backed off. Little by little, they shuffled toward the knoll from which they'd first launched themselves. The woman sent a third projectile in their direction. Begrudgingly, these self-appointed lords of the territory withdrew.

"I'm sorry," Marci stammered when she recognized the danger had passed. She had no idea what she apologized for.

"Good," her benefactor said.

Marci stared at the woman for several seconds. "I've never been so scared in my life."

The Peruvian took her hand. Her palm was dry and rough, her grip strong. She pulled Marci away from the scene of battle.

"Talk about mean dogs," Marci babbled, stumbling after her rescuer. "There are leash laws where I come from. Those two wilders need to be apprehended and euthanized."

The woman bobbed her head sympathetically. Marci hardly noticed where she was being led.

"Those two sons of bitches wanted in the worst way to rip me to pieces. They would have too, if you hadn't come along. What about the children who live around here? Who's looking out for helpless children? Don't you have a Humane Society in Peru? Who do you call to report vicious dogs? My god, there must be horrible incidents."

The woman stopped and patted her on the shoulder. She wanted Marci to sit down.

They had entered a circular enclosure through a doorway topped by a gray stone lintel. The wall they sat on was uneven; at its tallest, on either side of the doorway, it reached no higher than five feet. There were gaps in the circle where unmortarred blocks had fallen over. A massive black boulder, chest-high and flat on top, dominated the plot.

"Sun temple," Marci's companion said once she could get a word in edgewise.

Marci stared at her.

"Mans pray here," the woman added with a sweep of her arm. "Moon temple, for womans. Star temple, childs. Rainbow temple, for priests."

Marci remained dumbfounded.

"Ten soles, I show to you."

She had no idea what the woman was talking about. "Ten soles?" she questioned, merely repeating what she'd heard.

The woman shrugged. "Regular price."

"Ten soles," Marci iterated. "Regular price."

Then it hit her. Apparently the event that had scared her witless merited no further concern from the local woman. For Marci's chance champion, it was on to more important matters, like offering guide service.

"Hang on, girl," Marci said, raising an index finger. At this pass it seemed to her appropriate that she and the Peruvian introduce themselves. She also wanted to tell this impressive example of the female gender how grateful she was for her timely aid. "You know you saved my life?"

"Not know. Ten soles."

"Well, you did. I'd be gushing blood, if not for you."

"Yes?" said the woman.

"Better believe it."

"Yes?"

"You don't understand what I'm saying, do you?"

"Ten soles, yes?"

Okay, screw it. Ten soles. What did that amount to in dollars? Marci did the math—less than five bucks.

"My name, Alícia," the hopeful guide added and waited for her prospective client to answer.

"Marci."

Alícia wore tan trousers and a blue denim jacket over a green and brown wool sweater. Her clothes smelled of dust and dried sweat. Her long black hair was parted in the middle and pinned up behind a roughly square-shaped head. She had round cheeks, a flat chin, and a blunt nose. Since arriving in Peru, Marci had glanced over many such visages without pausing to examine a single one in detail.

"I show to you Intihurtana," Alícia said with another sweep of her hand.

"Show me what?" Marci questioned.

At which point, the good citizen of Peru determined that the two of them had struck a deal. She stood and beckoned Marci to follow.

They walked a short ways off the crest, upon which the sun temple was located, and then headed back the way they'd come. Alícia pulled up before another protuberance of black stone. Marci wondered what it would take to achieve common cause with her savior.

"Omen stone. Priests says *futuro* here."

She must somehow prompt Alícia to talk about herself. It had been abysmally inconsiderate on her part to have avoided neighborly conversation with any of the local residents before. Yet now that an opportunity to set things right was handed her on a serving tray, she could not think how to begin a dialogue.

Her eye swept the omen stone. Halfway along one side, a carved shelf supported rows of blocks the same beige color as those that formed waist-high walls guarding the outcrop. Behind the black boulder rose a higher rounded wall. To the right was located the squat remains of a building whose outer edge met the upsweep of a deep ravine.

"Inca people building high on a mountain," Alícia said, continuing her presentation. "Much water *abajo*," she went on, pointing into the ravine. "Priest says *futuro*."

"Do you actually believe that?" Marci questioned, thinking she'd been granted an opening.

Her guide compressed her lips. "Not know."

While Marci wracked her brain for something else to say, the guide chose to continue the tour.

They returned to the sun temple, circled around behind it, and descended a flight of broken stairs. In the hollow below, another black rock, the most massive yet, served as foundation for more beige blocks that rose up its sides. Marci studied the contours of the dark outcrop and realized then it was actually an extension of the same one she'd seen in the sun temple. A single gigantic black boulder had been partitioned by Inca architects at various levels to establish separate locales of worship. Recalling Machu Picchu, Marci again marveled at the ancient people's genius for erecting buildings that merged with existing features of the landscape. Beneath the rock, a short triangular pedestal had been fashioned from the floor of the hollow, and upon the pedestal had been carved the three symmetrical tiers of the Inca cross.

"Inca cross," Alícia informed her unnecessarily.

Marci dropped to one knee in front of the artifact and placed her hand on its top shelf. At one time, she presumed, the figure's three tiers had been sharp-edged, but tens of thousands of hands, over hundreds of years, had dulled its shape.

Alícia dropped down next to Marci and patted the top of the cross. "*Futuro*," she said. "Condor kingdom."

Marci pondered on the instruction given. "The top shelf of the Inca cross represents the future," she said to show she was paying attention. Then she made a connection. "The condor's realm includes the afterlife. Makes sense, when you think about it."

Alícia let loose a gay, soprano trill. She found the difficulty of communicating with her foreign client hilarious.

Nonetheless, Marci persevered. Dropping her hand to the next shelf on the cross, she asked, "What does the middle step represent?"

"*Presente*," Alícia responded without hesitation. "Jaguar kingdom."

Okay, so that meant the lowest tier signified, "Past time."

"Serpent kingdom," Alícia agreed.

"Right," Marci confirmed and then had an idea. "My past," she said, tapping her chest and grinning. "My past has been the work of a truly devious snake."

Alícia squinted at her.

"My past," Marci repeated. "Bad serpent."

Alícia chuckled. Her laughter had range, from soprano chirp to baritone rumble. "*Mi pasado*," she answered and patted her chest as Marci had. "Bad serpent *también*."

Their dialogue had finally got going. After agreeing on disappointments in their lives, it was just a matter of considering what preoccupied all women no matter where they lived.

"Kids?" Marci asked, extending one hand to shoulder height. "You know, short people."

The guide raised her palm with index finger pointed upward. "Childs," she said and nodded. "*Niños.*"

"You have *niños*?" Marci asked.

"Four," Alícia answered and thrust four digits in Marci's face. "You?"

"Two."

"Three *muhachos. Una chica.* You?"

"I have a daughter, thirteen-years-old, and a son, sixteen."

"Good *niños*?"

"Very good *niños*," Marci answered proudly.

"I *también*," the guide agreed with an expression that affirmed, "Yeah, don't ya just gotta love your kids."

After a pause, Marci asked a more penetrating question. "How about your husband? He around?"

"*Me pregunta de mi marido ¿no?*"

"Yep." There was no confusion about the topic of their conversation now.

"Yep," Alícia mimicked Marci and then scowled. "*Él es todo cabrón. No sirve para nada.*" She tossed her hands out from her body as if ridding them of a substance both sticky and repulsive.

"Sent the bastard packing, I take it," Marci said. "Gone," she added and mimicked Alícia's gesture.

"*Ya se fue,*" Alícia answered. There was every bit of consternation Marci felt at times for her own marriage in the guide's frown.

"He not love I," Alícia added with an exaggerated pout. "He not love I, *así que*, I not love he."

"Sorry," Marci said.

"He fuck many, many womans."

Well, Alícia knew one pertinent English word all right. "What a creep," she said.

What a total degenerate, she could have put in as well. Another unfaithful husband. On the other hand, she hoped, this was where she and Alícia parted company. Jerry had strayed to be sure, but when confronted, he had dutifully and remorsefully desisted in his philandering. Since Marci had called him to account, he had towed the line, so far as other women went. Marci decided her husband was of a less irksome variety than Alícia's former mate.

Her guide must have sensed the meaning of the word *creep* because she repeated, "*Él es cabrón,*" and turned her head aside.

Sometimes love feels like loathing, Marci recalled.

"I show to you," Alícia said and rose suddenly, taking her by the hand.

"What?"

"I show to you," Alícia said, pulling Marci to her feet and urging her to climb back up the stairs they had come down before.

The track they followed atop the ridge passed through a narrow alley with roofless, single-story housing to either side. More stone steps, which Alícia ascended and descended effortlessly, were fitted into humps on the mountain's spine. Marci reckoned the woman must have bellows for lungs and calves of steel.

They emerged upon an open height that gave a view of a paved road snaking through sweeps of trees at the bottom of a ravine. The road followed a stream that flowed toward the Urubamba. About a third of the way down the near side of the ravine could be seen remains of a hamlet. Marci pulled up when she discerned the village outline.

"Condor?" Marci called while Alícia continued on ahead. A footpath ran along the top edge of one of the village wings. Curved farm terraces under the wings stepped down toward the blue stream below.

"No," Alícia answered without pause in her march. "*Caracara.*"

Surly she gave the name of some sort of bird, Marci concluded, because if the hamlet she saw wasn't avian in shape, she couldn't trust her vision.

"*Venga,*" Alícia shouted, commanding her to catch up. "I show to you."

The woman stopped before a twenty-foot-tall cylinder of blocks, which stood by itself on the brink of a precipice.

"Boss house," Alícia said.

Marci shrugged to let Alícia know that she'd lost the thread of their talk.

The woman raised her middle, ring, and pinkie fingers. Her knitted brow implied that the lesson she was about to impart was the most important of all. "Three *reglas para esclavos,*" she began

What did the word *reglas* mean? Marci questioned. Had to do with the boss's house, which overlooked the river gorge. From his platform, the boss could watch what was happening on the terraces.

"Three regulations," Marci said aloud, proud of herself for deciphering Alícia's meaning. The boss was charged with making sure that farm laborers (no, *esclavos,* dummy) adhered to three rules. Her guide was about to teach her the three rules Inca slaves were compelled to follow.

"Work," Alícia said and retracted her middle finger.

Marci bobbed her head. The first rule required that slaves do the work assigned them. In lieu of financial incentive, what else but a command to toil would keep them in line?

"Not lie," Alícia added and dropped her ring finger.

Thank goodness the woman knew the English word *lie,* for how the concept might have been conveyed with hand signals Marci could not imagine.

"Not steal," her guide said, and down went her smallest digit.

In this way Marci learned the three slave laws. They were few and easy to comprehend. If you had the rotten luck of being made a slave in an Inca community, at least you knew where you stood with your captors.

When Alícia was satisfied that Marci understood instruction imparted thus far, she held up both hands to indicate that there was more to the lesson.

"Three *chanzes*."

Surely. Here came consequences for not being a good slave.

"One *chanze*," Alícia told her, extending middle fingers on both hands, which stuck Marci as comical given what a raised middle finger meant in the States. "One *chanze*, boss talk."

At first offense, the misbehaving slave was issued a warning.

"Two *chanze*," Alícia said, snapping up doubled fourth fingers, "work *solo*."

A two-time offender was made to work a piece of land in solitary. No one to talk to and no one to help with the heavy lifting. It was easier, too, for the overseer to keep an eye on a miscreant isolated from his fellows.

"Three *chanze*," Alícia said and paused. She cast about until she located a stick lying on the ground. Taking up the switch, she gave her leg a couple of stern raps.

Marci watched the performance with lips compressed. This was bad business, if the expression on the Peruvian's face was any indication. A slave who broke the rules a third time could expect a beating. After that he would certainly be aware that he'd used up all his chances.

"*Después tres chanzes*," Alícia added and pointed down the precipice. A pair of creases formed between her eyebrows. Wasn't hard to figure out what she meant. Break the rules a fourth time, slave, and you're toast. It's off the top of the boss's house without a parachute. Marci recalled the look on Simon's face when he plunged off Huayna Picchu. She turned away from Alícia, her heart fluttering.

"*Mi marido tenía mucho más que tres chanzes*," Alícia went on, compelling Marci to look back at her. "*Mi esposo ¿no? El cabrón.*" Her constricted expression bespoke summary judgment. She was talking about her former spouse.

"He not work," Alícia said. "He lie," she added to his list of offenses. "He steal." For Alícia, the rules slaves must obey applied as well to husbands. "He fuck many, many womans," she threw in for good measure. The Peruvian crossed her arms on her chest and thrust her chin upward.

Oh Jesus, Marci realized in shock, the woman had whacked the father of her children. She stared back at Alícia open-mouthed. Here she was in the middle of Peru, alone on a mountain, standing within reach of a confessed killer.

The guide glowered at her. While the two of them remained motionless, Marci calculated the distance between them. Take off and don't look back, girl, her brain commanded. Don't even think about how scared you are because fear will only slow you down.

Before she managed to even spin around, Alícia rushed up and grabbed her by the arm. A whine broke from Marci's windpipe. "Please let me go," she begged. "I won't say a word."

"No," Alícia cried, and Marci cowered. She thought of Jerry and her children. They, who were her greatest reason to go on living, would never know how she'd met her end. She thought of Simon and prayed the boy had felt no pain when he crashed on the rocks beneath Huayna Picchu.

"*Muchas chanzes,*" Alícia said and released her arm. "*Pero ¡ya!*" she shouted and split her hands apart, ridding them again of her trashy ex.

"But why me?" Marci pleaded as hot tears ran down her face. "I'm not your enemy."

The guide's visage constricted and her eyes hardened.

"I don't speak Spanish," Marci stammered. "The police wouldn't understand me even if I did rat on you."

Alícia failed to comprehend the argument, but her lips parted suddenly and the crease that had formed on her brow disappeared. She slapped Marci's hand and then her own forehead. "I not killing he," she squealed, leaning forward. "I not killing he," she repeated, her head wagging back and forth.

Marci dared to exhale.

"*Calma,*" the guide told her and patted her shoulder. "*No hay problema. Calma. No hay problema.*"

"Thank goodness!" Marci exclaimed aloud. She wasn't going to die today. Alícia had refrained from whacking the bastard, much as he deserved the ultimate chastisement brought to bear on unrepentant Inca slaves. Bad mojo between those two, Marci admitted, but thank goodness Alícia had let the degenerate live. He was a lucky man. More importantly, so much more importantly, Marci was one fortunate member of the pampered American middle class.

"I'm so sorry," she mouthed, ashamed of herself for judging the righteous woman capable of murder. She wanted to sympathize with Alícia's plight, but what do you say to someone who'd married an utter cad? You're better off without the jerk? Yeah, right. Four kids and your only means of support hustling tourists at one of the secondary ruins on the gringo trail. Government's not going to send you a check, is it? Relatives are doing all they can to scrape by themselves. Well, at least you don't have to feed the dork anymore. You're still young; go back to school. Maybe you'll find a better mate, someone who wouldn't mind raising another man's children. Yeah, right.

Marci's gaze dropped to the ground between them. She felt terrible for the woman who had, that very afternoon, saved her life. Did Alícia regret having told her troubles to such an ingrate? Marci hadn't foreseen the distress she'd cause in attempting to befriend her savior. Such a vague purpose, or lack of purpose, had led again to proof of her ineptitude. There was nothing she could do for Alícia, as there was nothing she could have done for Simon either. Again the lesson of hopelessness, the clumsy part she played in other people's misery.

"*No se ponga triste,*" Alícia uttered and gave Marci a wan smile. The good woman dropped down upon the gravely ground in front of the boss's house. Enough, said her resigned demeanor, enough talk of faithless husbands. What can one do about bad choices already made?

Marci lowered herself on the ground too. She wished Alícia hadn't made the acquaintance of someone more capable of assistance.

From the daypack, she retrieved her water bottle and offered Alícia a drink. They both had a swig of water and snacked on the *habas.* They chatted awkwardly about how water from springs and from the Urubamba supplied the daily needs of people who had lived long ago at Pisac.

Resuming the tour, Alícia pointed out stone stalls where the Incas had taken ritual baths. They visited remains of smart domiciles where royalty had pursued privileged lifestyles. They made their way up stone steps that climbed through a narrow tunnel hacked out of solid rock. On the far side of what was called the serpent's tunnel, they ran into a party of five Peruvian males who were also touring the ruins. Three of them were young men, two middle-aged.

Hundreds of holes gaped in the brush-strewn face of a ravine on the other side of the mountain. Grave robbers had stripped the tombs of valuables. A gravel track led to a spare pink façade that fronted the royal family's crypt. As Marci scanned the cemetery, she noticed that the sun had dipped toward the horizon. She needed to start back for Cuzco soon. Jerry was probably wondering what kept her. The Dutchman at the café had advised her that the last bus to Cuzco departed Pisac in the late afternoon. It was time to settle accounts with Alícia. It pained Marci that they'd probably never see each other again.

Unfolding her wallet, she discovered to her dismay that a single twenty-sole bill was the only cash she had on hand. What had happened to the rest of her money? Hadn't she been supplied with plenty of the local script when she boarded the bus that morning? Evidently not. Jerry (oh, damn him anyway) must have got up during the night and dipped into their stash. Didn't want to be troubled with a trip to the ATM, did he? If he'd let her know they were short, she would have stopped by a bank that morning. But no. Her husband had too much *carbon* in him to consider other than his own needs.

Removing the bill from her wallet, she shrugged apologetically to Alícia. Their deal was for ten soles, but her guide was unable to make change. Nor could she be expected to forego payment for her services.

Marci solved the quandary by forking over the twenty soles. What the hell. Worst case scenario, she'd hail a cab in Pisac and instruct the driver to stop by a bank. No big deal.

And yet Alícia expressed gargantuan gratitude for the decision Marci took. She seemed to consider it a huge sacrifice. Upon receipt of the money, the woman pressed the bill to her forehead as if it were a gift from the gods. She took hold of Marci's wrists and kissed her on the cheek. When Marci turned to go, Alícia would have none of it.

Her benefactor scampered up the path that led to the cemetery and spoke to one of the men in the other tour party. Their conference lasted no more than a minute. Upon her return, Alícia signed to Marci that she'd arranged a ride for her to Cuzco. Marci enveloped the amazing woman in her arms.

Good day after all, she affirmed, as wind rushed over her face and shoulders from the open front windows of a rattletrap sedan. She sat wedged between a pair of teenagers who tapped their feet in time with heroic pan flute strains emanating from a tape deck jerry-mounted to the dash. Contentment settled over her person, a sense of accomplishment lifted her spirits. Instead of staying at the hostel and spending the day bickering with Jerry, she'd struck out on her own, and damn if everything hadn't turned out just fine.

Wasn't there a Chinese proverb that advised when a student is ready to learn her teacher will appear? Unbeknownst to Marci, she'd got out of bed that morning ready for Alicia's lesson. Not the bit about worthless husbands (small change, really), but about the revelation of female strength and power. It's not enough to rise complacently in the morning and presume the world will come to you. Or hang back and gripe about mistreatment. You must exercise the prerogative granted you as a creature born with intellect and will. Every day of difficulty, every desire to make things better requires decisive action. If you don't exercise your options, you're wasting your talents. And do take heart. You will find in striking out on your own that there are others in the world of the same mind and be pleased to learn they make excellent company.

The man who owned the car dropped her off in a bustling commercial district unfrequented by tourists. No matter. Marci now felt quite capable of finding her bearings in the unfamiliar neighborhood. Overcast had thinned; a brilliant evening sky shown through wide gaps in scudding clouds. She stopped at the intersection of a narrow street that dropped steeply between the whitewashed backsides of single-story residences. A section of Plaza de Armas appeared at the bottom of the declivity.

When she arrived at center city, a public demonstration held sway. Marci kept to the edge of the crowd, content to observe the spectacle from a distance. Against the ripple of several white fabric banners, an elementary-school-aged girl with long dark hair tied in ponytails either side of her head displayed a tag board sign. The youngster wore a long-sleeved white blouse and a red knee-length skirt with three green stripes running parallel to its hem. *"No contamines las aguas de los rios,"* read the little girl's slogan.

Such a determined expression on her countenance: full cheeks and sloe eyes committed to protection of Peru's sacred land. Look, Marci told herself, pressing her lips together, as were the lips of the child compressed, watch, and learn. In a land where conquistadors laid waste to a thriving culture, you see how survivors of the devastation proclaim that life is never hopeless. Without the slightest hint of giddy self-congratulation, they act upon the dictates of their conscience and, in doing so, affirm an enduring mettle. Marci felt humbled by the people of Peru. The tenacity and gumption they displayed despite their plundered history brought mist to her eyes.

Standing under an arch, one of several lining the street tending from the cathedral, she surveyed the crowd, her gaze lingering on one face after another. While committing to memory this singular moment of learning, her eyes chanced to fall upon a familiar profile. Firm browed, knob nosed, he was seated at a table outside one of the restaurants at the north end of the square. Marci was so thrilled to spot Jerry in the crowd she couldn't possibly join him quickly enough. Though unaware of her presence, he threw back his head and laughed, as only Jerry could laugh. With chin up-thrust and eyes pinched shut, he flung gaiety upon a gathering of proud souls from the depths of his belly. Marci rejoiced along with him. The dense mood that had weighed upon them since the Machu Picchu tragedy had lifted like shredded overcast. What a perfect moment to be reunited. Then Marci saw that her husband was not alone at his table.

The mere glimpse she had caught of Jerry and his pals as they rounded a corner the night before, was sufficient to establish the identity of the sprightly bundle seated across from him. The blonde package chortled at some joke he told, a remark of merry wit judging from her delighted visage. Many such jocular remarks had transpired in Marci's absence, or so it would appear, what with their hands touching at the center of their table, what with heads drawn together when the laugh was done. Her first impulse was to vent the outrage that swelled her breast and flushed her cheeks, to storm across the cobbled intersection that separated her from the pair and loose havoc upon their jolly party. She would inform that *cabrón* he'd blown his chances one, two, three. She would level final judgment upon his faithless scalp.

What intercepted the hot blast projected from her quaking center, she couldn't say. What caused her fury to lose force even as it flew back in her face, she would never bother to parse out. Instead, she absorbed the cooling ricochet, sucked in one big breath of resignation, and blew out poisoned air. To what end a melodrama?

she asked herself as her shoulder muscles slackened. "That dork," Marci muttered wearily, the word drained of rancor.

She tittered at the joke she hadn't heard told at a table across the way. She found the joke, even though she didn't get it, too rich not to laugh at. Fatigue wrapped its downy tendrils about her neck and wound smoothly across her belly. Rest, at the moment, seemed a more encouraging course to embark upon than the rutted road to vengeance. To sustain the bitter taste of acrimony obligated much more effort than it was worth. Besides, another joke, one her husband hadn't heard, was in the offing. Undistracted by a public scene, Jerry would be much better able to appreciate the irremeable extent to which he'd screwed himself.

It was dark when she opened her eyes to mingled fragrances of alcohol and an unfamiliar brand of soap. Her head on the pillow, her face turned toward the wall, she smiled. No doubt he believed he'd been clever to shower before his return. He thought he'd sneak to bed, nod off unobtrusively, and greet his wife cheerily in the morning.

"How's it going?" she asked from the darkness.

His feet shuffled. "Scared me," he said as she rolled onto her back. "Didn't know you were awake."

"I wasn't," she answered.

"Sorry. Tried to be quiet."

"You were quiet, but I felt you come in."

"You felt me?"

"Yeah, I felt you."

Her husband wasn't quite sure how to respond. He opted for affection.

"Nice thing to say," he cooed then stumbled to the side of her bed and bent down clumsily to deliver a kiss.

She let him peck her lips.

He made to rise, but she stopped him by wrapping her arms about his neck.

"Come to bed," she said.

Not knowing what else to do, he stretched out beside her and flung an arm over her waist. Then he gave her another peck, this time on the cheek.

"Good time in Pisac?" he asked.

"The very best I've had so far."

"Sorry I missed out."

"When I came back, there was a political rally going on in the square. Did you see it?"

He hesitated briefly. "Heard a noise from the bar."

"Jeeze, Jerry, you can go to a bar anytime back home."

"Sure. But got up late. Felt like hell. Went out to bite the dog that bit me."

How funny. Seemed all kinds of mean dogs slunk about Cuzco and environs.

"One thing led to another I'll bet."

"Yeah. Met up with those two Frenchies. Great guys. Mistake to think the French hate Americans. Matter of diplomacy."

Diplomacy, you call it, Marci thought and smiled to herself. She flexed; Jerry responded by raising his head so she could free her arm. Then she unbuttoned his shirt halfway down and teased the hair on his chest with her fingers. His body tensed.

"Easy," she said and settled her hand on his rib cage.

With a sigh, he relaxed. Sweet smell of alcohol on his breath. When his breathing settled to regular rhythm, she slipped her hand over his pudgy belly and undid his belt buckle. She unzipped his pants, eased her palm under the elastic strap of his boxers, and began stroking his lax penis.

"Marci," he protested.

"Let's fuck," she suggested brightly.

He lifted his arm off her waist and dropped it behind his back. "Want to, babe. Want to, but drank too much. Better in the morning."

"Ah com'on, lover boy," she said, continuing to massage his lower head. "You know these lips could straighten a garden hose."

"Sorry. Really am. But not tonight."

"Not tonight?" she answered sweetly. "Let's take a chance and see what happens." Giggling, she began to lower her mouth in the direction of his groin.

With that, he pushed off the bed. "Can't, Marci," he pleaded. "Really can't." He was ashamed of himself.

"Not possible, huh?"

"No, sorry. Can't."

"You haven't even tried. How do you know you can't?"

"Just know is all."

Barely making out his face in the darkness, she knew nevertheless his features were clenched. Poor Jerry. Got himself in a pickle, hadn't he?

Not the sort to pull the wings off a downed butterfly, she decided to let him off her hook, but not before he dangled a few more moments in suspense. What was the point she was trying to make? Simple. Love didn't feel like loathing anymore.

"You really can't?"

"No. Really really can't."

"Well then, you better go to sleep."

"You mad?" he asked.

"Why should I be?"

"Well, because," he said, wrestling with shame. "Because, you know, I can't get it up."

"*Calma*, my love. Can't help yourself, can you."

"Can't help myself."

"Then go to bed and have a nice, long, restful sleep."

"You're the greatest, Marci. In the morning, I'll reward your greatness."

"I know you will. You're a good man, Jerry. Always remember that you're a good man."

"Thanks," he answered honestly. "Nobody treats me good as you."

"Go ahead now," she said as if speaking to a child. "Go ahead and sleep."

Her husband dropped onto his bed, struggled out of his boots, then fell back onto the mattress and went to sleep as he'd been told to do.

Marci lay awake, pondering her next move. She was still awake when first light filtered through their curtained window. It was the standard light of new day, nothing in particular to distinguish it from the marvel that attended each new day. Its ordinary dawning instilled her with gladness. What happen next required the normal, ordinary, mysterious context born of every day. Such was the proper air for any sensible action.

She got out of bed while Jerry snored away. He was still snoring when she finished her shower. Sunken into innocent sleep, he didn't see her pack. He was unaware that she paused long enough in her occupation to stand over his supine body and study his truly likable mug. He would find the note she left on the small table that stood between their beds and puzzle over its meaning. He would know very well the message was for him. A single line graced the page:

When loathing stops, only love remains.

It would take him a while (if he ever did) to figure out what Marci meant by those six words. To do so, he would have to piece together events that had come to pass during the whole of their marriage; he would have to somehow glimpse the world through her eyes at a dozen crucial instances. It was doubtful that such an enterprise was within his power of recollection, never mind his capacity to see beyond himself.

Certainly they would meet again—they were the parents of two children after all—they'd meet again for sure, but not before he had ample time to mull the enigma of his wife's sudden departure, and not before she had determined to what extent he was capable of understanding what it took to overcome hopelessness.

Por el amor de amor

(For the Sake of Love)

A German tourist Simon met on the bus from La Paz told him about a town called Copacabana where he could hire a launch and ride out to the Island of the Sun. If the German had known Simon was on the lam, he might not have been so eager to flap his jaws. But the dude didn't know, and so Simon got an earful about lake territory and ended up wasting half of what he'd paid for a ticket to Puno. So what though? Money was no big deal. By now, he was traveling on a rat's stash anyway.

Copacabana seemed cool enough, but the town didn't really wow him until he spotted a certain dime lady standing in front of a white wall that ran around church property. Purple blouse with buccaneer sleeves, calf-length skirt, half a dozen flower colors draped over her hips; she was one *mamacita* who knew she be fly. Simon did a double take when he saw her. Then, so as not to jinx himself, he swung his gaze upon fifty or so vendor stalls ranked in a wide open space outside the churchyard. Shade cloth riffling in a weak breeze above the stalls reminded him of boat sails. And with all the white around, that *chica* set the ships at the corner of his vision ablaze.

In addition to her other bright colors, she wore a pink silk scarf pulled tightly across her forehead and knotted at the back of her head. Lank strands of black hair tangled with the scarf's ends that fell past the nape of her neck. Her *café con leche* complexion matched his skin shade. He checked out her pointed nose and arched eyebrows and then got distracted by her feet because she pivoted suddenly on her toes and glided toward the church gate. She had on black slippers like the kind stage dancers wear, and those buns of hers—ohmagod, tight as bongo drums.

As dancer girl slipped from sight, Simon's eye was drawn to the religious enclave, which didn't look much like any other church he'd seen on his run through Bolivia. A small tiled cross affixed to the apex of a freestanding pediment that marked the entrance was the only sign that represented the grounds as Catholic. Instead, its architecture recalled photographs of Arab palaces he'd gandered in high school geography books, which hardly surprised him because where else would a princess be hanging out except at a palace?

A sick palace it was too. Alabaster, Jake might call it if he were still around, alabaster with dome roofs all over the place. The domes looked like the top halves of planets hovering against blue sky; they were covered in ceramic tile checkerboard style, only the colors weren't just black and red but jade green and yellow, orange, and olive too.

When he followed the princess into her palace, Simon saw that the largest dome, located in the middle of a wide concrete courtyard, was mounted atop four square columns that made a kind of monster shrine. Her Highness stood to one side of the shrine checking out three tall wooden crosses set up under the arch roof. He was going to walk up to her and lay on some rap but got the impression that she didn't want to be bothered at the moment. So he held back. Maybe she intimidated him a little, whatever; while he was waiting to make his move, this eerie music started up.

Since the music was hard to hear, he thought maybe it had been playing all along. He listened more closely and decided that the noise sounded more like a wail than music or more like a whine than a wail or more like a whistle than a whine. Anyway, he figured out where it was coming from. Five beggar women, humped like rag bundles on line with a walk that led from the cross keep to the main palace building, made the sound. He couldn't tell whether the old women were singing, praying, or crying, but they were definitely spooky.

After a few minutes, the dancer girl headed toward the palace proper and disappeared under its arch. Simon sauntered in the direction she'd taken but pulled up level with the shrine. He was curious to know what there was under the dome that had grabbed Her Highness's *ojos*. Nothing he could see but the crosses—three of them, tallest in the middle as you'd expect. There were circles carved one atop the other on all four sides of each cross and spheres the size of softballs stuck out at their extremities. Real art most likely, but he still couldn't see what made 'em special. About the time he decided to quit hanging by the crosses, a man walked up near him, glanced his way, and then raised his chin toward the Calvary setup. The guy was in his fifties Simon guessed; he had faded blue eyes and a sad face. A light-green flannel shirt drooped loosely over his basketball-sized paunch. Simon was about to wander off after the *chica* when the dude started mumbling.

> Me equivoqué
> Me equivoqué
> Me equivoquo otra vez.

Something about a mistake, Simon deciphered on the basis of his sketchy Spanish. Old guy didn't seem all that upset about the mistake though, sounded more like he was just remembering something stupid he'd done or something stupid that had happened to him. But he made Simon think about his own week-old screwup, which if he went ahead and got all serious about would have brought Jake back on the scene and then here comes bummer city. Better to slip off after the *chica* before a dead man showed up, which he'd been planning on doing anyway.

He didn't have to go far. Right as he turned away from the crosses, Her Highness stepped out of the main palace building. She had finished checking out whatever was inside, which couldn't have been much since she hadn't been in there long. Whatever, here came the princess in all her finery, and now she was actually walking toward him. Could this be the chance he'd been waiting for? They might be about to meet. Passing at a distance of ten feet, Her Highness glanced in his direction, and he nodded to her. Too bad she walked on without nodding back.

Maybe the princess thought she was too good for him, and you know, maybe she was right. Had to admit he wasn't exactly what you'd call prince material. And just as his hopes headed for the crapper, sure as hell that weird music started up again. Only this time, talk about a shocker: suddenly there was this really wasted old lady bent over right in front of him with her claw hand stuck out. Ohmagod, one second he'd been looking at flawless beauty, and the next this hideous face swaddled in tattered, grungy wool—skin blackened by the sun so wrinkled it looked like it belonged on a dried fig. The crone had tiny eyes, a shriveled nose, and dried spit caked at the corners of her mouth. The squeak she emitted made him think that somewhere within the many folds of her rags bled an open wound.

A terrible thing, he lamented, out of pity for the old woman, although damn if he could imagine how the terrible thing had happened. His next thought was, just don't let my luck go so completely to shit. He knew he was looking at a living example of how cruel the world could get; he figured the wasted creature crouched in front of him had a better idea about being totally screwed than anybody he'd ever met. Before she could leak bad luck onto him, he jammed his hand into his pocket and grabbed up all his loose change. The beggar woman's crooked fingers snapped shut on the coins, and he wrenched himself away from her.

Her Highness had stopped right outside the gate, and she was haggling with a fat lady in a straw hat at one of the sail-covered stalls. Simon was so relieved to see her after his run-in with scary-ugly that he didn't even try to be coy. He looked right at the *chica* and didn't care if everybody around there took him for a loser. But the princess acted like she didn't even see him. She held up several fake carnation necklaces, trying to decide which to buy. He would have recommended the light blue plastic lei because it'd go good with the yellow beads dangling already from her shirt collar. When Her Highness selected the blue lei, Simon wanted to believe her choice was a sign that everything from here on out was going to be happy trails.

After making her purchase, the dancer girl sauntered off down a street that sloped toward lakeshore. He waited till she was half a block gone before stepping up to the stall himself. The rainbow lei he bought made him look like a dumbass in his Oakland Raiders sweatshirt. So what? The princess had decreed a day of festival and no way was he going to miss out on the party.

Next to a beach strewn with rocks the size of dinner rolls, Lake Titicaca appeared murky green, then farther out, its water shone true blue. Several motorboats skimmed the glittery surface of the lake, while others bobbed gently in Copacabana's bay. Arriving at shore, Simon watched the princess step onto a narrow, sagging dock at the end of whose planks rocked a tour launch. Determined it was high time to either fish or cut bait, he sucked in his belly, threw back his shoulders, and strode toward the royal bark.

Too bad other revelers got to the dock before he did. From his spot at the tail end of their line, he got all worried the boat would fill up before he had a chance to board. The princess was first on deck of course, and she was guided to a seat for privileged people near the bow. The rest of her retinue piled onto benches bolted to both sides of the boat. Desperate not to be left behind, Simon pushed past four people ahead of him and jumped into the last space left for ordinary passengers.

Their captain, a hooknosed, bareheaded dude about Simon's age, who definitely had his shit together, steered the launch from the front, while a grade-schooler shuffled up one row of riders and down the other to collect fares. Gaining cruising speed, the boat planed out smooth as a *refrito*, except when it bounced across the wake of another boat, which blew spray against the side of Simon's head. On the second or third splash, he leaned out beyond the back edge of the launch's fiberglass cover to catch the spray full in the face. Felt good too, you know; like, hey, when you're cruising a lake big enough to float an aircraft carrier, you oughta go ahead and soak up some wet air.

They were headed to that island the German had told him about. One thing he would definitely do when the boat docked was to strike up a conversation with Her Highness. He hoped the island was small enough that it'd be easy to hook up with her. And he hoped too that once he did, she'd finally cut him some slack.

So as not to let on how he'd boarded the boat only because of her, Simon glanced around nonchalantly at other passengers. He happened to notice the geezer he'd seen praying (or whatever) back at the church sat next to him. Wind whipping around the edge of the boat cover mussed the old fart's thin wisps of gray-brown hair. Guy blinked now and again, reminding Simon of a tomcat that used to post up next door to his mother's house in Calif. Funny thing about that dumbass animal was it ended up getting stuffed down a culvert.

"Why are you smiling at me?" the old guy shouted suddenly.

Simon looked him in the eye. Geezer wasn't getting in his face though; he just wanted to be heard over motor racket. Other thing was that the man looked so harmless he made vanilla pudding seem dangerous. "You remind me of a cat I used to know," Simon shouted back.

"A cat?" the guy hollered. "Do you mean a jazz musician or a domestic feline?"

"I mean the sort of hairball that sits on a porch looking like it died with its eyes open."

Wrinkles appeared at the corners of the geezer's peepers. "How astute," he said.

Simon didn't know what the word *astute* meant. "What'd you expect?" he went, to find out where the dude was coming from.

"Nothing, I'm sure," the guy said and waited for a tic or two. Then he thought he should say something else. "You're an American, aren't you?"

"Yeah. What are you?"

"I'm Swiss, and my name is Jean."

"Sounds French. You speak French?"

"Of course. French is one of the official languages of Switzerland." Jean's attitude tickled Simon. The man acted so bored, like you'd have to whack him upside the head to get a rise outa him.

"Spanish the other one?"

"No, German."

"I heard you talking Spanish at the church."

"Yes, I was confessing my sins."

Simon could have mentioned a thing or two about sin, but he held off because that was Jake's department. Jean leaned closer so he wouldn't have to shout. He had coffee breath. "Are you a sinner?" he asked like it was a regular question.

"Who isn't?" Simon returned sharply. Guy oughta know you didn't go jumpin' in a *bato*'s personal life right off.

"Do you find it difficult to live with sin?"

What a dumb ass.

"The reason I ask," Jean went on, "is that I don't find it difficult to live with sin. Or perhaps it is more accurate to say that I rarely regret my sins. What do you think? Is it possible to sin without regret?"

Simon narrowed his eyes at the man. "Why you telling me this shit?"

Geezer caught on then he was messin' with somebody didn't appreciate it. "Please, excuse me."

Okay, so there was no call to square off against the codger. The dude was just one of those fools went yakity yakity yak. "No problem," Simon said and eased off.

"May I ask your name?"

"Simon."

"Where are you going, Simon?"

"Wherever this boat's headed."

"Will you stay on *Isla del sol?*"

"Don't plan on it."

"May I ask where you plan to go after visiting the island?"

"Peru," Simon said, and then it hit him that he shouldn't be broadcasting his escape route.

"I believe I shall return to Chile soon," Jean said without being asked.

"Been to Chile," Simon said, figuring news that old couldn't be used against him. Chile happened way before his run-in with Jake. "By mistake," he added, for the hell of it.

"How is this possible?" Jean asked, showing a tiny bit of amusement around his mouth. "How does one arrive in a country as large as Chile by mistake?"

"Easy. It's such a big country, if you take a wrong turn, you wind up in Chile."

Jean's lips widened slightly more, probably about as close as he got to smiling.

Simon leaned over and rested his forearms on his thighs. He glanced toward the front of boat to see what the princess was up to. She caught him looking at her. As he started to look away, she smiled at him and fingered her plastic necklace.

"You should speak to her," Jean said next to his ear.

Simon shot him a hard look. He thought he'd disguised his interest in the *chica* pretty good, and exposure shamed him.

"Are you going to speak to her?" Jean went on.

"Why don't you shut the fuck up?"

"Pardon? I didn't hear."

Simon caught himself. He wasn't in the right place to turn all huffy. "I said keep it down, will ya?"

"I think she expects you to speak to her," Jean responded at lower volume.

"Hey, man, why do you care?"

"I'm simply trying to be helpful."

"Thanks," Simon strained to answer, "but I'd just as soon handle life my own way." He figured a hint should be enough to back the guy off.

But no, the Swiss kept on. "Her name is Carol."

"How the hell you know?"

"She is Swiss, as I am Swiss."

"Like that explains how you know her?"

"Ours is a small country."

"Man, you must think I'm a dope," Simon muttered, totally exasperated.

"Have I offended you?"

"No, man, forget it. Do me a favor. Forget the whole thing."

Jean straightened and shrugged in the direction of the dancer girl. In response, she dropped her gaze. Well, wasn't that terrific. He didn't know whether to blame himself or Jean, but his chances of hooking up with the fly *mamacita* had definitely gone in the crapper.

An island appeared on his side of the boat. Near the bottom edge of yellow-brown hills shimmered streaks of reflected light. Without throttling back, their captain drove into a cove. There were trees in the cove, their trunks standing like sentinels behind thick bunches of leaves.

Once docked, passengers disembarked and made their way along a flat path that met the base of a stone staircase. Parallel to the path, across a patch of close-cut grass, water flowed down a rock channel. . Simon stopped on the path to allow his shipmates to get on ahead of him. He watched the dancer girl mount the stairs, her skirt hem lifting with each step she took, giving a flash of trim calf muscle. Seeing her rise into the greenery, looking like a tropical bird returned to its natural habitat, he regretted missing out on rapping with her. It sucked, but what could he do about it now?

"Aren't you coming?" Jean called from the rear of the group heading up the stairs. His hand rested on a stone banister.

Simon snorted. Looked like he's going to spend the day with a clueless yaker.

Titicaca spread out at ten thousand feet above sea level. The stairs up the island hill were steep; the air thinner than Simon was used to. He and Jean stopped often to catch their breaths and eye the climb ahead. Higher up, the staircase was busted—weeds had lifted and canted its steps, the banister to the right had fallen to ruin. The irrigation ditch to the left tumbled down an eroded rut. Brush, clumps of flowers, and encroaching trees overwhelmed terraces to either side. At one time, Simon figured, the stair had made its way through a well-tended garden of several acres, but the garden had become overgrown. Midday light, though, spilled a soft glow upon the greenery and exhibited a loveliness that might never end.

When the stairs ended, a mountain range came into view far across the lake. Snow on the distant peaks and ridges hovered like low-flying clouds against clear sky. A well-trod dirt track with raw stone stacked to either side curved along the slant of another hill. Simon and his hiking partner passed hovels with thatch roofs, walked by lone-standing trees, flowering bushes, dry patches of grass, and clumps of cactus with nearly flat leaves. Within laddered sweeps of field all around grew corn and stubby plants Simon could not identify. Some of the lots lay fallow.

"No tractors," he mused aloud.

"What's that?" Jean asked.

The two of them had stopped on a height overlooking a neighbor island.

"Farmers don't use tractors here. The plots are too small."

"No, they don't use tractors," Jean agreed.

"Not many of them either."

"Many what?"

"Farmers."

"No more than five hundred or so, I'm told."

"Seems about right," Simon concurred. They had passed a couple of women in bowler hats on their climb and a man in a worn cotton shirt who carried a load of firewood bound by strips of cloth on his back. A few children halfway up had pestered the other boat passengers for money, but for some reason hadn't bothered him or Jean.

"This is where creation began," the Swiss said, which distracted Simon from his examination of a patch of corn growing on a hill to their left.

"Creation huh."

"The sun was born here. Along with Manco Capac and his sister, Mama Huaca, who were the first Incas."

"I don't know much about Incas, but this is a good place to get a start."

"Why do you say that?"

"Feels special."

"Does it?"

"Sure. Don't you think?"

"*Isla del sol* fails to move me. It's an island on a lake. There are other islands on other lakes."

Simon wondered what Jean was trying to prove by acting so blah. "Sorry for you then," he said. "Me, I'm glad I came here." Glad even though he'd blown his chances with the dancer girl.

"I had hoped the island would inspire me."

He looked over at Jean. A strange vibe, the Swiss gave off, almost like he was a retard. His deadpan face wasn't what you'd call conspicuous; to get a read on the guy, you did a double take only to find out that you hadn't missed anything on your first look. "That's a bummer."

"The worst," Simon's companion admitted.

"I don't believe you though."

"Of course you don't."

"You can't say that stuff about creation and not feel anything."

"Can't I? I spoke of Inca mythology. I could relate many facts about the people who lived here long ago. I could say the Incas built this settlement. That's the truth, unadorned by mythology. They built those stairs back there. That's the truth too. They constructed terraces on the sides of hills to impede erosion but which, as you pointed out, resulted in patches of land too small for tractors. The Incas failed to anticipate the invention of farm machinery, but they designed and built an excellent irrigation system, and they erected temples to their gods. We could walk to the far end of the island to visit remains of their empire. But there are better ruins in Peru."

"Peru?" Simon questioned with interest. "What about Peru?"

"You don't know, do you?"

"No I don't." Simon answered, keeping his cool. "What's in Peru?"

"Cuzco's in Peru." Jean informed him. "Machu Picchu's in Peru," he added, "the jewel of all Inca ruins."

"What's so hot about Machu Picchu?"

"Nothing other than the outpost sits atop a mountain and emerges from morning haze like a cloud citadel."

Jean might act bored, but his latest news definitely gave Simon a thrill.

"That's like a fort, right? How you get there?"

"Don't worry, you'll find it."

"How?"

"Go to Cuzco. Follow the crowd."

Was the man working at it, or was he a natural pain in the ass?

"Oh, I get it. Tourists piss you off."

"Hardly. I am never angry anymore. I might as well be dead."

"Yeah, right."

"Would you like me to explain?"

"Don't hurt yourself," Simon answered, not caring one way or the other.

A pair of wrinkles that almost touched appeared between Jean's pale eyebrows could have constituted a grimace. Simon wasn't sure. He hadn't been sure either of the look on the tomcat's face when he'd stuffed it down a sewer drain.

"On this island," Jean told him, "simple farmers began to build an empire. They were destined to become warriors and conquerors. They defeated and enslaved their enemies, learned the secrets of the stars and the seasons, and built cities of such grandeur as to confound architects today. The lands subjected to their rule, at one time, comprised the world."

"Sound motivated," Simon joked.

"You're mocking me, aren't you?"

"What do you care if I am? You being so dead and all."

"It's important that you take the question I'm about to ask seriously."

Simon waited on him.

Jean didn't ask the question right away; instead, he raised a hand to trace a semicircle at the level of his chest. Or maybe the move was meant to convey the question, Simon couldn't tell. Whatever the Swiss meant was lost on him.

"Where is the Inca empire now?" Jean asked.

Simon held off because it sounded like a trick. Then he decided what the hell. "Gone," he said and shrugged.

"That is correct," the Swiss commended him.

"Not like it ain't obvious."

"Everything is gone," Jean added. "Everything is lost."

"That's heavy, man," Simon answered, deadpan. "Sorta makes you wonder where it all went."

"It has fallen into an abyss," Jean stated solemnly.

The word startled Simon. He'd seen a movie once about an abyss. In the flick, there was this deep canyon at the bottom of the ocean. Angels lived in the canyon. They'd built a sparkling city down there. Did Jean believe there were Inca angels swimming around at the bottom of Titicaca? Wouldn't surprise him. The more the dude talked, the more he sounded like a nutcase.

"I too have fallen into an abyss," the Swiss told him.

"Right," Simon said. The guy was crazy.

"Look around. Tell me what you see."

"What for?"

"Do you see a lake?"

"Wha'daya think?"

"Do you see rocky hills and sky?"

"Com'on, what's your point?"

"That what you see is an illusion."

Simon had no answer.

"None of what you see is real," Jean went on, regarding him with his empty look.

"Guess you're not real either."

"At one time I was."

Simon barked out a laugh.

"Go ahead," Jean said. "One day you too will face the abyss."

"You're talking about death, huh."

"I'm talking about living death."

The guy was starting to hack him off again. Back on the block, he might have grabbed old Jean by his green shirt and made his teeth rattle.

"Did you hear me?"

Man just didn't know how close he was to having his body parts rearranged.

"Yeah, I hear you. You're a zombie. Pretty soon I'm gonna be one too." Simon thought about the dancer girl to crowd out a sudden recall of Jake. No way would that *mamacita* ever be a zombie. She might never die.

Jean turned to walk away, as if his listener was too dense to bother with. Simon felt dissed but reminded himself the guy was a wacko.

Their path wound about the hill country. After a while it dipped down a gentle slope and then climbed up an equally shallow rise. The going was easy, not too steep. A cove appeared below, narrower than the one their boat had docked in. The lake glittered between a pair of hills, one terraced, the other a cutaway of layered sediment. A green skin of vegetation grew on the far hill. The cove had a sandy, concave beach to which the two of them could have descended by way of a well-traveled side route. But Jean pulled up at the fork; he had something else to say.

"Life is nothing but pretense. We are characters in tales we make up to realize ourselves. When our tales lose meaning, we cease to be."

Simon decided to set Jean straight once and for all. "Look, I don't know about you, but I'm not playin' around."

His companion blinked, and his lips formed his usual fake smile. "Forgive me. I did not mean to offend you. It is good to be alive."

"Relax, bud," Simon responded wearily. "You're alive too."

"No, I'm not so lucky."

Simon shook his head. "You sound so bummed, you oughta just go ahead and off yourself."

"One must have a life to end it," the Swiss pointed out.

"Get off it, man. Take a chill pill. Have a look around. Can't you see this place is beautiful?"

It was too. On the lake, beyond the mouth of the cove, flowed long undulating waves as smooth as folds of velvet. Beyond the water, ice-topped mountains lifted into sky that went on forever.

"I am well aware the island is beautiful," Jean granted. "But for me beauty has no savor. The world has become a sham."

"A sham, huh."

"Layer upon layer of fakery, swindle, and fraud. A hoax. These are excellent English words, don't you think?"

"How come you speak English better than I do?"

"Would you like to know?"

"That's why I asked," Simon said, though he was beginning to become bored too.

"You ask excellent questions. I said to myself when I saw you at the cathedral, 'Here is a young fellow with many interesting questions.'"

"You gonna answer me?"

"Of course," Jean said.

"When?"

"Soon. But wouldn't you like something to drink first? Aren't you thirsty? Would you care to have a beer with me? I noticed a restaurant back by the stairs."

"You buyin'?"

"I have extended an invitation, no?"

Simon had a sudden wormy thought. "Are you gay?"

Jean broke up, his shoulders shaking. The sound he emitted reminded Simon of the whine he had heard the beggar women make.

"Just so you're not hitting on me," he said.

"Don't worry. I am a committed heterosexual."

"Okay, I'll trust you. Let's go have a beer."

At the restaurant, however, they didn't get a chance to drink beer. A waiter approached their table, which was set up on a small patio at the edge of a drop-off above the dock. After Jean asked what drinks were available, the waiter rattled off a list that included large-sized bottles of beer, but when the Swiss ordered one, the waiter said he had sold out an hour ago. Jean ordered *refresco*.

While they waited for the waiter to return, a pair of foreign chicks arrived and sat down at a close-by table. Simon could tell they were gringas because of their skin, and he could tell they were travelers because of their dingy dress. Hard to keep clothes clean on the road. He recalled the dancer girl's bright apparel and wondered how she managed. Then he noticed Jean had on fresh duds too. Must be a trick only Swiss people pulled off.

The waiter walked up to ask what he could bring the ladies. He rattled off his list of drinks again. When the chicks ordered beer, he repeated his apology that the restaurant had run out. Simon nearly cracked up. Either the dude got off on taunting his customers or was too stupid to think beyond his spiel. Either way, he was a stitch.

"I make my living as a novelist," Jean said when the waiter placed a plastic bottle of a lime-green liquid and two glasses between them.

"Good for you," Simon said, having forgotten what the Swiss had promised to explain before.

"You asked about my knack for languages."

"Yeah, you talk good English."

"A talent I was born with and which I have successfully exploited."

"That means you make a lot of money writing books?"

"Not a fortune, but a comfortable sum."

"Enough to invest in stocks?" Simon had heard that rich people got involved in the stock market. He knew he'd never be rich. He'd always blow his money no matter how much he had.

"Yes, I maintain an investment portfolio."

"I have a portfolio too. I keep it under my bed at my mom's house. Mine's full of pictures of naked women." Jean acted so seriously tight-assed, sitting there with his shoulders squared and his back held rigid as a tent pole that he needed to have his chain jerked.

"My investments are of no consequence," Jean informed him and took a swig of the green soda. "They are no more important than piles of sand."

"Okay, you got me. What's important?"

"How my talent has become a curse."

"You know what? I'll bet your books are about curses too."

"You really are a perceptive young man. I am not disappointed in you at all."

"Sure you're not gay?"

Jean sighed. "Would you grant me a favor?"

"What's that?"

"Pay attention to what I'm saying?"

"Okay," Simon sighed and leaned back. "I see how you are."

Once Jean became convinced his listener would behave himself, he continued. "I have written several novels of intrigue. In them, pernicious men conspire to rob, rape, and commit murder. I have become a successful writer by exploiting the curiosity and moral scruples of my readers. Each wants to be the first to discover whether good or evil triumphs in new editions of my work."

"Good guys always win," Simon stated.

"They must, mustn't they?" said Jean.

What a riot, Simon thought. The Swiss made out like it was the worst thing in the world that good guys came out on top. "Bummer," he said to humor the old wacko.

"You and I both know that such stories are false. In reality, evil triumphs often."

"Well, sure stories are fake. That's why they're called stories."

"No, some are true. I'm just not able to write them."

Simon refilled his glass and topped Jean's off. In keeping with his high-class style, the guy drank soda pop a sip at a time. If he didn't get a move on, he was going to miss out on what he was paying for.

"Is that what you're bummed about? You can't write true stories?"

"I can't write at all anymore."

"Why not?"

"Because I finally discovered a story that put me to shame."

"No joke? Wow, that's so cool. You gotta tell me this story."

"I do the story little justice when I tell it."

"What's the story about?"

"I don't know."

"That's bullcrap."

"Not really. In the beginning, I thought I knew what the story was about."

"So tell me, and I'll let you know what it's about."

"Could you? You would be doing me a tremendous service."

"Think so?"

"More than you could possibly imagine."

"Well, here I am. Go for it."

As Simon suspected, Jean was dying to relate the tale.

"It happened on the gulf coast of Mexico," he said. "The owner of an open-air restaurant, much like this one, located on a sandbar at one end of a bay, told me the story. He didn't know what it was about either but thought I might find it amusing. The man kept toucans and a howler monkey at his restaurant to entertain his guests. But there I go, giving details instead of telling the story. And yet the meaning of the story lies hidden behind its many details. How do I get beyond the details?"

"By telling the friggin' story," Simon hissed in frustration. Jean better damn well do what he'd promised, or one perceptive young fellow with many interesting questions would smack him upside the head with a third-full bottle of soda pop.

"A man who ferried clients to the restaurant joined a poker game one afternoon. He was not a gambler but a gringo tourist, and another boat owner talked him into joining them at one of the tables. They needed a third player."

"What was the man's name?" Simon asked.

"Do you think that detail is important?"

"I want to know something about the guy."

"Very well," Jean complied. "His name was Arturo. He had a wife and two children, both boys, ages eight and nine. The younger boy had a cleft palate. Arturo owned a boat, a three-room house with a dirt floor, a few chickens, and a pig. Also a donkey. Arturo planned to butcher the hog and then buy another one. He had a hard time earning enough money to feed his family and maintain his boat. In the village, there were many other—"

"Okay, okay," Simon interrupted. "I see what you mean about the details."

"Yes," Jean answered. "One can make up a mountain of details to disguise the fact that one has no idea what his story is about."

"You're making all this up? I thought you said it was a true story."

"It is a true story, but I'm making up some of it."

"Did you make up the poker game?"

"No, the poker game is real."

"What happened at the poker game?"

"Of course. I should tell what happened."

Simon shook his head in disbelief.

"Arturo won a small fortune that afternoon. The gringo tourist became upset, but Arturo didn't feel sorry for him because he hadn't wanted to play poker in the first place. Besides, his gain was purely a matter of luck. It wasn't his fault he ended up stuffing the gringo's money into his pockets when the game ended."

Simon liked the idea of a Mexican making off with a rich gringo's money. So far, it was a pretty good story.

"Night had fallen by the time Arturo pushed his boat off the beach. Excited at the prospect of returning home with good news, he gunned the boat engine and headed for open water. Very soon, however, his motor conked out. He pulled the starter cord, but the motor failed to restart. This was not a surprise because Arturo had been fiddling with the engine for the past many weeks. Removing the cover, he adjusted the choke and throttle, yanked the cord, but with the same lack of result. As Arturo continued to work on the motor, his boat drifted farther out to sea. It was a moonless night, and all but one or two stars were hidden behind a heavy cloud ceiling. By the time the engine caught, Arturo had floated far from shore. He swung his launch toward the single dim light left on at the restaurant. Then the motor gasped and quit again.

"A storm broke and quickly intensified. Wind howled and waves rose. Even with his engine running, Arturo would have had a hard time navigating the swells, but without power to steer by, he was completely at the mercy of the gulf. One giant wave lifted the launch up into inky darkness and pitched it over. Arturo was thrown violently into the sea. Clawing to the surface, he reached out desperately for the capsized boat. He prayed to the Holy Virgin for deliverance.

"Fortunately, he located his craft in the darkness and was able to cling to it for quite a while or he would have become exhausted and drowned. But even then, he was in a bad way. Waves crashed so violently upon him that they ripped off his sandals, tore away his loose-fitting trousers, and shed him of his shirt. For hours, he clung naked to the clumsy craft, knowing that it would eventually sink. The storm raged on, indifferent to Arturo's plight. Not until pale light of dawn broke upon the horizon did the wind subside. By then, Arturo floated in the sea all alone, his boat having sunk into the dark depths. He had swallowed and vomited a bucket of saltwater. He was delirious and weak, but at last, the sea finished with him. The tide dumped his limp body back on shore.

"The restaurant owner who told me the story found Arturo stumbling along the beach in the early morning. He took hold of the nearly drowned man's arm and led him to his kitchen. There he wrapped Arturo in a blanket and gave him a hot cup of chicken broth. Later, one of the other taxi boat captains ferried Arturo home."

A minute passed before Simon realized that the story was finished. Jean sat there waiting for him to say what it was about.

"The world can go completely to shit anytime," he suggested off the top of his head.

"I considered such an explanation," Jean answered him. "I also thought about how we can never know whether what happens to us is good or bad."

"Sounds all right. Why can't that be what the story's about?"

"I urge you to tell it sometime. Tell it fifty times. Each time you'll reach for meaning, but come up empty-handed. Finally the story will leave you flat."

"So what if it does? It's just a story."

"Where else do we find meaning except in stories?"

"Well, I'd never let a stupid story get the best of me."

Jean emitted a nearly inaudible squawk that seemed half sigh and half weeping. "'The best of me,'" he repeated. "I believed once the story would bring out the best in me. It caused me instead to become disgusted with myself. I became appalled at my conceit in writing all those novels. I loathed my pretensions. The meaning of Arturo's story, which once, for the briefest moment, held such promise, in the end took away my ability to write. When the meaning of the story vanished, I was left, like Arturo, stripped of all my valuables on an isolated shore. It seemed I never had truly understood anything. My life was a fake, and I, a fraud. As a result, there was nothing at all about me to admire. What good my ambition or my life? Worst of all, I no longer cared."

Simon didn't have anything to say for a while. He knew about the world going to crap all right. He had faced the prospect of nothing good coming along and never coming along again. It was the black sorrow Jean was stuck in. He called it the abyss.

"I'll tell ya, man," Simon said at last. "You're making me feel pretty low right now."

"Don't allow that to happen," Jean answered with unexpected conviction. "Forget everything I've told you. When you want something, reach out and take it. Don't consider for a second why you should."

"That's what I always do. It only gets me in trouble."

"Be thankful for trouble."

"Nope. I'm through looking for trouble."

"No, you're not. You're still alive."

He didn't want to argue with Jean anymore. The bottle of pop was empty. He thought about leaving, but it wouldn't feel right to run out on the Swiss.

"A poor man would be happy to be given a few coins," Jean continued quietly as if ashamed of his voice. "I used to think such a person had no hope, but now I'm not so sure. A starving man wants to fill his belly, nothing more, but he has reason to live. A dying man wants to awaken to one more day of life, and rejoices if he does. An ambitious man seeks power and profit and revels in the trouble both cause him. A man betrayed glories in vengeance. And then there is the man who loves, who dreams of dwelling in the light of his beloved."

Simon looked away. Fair or not, he would leave Jean to his misery soon.

"I've lost all passion for life," he heard the man say. "Do you understand?"

"I can't help you," Simon said facing back. He might have passed the guy a couple hits of Seroquel if his supply wasn't running low.

"You want to help me?"

Against his better judgment, Simon answered, "Sure," and then braced himself.

"Remember that you wanted to help me. Because you will, you know."

That sounded like a prediction that made no sense whatsoever. A witch had volunteered Simon a glimpse into the future a couple of days ago, and he'd found out the portent made sense only after it came to pass. That's the way portents worked. Possibly he'd understand what Jean meant by his prediction later on, but right now it sounded like no more than a slip of the tongue.

"Now go," the man said.

Simon obliged him. He nodded to the Swiss and got up from the table.

He was still thinking about Jean when the boat he caught at the bottom of the stairs cruised into Copacabana bay. There were few people on shore besides the boatmen because it was too late in the day for tourists to set off on an excursion to *Isla del sol*. So there was little by way of bustle to put him off his brood about Jean's dark mood, though luckily, at a distance from the island, he was able to consider sorrow without it creeping into his own guts. The man he'd left behind carried nasty stuff around with him; he was one of those deep thinkers who couldn't quit fiddling with crazy ideas. Jean hadn't figured out yet that the way to climb out of the black sorrow was to quit noticing you were in it. After a while, your eyes adjusted to the darkness, and though you still felt rotten, you could get around okay. But the Swiss was all convinced that he didn't feel anything, neither depression nor sorrow nor anything else, which made Simon wonder what he had to complain about. It seemed to him that Jean was bothered mostly because he didn't feel rotten enough.

With nothing else to do, Simon climbed the higher of two hills that braced the bay. A dirt path led to the summit of the hill he chose where he found a row of cement grottos with fancy crosses mounted atop their arches. Stations of the Cross again; damn if every town in Bolivia didn't have at least one hill dedicated to the Passion story. Unlike others he'd seen, though, these crosses were situated close together. The ones in that other town (whatsitsname?) where Jake had taught him the penance ritual were more spread out. No sense in lugging rocks up this hill because the short steps between the stations required no effort. "What do you think, Jake?" he asked, seeking the dead man's advice as to whether he should perform the penance ritual anyway. But Jake had gone mute ever since Simon got on the bus out of La Paz.

The hill gave a good view of Copacabana with its flat-roofed buildings, narrow streets, and its glossy-domed Arab palace. Trees taller than most the buildings dotted the terrain within city limits, and there were a few thicker stands of them growing in the wider valley that spread out from the bay. A humped line of hills formed the landside horizon. The bay had changed color this late in the day to deeper blue, almost purple. The water reminded Simon of the dancer girl's flouncy blouse, although the lake was nowhere near as bright. Remembering the girl, he felt sorry again he hadn't got up the nerve to talk to her when he had the chance, which made him feel lonely, as if he had a reason to miss her. For a while, he pretended he had a reason to miss her, even to the point that the missing became a good enough reason for him to feel lonely. Then he got to the point of wishing he would see the dancer girl again for old times' sake. In remembrance for what might have been, he hung his rainbow lei on the arm of the cross at the last grotto in line.

Down in town, bus and automobile traffic was all but nonexistent, so he walked up the middle of a street paved in concrete without fear of getting hit. He noticed four parked cars, clean and shiny Japanese models, which meant there were at least a few people in Copacabana who had cash. Of course, why should that be a surprise with all the tourist dollars flowing in? No matter where you went, you could bet there were always some people around who made out.

Up another street, a row of beach umbrellas stood open along the sidewalk. Up another, whose flat-faced buildings were painted pastel colors, several Bolivians, mostly women, hung out. Then he passed a bunch of men milling around on a corner. A few of these guys wore red baseball caps; two pushed bicycles along. Then he saw the dancer girl.

She was standing next the entrance to a three-story hotel with yellow walls and white-trimmed windows and plaster flowers spaced about ten feet apart beneath a white cornice. The front door stood in a curved recess at one corner of the building. Simon was so thrilled to see the fly *mamacita* standing there in her pink scarf and purple blouse with yellow beads and blue lei hanging from her neck that he froze in his tracks. But she didn't appear surprised to see him at all; she looked as though she had been expecting him to come by any second. Turning away from her, he could still feel her eyes probing the side of his head. What should he do? The answer came that he better do something quick or else. Or else what? Damn if he knew.

When he turned back to her, the dancer girl stared at him hard, daring him to look away again. Then, sure that she had his attention, she swiveled on the balls of her feet in that dancer way she had, pranced to the door of the hotel, glanced back over her shoulder, and stepped inside. He followed like a dog on a leash.

There were chairs set against one wall of the small lobby inside the hotel, a hardwood desk faced the chairs, and a man in a white shirt sat behind the desk. The man was reading a newspaper as Simon entered and didn't look up. Simon took the stairs to his right, figuring that's where the dancer girl had gone. He slid his hand along a smooth, dark wood rail as he climbed, lifted it over a newel post, and then dragged his hand up the rail to the first landing. There, he scouted down an empty hall. Not this floor, he surmised. The stairs jogged left and entered a well with a pale green wall illuminated by a small shaded lamp mounted at the level of his head. On the second floor, he peered down another empty hall. Still no sign of the dancer girl. He made his way to the top of the stairs, anxious as a man who'd been granted an audience with a queen.

As on the lower levels, a double row of doors ran along a hallway to a curtained window at its far end. He started to second-guess himself, worried that the dancer girl had slipped into one of the rooms below. Since she hadn't shown herself, he wondered if he had misread her signals. Or maybe he was supposed to knock on doors till he found her. But there were a lot of doors in the hotel, which meant a lot of knocking and a lot of apologies. He was unprepared to backtrack and ask for the girl at the lobby desk, especially since she may not have invited him to join her in the first place. He didn't know whether to blame his confusion on the *chica* or himself. Probably he'd screwed up, but he couldn't guess how. That is, if he'd been right to follow the dancer girl at all.

Then the last door on his right opened inward and muted sunlight from the room merged with the glow cast from the window at the far end of the hall. He held his breath. The dancer girl appeared at the door, leaned against the jamb, half-in and half-out of the room, with her hands clasped behind her. He returned her look and waited for her to speak. She drew him toward her without saying a word.

She'd taken off her pink scarf and purple shirt. Her hair was mussed; her collarbones were exposed beneath the spaghetti straps of a black halter top. Simon pulled up at the length of the shadow her body cast to the opposite wall. She waited on him. Her shoulders were as olive-tan as her face and looked as smooth as suede. He could see by the wrinkles at the corners of her eyes that she had more years on her than he'd thought. Rather than disappoint him though, he found her age captivating, her maturity the curtain of a mystery seldom revealed to boys as young as he was. He inched toward the woman—Carol was her name—and when he crept close enough, she took hold of both his hands, slipped them under her halter top, and pressed them against her breasts. Her fingers were cold but her breasts were warm, and his palms itched when they touched her nipples. She rubbed his hands against her boobs in circles. He couldn't believe what was going on but didn't try to figure it out. She backed into the room with his hands firmly in her grip so he had no choice but to follow.

Carol sat down on the only bed in the room, its frame extending parallel to line of sight from door to window on the far wall. Once settled, she released his hands, and when she lay back crosswise on the mattress, they slipped from under her halter-top. She scooted farther onto the creaky springs, creating long wrinkles in a turquoise-colored bedspread. Folds her body raised in the cover reached to a pair of pillows plumped beneath an ornate wooden headboard. When she lifted her heels to the edge of the mattress and parted her knees, Simon could see she wasn't wearing underpants.

Her skirt was hiked to her thighs, but evidently that wasn't high enough, for as he gawked, she arched onto her shoulders and heels, pressed her chin to her chest, and slipped the hem of her skirt under her butt. Simon was about to erupt. When the dancer raised outstretched arms to him, he shoved his drawers to his ankles, which sprang his yanger free of his boxers. He lowered himself upon her, stuck in his dick, and let loose as directly as if the *mamacita* had turned on a water tap.

Oh man, what'd I ever do to deserve a bonus? Simon pondered fitfully as the pinnacle interval of their joining lapsed to spasms. When reverberations in his groin subsided, he propped himself on his forearms. He wished he could collapse upon Carol fully and wrap her in the warmth of his gratitude and devotion. What held him back was fear that he'd crush her. It had all happened so fast. He didn't know why she'd let him fuck her. He wasn't sure how much of her came with the prize. Hope for understanding swelled his heart. Confusion and amazement spun around in his head; wonder and disbelief arrived all scrambled together. Her many smells—of deodorant and lake water, of sand, fresh air, sweat and sullied breath—rose to his nostrils and clouded his brain. The porcs on her unblemished cheeks and slender nose entranced him. Several strands of hair had fallen across her forehead. Omniscient eyes regarded him unflinchingly.

He pushed up onto his hands to frame her face better. She looked anxious, as if more intent on what might happen next than on what had come to pass. What did she want now? Was he supposed know? Reproach in her brown eyes bewildered him.

Well, of course. How stupidly insensitive of him. But really. Look at what they'd just done together. Did she really not sense how much he loved her? No matter. *Chicas* were *chicas*—even the older ones—and you had to give them what they wanted. In his defense, he could have pleaded forgetfulness, and it'd have been the truth. In any case, his oversight could be remedied easily. He descended to kiss her tenderly on the lips as he'd meant to do all along—no kidding.

Yes, that was what she'd been waiting for, though not in the way he'd supposed. Instead of lying there to receive his kiss, she propped up on her elbows and met him halfway with a peck on the cheek. "You must go now," she said immediately after as if some schedule had been arranged beforehand.

But hey, wait a sec, he protested silently, as she made to roll from under him. Okay, admittedly he'd been a little hasty on the first romp, but he'd do better second time around.

"Could you move, please?" Carol said though, before he was able to present a case for leniency.

No, he was too stunned to move, and while he dallied above her, there came a soft knock on the door. Christ, he'd forgotten to shut the friggin' door.

Her eyes accused him: "See now, you've done it. You were supposed to be out of here by now."

Tap, tap, tap went the sound behind him, fingernails drumming apologetically on wood. Carol hastened to scoot from under him, her eyes avoiding his. Simon sensed other eyes focused on his bare ass. He rose from the mattress filled with shame and panic, wriggled into his pants, and fumbled with the zipper. It took guts to turn about and meet the desk clerk's censure. Only it wasn't the desk clerk standing in the open doorway.

Tears slid down Jean's cheeks, and his shoulders slumped like a pair of sodden twigs. The man felt something now all right, rottenness of a kind that made him wish he'd never been born. Jean stood at the threshold of life with the pain of rebirth buckling his knees. The hand he'd used to *tap, tap, tap* flatted on the doorjamb, barely keeping him upright.

Simon got his pants fastened just as Jean's imploring eyes fell upon him. He couldn't hold the poor guy's gaze. Glancing Carol's way, he saw she had risen to her feet on the other side of the bed and was looking past him. There were lines on her forehead and next to her eyes, and her lips sagged like limp curtain lace.

"I'm so sorry," Jean said, as Simon, head down, took his first step toward the exit.

He froze and felt as though he'd just been run through with a lance. "Sokay," he mumbled idiotically, but the Swiss wasn't talking to him.

"Can you ever forgive me, Carol?" Jean said in a voice barely above a whisper.

Simon took another step toward the door, wanting to break into a run.

"I will always forgive you," he heard the woman answer.

"I know," Jean said, his voice cracking.

Simon pushed past the Swiss but could not get out of earshot fast enough.

"Come inside, husband," he heard Carol say.

Cascading bowling balls raced Simon down the stairs. When he stumbled into the lobby, the desk clerk glowered at him. "Have a heart, dude," he shot back. "I just got my nuts hacked off with a dull butter knife."

Then he burst onto a street where one day in Copacabana was dying. Or if not, he was at a loss to come up with a way to finish it off. If pressed, possibly he could trap a small, furry animal and torture it to death. Or spin around in circles until he drilled a hole to China. Or grab hold of the next gringo passerby who came along and demand to know if he'd caught the name of the last sheep he'd sodomized.

Simon stopped before the stampede of insane visions overwhelmed him. Who the hell was he kidding? What'd he have to joke about?

As if emerging from a raging storm, he became aware by degrees that he had washed up onto a narrow concrete strip of beach where four adult Bolivians hunched over a *fusbol* game. Other battered wooden contraptions had been set up in the open air, and other enthusiasts contested among them. A red, white, and blue Pepsi sign painted broadly on the stucco wall behind the players deflected their bursts of energy. A stout woman in the group he had first centered on—flat-crowned felt hat scrunched down tight on her brow—let loose a joyous whoop when she shot to goal a miniature soccer ball.

Down the street appeared vendor stands with flat white sails rigged above them. Farther on, a hill slanted from behind a three-story bare brick building across blush cloud and indigo sky. Three boys at one of the *fusbol* benches vied for his attention. They called in Spanish and motioned for him to make a fourth in their game. He wasn't much of a *fusbol* player, but how could he refuse? Just now, the whole world had become too insistent for him to deny it anything.

Cosa de tiempo

(Matter of Time)

While naked Chama boys scooped a hole by hand out of the riverbank, Fulgor Armanza posited his theory of the atom. One of the two *muchachos* at play squatted in slop at the bottom of their excavation while the other leaned on an arm above the hollow and ladled loamy earth from its collapsing sides. Albert had learned previously from Walter that members of the Chama clan made their living by scavenging what sustenance they could at the shores of the Beni. From Sharp's crapulous perspective, these unobtrusive individuals (in prepubescence, they resembled eels) came off as a transitional species among the jungle fauna, a vague link between tame and wild critter as yet uncompelled to follow one evolutionary line or the other.

Fulgor too turned out to be an exotic inhabitant of the Rurrenabaque rain forest, although not so much for the way he looked as for the uncommon notions he espoused. At first, Armanza had seemed to him one of those busy jobless fellows one spotted in any small town; a middle-aged lifelong resident of a *pueblito* who traded in good manners and village gossip with other local idlers who spent their days wandering in and out of small shops and grocery stores. A couple inches shorter than Albert and expanded through the middle, he appeared constitutionally fit and mentally alert. Not a single strand of gray marred lush dark hair that curled over ear wings beneath the brim of his straw fedora. Bent nose, straight teeth, easy manner, Armanza struck Albert as an unremarkable *fulano* until the so-and-so made mention of his genealogy, told about a certain mechanical contraption he'd engineered, and then presented the results of his philosophical research.

Recently returned from a four-day jungle trek, Sharp had made the man's acquaintance at a patio table overlooking the Beni. The fish Albert ordered from the restaurant kitchen arrived overcooked, though when prompted, and in order to promote himself as gracious guest, he complimented the chef on his culinary skill. While Albert separated flesh from spines, Armanza related how his grandfather had assassinated the third president of Bolivia. No student of the country's history, Sharp could neither verify nor dispute Fulgor's assertion, and so their conversation lagged. Then Armanza called attention to his button-down, off-white shirt, and to the pair of flaccid trousers of indeterminate color he wore, and remarked that he owned a laundry, where a washer-dryer of his design operated more efficiently than the machines from which he'd cannibalized parts. The limp and dingy character of the Bolivian's apparel—a coordinate to his sagging jowls—aroused Albert's skepticism. Either the man's clothes contravened praise of his invention or they disputed Sharp's prejudice for bright crispness in freshly washed fabric.

Critical too was his reaction, at first, to Fulgor's metaphysical musings. Not because the man envisioned the atom as an entity so small as to be invisible (a common enough conception), but Armanza went on to describe this elemental nit as comprising infinite scope and expanding from a nucleus wherein resided time. Fulgor's brown eyes bulged like binocular lenses when he propounded, "UFOs are not from outer space," which Albert took for a digression in their discussion until his acquaintance added that the famous glowing saucers, or cigar-shaped transports with red and green blinking lights, actually navigated a future dimension at the atom's core to which present-day observers accidentally transitioned unawares. It was at this juncture in their talk that Albert wondered whether the theorist meant to explain the existence of UFOs by means of his thesis or cite the anomalies as proof thereof.

Only when the restaurant table had been cleared of lunch scraps, and Albert had ordered his fifth medicinal beer, did it dawn on him what was really going on in theory. The atom, as conceived by Fulgor, amounted to a subjugation of space at the behest of time. Or maybe one could say that time and space flip-flopped priorities in Armanza's universe. In either case, if you believed the theory, cause and effect became unchained, locale took a hike, chronology dropped several beats, and objective determinations gave way to random awareness. In essence, the eccentric proposed that the cosmos should be understood not as a concatenation of uncountable celestial bodies but as a single, eternal being.

Well, being the sort who found dealings in the usual universe awkward and messy, who could recount numerous upsetting episodes that had befallen him in normal space, Fulgor's conceit at last appealed to him. Spatial entities after all were prone to impose themselves rudely upon a body, and then, just as some body began to accept their integrity, care about, and even cherish them, these entities either died, degenerated, or otherwise slipped away, leaving behind a haunting aftermath that perpetuated regret. In Fulgor's atom, on the other hand, persons and things abided in a state of suspension (accessible as everlasting tics) that bypassed disappointment and assumed no specific weight.

Thus, Albert concluded, he might very well transition to a certain jungle trek in the cloud of Armanza's theory. Without ordinary space as its determining factor, the excursion might proceed devoid of consequence, which he had been suggesting to himself all along, and which proposition Fulgor now unwitting confirmed. In other words, the adventure will have happened in his life with no requirement that he admit any moment of authorship.

Thus, at a dark time unfounded, a trio of capybaras (heading nowhere in particular) swim noiselessly in the Tuichi River while flamboyant Riki gigs frogs for bait from the floor of Walter's canoe. At no specific time, a tug on the thick line wrapped once around Albert's right hand and festooned to his left suggests that were he to act quickly and forcibly enough, there would begin a fight to the death with a thirty-pound catfish that wallows in the rustling black depths before him. But the fish spits out the hook and peace envelopes Sharp instead. A calm purr of loneliness resonates in his head, setting him apart from the chatty jocularity of his cohorts, from which sound he distinguishes the supple, supercilious ripple of Ana's laughter. Concurrently, he sums up events populated by howler monkeys and parrots, ants and butterflies, snakes and mosquitoes, and consigns himself to a singularity that elapses uninhibited.

Transition underway.

They are six in all when they set out, six plus one when they find Marci hugging herself at the cavernous base of a *mapaso* tree. Walter leads them. On the river, he guides them from the stern of a forty-foot-long canoe with his fingers wrapped around the outboard tiller. On foot, he breaks trail at their head, employing a short-bladed machete to hack though undergrowth. He shows them how the seeds of abundant wild mangoes (a favorite food among the monkey clans) can be drilled out and polished in sand to make attractive finger rings. He teaches them how to weave carriers for their water bottles using long segments of palm leaves. He also demonstrates implicitly thereafter the redundancy of their burden. For bark-skinned lianas, the width of a grown man's wrist, when lopped apart, send forth gushes of water as clear and reliable as if from a kitchen tap. Why carry water in the middle of an endless stream is Walter's tacit lesson.

Albert snaps a digital photo of their guide as he steadies the severed end of a vine above Ana's open mouth. "Poor man," she designates Walter when celebration for the trek's success ends outside a karaoke saloon in Rurre. But the guide has forgotten her by the time she pities him and suffers not the slightest regret over her rebuff. He joins his river mates in the street outside the bar and spills from his heart raucous declarations of lusty love that puddle at the feet of a more willing recipient of his affections. "Not so hopeless," Albert observes for Ana's benefit as their guide flings his arm about the shoulders of a spry village talent. And Ana feels better after that, not so guilty for being blessed with the sort of beauty all men desire to touch and fondle. Men are not so delicate as you think, Albert has meant to convey and thereby shake loose from the silly girl's mind fantasies she entertains about her fate. It is Ana's conceit that she will disappoint even the boyfriend she has left back in Sweden once he realizes that she doesn't love him.

"That woman's a pain in the ass," Steven says.

The three male clients from Walter's boat consider Ana's attributes while she walks ahead of them toward a clapboard hostel where this one night Albert is bound to share a room with her. Sharp concurs with the Australian even though he hopes that the pretty lady's twisted knots of personality can be loosened. He grants Steven the accuracy of his appraisal not only because the Aussie is a likeably prim sort of chap, but also because anyone who meets a man as wise as Walter, schooled in the naked truth of the *selva*, and takes his humility and contentment for impoverishment, has to have missed a turn somewhere along her narrow road.

And somewhere down his road, Riki, their cook, presumes that he too will become a guide. The young man confides his aspiration to Albert while splitting wood for the camp stove with an ax that will soon have played a crucial part in a transcendental event. He has already demonstrated his knowledge of the territory and the clarity of his prescient vision. The cook recognizes, for instance, that a certain jealous monkey whose red eyes are caught in the beam of a flashlight only after the fact will spray Steven from jungle canopy before Walter takes precautions. Riki's screech of laughter, like the prolonged exultation of a madman, verifies his superior sight. And the Aussie, who bolts too late to escape foul bombardment, has recourse only to complain most woundedly, "Something up there shit on me!"

In contrast to Walter's circumspect reserve, Riki submits to impulse. Notwithstanding the shapelessness of Fulgor's universe, physical comparisons between the two are also noteworthy. Riki's head reminds Albert of a sun-dried husky coconut set atop a side of sated beef. He wears blue print Bermudas and retro-Jagger T-shirt. Walter's shaman face, by contrast, is sculpted diamond-shaped from knotted mahogany and features a wry mouth sans incisors. A light-colored collar shirt with ersatz pearl snaps hangs loosely over his wrangler torso. Rolled sleeves expose forearms lithe and strong as braided hemp.

Yet while this pair of forest experts are dissimilar in demeanor and physique, they bear like scars of their profession. Welts raised upon their arms, calves, and ankles demonstrate that all flesh and blood in the jungle are ready food for its infernal insects. Carnivorous centipedes, mosquitoes immune to repellants banned in developed countries, ants whose bite on the hip will deaden a leg for half a day, lurk and swarm in a riot of vegetation living off its own layered rot. One way or another, the rain forest takes its toll on all and sundry, such that if compared in the abstract (which Albert is wont to do) to a struggle set upon a temporal plane (*a traves de* Fulgor), discoveries can be made of intriguingly distinct tactics and strategies of survival pursued within periods dark and light, but never will there step forth any contestant in the deadly game who will have mastered all its perilous variations.

Multiple transitions interrupted.

Fulgor Armanza reminded Albert that their discussion had reached a scheduled interlude. It was news to the gracious guest, who knew of no objective time frame assigned their meeting. He was therefore somewhat miffed when the charlatan proposed to set aside atomic paradox, overlook UFOs, and ignore the Chama excavation in order to rendezvous with his business partner. This afternoon, the two will firm up plans to build not far from Rurre a luxury hotel, complete with spa, swimming pool, and tennis courts. For Albert, the distraction didn't work. Exactly when Fulgor scooped the paradox aside, uninhibited time seeped back into the hollow of Sharp's consciousness. He wanted to grab hold of Fulgor's wrist as he rose from their table and wrest from him an admission that in truth he didn't know the first thing about eternity. But instead, Albert let the man go his way and ordered another beer. Truth to be told, he could not have cared less about luxury hotels with tennis courts; for diversion, he preferred a game of chess.

Overarching transition regained.

The night of the fishing trip, before the party beds down, Riki challenges him to a match by lamplight. As they set up chessmen on the miniature pegboard Albert retrieves from his traveling bag, the riverman warns the gracious guest that his father, a national champion, taught him to play. Not to belittle the cook's instructor, five moves into the opening, with Riki playing black, Sharp nonetheless recognizes his opponent's inferior grasp of the royal game. His style of engagement is consistent with his mode of life, what with one plan begun and abruptly abandoned when another plan snares his fancy. (Riki has boasted previously that he changes women, too, at least twice a year.) He is a tactician exclusively, in other words, with no devotion to career beyond a flare of spirit that trusts in advantageous fortune. By the twelfth move, in other words, Albert has snatched two of Riki's hanging pawns and constructed a strategic redoubt.

In the early going, Albert suffers second thoughts to be sure, but as he trades down—bishop for a knight, queen for queen plus a bonus pawn—an emerging picture of the cook's defeat achieves stability. Then Albert feels as if he takes unfair advantage of his opponent's valor and élan, as must even a master statistician regret at least once in while the cold laws of probability. Riki's last chance to win, a long shot to be sure, fades just before the endgame. He sacrifices his queen bishop to free his rooks and will have secured counter play if he but follow out the combination he initiates. But a spurious vision of Albert's immediate annihilation inspires him instead, which results in a scattering of his forces and allows the gracious guest to firm up a material advantage. Sharp will have resigned in Riki's position after that, but of course, the riverman fights to the bitter end, whether out of obstinacy or hope for a miracle Albert, by now steeped in self-reproach, makes no attempt to learn.

They emerged together from beneath a canvas awning that roofs the camp mess, where, a few hours earlier, the cook has served a repast of chicken, noodles, and vegetables appetizingly arranged on each paying customer's plate. Riki breaks away from Albert as they meet the questioning eyes of the rest of the crew and takes to flinging a carving knife at a nearby tree. "*Me ganó*," he informs the others, to put a brave face on his defeat, and then lands the blade in softwood from ten paces to prove that his pride remains unvanquished. Albert is forced to interpret Riki's statement since he is the only gringo present who speaks Spanish.

In the uneasy silence that follows the cook's painful admission, Walter places a can of kerosene on an upturned log and sets it alight. Albert and the other clients form a circle around the fire while Riki continues to sulk a ways apart. Peter, the twenty-some-year-old Christian in their party, who recognizes the existence of Almighty God but cannot explain why he has fashioned life on earth part to part with the irresistible epoxy of suffering, begins to intone in his native German a melody the other travelers have heard before. In Ana's Swedish, an eensy beensy spider's journey up a waterspout sounds like the tinkle of little bells. When Albert requests an encore, Riki puts a stop to the sing-along. He flings his knife from outside the chorus circle and sticks it in the log next to the flaming can. He laughs as the singers scatter and moseys like an outlaw into an abandoned glow.

Briefly, Albert considers voicing an objection but, rather than risk getting soundly thrashed in one game he has never mastered, decides to follow Walter's example by ignoring the cook's crass behavior altogether. To draw everyone back into firelight, the guide tells a story about a tourist from another trek, again, with Albert translating.

It seems the fellow pestered Walter to locate a jaguar for him to photograph. The guide patiently explained to the man that big cats are cunningly elusive, and that in all his years of jungle work, he has spotted only one jaguar roaming free in the wild. But the tourist continues to inveigh Walter to produce the desired subject for his lens, and one amazing night, they do stumble upon a formidable member of the feline genus, whereupon the guide commands his charge, "There, now take your picture." *Pues*, the man becomes so terrified face to face with the beast that he can't even lift his camera.

While his listeners laugh at the story, Walter secrets Albert a look. Sharp reads the innuendo, retrieves his digital from the side pocket of his travel vest, and snaps a shot of Riki's blade. On the miniature viewing screen "Knife in Burning Oil" fails to achieve the dramatic effect Albert has envisioned, but as the cook studies the artwork, his features soften and his resentment subsides. Walter lets Albert know that he has done a good thing.

So many photos have been taken of the guide and the cook over years of jungle treks that Albert reckons the two must be famous as movie stars among friends and relations of their dispersed clientele. When he mentions the idea to Walter, their leader smiles knowingly, clearly having surmised already that his image is preserved in photo albums in more far-flung countries than he could possibly visit even should he live a hundred years.

On the morning after the fishing trip, Albert adds to the legend; he takes pictures of Ana's zircon smile, of Peter's slender figure suspended from a vine above a rill, of Steven contemplating an exotic flower, and he has just recorded Walter playing savage with fingers curled like claws above his head and machete clasped between gapped teeth, when Riki steps around the giant trunk of the *mapaso*, under which their guide poses, only to discover a lost white woman cowering in shadow like a panicked child.

She trembles as members of Walter's crew mince toward her and whimpers when Ana extends a hand. Drawing back, the Swede mumbles something sorrowful. Walter motions to Riki, and the two of them step forward. Marci fastens upon their sympathetic murmurs, ever though, most likely, she fails to understand a word they say. Each riverman takes hold of a shoulder to ease the orphan upright, but when her legs fail to straighten, Riki issues a command, which spurs those holding back to action.

Steven wraps his arms about Marci's ankles and draws them slowly out from under her, and then Walter and Riki set her down again gently on her hams. Ana kneels to massage the waif's cramped appendages. Peter steps behind the woman to support her back while Albert bends at the waist to address the poor soul in English.

"How long you been out here?" he asks and, when Marci meets his look, goes on. "Rough go, huh. Easy now, you've had the worst of it. It can only get better from here on out."

Riki demands water, Steven produces his bottle, and Marci drinks. Maybe she is not so far gone, Albert dares to hope as he watches her imbibe the liquid greedily. She croaks her thanks when Steven steps back. Her legs responded to Ana's ministrations, straighten little by little, and she grimaces at the pain of their rejuvenation. Shuddering the length of her body, she blinks at Albert, and then inquires, "Could we leave now, please?" as if the two of them attend a social function that has become somewhat tedious.

Riki proposes to carry her back to base camp, but Marci wants to remain fully upright and hobbles along in the group's clutch one slow step at a time. They followed a narrow track that winds among trees and brush. Birds chatter, insects whine and buzz, and the sudden screech of some hidden animal gives Marci a start. Among the rescuers, there is a tingling of nerves as in moments fraught with mortal danger.

Once the woman settles at the mess table, Riki prepares a rice and tuna salad, which Marci ravenously consumes and washes down with two hot cups of *mate*. "That tastes so good," she comments. "You would not believe how cold it gets out there at night."

Ana wonders aloud how the orphan came to be alone in the forest. "I kissed a frog," Marci confesses, which statement, as Albert translates it, makes perfect sense to the rivermen. "*Sedano*," the cook says, and Walter nods in agreement. "*Drogas*," Riki adds, "*Sedano se las da drogas a sus clientes*." Albert grimaces. "You took hallucinogens in the *selva*?" he asks Marci incredulously. "Seemed like a good idea at the time," she sighs, and at a later time, it seems a good idea that she spilled her guts.

Darkness has begun to fall some little while before Sedano and his crazies emanate from the trees and the freaky battle between warring bands will have begun. The orphan parts from a long talk with Ana and takes Albert's hand. With furtive glances cast toward deepening shadows, she begins a disjointed ramble. Sharp can't understand why Marci chooses him to be her angel, where she gets the idea that he is stalwart, brave, and true. Must be he serves as substitute for someone else: a husband, boyfriend, father or brother she has clung to before in crisis.

"It's over now," he mouths to assure the woman that she has joined safe company. "Quiet, dear, you've no call to upset yourself."

But Marci will not be calmed. She's convinced that out beyond camp prowls a phantom whose poison darts drizzle yet about her head and body. Someone has died; this much Albert determines from the troubled woman's scattered recollections. She has seen the man die up close as you can get to death; she is the last person the deceased sees as well before he takes the plunge. Though she has not caused the man to die, his demon hovers like a predator at the edge of base camp. With eerie vigilance, the haunt bides his time, waiting for her to wander away from Walter's troop.

"What's he want from you?" Albert asks calmly, though he too senses an incorporeal presence lurking nearby.

"He wants me to do as I promised," Marci blurts out pitifully.

"What'd you promise?" Albert questions, and the woman shudders.

"I promised to stay with him if he fell."

"But you didn't."

"No, he was dead."

"Well, what can you do for a dead man?"

"It would seem so, wouldn't it? But a promise is a promise, to his way of thinking."

"Forget it. You have no obligation to serve the departed."

"Turns out, that's wrong."

"Right or wrong, he can't harm you now."

"Don't be too sure."

Marci confides that the haunt has allies in the jungle. All manner of slinking beast creeps around in the dark and presses close every time she pleads for release from her promise. Swarms of flying pests sweep about her head at every hint of resistance.

"There must be a statute of limitations even in the netherworld?" Albert speculates.

"I promised to stay till help came. Since there was no help for him, I left."

"Makes sense."

"Not to Simon."

The dead man's name, Sharp guesses.

"Why me?" she pleads and, since Albert can give no answer, supplies her own. She was last to catch the boy's eye before he fell and will never forget that horrific, mocking look on his face. The look binds her forever to a promise impossible to fulfill, but Simon denies the contradiction. For him, her pledge is his only hope to complete his destiny. And that's the part she really can't understand. You'd think if Simon knew the destiny she was assigned to help fulfill, he would have told her what she was in for before he died. Which makes her think he didn't know, that he only perceived the meaning of the promise after he was crushed to death.

So what's she supposed to do? It's too late to keep the pledge, and yet the ghost is too stupid to understand that he's been cheated, that once something happens, there's no turning back. Damnit, can she help it if Simon's caught between what should be and what can no longer come to pass? Well, to be fair, he's not blaming her; he just doesn't know where else to turn. The flippin' ghost is stuck with a destiny untimely terminated. She feels sorry for Simon, but what can she do? And what can Simon do but torment her?

Albert doesn't know what to tell Marci; her question, "Why me?" echoes his own bewilderment.

Transition.

Before Fulgor told him about the atom, there was no way he could have solved Marci's dilemma. Post-Fulgor is another story. Post-Fulgor he might explain that time's pilot is under no obligation to chart a consistent heading. Destiny and fate are therefore mere illusions because time is a tactical unfolding, not a strategic map.

To be sure, Albert could have explained Fulgor's teaching to the woman, had she taken a seat at the restaurant after the metaphysician left. But following the return to Rurre, she had broken off from Walter's troop, claiming it was high time she went home to tend to her children.

"Sure that wasn't your husband that you imagined slinking around in the jungle?" Albert had proposed just before she boarded the plane to La Paz. "Maybe you were feeling guilty about being too long away from your family."

"My husband's alive and kicking," she'd scoffed. "At least he was last I saw of him in Cuzco."

In his ignorance, before he'd learned that space was a secondary cosmic category, and before he could have explained that destinies and ghosts might just as soon pop out of existence as pop in, Albert gave mundane examples to allay Marci's terror. Out behind Riki's camp stove, for instance, lived a black spider the size of a salad plate, which any sensible person would give a miss. Should Marci, however, dare to sneak up on the critter, it would skitter back into its hole before she got within ten paces. And there were at least two bands of howler monkeys not half an hour's walk from where he and Marci sat, which kept to the trees while human beings were around. The point being, even venomous snakes, jaguars, caiman, and raptor birds kept their distance. Furthermore, he bathed in the river every evening without having been assailed by piranha yet. Of course the insects were fearless, Albert had to admit, but Marci could see that the camp shelters had screened windows and the cots inside were equipped with mosquito nets. So even though obnoxious and dangerous creatures did inhabit the jungle, they were more alarming as imagined than in reality. A ghost? *Pues*, Simon's wraith terrorized her only in darkness, didn't it, and the phantom attacked her only when she was alone, which should tell her something about the demon's potency.

He gave these reasonable arguments to assure Marci she had little to fear from any substantial beast, let alone a ghost. But then a hellion came screeching into camp, and Albert experienced first-hand the woman's fright.

Another beer, another transition.

The specter flashes by the can of kerosene Riki has newly set aflame. Its bloodcurdling scream trails into brush by the river. Then here it comes howling again and darts past flickering orange light before remelding with the trees.

Albert leaps to his feet. Marci flings her arms around his waist and buries her face in his chest. Riki ducks beneath the mess tent and reemerges with his trusty kitchen knife clasped in his fist. Walter, from near the path that leads to the latrine, appraises the disturbance unperturbed. Ana's face is an endearing snapshot of astonishment and alarm. Steven is more amazed than scared. Peter's thin eyebrows scrunch together in puzzlement.

"What was that?" Albert manages to croak, but no one answers him, for as he speaks, two more phantoms materialize from the gloaming. They are naked but for loincloths, with faces and torsos painted camouflage green and their nipples circled in red.

The original apparition, a lanky haunt, returns to the light, pounding the butt of a spear on the ground between his bare feet. His long, limber body contracts at the waist, and he jerks his head up and down, whipping shoulder-length hair in repeated arcs.

Screeches subside to rhythmic chants as the raiders take the measure of Walter's band. Another invader slips out of the trees at whose appearance the first three howl and whoop as though announcing the arrival of a dignitary. He is nearly as tall as the spear bearer, though more muscular through the shoulders. In the glow of burning oil, his skin assumes a caramel hue. He holds himself erect, stately even, with black hair trimmed in the shape of a Nazi helmet from which protrude multiple downy feathers.

Riki emits a disdainful huff from pursed lips and lowers his knife. Walter greets Sedano nonchalantly. It takes Albert less than a second to conclude that the invaders are high as kites, and unlike the guide and cook, he is not made easy when the feathered chieftain is identified. He recalls nastiness that bad drug trips precipitate. Charlie Manson and family come to mind as well as tales of cannibalism, said to be practiced yet hereabouts. The flutter of Marci's heart against his chest convinces him to remain on guard.

And then Sedano charges up to Albert, grabs hold of Marci's forearm, and attempts to yank her away from him. She screams. Sharp and the savage pull her back and forth while the other warriors square off according to alliance.

Ana enters a wrestling match with the smaller female raider; their palms join with fingers intertwined as each attempts to force the other to her knees. The Swede invokes her Viking ancestry as she does battle, and it is not the first time Walter's crew has heard her boast of her prowess (which before has brought mocking scoffs from Riki), but during the set-to with the raiders, she is at last afforded an opportunity to prove her worth in combat. Steven and Peter are less successful than she in meeting the enemy. When the heftiest of the invaders begins taking swipes at them, they are reluctant to strike back. They do attempt to restrain the thrashing dervish, but in reaching for a secure hold on her naked flesh, big boobs and pronounced posterior thwart their maneuvers. The Amazon latches onto Peter's long locks and swings him around in a circle. When Steven lunges in her direction, she smacks him in the nose.

These skirmishes run their course on the fight's periphery. At its core, Sedano battles with Albert to reclaim Marci as a member of his band. Riki's willing to spill blood to defend her liberty, and the gangly raider would just as soon poke his spear in the cook's guts if the latter insists on being contrary. They circle one another, Spearman howling and vying for an opening, Riki inciting him to bring it on and spicing his challenge with remarkable profanities.

Transition in time to reorder refreshments.

On a cool-headed metaphysical level, the battle was joined not only between agitated human beings, but also amounted to a conceptual struggle within the atomic paradox. If space dominated, enduring physical evidence would permit Albert to trace cause and effect to a sensible summation. That was the province of space: to keep facts about the world on hand, to store them in a huge file cabinet dedicated to objectivity. If, on the other hand, time held sway, well, with time it was always either all or nothing in any given instance. Space reports, in other words, while time comports. Therefore (is that the right word?), something happened to be sure, for something always happens, though whether verifiable as fact or accessible only through enigmatic transport had yet to be determined.

At some point or lapse, Sedano released Marci's arm, and Albert scooted the woman around behind him. And at some point or lapse, Riki threw his knife at the tree he had targeted following the chess match with the same impressive result. In its flight, the weapon passed so close to the spear bearer's head that to avoid being skewered he dropped to one knee. Thunk went the knife; "Yeeeee!" went the painted warrior. Walter turned his palms toward Sedano as if to say, "I rest my case." So even though time might not be held to spatial determinations—the knife was not required to stick in the tree, it could just as well have been vaporized in flight by a UFO ray gun—the knife did stick in the tree and ever after was established a moment, whether founded in the physicality of space or repeated and repeated in an echo of time, Albert was at a loss to decide and fascinated by his inability to decide.

Swig of beer, next transition.

The knife sticks in the tree, and it is followed by a spear's sticking in the tree as well. Then Sedano makes signs by pointing at his head, the spear, the tree, and each member of his tribe in turn to convey that not only do his followers talk to each other without using words, they also practiced telekinesis. Walter catches on first to the meaning of the chief's mime and, since he is not prejudiced against the use of intelligible speech, explains his finding in Spanish (which Albert translates) to sober members of the gathering.

The fighting halts at the thunk of the knife, and the whack of the spear underscores its cessation. The Amazon lets go of Peter's hair and hastens to console with caresses and kisses the weakest of the raiders (a rather svelte, attractive primitive in Albert's estimation), whom Ana stands over like a Nordic conqueror. Steven doubles at the waist and presses both hands to his bleeding nose. Riki strides resolutely to the tree, pulls the spear out of its truck, flings it to the ground, and will have retrieved his knife has not Walter ordered him to leave it be. At this pass, even Sedano waits to learn what's on Walter mind, for without a doubt, the guide commands respect. Walter is about to propose a course of action that will resolve the dispute.

(Whether time allows his idea to be realized, it is at least one of those times that permits foreshadowing.)

When he has everyone's attention, Walter steps under the kitchen awning to retrieve Riki's ax. The tool has a heavy iron head and a truncated handle. All the warriors form a semicircle near the tree while Walter scratches a line in the dirt with the toe of his sandal. He gestures a throwing motion with the ax and thereby establishes the rules of a contest. "Closest to the knife," he says and hands Spearman the hatchet.

Though Sedano appears reluctant to give consent, his long-limbed enforcer lets out an enthusiastic screech, and the women among the raiders chortle and chirp acquiescence. Marci sidles away from Albert and nods bravely at Walter. It seems the duel will take place despite the chief's misgivings.

For the longest time, Spearman concentrates on the target. No doubt he waits for stars and planets to align just right and for numinous forces to enter his throwing arm. Tension mounts. Albert shifts his weight from one foot to the other, silently willing the beanpole to let fly. Finally, the renegade swings the ax back and forth next to his thigh. Its iron head reaches the level of his shoulder, whereupon Spearman windmills the missile over his head, not once but half a dozen times, and either releases the handle willingly or can no longer maintain his grip. At any rate, the ax spins end over end in flight, fascinating in the way it tumbles through firelight and riveting in the way it slams against the trunk of the tree. But then, the ax ricochets back in the direction of the thrower, and everyone scatters to avoid being hit. Riki laughs his head off; Sedano shoots him daggers of contempt. Walter's expression remains placid as still water.

Following the abysmal failure of their champion, the raiders appear downcast. If Albert hears correctly, Spearman swears under his breath in Dutch, but maybe not; perhaps the wild man mutters a mystical oath channeled through his soul by indigenous phantoms of the forest. Whatever. Riki seizes the opportunity to strike while the opposition regroups.

The cook snatches up the ax and pitches it without preamble at the tree. It lands blade first and holds, its handle frozen at an obtuse angle to the trunk. "*Ahora ¿qué?,*" Riki proclaims, for the missile comes to rest a scant two feet below the point of the knife. He steps forward to retrieve the ax, but Sedano halts him mid-stride. Riki makes to push by, but the chieftain snags his arm, and it looks as though hand-to-hand combat will again break out.

Reflective transition, somewhat wobbly.

It could have, too, because there is no necessary order of events in time that Albert can discern, no precondition of moment to prevent blood from being spilt, UFOs to land, or human flesh to be eaten; there are only those events that do take place, though how is anybody's guess. One could say that Walter prevented a regress to helter-skelter violence by urging Riki to give ground. But then, one would have to admit that the cook's deference to his boss's coaxing also played a part. Consider this: Walter was not compelled to advise discretion, nor Riki to submit to counsel. And what about the chieftain's notion that it was in his power to magically erase a disadvantageous incident? If Sedano hadn't positioned himself before the ax, raised his hands to either side of its head and begun to hum at the tool, if his shoulders hadn't swayed as he sang out, and his followers hadn't joined in the chant, if, lo and behold, the ax handle hadn't begun to move, if it hadn't drooped and quivered, if the iron edge of the hatchet hadn't slipped free of its crease and fallen to the ground at Sedano's feet, well, what manner of wretched chaos would have transpired instead?

Okay, let's transitionally relocate ourselves.

By now, night has fallen over the forest and vision is limited to a wavering aura produced by burning kerosene. Riki cries, *"¡Mierda de caballo!"* with conviction, accusing the enemy chief of performing a slight of hand under the cover of darkness. Albert knits his brow in consternation. Sedano's adherents ooh and aah in monkey talk over their leader's awesome feat. Sharp wants to call for deliberations, but before he can, Sedano picks up the ax and backtracks to the throwing line. Though it hasn't been established beforehand whether a contestant's toss, once completed, can by any means be annulled, Sedano hefts the ax and lets fly, thus rendering the question moot. The missile whacks against the tree right solidly and sticks a mere three inches below and left of target. It's too late to petition for redress once Sedano pitches the ax, especially since his warriors dance wildly around the fire and howl and holler madly to celebrate their paragon's masterwork.

Besides, Riki, ever the tactician, has other ideas. He accepts immediately Sedano's play and marches up to the ax. He curses the instrument with all his might, shouting at it a string of invectives too beautiful to be believed. Contrary to the result Sedano has enjoyed, however, the ax holds firm, and the enemy mocks Riki shamelessly.

It is in this atmosphere of ridicule that Martha, for such is the hunk's name, which Marci reveals later while she stanches the flow of blood from Steven's nose ("Martha caught you a good lick," she will have said); this Martha hussy shoulders Riki rudely aside, wrenches the ax from the tree (ripping loose a chunk of wood roughly the size and shape of a grown man's testicle), and directly pitches a heater. Arrogance notwithstanding, the shot goes wide, and her missile clatters into vine and brush beyond the target. Well, crap. With loss of the ax, the good guys are in danger of losing by default.

But no, Walter's faithful follow him into the forest, taking consolation in Martha's misfire to be sure, yet suffering dejection too, for even if able to locate the ax, who among them might better Sedano's mark? Luckily, it is not in their leader's makeup to admit defeat; his wordless message to his *compadres* as they beat about the bush is to take heart, the battle is by no means lost, through courage and perseverance they will realize their finest hour. When Peter locates the ax, they return to the clearing, taking solace at least in the game's continuance.

Peter goes bravely to the line and shows no sign of surrender when his attempt falls short, and neither does Steven slump in defeat when he misses. Then Ana's shot lands halfway up the tree trunk—in no way challenging the chieftain's toss—but the team's spirits rise. They hold their collective breath as the ax leaves Walter's hand and whirls straight for the knife blade. Most of its trajectory, the missile flies precisely on line, but then inexplicably on its last spin, the ax drops off course and lands low, though so close to the other gouge as to require a string measurement. Once made—goddamn the luck!—and once calculations undergo review—*¡Hijo de su puta madre!*—Sedano's disciples erupt in wigged-out jubilation.

For the next few moments, no one but Albert remembers that he has yet to take a turn. Members of Walter's band exchange anguished looks while the savages romp around camp like lunatics just released from a locked ward. Sharp keeps quiet, deeply regretting the inevitable. When Riki catches his eye and shouts for the group's attention, he looks away, wishing to be anywhere other than where he is.

Transition.

At a patio table in a restaurant that specialized in overcooked fish, Albert remembered Marci handing him the ax and telling him not to worry. No one suspected her of knowing a secret that guaranteed their success. "Trust me, Albert," she said. "I have the power."

"What power would that be?" Sharp mumbled sarcastically.

"The power of love," she answered, which made him cringe.

What a ditz, he'd thought at the time and shrank sheepishly beneath the raps Riki delivered his back. He could have cried remorseful tears at Steven's encouraging words, "You can do it, Albert, just go ahead and do it."

Well, at the time, he didn't know about the power of love, wouldn't know until Marci joined him at the bow, on the boat ride out of the forest. He was hunched forward then on a plank at the bow, his body swaying as the brave canoe leaned gracefully into wide turns on the Beni. A quilted green jungle curtain swept by; oh my, the blinding sheen touched off by the sun on viscous brown water. Pink and black jags of protruding rock, the approach of a tree isolate in scarlet bloom; my, oh my, he exulted in a glorious elapse of beautified time, which he didn't know about then beyond color and sweep.

Transition to love.

Marci appears at his side and asks him to scoot over and make room for her on the bow plank. Hip pressed to his hip and facing sternward, she asks, "Have you ever been in love?" And then, when she spots the look of consternation on his face, she hurries on. "That was a dumb question, wasn't it? Everybody's been in love at least once."

He wishes she wouldn't place her hand on his forearm, though she is a handsome late-thirties female despite mosquito bites that mar her face. Her dark brown eyes shine with ardor. The gaze embarrasses him, and he turns back to the river. She remains silent through a full turn in the Beni.

"Once maybe," he obliges her at last.

"Only once?" she teases.

"Once, a long time ago."

She swings her legs in a half circle and scoots forward, using both hands to propel her hips. Their calves end up dangling either side of the prow, and they ride back to Rurre scrunched shoulder to shoulder.

"Seems to me love is definite," she says.

"Seems to me love is doubtful," he counters.

"I think you're being coy," she says, by which assertion he assumes that from her point of view they are themselves engaged in the preliminaries of love.

Well, this is definitely not the case, far as he's concerned; he isn't being coy, he has attempted to give an accurate response to her query.

"Tell me about the one," she suggests.

Only for the sake of clarification does he sum up his romantic history.

"She looked for love in me and was nearly convinced she'd found it."

"How poetic," she titters, poking fun at him.

"I know less about poetry," he assures her.

"Less than love?"

"Less than you."

And that inspires her to be out with her spiel.

To begin, Albert reminds her of her husband, which he has suspected ever since that night she told him about the ghost. It seems they are both balding men and self-possessed, and they both are sound of body, though Jerry is thicker through the torso and square-shouldered. Is Albert aware that his left shoulder slants below his right? An occupational affliction, he might inform her, if of a mind to justify his posture.

Furthermore, her husband's bearing is studiously erect (as opposed to his own stooped form, Albert conjectures, and begins to wonder whether Marci intends to cite more contrast than similarity between the two men she compares). Well, she loves Jerry to distraction (so maybe that's the crucial intersect, though Albert hopes to hell not). He is relieved when she goes on to explain that she and Jerry have been together for fifteen years through thick and thin, and it is only during the later stages of their marriage that he treats her crassly, which makes her feel worthless. (At this pass, Albert will have been only too happy to admit a contrast.)

And Jerry has gone off on a romp with another woman. But before that, though not long before, she has come to loathe as well as love him till the two passions became one in her soul and rage on till she chokes on resentment. The idea of the South American trip has been proposed to leap beyond their warring ways and circle back to the beginnings of love. But so much for turning back the clock. Marci knows now you can never backtrack on love, that the only hope for true love lies in forging ahead. That's what she's learned from the wise woman she met in Pisac who overcame loathing and resentment by taking stock in herself. Marci too has got beyond loathing. She's got beyond loathing by allowing herself to see that what her husband thinks of her is not what she has to be. "You see," Marci declares, "he has his path and I have mine, never mind what he thinks. You are what you are despite what anybody thinks, that's how you get beyond loathing and discover love's what's left over.

"You don't know where it comes from," she continues, "nor where it's going, only that it's there same as you're there." There is no reason to love, so love doesn't have to measure up to any standard. Nor does the love she's talking about want to be acknowledged or repaid. It goes out from a person, circles around, and comes back to itself. And in the going and the coming, it embodies a power that defies explanation, that shrugs off all encumbrances, and that emerges from captivity without looking back. It is this love that has parted her from Jerry. It is this love that Marci welcomes with every breath she takes. It is this secret power that she passes on to Albert when she hands him the ax. And the moment true love touches him, he becomes a hero.

Woozy transition. Who emptied all those beer bottles on the table?

Well, she might as well have taken credit for what happened next. He honestly didn't feel the ax's collaboration with the knife blade was the result of any skillful coercion on his part. In Marci's understanding of the event (if extrapolation served), the wedding of love to strife had spun off an urge whereby the ax found its necessary crease. In this way, Marci didn't take credit for the victory either (he supposed); in her view, she simply functioned as one essential element in the circuitry of love.

He recalled a sense of foreknowledge that accompanied his approach to the line, a kind of muted voicing that he hardly heard, which voicing was entirely muted once he arrived at Walter's mark in the dirt. Swinging his arm upward had been just something he did because it was expected of him. The ax flipped through the air when he released it and landed in the tree precisely where it was supposed to land. He did not feel particularly fulfilled when the ax struck the target; he did not feel anything in particular, even when Sedano marched up to the tree and raised his palms to either side of the joined blades and started in on the same routine he had performed following Riki's toss. While the others, especially Riki, got all worked up over the chieftain's interference, the gracious guest hung back, taking in the brouhaha from a figurative distance. Albert was of a mind by then to assume that his contribution to the contest had run its course.

Transitions becoming confused. Sometime or other transitions are bound to become confused.

Sometime or other too, Marci sidles up next to the witch doctor and counters his chants with blistering silence. Apparent in the trenchant stance she assumes beside Sedano is a surety that any attempt to alter the outcome of the contest will come to naught. It tickles Albert to watch this meeting of sorcerers and their subsequent telekinetic wrestling match. Neither ax nor knife moves a micrometer while the match ensues. Sedano hums and babbles, Marci edges closer, the chieftain glances her way, and she glares back at him. Sedano abruptly halts his incantation, and panic seizes his features. He crosses his arms over his chest and cries, "She steals my soul," which causes the rest of his band to shut their yaps and stand stock-still. And then Sedano bolts for the trees, and the other savages run after him. Only when the raiders have evaporated into darkness does the ax droop slightly from its purchase. As Albert watches, the hatchet drops out of the crease it has made in the tree and thumps to the ground. Riki laughs like crazy whenever that will have happened.

So Marci is saved from kissing any more frogs and from stripping down to her skivvies and painting herself green. She bathes in the river that night instead and accepts a change of clothes that Ana provides. After her cleansing, she partakes of a tasty canned meat supper Riki sets before the crew. Then, with her belly full, she succumbs at last to exhaustion. She sleeps like an angel in the camp barracks amidst multicolored moths and butterflies that cling to its airy screens.

Next morning, under a scorching sun, she helps lash together bamboo posts with strips of palm leaf and pole down the Tuichi on the return trip to Rurre. It is sometime after when their raft begins to disintegrate, after they will have worked their way through cross currents in the river to enter the mouth of a cave where light quickly fades and Peter lets out a deep-throated Dracula rumble, which echoes off the chamber walls and wakes a battalion of resident bats that peep and squeak in a mad dash to safety, and Ana dives into the water to escape their raucous onslaught, screaming as soon as she resurfaces that she is being eaten alive by piranha, and Marci shrieks, which causes Albert to damn near spit up his liver because if there is one thing that churns his innards it is the sound of a woman's shriek, which in no uncertain terms, he lets Marci know, "Hey, lady, goddamn. It's only flying rats and ravenous fish." Only after Walter will have fished them one by one out of the river does Marci meet with Albert in the bow of the canoe, now having motored onto the Beni, to tell him about the amazing power of selfless love.

Transition to whenever. Everything happens at the same time in the same atom anyway.

Frankly, he would have preferred to participate in a more carnal variation on the passion. Back in Rurre, following the karaoke party, the evening after Marci had been sent home to be reunited with her children (and perhaps a contrite husband), he had shared accommodations at one of the town's inexpensive hostels (a dump, that is) with Ana. There were only two rooms available at the time of the crew's retreat, and while Steven and Peter secured one, he volunteered to bunk with the Viking.

Her amenable endorsement of the arrangement made him think that, sonofagun, he was being given at last an unexpected run at some stellar pussy. He believed his chances were still good even though, once reclined between the sheets, Ana failed to invite him with outstretched arms to cross the gap that separated their beds. Instead, she mused aloud on her state of life, her search for meaning apart from conventional involvement, and her lonely commitment to the stern discipline of self-completion. For his part, he listened patiently, flattered her shamelessly for undertaking the difficult quest, sympathized with her dismay, and expressed admiration for her courageous determination.

Before finding a graceful way to approach her bed, however, he fell asleep. When he felt her hand on his shoulder in the middle of the night, he dared to imagine that the blessed hour had arrived for him to rise and strike out upon a dreamscape of perfect lechery.

"You were snoring," she informed him though.

"Sorry," he apologized for his unworthy behavior.

And in the silence that followed, he agonized over whether she meant what she said, that he had disturbed her sleep and would he please roll over and be quiet, or whether she actually meant for the interruption to be a prelude to salacious embrace.

Because he couldn't stand not knowing, he slipped finally out of bed, crossed the floor, and leaned over her. She gave no response until his lips had descended to within a hand's breadth of her lips and the next step he took could only have lifted him to the wet acme of carnal climax. Only then did she tell him, "I would never betray Marci."

Straightening and turning away, he regretted deeply her error in judgment, for on the one hand, her loyalty was misplaced—he had made no pact whatsoever with the woman named—and, on the other, rejection was no treatment for a hero.

He is a mere stumbling sot by the time he meets up again with Fulgor Armanza in a bar on the other side of town. By then, the philosopher is in his cups as well, so that when Albert prompts him to hold forth further on the subject of the atom, the man sounds like a broken record. It takes less effort to listen passively to the brass band playing in the tavern than to actively engage in fractured metaphysics. When Peter joins him at the table, Albert learns they are the last adventurers from Walter's crew left in Rurre.

Somewhere along a temporal lapse, a diverting past has transitioned to a disheartening present. Peter accepts Albert's invitation for a nightcap, and they speak of the trails they will have set upon in the morning. The German will have boarded a third-class bus that follows the most dangerous highway in the world, from which graded surface on average (Peter reports with subdued bravado) two loads of passengers per year plunge to their deaths. The American will have flown out in a Fokker F-27 (as noted previously in the lounge at the military airport in La Paz), which name of aircraft recalls to Albert's mind flying machines that resemble kites. In any case, Peter makes his separate way at their parting, though the two of them promise to meet up again in the capital if the young man will have survived his bus ride. At closing time, Fulgor Armanza goes his separate way, too, to sleep with the lumpy jolly wood nymph who owns the tavern. Everyone goes his separate way but Albert, who cannot be separated from himself despite the centrifugal force that currently entropies atoms in his brain. It is too late in transition and he too inebriated to reconcile a matter of time other than the one that has caught him up.

Pleito por plata

(Fight over Money)

He awoke on guard, rolled out of bed in his boxers, and hustled to the hotel window.

"Check the perimeter." Jake was awake too.

A clattering minibus pulled onto the street below, swerved toward the far side curb, and braked. The van's side door banged open, and two women in bowler hats and tasseled shawls that reached to their knees stepped onto black paving bricks. The van lurched forward but screeched to a halt when the second woman out of the bus hollered at the driver. After she retrieved a wool-wrapped bundle from the floor of the vehicle, the driver took off for reals.

"Clear," Simon said.

"Stay alert," came Jake's response.

From behind the glass, he couldn't hear the women's footsteps as they trudged up a steeply slanted sidewalk. They made their way between dingy roll-down shop doors and widely spaced, stunted trees that followed the line of the curb. A man in a blue denim jacket started up the hill behind them. Two schoolgirls descending, with pink book bags riding on their backs, walked past the climbers.

"No sign of heat."

"They're out there, recruit. Bet on it."

Following a trip to the commode, Simon pulled on a pair of dark brown denims that snugged his thighs and pinched his waist. He returned to his post. A wooden power pole, supporting a tangle of wires he couldn't make sense of, stood directly beneath the window.

Black bricks that surfaced the street were laid in a pattern that reminded him of a design he'd once seen stamped in old leather. Stores across the street started opening; a kabob vendor parked his cart on the sidewalk half a block down. In the intersection at the bottom of the hill, a fair-sized crowd coalesced. Broad advertisements for soft drinks and cooking oil were painted on the side of a tall corner building. Thick overcast roofed the city.

Simon reckoned most people in the capital would keep hunkered down on such a dreary day. Nobody knew him in La Paz, and he hoped nobody knew he was in La Paz either. Jake would continue to harp on stealth, which was fine, but if he started in on shame and blame again, Simon planned to shine him on. He believed the old jarhead couldn't hold murder against him because he'd all but admitted to such wholesale slaughter as Simon could only imagine.

A gray-haired clerk on duty at the front desk was talking on the phone when he handed over his key. So far, so good. Any description the clerk gave of him, based on one quick glance, would be of no use to the cops.

"Relax," Jake whispered, "not that hard to be invisible."

"You oughta know," Simon mumbled as he slipped out the door. The situation was under control.

Wouldn't you know it, though, the first people he came upon at street level were the very sorts who paid close attention to everything. Two children locked onto him as he emerged from the lobby, their expression so severe you'd have thought their faces were rough-cut from granite. The girl wore the usual bowler hat along with a hoop skirt and shawl. She had a round head, pug nose, and thin lips. The boy standing beside her was a couple inches shorter, bony and bareheaded.

Simon figured them for a pair of runaways and guessed right off what they were up against. A rolled blanket stowed against the hotel front verified that they'd spent the night on the sidewalk. It was a pretty good bet too that they didn't have a cent to their names.

"Snap out of it," Jake ordered.

Simon shook himself inwardly. He knew where he was at and didn't need Jake getting on his case. "Chill, man," he told his partner. "Those two could use a break."

"Forget 'em. We gotta move out."

"That's hard, man."

"Been cold and hard since I took a tumble."

Simon ignored the jarhead's last crack. He fished out his wallet, unfolded it, and checked his stash. It was then he remembered he'd spent the last of his *bolívares* on rice and chicken the night before.

"Bummer," Jake flipped off.

Not funny. His partner either didn't know what it was like to be broke or didn't care so long as he wasn't the one *jodido*. Seemed like a dozen times a day Simon found out something else about Jake that ticked him off. Ever since the killing, they'd been stuck with each other, and there didn't seem to be any way for them to get unstuck.

At the bottom of the hill, the street opened onto a split-level plaza where portable stalls had been set up since he'd rolled out of bed. City residents shuffled about the half-circle as if they had nothing better to do than hang around a chill, open-air market all day long. Local homeys posted on a block ledge at the back of the plaza's upper tier reminded him of blackbirds strung along a power line. There were sculptures at either end of the raised shelf. One looked like nothing more than a stack of rocks; the other depicted a ten-foot-tall stone head with a big nose and bent brow. A billboard beyond the layout pictured a pink-skinned *chico* smiling like the Mona Lisa.

Simon turned his back on the market, walked by a church, crossed the main drag, and ducked among tall commercial buildings. Row upon stacked row of window glass either side of him gave the impression of diamond facets.

"Where we going?" Jake demanded.

"A bank, if that's okay by you."

"Bad idea. Gonna wanna see your passport."

"Where else am I gonna change money except at a bank?"

For half a block, Simon enjoyed a respite from Jake's blather. He leaned into the sidewalk slant, turned a corner onto level ground, and made for a row of square columns that ran to the next intersection. The columns presented the type of building front he expected to see at the entrance to a bank.

"Don't look now, but we've picked up a tail," Jake cut in.

"Yeah, right."

"Okay, don't believe me."

"You're serious?"

"Hey, man, forget it. What the hell do I know? Like I don't have eyes to see with or ears to hear? Then again, I don't. Thanks to you."

"Would you please—?"

"Please what? Let you go ahead and walk into an ambush?"

To shut the jerk up, Simon swiveled his head casually to one side and scoped behind him. Okay, so the boy and girl from the hotel traipsed along ten steps rearward, but so what?

"Oooo, we're in terrible danger," he mocked his partner but then realized Jake had a point. Last thing they needed was to attract a couple of strays, not only because some degenerate might think Hansel and Gretel back there had glommed onto a soft touch and join the parade, but also because sooner or later, the heat was bound to spot the freak show and want to know more about the gringo leading it. So he was about to turn around and run the kids off when this pushy type stepped out from behind the line of columns and yanked a wad of bills from the inside pocket of his brown leather jacket.

The first idea Simon flashed on was that the dude wanted to buy his two kids. That being a really dumb idea, he rejected it. The man had bushy black hair, fleshy cheeks, and carried a good bit of weight abound his midsection. Could be he had backup too since two other wise guys in collar shirts and sweaters hung by the columns with their eyes peeled.

"Change dollars," the dude with the roll said.

"Knew it all along."

Simon ignored Jake's useless comment, which was only his latest echo of the obvious. Given a chance, his partner could be counted on to get all trippy about how doing business with a money changer avoided hassles at the bank. Simon reached for his wallet before Jake got worked up.

As his hand cleared his pocket, he felt a gentle tug on the sleeve of his sweatshirt. When he swung around, the boy drew back and raised clawed fingers to chest level. Simon squinted at him. The kid's kung-fu move came off borderline ridiculous.

"No problem," the moneychanger broke in and flipped the back of his hand at the runaway. "Five thirty, one dollar," he added, thus stating his business.

"Going rate," Jake advised as if he were a currency expert.

Simon hesitated. Something about the *muchacho*'s Bruce Lee pose bothered him, something he maybe should think about.

"Wants a piece of the action," Jake speculated.

Yeah, no problem. "*Calma,*" Simon told the boy, planning to get back to him later. At the moment, he had a more pressing matter to attend to.

Being nobody's chump, he held onto his hundred-dollar bill until *bolívares* crossed his palm. Smart decision as it turned out since in counting the money, he discovered the stack was light twenty Bs. The changer apologized profusely for his mistake, took back the multicolored bundle, added an orange bill, and counted the stack slowly with Simon watching.

Satisfied at last that the sum was correct, Simon stuffed the Bs into his front pants pocket and headed directly up the street. There was no call for him to get chummy with a moneychanger.

"Smooth," Jake observed sarcastically.

Yeah, whatever; his partner could get bent. He rounded a corner feeling slightly miffed at Jake's remark, which emotion torque up a notch when the kid tugged on his sleeve again. Where'd the twerp get off acting like he was owed a cut? When he turned to glare at the runaway, there was a surprise waiting for him.

The boy didn't look like he expected a tip, more like he was disappointed in the foreigner, and his sidekick looked disappointed too. Their features remain steady, but Simon caught their drift. The boy repeated his claw gesture and pointed to the pocket where the Bs were tucked away. A nasty premonition nipped Simon's brain as he reached for the bills, but he relaxed when his fingers closed on cash. To show everything was cool, he pulled out the folded wad and held it up for the boy to see. The kid signed for him to do a recount. When he flipped through the notes again, they worked out to a hundred and sixty light. He thumbed though the jack once more with the same freaky result. Oh man, was he now truly pissed.

He charged back around the corner with his fists doubled and his jaw set. The two wise guys who had hung back while the scam went down were there, but the other scumbag had dipped. Simon grabbed the nearest fool by his sweater front and demanded to know where the main ratbag was hiding, but of course, the dude acted all innocent, and of course, his homey charged up like it was bangin' time.

With temples throbbing, Simon was plenty ready to get it on. Might have too if he hadn't remembered the heat just then. Cops walk up on the dust up, and he'd be one clueless sap looking for a rathole to dive into himself.

So instead of trading blows, he let go of the jerkoff's sweater and swatted the other moron's hand off his shoulder. Sure as fuck, these two worked the same grift as the main rat, though what could he do about it after the scam went down? "This thing ain't over," he growled and stared acid at the pair of shills. They looked back at him like he was nuts, but behind their stupid faces, he detected smirks.

He walked away feeling like a total loser. Back around the corner, the children waited on him. They'd known the score all along, and he blamed himself for not heeding their warning.

"Guess we got an appointment with one sorry-ass rip-off," Jake drawled hard.

"Right," Simon answered and forced a grimace. It'd be a big mistake to let the jarhead think he was in charge. "Dead man comes up with another bright idea."

"You seriously blaming me?"

"Said the *muchacho* wanted to get paid."

"Still say it."

"Wrong. He was looking out for the team."

"Since when he join up?"

"Since just now."

"Gimme a break, newbe. Like we need a couple of civilians tagging along."

"You're so full of crap."

"That your answer?"

Simon noticed the kids were watching him. They appeared neither surprised nor puzzled by his monologue. Street smart, these two, way beyond their years. Too bad their talents were wasted on his dumb ass.

"Matter of honor," Jake argued.

"Semper fi, right?"

"Time to walk the walk."

"Wish you'd walk your sorry ass outa my face."

"Not going to happen, recruit."

"Oh, man," Simon moaned. "Why can't you make for the light same as other stiffs?"

"Like I got a choice. Like it's up to me when I rotate."

"Okay, how about this deal. I take the mission, and you hit the bricks."

"From the man who sent me packin' to begin with."

"Why you still casing my ass then?"

"Beats the hell outa me," Jake answered like nothing in the world was his fault.

To tweak the jarhead, Simon reached into his pocket and withdrew the first bill he touched, read a tener, and motioned the boy to come over and take it.

"Terrific," Jake squawked.

"Go haunt yourself," Simon shot back as the boy passed the note to his sidekick, which she rolled up tight and tucked into a pocket among the folds in her skirt. He expected them to bounce after copping a handout, but they hung tough.

Well, ain't this a peach. Lost in enemy territory with bad guys closing in and a couple orphans glom him for a meal ticket. They have any idea what was up? How could they unless they heard Jake's yammering?

"You speak Spanish?" Simon shot at the marine vet.

In the silence that followed, he shook his head. Christ, he was losing it.

High-rises towered either side of the street with their cornices about to float into the sky. Jake oughta take the hint and fly up to heaven himself. Hell, maybe he'd already been air mailed and returned-to-sender. Thanks, God. No offense, but you've got some sick sense of humor.

"Saddle up," Jake ordered, rude dog he was.

"We got a deal?"

"Go for it. See what happens."

"I wanna hear you say we got a deal."

"How should I know? You're the one in tight with the commander."

Simon laughed mirthlessly. Hell of a way to start a mission. No FO intelligence, no battle plan, and a proven fuck-up in change. But there it is, kiddies. Sure you wanna hang with a twisted gringo? Sure you wanna run a rat down on his own turf? Oh cripes, apparently they did.

The only way he could think to launch the mission was to return to the crosscut where the scam had gone down. A few Bolivians occupied the intersection, but the target wasn't among them. Great news. Meant the ratbag might be anywhere in La Paz by now.

Groping for a search strategy, Simon recalled his bus ride into town the evening before. From a plateau above the capitol, he'd scanned a broken maze of red-roofed buildings that sprawled up the city's bordering crater walls. He remembered catching a glimpse beyond the hoop of a mountain peak majestically encased in ice. From the valley floor, high-rises blocked his view of the landmark.

Without a prominent point of reference to steer by, he had no idea where the hell he was. Looking around, he could almost hear a hundred sighs emanating from a hundred doors and windows. "Simon," hissed a chorus of voices. "Simon, are you afraid?" He shuddered at the creepy taunt and checked with Jake. His partner had got creeped out by the voices too. Terrific. Here he was, lost in enemy territory, and the scuzbag who dogged him at every turn zipped a lip.

Strange airs circled overhead. A flock of pigeons flew around a street corner heading who knew where. The birds circled back and tried another route. Strange air, not even birds could find their way in it. Exhalations rising from city floor collided with overcast and rebounded upon other stirrings. When he spotted the pigeons again, still circling and looking for a place to alight, he had half a mind to say, "Ah, screw it, better blow this pop stand while the heat's still out to lunch." He knew though that once clear of La Paz, Jake would commence to ream his ass. If he retreated from battle with the rat before he'd got so much as one good lick in, shame and vengeance cravings would hound him clear to Peru. What devil dog cries uncle, middle of a fight.

"None I know. We're talkin' chicken shit." Oh yeah, the triumphant return of Jake.

The patrol headed out. He took point; the kids guarded flanks from a step or two behind. Simon had no idea why the runaways followed him. Maybe they had nothing better to do than watch a gringo jack himself up.

Whatever. The three of them plodded up a steep incline where raised lips of paving bricks stubbed the toes of Simon's boots. Gray light cast stone, stucco, and wooden buildings in dingy hues. Atmosphere up the byway grew dank and cramped.

On a track that ran perpendicular to the city's crater wall, they passed a pharmacy where a skinny codger in a white smock eyed them from behind smudgy plate glass. When Simon met his gaze, the druggist looked away, refocused across the street on a building with broad clean windows and a polished wooden entrance above which a black-lettered yellow sign identified the establishment as a bank. A steady stream of customers ambled on and off the premises. Well, he knew already he'd screwed up and didn't need to be reminded.

Angling his head away from the bank, he spied a knot of idlers stationed up the sidewalk. Five or six fools yakked it up without a care in the world. He looked away from them and kept walking, but one face among the no accounts sucked his eye back. Damn, there stood the moneychanger swapping lies with his cronies, like he didn't have to worry about being made by the sap he'd just ripped off.

A car horn blared from the left as Simon cut diagonally across the street. The rat cranked his head in the direction of the noise and froze when he saw Simon. Up close, Simon slammed his palm against the hustler's shoulder and fisted wool. Just before dropping the hammer though, he realized a case of mistaken identity. The man he'd grabbed was around the same age as the ratbag and of similar build, but a thin mustache lined his upper lip, and he wore a maroon sweater, not a brown leather jacket. Simon dropped his hand and stammered, "My mistake."

Before the guy's backup could throw down, he about-faced and scurried back the way he'd come. Across the street, his team fell in line and double-timed with him downhill. Sheer faces of buildings to either side suddenly seemed so certain to tip over that they were already falling. Simon reckoned he'd better get out of canyon land before big bad La Paz crushed him dead.

Okay, so flying off the handle was definitely not smart. Okay, so without a battle plan, chasing after a rat on his own turf was nuts. Okay, so what he needed was time to think. "Excuses," Jake accused, as Simon hustled down the hollow. "You're gonna wimp out like a punk."

"Wrong," was his adamant response to the devil dog. "I'm going to nail that sucker if it's the last thing I do."

Several minutes later, he stumbled onto the capital's main artery. Bus and automobile traffic raced along the paved concourse; sidewalks both sides of the drag thronged with pedestrians. Looking right, he caught sight of the stone head resting on its squat pedestal three blocks distant. Finally, he'd found a landmark; there was hope for the mission yet. Given time, he'd come up with a plan to trap the rat, seize him by his spindly neck, and shake his bones till they separated.

It took only one glance rearward, however, for his vengeance fantasy to fade. The female member of the strike team remained with the program, but the boy had beat feet. In his absence, the girl toted their rolled blanket over her shoulder. Simon raised his arms and turned his palms outward in query, but the child regarded him with her usual flat expression. To her, the loss was no big deal. "*Calma,*" Simon admonished himself. "The girl's not upset, so where's the big whoop?"

To steady his nerves, he headed up the main strip toward the plaza. The girl followed for three blocks and climbed with him onto the flat concrete platform that fronted the severed head. There they traipsed among plastic-draped market carts where blankets and T-shirts, roasted meat, soda pop and hot tea, cigarettes, and cotton socks were sold. He bought his partner an ear of corn. He watched a shoeshine boy whose face was hidden behind a black ski mask run down trade. Why the dude worked incognito, Simon couldn't guess. An altercation between a minibus driver and his fare started up. The dispute went on for about a minute before both parties flung up their hands in disgust and departed from each other in a huff.

While he and the girl lingered among the crowd, and while Simon numbered his options (which made for a lengthy list so far filled with blanks), a short, pudgy man wearing a white shirt and black nylon jacket unzipped to his navel marched up. Once stopped in front of Simon, without so much as a nod, he demanded that the foreigner produce his passport. Simon balked, though his confusion lasted only so long as it took the intruder to whip out a billfold and display police identification.

"Holy shit!" Jake exclaimed while Simon's mind tore off. The loafers outside the bank must have dropped a dime. He cursed clustered carts and milling lumps of humanity that hemmed him in. Worst case scenario materialized: dead straight path to a locked door with iron mesh over its tiny window.

As he scrambled to reorganize and refocus, the cop pressed closer, got all huffy and intimidating, which act came off lame since he had to stand on tiptoe and bend back his head to meet Simon face to face. "*Pasaporte,*" the runt repeated and, when Simon showed no sign of cooperating, issued a third command. "*Venga,*" he ordered and thrust his chin toward the street where a taxicab waited at the curb with nearside front and rear doors thrown open.

Being hauled to jail in a taxi struck Simon as downright bizarre (for one thing, he wondered who was going to pay for the ride), but he blew off inconsequential thoughts and got set to whip up his fist, smack Shorty between his gerbil ears, and sky out for the nearest exit.

"Piss off," someone barked at his side, which made him jump, which wouldn't have made him jump if it was Jake talking.

Made the cop jump too. Simon took a step backward, amazed at all the weird shit coming at him all at once. While he zoned like a retard, speaker and cop started up a word fight. Spit and Spanish shot back and forth between them. The cop flashed his ID again and (no surprise, second verse, same as the first) ordered the other foreigner to produce documents. Anyway, it was nothing doing this time around either since the new arrival laughed in *Señor Policia's* face. Funna dip, Simon decided, having regained his wits sufficiently to look out for *numero uno.* Then he noticed *Señor* Badass had started to mince sideways, like maybe he had second thoughts about the bust.

"Arsehole," the other foreigner flung at the cop as he sidled toward the waiting cab.

They both watched the cop slam shut the taxi's rear door and climb into the front passenger seat. Simon expected more trouble even as the cab driver hit the gas and shot into traffic. Back to the headquarters to muster reinforcements, he feared.

"Having a lend," the guy beside him commented.

Simon turned. The stranger stood taller than him by four inches with shoulder-length blond hair falling from a part top-center of his noggin. Goldilocks, Simon immediately christened the dude. He wore his tan jacket flung open so that his peach colored flannel shirt was exposed from collar to untucked tails. He had pale green eyes, a flat chin, and a nose shaped like a *chile.*

"Don't know about you, but I'm outa here," Simon said.

"Easy, mate, bloke's not coming back."

"How you know?"

"Having you on was all."

"Not a real cop, you mean?"

"Don't imagine he was. Fancied doing a robbery once you climbed into the taxi."

"I was about to dust him," Simon answered to let the stranger know he could handle himself.

"Should have waited then. Proper riot that, I expect."

Annoyance replaced initial relief. Simon wondered what it was about himself that made lowlifes in La Paz take him for a pushover. It couldn't have been his size that attracted rip-offs. He'd had a good sixty pounds on the moneychanger and outweighed the fake cop by at least fifty. Nor did he believe his close-cropped hair and Chicano mug marked him a wimp.

"Do I look stupid?" he demanded of Goldilocks.

The guy made a deal of examining him. "Well, you're not from a university, are you, mate?"

"That make me a dope?"

"Didn't say you were."

"I look stupid, you said."

"Did I?"

"What do I look like then in your opinion?"

"Like a Yank drug pusher. Sorry, you asked."

Well, there was no need to apologize because the description painted him in banger colors.

"Care for a parley in the underworld?" Goldilocks inquired blithely.

Simon screwed up his face. The dude sounded friendly, but around here, things could go screwy in a hurry. "Where's the underworld?"

"You're standing in it, mate."

Jake interrupted. "College boy," he warned, "take it from me, he's dead weight."

Which made Simon remember swearing that morning to avoid hook-ups during his stop in La Paz. On the other hand, he had not foreseen run-ins with rip-offs either. "Beat it," he ordered his shadow.

"Pardon?" Goldilocks said.

"Not you. I was thinking aloud."

"That's what I call speech, mate."

"Whatever. I'm not feeling too safe around here."

"Where might you rather be?"

Simon didn't know.

"When you think about it," the stranger added, "around here is as safe as anywhere else."

Which inclined Simon to review where he'd been so far that morning. The streets he'd got lost in, pigeons he'd seen circling in skyscraper canyons, eerie sighs and whispers coming out of nowhere. "Okay, I get it. From where we're at, we scope the smart guys before they jump us."

"In a manner of speaking."

Virgil was the guy's name, he learned, when the two of them took seats on the back ledge of the plaza near the statue of the head. The raised vantage gave a bird's eye view of surrounding terrain. Taxis came and went; merchants conducted low-key business. Three or four shoeshine boys worked the crowd below. Up the main drag, a large Coca-Cola sign was hung on the flat face of a ten-story apartment building. He scanned traffic for a tic; he spied no cop cars. He glanced at Virgil once or twice and then beyond him to the knot of homeys who sat on the ledge, representing total boredom. His attention drifted back to the shoeshine boys.

"They look like terrorists," he mumbled.

"Don't want to be recognized," Virgil answered, catching on somehow. "Supposed to be in school, aren't they?"

"Oh yeah?" Simon answered. "They the reason you call this hangout the underworld?" Could be there were plenty of fugitives besides him in the crowd looking to keep a low profile.

"Hadn't thought about truants actually, but they do fit. If you take my meaning."

Simon crinkled one corner of his mouth and puffed out a breath through his nose.

"Brilliant. Challenging my metaphor, aren't you, Simon?"

"Challenging your—?"

"Comparison, as your old grammar has it. But that's not much help. Think compass, then you're off. Locate game sites on holiday with a proper compass."

The way the guy talked cracked him up. He sounded either like a college professor, or what a college professor was supposed to sound like.

"Spirits wander the underworld," Virgil prattled on. "Divine *Illimani* looms above the city, and deep beneath the mountain, spirits roam besotted in the spell of Death's own brother, Sleep."

Did the professor hear the voices too? Simon cringed when reminded of the voices. "All I see around here are shoppers," he said to hide his anxiety.

"I could lead you to a discreet corner where spirits knock about unhidden."

"Sure you could."

"You game, mate?"

"Ah, man, I probably know more about dead people than you do."

Rather than answer, the man pushed himself to his feet.

"What's up?" Simon sputtered and spun toward the backside of the plaza. He was afraid his companion had spotted trouble.

"Thought I'd go for a stroll."

Oh. No problem then. "Mind if I go with?"

"Assumed you would."

Following Virgil off the ledge, he remembered the girl. She was posted over by the rock tower. He caught her eye and motioned that she join him.

While the Englishman gave account of the area, Simon gathered info. The church he'd passed on his ill-fated trip to the bank that morning was called San Francisco. It was built in the 1500s, collapsed under heavy snow in 1600, and was rebuilt during the 1700s. "A fine example of simplicity's elegance," Virgil gushed in praise of the church's single square tower.

The plaza they left behind was named after the church and served as a hangout for both locals and tourists. A few blocks east, they'd find Plaza Murillo, where government buildings were located, along with memorials to the country's political ideals and heroes. Most long-distance bus stations and a rail terminal lay to the northwest; shops, restaurants, and hotels were situated all up and down or just off the main strip.

But Virgil was more interested in dodgier facets of the capital. He led Simon up a steep slant behind the church and turned onto a narrow, cobbled alley.

"Welcome to the witch market," his guide announced.

Simon gave the area a quick visual. "Doesn't seem like much."

"Open your eyes to the genuine article."

Halfway up the alley, a swarthy, sloe-eyed fat lady, peering from around two neat stacks of varicolored blankets, gandered their approach. Other side of the woman stood a folding table with green baize draped over its front. On the table slanted an assortment of drab figurines that reached higher than their owner's medium-length Afro. She was seated with pudgy arms flopped at her sides and hands resting in her lap. A sack dress drooped over her belly and extended from knee to ankle. Under the blue bodice, she wore a faded brown sweater with long sleeves bunched to her elbows. The woman grinned at Simon as if given the slightest excuse she'd change him into a cockroach.

"One of *Pachamama's* disciples, I expect," Virgil commented, tracing his companion's line of sight.

"Yeah? Who's *Pachamama?*"

"Roughly speaking, Mother Earth."

"Mother Earth's a witch?"

"Didn't say that, did I?"

He stepped toward the fat lady's setup, letting her know he wasn't intimidated. Close up, her fleshy face assumed a more welcoming guise. With a wave of her hand, she invited him to examine goods on her table.

A dried frog with a cigarette jutting out of its mouth drew Simon's interest, and he extended a finger to touch the dead amphibian's shiny skin.

"*¡Ja!*" the woman barked and cackled like a grandmother when he jerked back his hand.

Simon laughed too despite being startled. "What's so great about a stuffed frog?" he challenged.

The *señora* answered conversationally in Spanish while studying his face.

"The frog will make you wealthy," Virgil translated.

"She said more than that," Simon countered. His educated friend was unaware of the affinity developing between him and the frog vendor.

"Right you are," Virgil admitted. "She offered a special price as well."

"Still not all."

"What you on about, mate?"

"My Latin blood's kicking in," he answered and started fingering other bits of merchandize.

All manner of charm could be had for a price at the magic stand. Statuettes of dusky clay promoted by turns romantic love and fertility, good luck and retribution, success in business ventures, cures for disease, and robust health generally. A desiccated llama fetus buried on site of your home insured protection against misfortune. Armadillo carcasses prevented burglary. There were potions herbal and mineral apportioned in clear plastic baggies arranged in a rack of cubbyholes leaning next to the figurines. Simon asked after properties of the items but was drawn more to the *señora* than to the odd paraphernalia she sold.

"Find out how she became a witch," he commanded Virgil.

The guide inquired. Following a lengthy narrative from the vendor, he gave a condensed report.

"Evidently, her family has been in the sorcery trade for quite some time. She has a cousin who can turn himself into an owl, an aunt who talks to serpents, and her grandfather predicted the day and hour of his death."

"I'm sure. What'd he die of, suicide?"

"She didn't say."

"His prediction had to come true though, or everybody'd know he was a fake."

The witch chuckled when he said that. She must have known some English.

Simon straightened, hooked his thumbs onto the hems of his pants pockets, and thrust his chin in her direction. He meant to test the witch's powers.

"She predicts you won't buy anything," Virgil said.

"That supposed to impress me?" Simon snorted.

"You'll be back later," the man added. "She'll have a charm for you then."

"Really."

"Seems you need protection. The ghost standing next to you told her so. Imagine, mate, there's a ghost standing next to you."

Lucky guess, Simon wanted to believe, but he caught a creepy head rush from the witch's remark. Needles pricked his face and neck, then the assault took the form of an electric surge that traveled down his spine to his groin.

"Something wrong?" Virgil asked.

"Tell her she's full of crap," he shot back. The witch met his eye. They sparred silently for several seconds.

"*Por ti es tarde,*" he heard the fat lady say to the back of his head when he about faced.

Virgil hurried to keep up with him. "Steady on, amigo. No reason to get upset."

"Do I look upset?" he countered without looking back. By way of the first street that led downhill, he quit the alley.

"Where's the fire?" Virgil joked.

"I'm sick of being taken for a dope."

They dropped wordlessly onto level ground, stood together at one corner of the San Francisco block, and watched ambulant and motor traffic pass by. Simon didn't know about Virgil, but he needed to get a grip. Grandma Witch had given him a pretty good shake. Blow it off, he told himself, just another scam. He expected Jake to start in again.

"*Por ti es tarde,*" Virgil mused.

"Huh?" Simon barked, thinking for a second the guy meant to rattle him too.

"It's the last thing the *señora* said before we sodded off. You hear?"

"Yeah, I heard."

"'For you it's late.' Peculiar, don't you think?"

A gang of travelers with heavy packs on their backs stopped a few paces in front of him and Virgil. They circled up and consulted a guidebook. One of them pointed up the street toward the hotel where Simon had a room.

"Tell ya, man, she was setting me up for a con. Like those other wise guys. Only this time it didn't work."

"Reckon you're safe then," Virgil said. If Jake had made the same comment, Simon would have read sarcasm. He had a bone to pick with the jarhead. Where'd he get off tattling to a witch?

After about a minute, his friend, or he hoped Virgil was a friend, suggested they go for a bite to eat. Simon admitted then he was running on empty. What with travails that had befallen him so far that day, he'd hardly thought about his stomach. Virgil was a cooler hand, but then, he didn't have a murder to his credit, did he. Simon wondered how long the two of them would remain friends if the professor found out he was hooked up with a killer.

The man led him to a restaurant where a row of booths upholstered in red vinyl ran along one lengthy wall. Aromas of soup and bread met them at the door. Simon sat down facing the front window of the eatery. Through plate glass, he spotted the girl-child on the sidewalk outside.

"Hold a tic," he told Virgil as a waitress brought them menus. He slid off the bench and returned to the street. The girl shook her head when he motioned for her to accompany him back inside. Even when he wagged his hand insistently and held the door open, the girl refused to follow.

Their waitress brought chicken soup served in wide, shallow bowls with blue flowers stenciled around their rims. Thin strips of white and dark meat swam in a yellow broth that included rice, sliced carrots, diced onion, and green beans. Soup vapors alone soothed his stomach. When the waitress brought a plate of crusty rolls, Virgil ordered cheese. Then he suggested they have a glass of wine with their meal.

Simon opted for hot tea instead, and when a steaming cup was set before him, he retrieved his pill bottle from his pants pocket and shook out two ochre tablets. Before screwing the cap back on, he studied his dwindling supply of meds. He couldn't recall the last time he'd taken his pills.

"Who's the child?" Virgil asked while they ate.

"Don't know her name. She and a boy were posted up outside the hotel this morning, and they followed me when I went looking for a bank to change money. After I got ripped off, the boy disappeared, but the girl's been tailing me ever since. Don't know why."

"She's Aymara."

"What's that?"

"Over half the population of Bolivia descends from Aymara Indians."

"Not like I don't believe you, Virgil, but my tag-along isn't dressed like an Indian."

"Well, there are different sorts, you see. The Aymara started wearing European garb following service in the Chaco War. Earned the right to dress like gentry, they reckoned."

"Bolivia win the war?"

"Ended in a draw, actually, although by terms of the peace treaty, Peru annexed a good bit of territory. It's a sad history, I'm afraid.

Over the years, Brazil and Paraguay have sliced off chunks of land too. Chile stole the country's coast line."

"Sounds like these Indians could use a couple squadrons of F-16s."

Virgil scrunched up his *chile* nose.

"A trip to Parris Island wouldn't hurt either."

"Heaven help the poor dears."

After a sip of red wine, Virgil came up with another question. "How'd you get ripped off?"

"By being stupid. I changed money in the street instead of going to a bank. Met this joker thought he was slick. We'll see who's slick."

"Might be better to cut your losses," Virgil opined.

"Not a chance."

"You'd have to be on your game to run a *ratero* to ground in the underworld."

"I've done some hard stuff in my time."

"Have you now?"

Simon was tempted then to lay down his cards. Might be his friend would understand that the murder had been unavoidable. But then, Jake went berserk, and it was all Simon could do to hold steady. "Personal matter," he said aloud to shut the creep up.

"Have to do with a ghost?" Virgil inquired after the waitress had cleared the table.

Simon was proud of himself for not flinching. He must be getting used to dealing with all the smart guys in La Paz. First, the witch had read his mind and now Virgil poked around in the ol' brain pan too. Scam artists on the streets marked him for easy pickings. Before he'd got used to all the smart guys around, he might have freaked at Virgil's question.

"What you talking about?" he answered brusquely.

"*Pachamama's* disciple mentioned a ghost."

"She's nuts. I don't believe in ghosts."

Jake started laughing his head off when he said that. Simon wanted to laugh too because his nemesis didn't have much of a head left to laugh with.

"Sorry, mate. Didn't mean to pry."

"You can pry all you want and still not know what you're talking about. *Pachamama* didn't know what she was talking about either."

"Fancy you'll return to the witch market, as foretold?"

"I'll have both my legs amputated first."

They calculated shares of the check and paid it off. Outside the restaurant, Virgil sidled up next to the girl and started probing her with questions. The little lady told him nothing. Her silence made Simon feel privileged, as if the two of them shared secrets. He might read like an open book, but his trusty partner revealed no more than one blank page in hers.

"I imagine the game's afoot," Virgil droned after he'd quit trying to interrogate Simon's loyal follower.

"Yeah."

"In for a dicey patch, I expect."

"Been there, done that."

"Can't change your mind?"

"Not even."

"Bit of a word then, if you'd care to hear."

"Go for it."

> Never shrink from blows.
> Boldly, more boldly where your luck allows,
> Go forward, face them.[1]

"That sounds like something somebody else said first."

"It's a voice from the underworld intended to embolden a hero."

"You see a hero around here, kiss his ass."

"Think I'll toddle along instead, mate. Glad we had our chat."

"You from England?"

"London, guv."

"Figured you were from England."

"Where in the States are you from?"

"Calif."

"My first guess," Virgil said and fell briefly silent before deciding he had nothing to add. "I'll be off then."

---

[1] Virgil, *The Aeneid,* trans. Robert Fitzgerald, 163. The author of "Pleito por plata" has also lifted other imagery from the section entitled "The World Below" for use in his story.

"*Hasta luego*," Simon said as his friend walked away. He guessed it was the last he'd see of Virgil and, at their parting, realized how much he liked the man.

"You like him as much as me?" Jake goaded when the Englishman had wandered from sight. Simon laughed out loud. Every so often, his shadow told a decent joke.

"Nobody likes you," he answered Jake.

"The Indian girl thinks I'm terrific," Jake countered.

"In your dreams. She doesn't even know you exist. You're a figment of my imagination, not hers."

"No offense, but I'd rather be in her head."

"Sorry about your luck."

"We saddlin' up or what?"

"Yeah, let's get it done."

He and the girl crossed the street and climbed back toward the *ratero*'s hood. Chicken soup weighed him down. The climb hardly winded his companion, whereas it made him pant like a dog.

He didn't know how much he still counted on jumping the rat at the scene of the crime until he stood once more next the square columns. Not only the moneychanger wasn't there but nobody else was around either. The silent emptiness of the street gave him a case of the downers.

"Somebody promise you a cakewalk?" Jake teased.

Simon started walking again, and the girl followed along behind him. He'd never met anyone so persistent. It seemed not to cross the child's mind that their mission was looking more and more like a bust. Soon, visibility would be limited to the reach of streetlamps, and once night fell, chances of cornering the chiseler in murk beyond the lamps would reduce to zero. Probably the most sensible course at this pass was to call off the hunt till morning. He exchanged glances with the girl, and as usual, she kept her opinion to herself.

Back down in the plaza, vendors were packing up their carts and preparing to wheel off. A quartet of musicians fell together on steps near the stone head, and the twitter of their guitars and flutes joined with encroaching darkness. Simon worried about his teammate. He didn't want her to spend another night on the sidewalk. Would she let him buy her a meal in a restaurant finally, and after, would she let him tuck her into a warm bed at the hotel? He doubted she'd go along, but he had to at least make the offer. As he mulled over how to communicate his concern, damn if the missing member of their patrol didn't reappear.

Simon failed to make out the boy's features until the girl tugged on his sleeve. Her *compadre* headed straight for them from the direction of the church, with a hundred rosy dots extending up the hillside above and behind him. The *muchacho's* timing made Simon wonder if his kids had set up a rendezvous without bothering to inform their leader.

Savvy members of the team touched hands and spoke to one another at length before facing in his direction. He got the impression they expected him to know what was up. Rather than disappoint his troops, he thrust his chin forward to signal, "Okay, let's dip." He had no idea which direction to take so it was a good thing the boy pranced out ahead. They crossed the plaza and the street in front of San Francisco. Then they walked by the church without paying any attention to the people seated on its concrete steps. The mopheaded point man angled onto the same steep rise Virgil had taken earlier. Simon experienced a shudder of foreboding as he climbed the hill. Couldn't be they were headed back to the witch market, could it.

Woolen and ceramic, with a tinge of packaged incense and musk of dried animal flesh, the smell of the murky alley reached his nostrils before he set foot on its humped base. *Pachamama* either hadn't moved since he'd seen her last or had returned to her stool in anticipation of his arrival. Same smug grin on her face in candlelight, only now the expression she pulled appeared more sinister.

He tightened his lips as he walked up to the witch. Let's get this over with, he wanted to tell her. She moved not a muscle to accommodate him.

"You have something for me," he barked in an attempt to motivate the fat lady.

She remained still as a Halloween ornament.

"*Por favor,*" he conceded, surrender in his tone.

The witch nodded at him ever so minutely. A tinny laugh rippled from the depths of her belly.

He expanded his chest.

The witch reached into the pocket of her dress and produced a round clay article the size of an arcade token. When Simon reached out, the *señora* pulled back. "What?" he questioned. She pointed to his left hand. He guessed she wanted his right hand free to fish for Bs, but he was wrong. When he retrieved money to pay her, she shook her head vigorously.

"Well, what you want then?"

"Por ti es tarde."

Yeah, he'd heard that one before.

"Qué le vaya con Dios," the witch added, and he knew then he was in for a world of hurt.

Her words stayed with him as he and the children left the market. The first phrase Virgil had translated for him, the second he was familiar with already. "Go with God." In Calif, the expression meant little more than "good-bye" or "take care." Put the two sentences together though and Grandma's message bothered the crap out of him. She predicted his time was up and he needed prayer.

Commotion on the main avenue distracted his thoughts. A public demonstration was taking place, of the kind he'd witnessed in Tupiza the week before. Paul, a gringo dude he'd met on the train out of Uyuni talked about the Water War. Here, the protesters marched twenty abreast with banners waving above close-packed heads and rockets exploding over their mass. He and his team had to wait for the mob to pass before they could cross the street.

And then it was up through canyon country yet again and, farther up, into an ever darker labyrinth of silent foreboding. The long passage pitched high into gloom barely relieved by circles of lamplight widening in the rising distance. Roofs of houses to either side slanted into the slope of the city crater, their walls compressed front to back and butted to the next riser. Small curtained windows periodically emitted pale, elongated rectangles flattened on black bricks.

Simon leaned forward as he climbed, of necessity shortened and slowed his stride while his breath came in quickened gasps. At first he held his head up to scout the ground before him, but the drag of fatigue soon pulled his chin to his chest, and he peered into clots of murk one cursory glance at a time. Sunken into the solitary effort of his labor, he couldn't say how long it was before the children had outstripped him by several yards, and then by more, until he no longer made out their shapes in the gloom pressing upon the hill. After losing sight of his team, he was sorely tempted to stop and rest. He kept on though, fearing that if he did stop, it'd be only that much harder to take up the climb again. At last the patrol's forward element halted and waited from him to catch up. His scouts had reached their objective.

He fell against a wall and wheezed, heart pounding in his chest and sweat streaming down his face. His wet skin chilled rapidly in the cold night air, but it took several minutes for him to regain strength. While his breathing regulated, the children peered down a street that traversed the gut-buster they'd led him up. Simon scoped the stretch too. Nothing moved from where he stood to the end of a residential block. Down there, a single pole lamp pooled light upon a narrow sidewalk and hump of cobbles. He waited, but nothing happened. "What's up?" he questioned the boy. The kid shot him a scolding glance and raised a finger to his lips. Yeah, okay, he was supposed to maintain silence. Also practice patience, which he wasn't good at.

To occupy himself, Simon removed the witch's token from his left-hand trouser pocket and examined it. The object was made of clay, circular in shape. Working his thumb back and forth across its surfaces, he discovered one side felt smooth as river rock while the other presented a raised image. He held the relief up to weak light originating from the distant lamp. By tilting the amulet back and forth, he was able to make out a roughly rectangular visage topped by either a turban or a lopped-off Shriner hat. The figure had lips in the shape of a squashed O-ring and eyes large enough beneath protruding eyebrows to represent a pair of sunshades. No idea of the amulet's significance occurred to him; that is, other than it had been handed him by a woman with whom he'd established sympathy and who believed he needed God's help. The witch's parting words echoed in his brain, again causing him to ponder anxiously their enigmatic implication. What had she foreseen that moved her to pity? Was his enemy a killer too? Up to now, he had presumed that kicking butt would be automatic. Because the rat had turned tail right after the rip-off, Simon hadn't given him much credit as a banger. But Grandma saw things before they happened. Was the amulet meant to protect him in battle or ease his passage to the underworld? Not Virgil's metaphor underworld, but the one where no bus stopped to take you out.

A tug on his sleeve dispersed scary thoughts. He stuffed the charm back into his pocket and raised his head.

Two men approached from down the street, and as they passed through the light on the corner, the one wearing a leather jacket tossed off a casual remark, which his buddy found hilarious. They proceeded unaware of the ambush they were headed for, just two dickwads out for a nighttime stroll in a neighborhood where they felt safe. Simon's cohorts retreated; he heard a faint ruffle of their clothing as they slipped back around the building beside him. He held his ground. The approaching quarry weren't going to make out his shape in the dark unless they looked directly at him. As the pair drew within twenty paces, he concentrated on the one in the jacket. The rat's hair attracted a whirl of black halo driven by the night. Grandma knew what she was talking about; he was about to come to blows with the baddest motherfucker in La Paz.

"Hold fire," Jake said, but Simon didn't need advice from a dead man. *Suck it up,* he told himself. *There's a scam rat coming close who needs to have his cage rattled hard. Now. Go now like a Mack truck.*

Simon jerked up both hands and slammed them against the moneychanger's chest. The man fell back, and his arms shot up instinctively. Simon reached for the lapels of the rat's leather jacket and shouted so the thief would know what was going down. "Change dollars! Remember?" He couldn't see the enemy's face but felt his upper body go rigid. The moneychanger knew damn well who grabbed him and why.

The other wise guy swung round behind and caught Simon in a bear hug. In the few seconds it took for him to free his arms, the rat flat-out booked toward the streetlamp.

He made it around the lighted corner better part of a block ahead of his pursuit. Simon ran faster, or thought he did, until the boy sped by. The kid darted out of sight while Simon remained still fifty feet short of the corner. When the girl reached level with him, he despaired of ever winning a footrace with a Bolivian. He slowed, trading looks with the girl. She stopped, and he pulled up alongside her. Her shoulders rocked rearward, reminding him of the wise guy they'd left behind.

Simon bolted in his direction. Gutless lowlife that he was, the rat's partner ducked around the building where the patrol had sprung their ambush. Just like that, he disappeared. After he was gone from view, one hard *bato* from Calif had no enemy to lose vengeance upon but himself.

Simon doubled his fists, threw back his head, and screamed into the black void overhead. The sound he made was pure outraged animal for one long burst and then settled into the dying whimper of a desperate human being. He took a couple strides toward the streetlight, stopped, spun on his heel, and shuffled again in the direction of the second man's retreat. He reversed himself a third time. The girl's image flashed through his field of vision as he spun in a circle. When Jake threatened to cut loose on him, he covered his ears with his hands. "I don't wanna hear it," he warned Jake. "I don't wanna hear it." Then he caught himself yelling down an empty street. My god, he thought, a man can drop off the edge of sanity before he knows he's falling. "Oh my god, I need help," he shouted.

He framed the girl's face between lifted palms, and she looked back at him, calm as you please. To her way of thinking, there was nothing around them to get all trippy about. Simon let lose a whine. The girl-child watched him deadpan while he moaned. Least she could do was show a little sympathy. No way, no how, her face answered. Yeah, she was talking to him finally, more or less as Jake talked to him.

To prove he was through freaking out, he dropped his arms, slumped his shoulders, and gave his head a good shake. There now, he was back to normal. Not totally, but close enough. He eyed the girl. "This thing ain't over, is it?" he said out loud. She went, "Yeah, this thing's been going on all day and probably go on all night too." What else? Simon admitted to his cohort. *Poco a poco.* Little by little we make progress though, don't we? We jumped the enemy, and he's not such a badass as we thought. Or I thought anyway. Turns out our enemy is lame. Shoulda figured. Never known a rip-off to stand his ground and fight. Grandma Witch—God love her—had been radioed the wrong info. Her lucky guesses misdirected the team for a while there, but now the truth jumps up. It's against the nature of a scam rat to stand and bang. A scam rat lacks all manner of balls.

Simon had solved one problem at least. Admittedly, not the problem of getting his money back, but right now, he didn't care much about the money. He cared most about his sanity. And with regard to sanity, he was doing fine. If he could see the truth about the rat, he wasn't crazy.

He smiled weakly at the girl. There she stood, patient and wise as ever, like a midget nun sizing up a very bad neighborhood. Where'd her partner get off to though? Still running down a thief, wasn't he? Simon at last comprehended what the kid had been up to all afternoon. Hate to have that bloodhound on my trail, he judged. That dog didn't have an ounce of quit in him. Well, if the boy wasn't ready to call it quits, who was he to wimp out? Owned it to the team to hump on. Ain't that right? Hell yes, that was right.

A short, sharp whistle disrupted his deliberations. The call came from above. The girl turned in the direction of the sound. Simon scanned upward from their corner and saw the boy.

Standing in the intersection one street above, the kid raised his hand and pointed, then darted behind a building. The moneychanger had doubled back on them. Simon and the girl crossed the lower intersection and strode parallel to the upper block. Since he wasn't required to climb at this pass in the chase, Simon found it easy to match steps with his partner. They must have advanced rapidly enough to keep abreast of their quarry because, at the next intersection, their scout motioned them excitedly to join him.

Simon ran even with the girl up the incline, ignoring a stitch in his side. Up top, while he sucked air, the children conferred in whispers, and then the boy signaled that the three of them should set out on the higher track abreast. Simon covered middle ground while the boy and girl kept to either sidewalk flank.

Halfway up the block, the boy darted over from the sidewalk and yanked on his sleeve. The girl froze like a pointer a couple steps beyond a single lighted window. A narrow gap in an otherwise continuous run of wall gaped in front of her. Simon stepped forward. After motioning the girl to back off, he projected his basso voice at low volume into the break. "Gotcha cold."

No answer rebounded from the pitch-black crease, so he rumbled louder. "Game over."

Still nothing stirred in the darkness, and for a long moment, Simon feared he'd have to plunge into the crack and grapple blindly with his enemy. Then he remembered the amulet. "Bless you, Grandma," he mumbled as he flung the clay disc into the rat's hidey-hole.

The thief broke from cover, doubled over, and with arms crossed in front of him. Simon shifted sideways to parry the attack and, as the rat swept by, flung out his left boot. The thief sprawled forward and landed in the street on his hands and knees. Before he could right himself, Simon lunged onto his back and smashed him flat.

As his captive began to thrash wildly about, he grabbed a fistful of hair, jerked up the swindler's head, and wrapped an arm around his throat.

Fingernails broke the skin on Simon's forearm. He felt no pain at all and squeezed tighter. The downed man gagged and churned his feet. To shield his groin, Simon crossed his ankles and spread his knees, trapping the man's calves between his shins. The thief slapped his hands on the street cobbles and attempted to lever up his chest. Simon threw his weight forward again, and the body beneath him gave way, rotated minutely to one side, muscles locked up from collarbone to waist, and then the thief threw his opposite shoulder against his captor's chest. Smell of dandruff shampoo, sticky sweat, and whiskey drool fogged the air around Simon's head. An artery in the grifter's neck pulsed rapidly against his forearm. When the body of his enemy went slack, Simon still maintained his strangle hold. He was unaware the fight was over until his best tracker tugged on his arm. Possibly the kid saved him from committing another murder.

He let go of the guy's neck and pushed himself to his feet. While the children stood by, he bent at the waist and rolled the lug over. He found what he was looking for in the inside pocket of the man's jacket. After straightening, he smoothed the roll of notes, split them without counting, stuffed roughly half the stack into his pants pocket and handed over the other half to the girl. The wide-eyed looks on the children's faces, visible in light cast from the nearby window, gratified him immeasurably. But it wasn't time to bust out high fives; it was time for the team to make tracks.

And so they did; he and his loyal followers scooted off the hill. Bugles should have been blowing a martial air and snare drums should have been snapping out a crisp military rhythm in accompaniment of the patrol's safe return from battle, but he and the kids marched down the main street of La Paz with no band playing and nobody noticing. They crossed the nearly empty avenue and headed for Simon's quarters. At the entrance to the hotel, the leader halted, turned to face his comrades, and considered what he might say to them if he spoke fluent Spanish. Or what he might say if they understood English. Or what he wanted to say in whatever language. Then he figured it was just as well he didn't speak Spanish and they didn't understand English because whatever he said would have fallen short of what he should say probably. They'd come together without words; and so, it shouldn't bother anybody that they were about to break up the same way.

He'd like to have found out why they'd followed him that morning though. Could they explain what had been on their minds at that time? Probably not. No more than he could explain why he'd kept going after the *ratero* when the mission turned hopeless. "We got lucky," he might say if he spoke Spanish. Yes, that's what he should say, if they could understand him. Not that it was much of a speech or anything.

Simon raised a hand in parting, smiled, and turned away from his cohorts. He entered the hotel and went up to his room to pack. He believed his loyal followers would drift off while he was gone. No reason for them to hang around as far as he could tell. He thought when he returned to the street with his duffel slung over his shoulder, they'd have bounced. So he didn't know what to say in whatever language when he found them stationed yet on the sidewalk.

With an exaggerated sigh, he flagged a taxi. While he loaded his bag into the trunk of the car, the two strays scooted onto the backseat behind the driver. Climbing into the front seat, he fussed over what his kids were up to now. Who'd they think he was? Mother Goose? "Hey, guys, mission accomplished," he wanted to tell them. "Go get some R & R."

Beneath the yellow ceiling vault at the station, he checked schedule boards of various transport companies for the departure times of buses headed north. The children followed along as though still under orders. When he stepped up to a counter to purchase his ticket, they fell in line behind him. Well, damn; he'd hoped he wouldn't have to get harsh. He was grateful for their help, couldn't have run down the rat without them, but no way was he going to take on a couple of homeless orphans when he was far from home himself. He'd like to break the news to his team gently. That's what he'd try to do. But if the kids forced his hand, well, what could he do but get harsh?

Turning away from the ticket counter, the last thing he expected was to spot the blond-headed guide from the underworld towering in line behind the kids. Virgil said something, but Simon wasn't listening.

"Tell these two I'm leaving and they can't come with," he blurted out.

"Easy, mate," the Englishman replied. "No reason to become distraught."

"They can't come with me, tell 'em."

"No, I don't suppose they should," the Englishman agreed.

Simon regarded the children. Their innocent return gaze made him feel like a traitor. "Go ahead," he told Virgil and faced away.

"Right-o," Virgil answered and began speaking Spanish.

It wasn't easy for him to draw the kids out, so Simon had to get involved after all. He gestured to the children that there was nothing to fear, that they should listen to Virgil. The boy responded tentatively, then the girl seemed to catch on. She laughed when it dawned on her what the conversation was about. Being the first time Simon had heard her laugh, he was startled by the shrill outburst. The boy chimed in, and the two of them competed for Virgil's attention. Repeatedly interrupting one another, their voices rose excitedly in volume, and Virgil had to speak loudly too to get a word in. Simon listened to the freely flowing babble once it started and reveled in the glee that burst upon the children's faces. Virgil gave up trying to keep pace with their chatter and faced back to Simon.

"Congratulations, hero," he said. "Or should I say Sir Drake."

"What'd they tell you?" Simon returned, ignoring the Englishman's joke, which he didn't understand anyway.

"Couldn't follow it all, but far as I can decipher, they don't live far from La Paz. Came here as a consequence of disaffection in the family. After a row with stepdad, the boy left home to seek his fortune in the capital. His cousin insisted on accompanying him. Lost souls when you happened along, mate, in dire straits, you might say. But a wandering pirate—bloke with the eye patch on your sweatshirt—took mercy on them, and they were saved. Bit about trouble with a robber and a reward. What reward, by the by, if you'll pardon my asking?"

"It's complicated," Simon answered, reckoning Virgil didn't need to know too many details. "You tell 'em they're on their own again?"

"Didn't have to. They fancied a return to their village all along. The boy reckons nasty stepdad is small beans now. Learned a lesson in valor, he did."

"Really."

"You'll be pleased to know he credits you."

"Kid's got more *bato* in him than I ever will."

"Scamp reckons you're his bloody champion."

Simon turned his attention on the children, who were jabbering back and forth between themselves. Catching his look, they fell silent. He shook his head in amazement at them.

"Thanks," he told Virgil.

"What for?"

"For telling me what they said."

"You going to flesh out the tale?"

The boy raised a hand to wave, and the girl waved too. They were saying good-bye.

"*Vaya con Dios,*" he bade his kids.

"*Qué le vaya bien,*" they responded in unison.

Simon hefted his duffel bag, ready to depart.

"Hold on," Virgil protested.

"Can't," Simon answered. "Got a bus to catch, mate."

"Going to play the mysterious vagabond, are you?"

"Not playing," Simon said as he walked away.

He felt strong when he boarded the bus. He'd felt pretty puny that morning, but a lot had happened since then. Mostly bad stuff that turned out mostly good.

"Just you and me again," Jake said in the confines of the vehicle.

"Just me, you mean," Simon answered. "Because you don't exist."

Though he couldn't know what travails awaited him down the road, he was surer than he'd been in quite a while that whatever turned up, he could handle. Might not be true, but that's how he felt. What worse trouble than what he'd taken on already? What worse trouble, huh, Jake?

Never mind, don't answer.

Juego de corro

(Ring-around-a-Rosy)

He smiled at her over his shoulder. She smiled back. She felt like a little girl, too embarrassed to speak, meeting a little boy for the first time on a playground.

"I'm almost finished," he told her.

"No hurry," she answered, a bit too enthusiastically, and jostled the small bundle of soiled underwear she held at waist level. "I don't have much."

"Good idea to keep up with laundry."

"I guess."

He turned away and went back to work. Broad shoulders flexed beneath a white, sweat-dampened T-shirt, elbows pumped back and forth vigorously. Bone-colored fabric and lighter soapsuds obscured his hands.

"You sure are good at washing clothes."

"Comes with practice."

He had a muscular body tempered by a soft outer layer of what she might have termed baby fat, mussed dark hair, blameless brown cherubic eyes and boyish lips. Peculiar thing was he couldn't have had less than a dozen years on her. This wasn't the first time she'd found an older man attractive, but it was odd how the attraction this time made her feel childish. She wondered what he felt when he looked at her.

So far as outer layers went, hers expanded more noticeably than his at the hip. She had narrow shoulders and a bosom less than voluptuous, but his eyes had fixed on her face, not her boobs. Wavy auburn hair trimmed neck length complemented bright blue eyes. A rabbit nose tended lips that her grandma had once said never told lies.

> Every day is wash day
> God bless—

"Well, not every day," she said.

In point of fact, the problem of keeping clean clothes while on the road was not one that preoccupied her. You could hire a maid to wash your clothes, but that incurred an unbudgeted expense. Better to wear what you had on for as long as you could keep from looking slovenly and only then locate a washstand. But her new acquaintance went on before she could hold forth about her secondary concern for apparel.

> Soak and scrub,
> soak and scrub:
> every day
> we drop our duds
> into a heady tub.

His arms moved in rhythm with the chant, and his voice followed a bouncing ball.

> We wait a spell
> before whirling well
> the raiment of our hub,
> then rub out shame,
> cast off blame
> plus other
> nettle sums.

Pausing, he checked to see if she dug the poem, maybe worried that the pun in the last line failed to justify a false rhyme. A playful grimace on her part spurred him on.

Rub-a-dub
we drain the crud
down a secret path,
with reverent frown
briskly pound
deep dark stains
from our past,
but bear in mind
kith and kind,
or lose baby
with the bath.

She drew breath to offer an appraisal, but there was more.

Every day
we drape our fame
along a windy way;
shed of us,
acclaim smells
sweet enough
to redress—
cleanli—
ness.

He lifted sodden cargo pants off the scrub stone, doubled them
over twice, and twisted the fold to wring out water and detergent.
She watched him swish his trousers around the rinse tank.

"It's sort of like ring-around-a-rosy."

"What a good idea," he answered, turning. "Think I should
change the rhythm."

"You want to?"

A frown belied his more handsome, younger guise. "Not really."

"Leave it then. It's okay the way it sounds."

"What do you think the rhyme's about?"

"It's about sprucing up our act and staying healthy."

"Don't forget self-image."

"Okay."

"And don't get me wrong. I'm not satirizing vanity."

"Never crossed my mind."

His gaze shifted to a point over her right shoulder, and she turned to see what he was looking at. In the near corner of the garden, a scarlet blossom whose four rippled petals fanned symmetrically from the top of a hairy red stem grew against a thigh-high hedge with leaves sharp and green as shards of jade. When she swiveled back in his direction, he came to a decision.

"Would you like to go to the zoo with me?"

Under the circumstances, it was the right thing to ask.

"When?"

"Soon as we're done with our laundry."

"Sure."

After he put on a clean yellow collar shirt with epaulets, they stopped for breakfast at a café; and over bread, cheese, cold ham, and fruit, they talked about how they'd come to join the traveler nation. Paul was on sabbatical from a teaching job in the States. For personal reasons, and despite there being no such clause in his contract, he had contrived a lengthy break. She played the cello in Toronto. Her gig with an amateur orchestra didn't pay the rent so she had been forced to take odd jobs. A month ago, for personal reasons, she'd volunteered to teach music to Bolivian children for a year. The village where she worked was located not far from Santa Cruz.

"Cello player, huh?" Paul commented.

"You find that strange?"

"Actually, I feel privileged to be in your company."

"Whatever for? You're teasing me, right?"

"Not at all. Everybody knows guitar and piano players, but how often does one meet a cellist?"

"Actually, I know people who play oboe and bassoon. And one or two who can whip out mean licks on a tuba."

"Yeah, but the cello. That's special."

Kristina wasn't used to being idolized.

"I guess I don't get around much, huh," Paul said, misinterpreting her laughter.

"Maybe that's lucky for me," she answered to clarify that he needn't try so hard.

After the meal, as they made their way along the wide streets of the city, Paul told her about his ride from Tarija. He complained that backrests on the bus were too narrow for his shoulders and he had slept during the twenty-four-hour trip only in snatches. During one interminable stretch, a woman sat next to him with two toddlers on her lap, and though she did her best to keep the scamps from squirming and fussing, they weren't about to suffer discomfort stoically. And then there was this kid seated behind him who kept practicing bird whistles. For a while, the sounds the boy made were amusing, but fifty kilometers down the road, Paul got tired of hearing the same tweets, hoots, and chirps over and over.

"I can't sleep on the bus either," Kristina put in as they strode abreast along the sidewalk. "Too many starts and stops."

"My problem is I snore. Sometimes I wake my own self up with the snorts I make. It's embarrassing."

She snickered. "Do you snore only on the bus?"

"Sadly, no. My former spouse complained that I sounded like I was choking to death."

"Divorced, huh?"

"Yep, and I wouldn't do it twice."

"She wake you up?"

"Who?"

"Your ex. I mean when you were choking to death."

"Rarely. Why do you ask?"

"Maybe she lay there quietly, waiting for you to stop breathing."

Paul found that remark hysterical.

They ducked under the branches of a tree laden with pink buds. Farther on, they stopped to admire a multipeaked white cathedral whose side columns lined an entire city block. Kristina suggested that the thin spires lifting off the façade and roof pointed seven times to heaven. Paul said it was a good omen.

Two of the intersections they crossed flaunted broad circles of curbed grass from which rose larger-than-life statues. On one pedestal, Jesus faced a spread of ten-story commercial buildings; on the other, a heroic woman warrior with long hair and full breasts bore in her strong hands a rigid banner. Few cars occupied the hexagonal cobbles of the streets. Translucent haze in the distance backdropped the crisscross geometry of several power lines.

"You know, this town feels as if it's on holiday," Paul said after they had advanced several blocks. "You'd expect Bolivia's economic center to be bustling on a weekday."

"Today's Good Friday," Kristina informed him cheerily.

"No kidding. How'd I forget? You think I'm losing my marbles?"

"You don't seem any more deranged than most people."

"And even if I am, so long as nobody notices, where's the harm?"

"Anyway, after dark, there'll be a procession and an open-air mass in the plaza."

"That's excellent news. I do love a parade."

"You're not Catholic, are you?"

"How can you tell?"

"You said *parade*. Like you expect the procession to include marching bands and baton twirlers."

"I didn't mean any disrespect. Are you Catholic?"

"I am."

"Will you forgive me for saying *parade*?"

Kristina busted up.

"Look, I'll spring for dinner if you forgive me."

A goodly number of city residents had chosen to spend their free afternoon at the zoo. Spacious paths meandered among wrought-iron animal cages beneath a flourishing canopy of trees. There were plenty of wooden benches on which to sit and enjoy the distracting atmosphere. Scads of children with *refrescos* and *dulces* clutched in their fists rushed about to marvel at macaws, parrots, and flamingos; to stare with titillated alarm at jaguars, ocelots, and pumas; and to grimace at the rattlesnakes, the boas, and other creepy serpents. Iguanas looked back at them and blinked. Nocturnal striped pigs couldn't be coaxed from their shelters. Armadillos kept their distance, but diminutive deer moseyed up to wire fences expecting a handout.

Soon after Kristina and Paul turned up, four small redheaded monkeys staged a jailbreak, which twitterpated the entire gathering. As ground-bound keepers attempted to corner them, the escapees dispersed among leafy branches overhead and taunted their pursuers. One among the outlaw band slipped down a tree trunk just ahead of the posse and snatched an orange section from a puffy-cheeked two-year-old balanced on a bench next to her mother. When a keeper rushed toward the scene of the robbery, the monkey skedaddled back to safety.

"What admirable bums," Paul mused.

"Don't they bite?" Kristina answered, pointing out what she thought an important concern.

"Not if they get what they want."

"Regardless, monkeys bite."

"If you like," he said.

A little later, they chanced upon a waist-high wire enclosure that confined several tortoises. Two of the captives were engaged in combat; the smaller of the hump-shelled pair seemed to be getting the best of an adversary twice its size. Periodically, the contestants snapped at one another, though mostly they kept their heads retracted and used the front lip of their shells to drive the opposition back. The smaller kept clawing forward and was gaining ground inch by inch until a bystander joined the skirmish on the side of the larger.

Within the cage, another sort of engagement took place as well. The largest of the tortoise clan, whose back reached as high as a car tire stood on end, had somehow managed to hoist his torso onto the back of a female and was attempting to mate with her. Because his love refused to cooperate and attempted instead to crawl from under his armored mass, the tortoise king appeared not only clumsy but also foolish as he shuffled forward on his hind pads and stretched his neck to maintain balance. One might have judged, however, that his endeavor was not entirely futile, what with deep erotic groans escaping from his throat.

"It's a no-go, bud," Paul advised the brute after watching him struggle for a while. "Back off and admit you're not her type."

"Could be she doesn't object," Kristina suggested. "She might want to go someplace private."

Her companion smirked. "Yeah. She's probably shy."

"Sensible, I'd say. Who'd want to copulate in front of a bunch of turtles?"

Paul doubled over holding his belly, which made Kristina wonder if she got her own joke.

They bought soft drinks and drew apart from the crowd. It wasn't possible to remove themselves entirely from the path of scampering children, but they found a spot at a corner of the condor cage away from the general fray. Fugitive monkeys continued making merry at the other end of the zoo.

"Those sure are ugly birds," Paul said, referring to the pair of scruffy scavengers perched behind the wire. "They remind me of Quasimodo."

She could see why. Scaly, callused folds of skin covered the condors' slanted heads, making them appear deformed. But the birds were also remarkable in size, and their alert orange eyes fixed upon her critically. "In flight, they're inspiring," she offered in defense of the condors.

"Dah, dah da, dah da, dah dah da," Paul intoned.

"Exactly what I was thinking. The way Reynaldo plays 'El Condor Pasa' on pan flute brings tears to my eyes."

"That's high praise coming from a cellist. Who's Reynaldo, if you don't mind my asking?"

Kristina smiled inwardly, believing that she detected a hint of jealousy on Paul's part. Could it be that he feared competition for her affection? Might their chance meeting be developing into romance? "He's one of my students," she reported evenly, keeping hope and amusement to herself.

"In that case, please be careful. You don't want to become too familiar."

"Reynaldo's only twelve years old," she informed the goof.

"Well, that's the point, I'm afraid," he answered, which, along with the compression on his lips, befuddled her. Certainly Paul didn't mean what she thought he meant. She knitted her brow in consternation.

"Are you saying—?"

"Came as a shock to me, too, when I was starting out. Luckily, a veteran member of the school staff led me aside and warned me of the regrettable hazards we face as teachers. Take special interest in a student, and next thing you know, you're the object of dangerous accusations."

"Have you ever been accused—?" she started to ask, but couldn't finish the sentence.

"No, thank goodness."

"Of course, I didn't mean to imply—"

"What? That I'm a pedophile?"

"Certainly you're not."

"Certainly you're right."

Supercilious looks from the condor pair made her wonder what she'd done to deserve their reproach. The birds had a bone to pick with Paul, not her. He's the one who had called them ugly.

"I think your concern is misplaced," she stated frankly.

He looked away and grimaced. One of the condors lifted its wings as though alarmed.

"Maybe we should talk about something else," she suggested, wanting to escape the briar patch that had suddenly sprung up between them.

"I was just saying lawsuits are a fact of life in our profession."

"I understand what you were saying, but I think you're wrong. These aren't the United States after all."

"You're right," Paul quickly agreed, sorry that he'd brought the irksome subject up. "Go on ahead then."

"What?"

"I mean. Oh cripes, I don't know what I mean."

Kristina was going to press her case but realized when she opened her mouth that it wasn't clear what their disagreement was about. Or if they were even having a disagreement.

"Have I offended you?" Paul asked and, before she could answer, added, "If I have, I'm sorry."

"You haven't offended me," she responded, pretty sure she felt only a little apprehensive.

"Well, that's a relief. For a second there, I thought we were going to quarrel."

A boyfriend-girlfriend sort of quarrel? Kristina asked herself.

"Wouldn't be a very good spat," he went on sheepishly, "since I'm prepared at the outset to agree with everything you say."

"So there wouldn't be much point in my saying that you don't have to worry about Reynaldo."

"None that I can see."

"Okay, I won't then."

"Good. Today, schools are closed for the holiday. We're free to have a good time."

"I started having a good time back in the garden," Kristina assured him.

"I did too," Paul said, glad to be back in her good graces.

A little later, he offered to dispose of her empty cup, and while he went in search of a trash bin, she studied people in the zoo. The mood among the Bolivians was upbeat; high-spirited children ran all over the place, and their parents took the opportunity to engage in relaxed conversation. It wasn't hard to figure out that the two smartly dressed women settled on a bench nearby brought each other up to date on the pursuits of relatives and mutual acquaintances. She could also determine which men and women were coupled and which among the wild Indian pack belonged to them. But she sensed acutely her foreignness among the local folk, her displacement from home environs where she too on a day such as this one would have been a full participant in festivities. On home ground, she'd have been able to relate in detail what so and so was about, what her problems were, and what she was doing to solve them. And so and so would know Kristina's worries too. Talk between her and friends back home started in the middle of a narrative with episodes both had heard about before. Both listened and contributed to the tale, and were, if not altogether pleased with unfolding events, entitled at least to assume their mutual importance within the melodrama.

But there was none of that for Kristina in Santa Cruz. Here she was a stranger whose significance among unfamiliar faces would never be determined. Still, she declined to dismay. The sense of being apart from the crowd drew her into another stage of distinction in which she included Paul when he sauntered back from his errand.

He didn't speak right away; rather, he stepped aside and conducted his own study.

"Something wrong?" she asked after going along with his silence for about a minute.

"I didn't want to interrupt."

"Interrupt what?"

"You appeared lost in thought."

With hands on the small of her back, she stretched her neck and shoulders. "Now I'm found."

"What would you like to do next?" he asked when she caught him ogling her boobs.

"I don't know," she answered, holding his gaze. "You choose."

"I was thinking of heading back downtown."

"Okay by me."

As they stepped toward the entrance to the zoo, he asked, "You want to walk, or should we take a cab?"

"How much for a taxi?"

"Does the deer have a little doe?"

"Huh?"

"Two bucks."

"Right," Kristina groaned. "Let's ride then."

In the cab, she asked him, "Have you been divorced long?" because curiosity had finally got the best of her.

"A little over six months."

"You miss your ex?"

"Total bummer. I'd like to forget."

"I lived with a boy for five years myself."

"He leave you or you leave him?"

"Both. It was the only time we reached complete agreement."

"That's some consolation, I guess."

"We broke off more than a year ago, so it's not a big deal anymore."

"Good chance then, in another six months, give or take, I'll be over my breakup too."

"Maybe it won't take that long. They say men recover from failed relationships more quickly than women."

"Sounds like a woman's complaint."

"It was true in my boyfriend's case."

"He found someone else, you're saying."

"Not exactly, but that's one thing I noticed."

"Rotten ingrate."

"Kind of you to take my side."

"Filthy swine."

"More or less."

"Promiscuous dog."

"Okay, enough."

"Ran out of invectives anyway," Paul said and smiled.

Residents of Santa Cruz gathered also in the city's two-block long central park on Good Friday afternoon. The atmosphere was more subdued at the city's hub than in its remote environs. Sunny palms lined the perimeter of the park and, by their lack of ostentation, contrasted favorably with formidable columns at the front of buildings that braced three of the enclave's outside streets. As she and Paul strolled by the park, Kristina could see that leafier foliage shaded curbed paths within its border of palm trees. The walkways intersected at right angles and were surfaced by tightly fitted, off-white tiles ridged on their top edges. Benches made of wooden laths screwed into wrought-iron frames stood at accommodating intervals in rectangular recesses notched out of grass.

Across the fourth street border of the park rose a cathedral. Beneath the tiered arches of bell towers that flanked its solemn entrance, half a dozen workers adorned an altar with red fabric facing. She and

Paul, among other strollers, stopped briefly to observe the workers' progress.

Around the corner of the cathedral, they came upon the effigy of a ghastly pale holy woman draped in a black, hooded cape. Bright white cloth within the dark wrap encased the statue's head and another stiff sheet covered its breast. With white-gloved hands raised and folded, and with murky eyes in heed of an entity unseen, the likeness represented a kind of suffering that deified humility and loss. In the presence of the statue, Kristina recollected sin, shame, and guilt that had tormented her formative years. She would just as soon have been away from such teachings.

"Is that Holy Mary?" Paul asked.

"No," Kristina answered evenly, "it's one of those saintly nuns as my mother used to say."

"Do I detect reproof?"

"You had to be there."

Paul laughed, and she appreciated the ameliorating affect of his ignorance. He clearly lived apart from religious reverence and therefore outside the statue's sphere of influence. "Would you like to do a paseo?" he proposed, and she was glad to assent.

Genial light, flung like a tablecloth beneath plotted trees, devised shadow shapes in a broad-stroke pattern that accepted animated contributions from unwitting passersby. Paul located an unoccupied bench along a walk that led away from the cathedral. Kristina settled her eye on the pair of stretched shadows they made when they were seated, and then she regarded a bright swath of sunlight that shone on scuffed tiles between the shades. Her companion had chosen to remain at arm's length when they dropped down, and his caution proved contagious. It would have felt awkward for the two of them to sit closer together.

"Your mother has reservations about Catholicism," Paul speculated to make conversation.

To his credit, he didn't miss much, but what he did miss might have been judged germane had his way of playing ring-around-a-rosy included motive. He truly took no notice of the neutral gap established between them.

"My mother is a devout Catholic," she answered. "But for her peace of mind, she wisely ignores selected dogmas of the faith."

Hoisting a knee to the edge of the bench, she swung her torso toward Paul and focused on his profile. Sensing her attention, he turned to her, urging her to continue.

After brushing imaginary dust from a pant leg, she obliged him. "For example, her first marriage took place in the church. I'm told a couple hundred guests attended the ceremony. Of course I wasn't there. I'm also told that during preparations for her second marriage, she pretended not to understand why the priest refused to readminister the sacrament. By the third go-round, she had surmised that it was useless to request a blessing."

"The priest objected to divorce, in other words."

"My mother thought he was being silly."

"Nothing silly about divorce."

"I couldn't agree more, and neither could my mother. But you move on, she'd say. To pretend what has happened can be reversed, or to insist that it shouldn't have happened in the first place is, in her opinion, absurd."

"What do you think about divorce?"

"I've never been divorced. But I think my mother's right about moving on."

Paul's expression darkened. His features lost their easy demeanor and, damn the luck, he seemed about to turn serious. "Do you mind if I tell you about my situation?"

Yes, she did, even though his "situation" had been on her mind all along. Ineluctably, they had slipped beyond the innocent pretext of their meeting. The way it worked was, you met someone, had a few laughs, and then got down to the business of exposing wounds. Even children got around to comparing boo-boos. "Go ahead," she allowed and believed her tone masked whatever regret or apprehension she felt.

Still he hesitated, not sure how to begin. He was determined to achieve sincerity, Kristina determined, which pretty much sealed his doom. She might have said so, but he wouldn't have found her attitude encouraging.

"My biggest mistake was thinking I could keep myself safely separate," he began. "I could go along with devotion so long as it remained an idea. That's cold, isn't it?"

"You didn't love her," Kristina concluded for him. In her opinion, discussions involving personal problems required simple speech.

209

"That's what Susan said."

"Well, Susan was right."

Paul's scrunched upper lip and pained squint implied disagreement, the possibility of a counter argument, and definitely remorse. In sum, the grimace delivered an admission of defeat. He wanted mostly to understand what he had been beaten at.

"If she was right," he asked, "how come I can't get over her?"

Kristina held her tongue, certain that Paul would elaborate. He'd gone beyond the point of no return in the discussion he'd started.

"I rarely dreamed of my wife while we were married, but now I dream of her every night. I wake up feeling grateful for her visit. When we were together, I felt terrible for not confessing I didn't love her, but there was security in the lie."

"You told her that you did love her," Kristina said.

"Yes."

"Well, believe me, she wasn't fooled."

"Wasn't she?"

"No woman's that simple-minded."

"My suspicion is we both were fooled. I think I loved her in spite of myself."

"From beginning to end?" Kristina asked with raised brow, remembering her own terminated relationship. Sam used to say, "We're as different as two peas in a pod," after simple speech had disclosed they didn't get along all that well.

"Must have been throughout, otherwise I wouldn't be haunted by her absence. Her rejection feels like betrayal. Twenty years of marriage—oh man, the chicanery of that institution is astonishing. Twenty years of uninterrupted masquerade bound us tight as mated pigeons."

"And yet you flew your separate ways."

"Yeah, okay. But what's divorce mean when you're not free to accept what comes after."

"It means you let go and soldier on. Take it from my mother, she should know."

"Right, and I thought it wouldn't be all that difficult. I had kept myself apart, you see. Then it turns out that to stay separate, I required her presence to be separate from. Her fussing over me, my fussing over her, her demands, my demands—they caused resentment both ways but established a pact as well. Dutiful husband, self-centered creep, patient housemate, shameless charlatan—that was me she sent packing and me who remains gone. Without her, I've become my own absence. I am no longer who I was and can't find a way to be anybody else."

Paul spoke at normal volume, kept his hands folded on his lap, maintained an even tone, but his speech sounded overwrought. He made the mistake of supposing that his case was unique. His current disturbing notions were to him unprecedented and, as a consequence, allowed no formula for casting them aside.

"Be patient," she advised. "Things will change."

"When? I've been wandering around four months now in South America and nothing's changed."

"Things have changed. You just haven't noticed."

"Really. And when will I notice?"

"When you stop looking."

Kristina surprised herself by what she'd said, and her next statement surprised her even more. "I have a theory about transformation."

"My mind's open to anything," he answered hopefully. "Or at least, I'd like it to be."

So she was about to unveil her deep thoughts concerning Paul's dilemma when a stranger walked up. A stranger to her, though not to Paul. By the familiar manner the man assumed in speaking with her companion, she presumed they had met before. Their exchange took place in Spanish, which language Kristina had only begun to learn. A word here and there she understood, but not enough of the dialogue to follow what was being said. The interloper had a slender frame, thick dark hair curling untended over ear wings and sharp facial features. His angular body somehow confided near tragic resignation. The long-sleeved, blue-striped shirt he wore had escaped the washboard for a day or two longer than Kristina would have recommended.

During the talk between the men, she watched twilight creep upon the park. Birds chattered in the trees; human traffic began to thin. The residents of Santa Cruz were setting off to prepare for evening worship. Lassitude slouched over her. She was a little bored but wanted nothing at the moment. Later, she was fairly sure, Paul would take her to dinner, not only on account of his previous invitation, but also due to a sense of continuity and momentum that defined their acquaintanceship. No hurry though. Neither schedule nor expectation disturbed her lazy state of mind until the man in neglected clothing broke away.

"I met Ignacio the other morning," Paul volunteered, supposing she was curious. "He's an eccentric. Then again, there are a lot of oddballs in Bolivia."

"He's not really eccentric, you mean."

"Whatever I mean, Ignacio's trying to get back to La Paz. That's where he was born and where he grew up. He's negotiating with Mormon missionaries for bus fare."

"What's he offering them in return?"

"I'm not sure. Maybe he proposes to join their congregation."

"Did he ask you for a donation?"

"Not a dime."

"He's dignified then, not eccentric."

Paul rocked his head from shoulder to shoulder with his lips scrunched together, implying that Ignacio's character defied definition. "He believes he has discovered a cure for AIDS."

"Really. Did he give you the formula?"

"Half a cup of vinegar with a splash of lemon, taken every morning."

"Seems far-fetched, don't you think?"

"Cured him, he claims."

"And surely a reputable physician diagnosed him."

"Maybe yes, maybe no. The concoction also cured him of diabetes."

She didn't mean to laugh, but where she came from, the poor fellow with multiple afflictions would have been judged a kook. Lunacy was the panacea Ignacio had discovered.

"Are you hungry?" Paul asked a little later.

Dinner, as she had foreseen, was in the cards.

Her friend led the way to a restaurant a block off the park. The waitress who met them at the door, a pretty girl dressed in a black knee-length skirt and a long-sleeved white blouse, guided them to a table just large enough for two. They situated themselves at the edge of a lawn garden with groomed bushes at its borders. Shaded light bulbs, mounted on the blue stucco wall behind Paul, provided dampened illumination. He ordered a bottle of red wine. When the young lady filled their stemmed glasses, he toasted Pascua, which was the Spanish word for Holy Week. Kristina smiled encouragingly at him as they drank. Pan-flute music, wafting from invisible speakers, swelled her heart with portent.

"My cab driver was wrong," Paul said as he examined the menu.

"Which cab driver and what was he wrong about?"

"The one who drove me from the bus station. He said restaurants here don't serve meat on Good Friday."

"Then I'll have fish, which we Catholics don't consider meat."

"It's a moot point. We had ham for breakfast."

"Yes, we did," Kristina said, remembering.

"My chauffeur was unaware of the affect tourist dollars have had on Santa Cruz tradition."

"Probably he doesn't go out to eat much."

"Lucky him. He has his own kitchen."

"I have my own kitchen too in the village. For me, being invited to a restaurant is a treat."

"For me too. Mostly on account of present company."

She acknowledged his compliment by raising her glass.

They ordered food, he a slice of breaded beef, she went ahead with fish. Soon their plates arrived, and there was plenty to eat: potatoes, green and yellow vegetables appetizingly presented, and a basket of salt bread set between them. The wine was not one of those libations that connoisseur's wax poetic over, but it had deep color, an honest aroma, and its flavor bolstered the spirit.

"Do you have children?" Kristina asked as they began their meal.

"Two daughters. One is in her second year of college, majoring in psychology. The older one works for the railroad and reads a lot."

"Maybe she intends to become self-educated, which, to my mind, is admirable. What subjects interest her?"

"History and politics. Everything from counter-culture zines to Plato's *Republic*."

"What do the two of them think about your divorce?"

"They think it best to keep clear."

"You and Susan remain at odds?"

"We communicate little. My choice mostly."

"Does she see other people?" Kristina asked, not sure whether her sympathetic interest had turned to prying.

"Men you mean," Paul responded easily. "From what I hear, though it's none of my business, in lieu of love, my ex has opted for variety. But that's unfair."

"It's funny the way you put it."

"Yes, I only meant to be funny. The thing's a riot really, even from up close. Divorce makes a person laugh big tears."

Kristina suspected that despite his lament, Paul made good use of what he called his "situation." He seized the opportunity to be shaken by unexpected emotions and welcomed exposure to the failure of his assumptions. But like the cab driver he had spoken of, he still denied a fundamental alteration in his world.

"Do you have children?" he asked.

"Not any that I'm aware of."

"Ho ho, funny girl. Ever tempted?"

"Now and again. Then I remember I could have been aborted."

Paul's knife and fork stopped working for a second. "That's a dreary thought."

"It's not speculation."

"No?"

"My aunt and my grandfather recommended that Mother terminate her third pregnancy. I believe they had several discussions about me. Before I became anybody, that is."

Paul set down his utensils, lifted his glass, and squinted at her curiously. "First report I've heard from a rescued fetus. Tell me, little one, how did you become a person?"

"Mother stood her ground, and Father concurred."

"And this was which father?"

"Second father."

"Whom she later left behind."

"She kept me though."

"You'd think she would have kept her second husband too."

"Oh? Why's that?"

"I don't know," Paul shrugged. "They did decide to have a child together?"

"You and your wife decided to have two children together."

"But we were never called upon to defend our decision."

"And that's why you broke up?"

He hesitated, realizing that whatever idea he'd been entertaining about how solid bonds were formed was a pipe dream. "Okay, I get it. The big question remains in every case. How can you be so sure that you belong with someone in one instance and then be sure it was all a big mistake?"

"Were you sure that you belonged with Susan?"

He cocked his head to one side. "Sometimes I was, sometimes I wasn't, and now it doesn't matter. We split the sheets, and there's no turning back."

"If you believe what you say, I think you've taken a big step toward moving on."

"Oh, I believe the fact all right. The problem lies in what follows."

"Becoming someone else," Kristina recalled.

"How do I become someone else?" he countered, ignoring her skeptical tone.

"By getting over your guilt for leaving Susan."

"Am I feeling guilty? Maybe she left me."

"And maybe it went both ways."

"Would you like dessert?"

The waitress, who had arrived to clear the table, provided him an occasion to digress. While the girl stacked nearly empty plates on her arm, Paul divided remnants of the wine between their two glasses and handed over the empty bottle. He tittered at himself for seizing upon the interruption. Kristina shook her head as if exasperated and then blithely asked what sweets were available. Fruit in a dairy sauce, he told her, after consulting the *mesera*. Sure, she'd have dessert.

"You might think what I have to say next is irrelevant," she ventured after the waitress departed.

"I might also think you're getting bored with the topic that keeps cropping up." He leaned back in his chair with half-filled glass in hand. "Go for it, darlin'."

"Well, okay," she flounced back at him. "Did I tell you I missed the bus to Santa Cruz?"

"No, you didn't. What'd you do, walk?"

"It's too far to walk, but here's the story. There was a crowd at the stop when the bus pulled up and everybody rushed the door. I couldn't get through the mob, which really upset me because I could see the seats were all filled up, and there was hardly any standing room left. I became cross, unable to imagine what would happen if I didn't get on that bus. I was convinced being left behind constituted a grave injustice." Kristina paused, hoping Paul could see the point she was trying to make.

"So what happened?" he asked.

"Well, I got here, didn't I?" she sighed.

"Don't worry, I understand what you mean."

"You do?"

"Yeah. You're still talking about my mess."

"Is that bad?"

"Yes, and it's my fault."

"Well, I just mean we can get awfully wrapped up in what we think is supposed to happen and, when we do, overlook other possibilities."

"Which could turn out better for us," he drawled, having heard such advice before.

"Or what we hoped for all along," she persevered.

"So I guess you wanted to get to Santa Cruz, and it turned out you didn't come by bus. And I presume how you did get here was, what, more fulfilling?"

"Actually, a farmer spotted me standing by the road after the bus left. I must have looked a wreck. He offered me a ride in his truck, and the two of us had a jolly time following the road to the city. Much more comfortable than the bus would have been. He gabbed on and on about who knows what, not caring a bit that I didn't understand a word he said."

Paul set his empty glass on the table and lifted a napkin to his lips. He had a punctilious way about him that Kristina had just realized. His every word and action resulted from circumspection, as if he edited his life a moment before he lived it. No, that was unfair. If he weren't capable of spontaneity, she'd have shined him on in the hotel garden.

"Look," he told her, wadding the napkin in his lap. "I know I'm being obsessive. But the nasty thing about this obsession of mine is I can't be rid of it piece by piece." He picked and pulled a corner of the cloth nested at his crotch and twisted it between his thumb and forefinger. "I can't just grab hold of the grossness either and toss it off all at once." He crushed the napkin suddenly in his palms and threw the offending object to the painted concrete floor.

Kristina started, and he laughed at the look on her face.

She continued staring at him.

"Sorry about that," he apologized a second later. "Don't worry, I'm not having an episode. Hell, I'm not even flustered. True, I have a twisted sense of humor, but where's the harm?"

In response, she pulled a clown's face, and he relaxed. When he stuck a finger in his ear and scratched the interior canal, his lips parted to expose gritted teeth. At that moment, Kristina felt she'd known Paul for a long time.

"You ever want to be president?" she asked.

"Maybe," he said, examining the end of his pinkie. "I don't know. Where'd that question come from?"

"I was just wondering what it'd be like to be president."

"You think the president is obsessed?"

"Surrounded by people who hang on his every word and agree with everything he says? He must be immensely gratified."

"Okay, sure. I'd love to be president."

"How about a person of True Faith."

"Maybe. What would I believe in?"

"Anything you want. Just so you were absolutely certain you were right all the time."

"Well, you know, I read a philosopher once who claimed faith requires an equal measure of doubt."

"Well, how about a traveler then, who's not sure who she is."

"Exactly why I'm on the road."

Kristina nodded confidently. What she had to say next concluded a notion she'd taken in the park.

"I was eight or nine years old, sitting alone in the school library after classes, reading a magazine about Africa. For some reason, I looked up from a picture of two elephants, and there, suddenly before me, was the librarian. A plain sort of woman with gray hair arranged in a sensible style that never changed, she catalogued books behind the circulation desk. Everybody knew the woman had worked at the school for years. As I watched, she moved around behind her counter so absorbed in her duties that she seemed unaware of anything else. And I became as riveted as she was to her chores and lost awareness of myself as a person watching her. It was as if I looked into a mirror and forgot what I saw was a reflection. Or the librarian was my reflection and her own reflection too. Everywhere the same reflection."

Paul regarded her intently. "You could read the librarian's mind?"

"No, nothing like that. The mirror was the only mind present."

"And you both read it?"

"I don't know. It didn't seem like I was reading anything, and the librarian was busy stacking books."

"But she was mindful, you're saying, the way you were mindful."

"That's not quite the point either. Later I had the same experience with the prime minister of Canada, while he was giving a speech on TV. A couple times with people praying in church. But sometimes with rocks. That's peculiar, don't you think, because how can rocks be mindful? I also once saw a butterfly fly into the mirror."

Paul's mouth fell open, and "ah" flushed from his breast. His pretty eyes gladdened. "Okay, I get it."

"You do? You've had the experience."

"Well, no. But there's this story about a Chinese man named Chou who went to sleep and dreamed he was a butterfly. When he woke up, he couldn't be sure whether he had been dreaming of the butterfly or the butterfly had been dreaming of him."

"I mean something like that," Kristina agreed.

"Am I your reflection at the moment?"

"Would you like to be?"

"Maybe you could be my reflection."

"Glad to oblige, if you wish."

"Better than being stuck with my empty self."

Kristina smiled, thinking Paul's insistent gloominess was kind of sweet, the way Grumpy of the Seven Dwarfs was sweet. "Oh, I think you like being stuck."

"Really," he answered and looked as though she'd given him something to think about.

Neither of them spoke further for a time, and during the hiatus in their give and take, a commotion from outside the restaurant reached their ears. The increased noise muffled music playing from nearby speakers. A growing sense of jostling human beings announced commencement of the evening procession Kristina had mentioned earlier. Paul arched his eyebrows and nodded to her as though they had agreed beforehand to attend the spectacle together. What else? He signaled the waitress to bring their check.

Such a crowd of fervent souls amassed before the cathedral on the square that it was hard at first to discern which were participants in the ritual and which were present in no assigned capacity. White lights with orange halos, streetlamps, and a greater concatenation of illuminators affixed to many ledges on the imposing edifice sloughed their glow upon the confluence of teeming faces. Palpable darkness overarched the glow, however, so that stark night prevailed upon the event, creating an embodiment of mortal consequence.

The saintly nun, whom she had spurned that afternoon, floated by on a pallet above an eddy of gently bobbing heads. Satin banners—white, burgundy, and royal purple fringed in gold—drooped from mastheads that followed in her wake. A statue of Mother Mary, standing on a platform swathed in mossy boughs, sallied forth, accompanied by an honor guard of blue-uniformed policemen bearing rifles at shoulder arms. Half a dozen men in black ties lugged a litter, upon which was erected a wooden cross, decorated with boughs of white rose and festooned with an ivory shroud. Two matronly ladies wearing smart black dresses and red scapulas prayed the rosary as they shuffled by. At the rear of the flow, Jesus Christ appeared, represented in two states of being. In the first, he lay supine within a portable sepulcher of polished hardwood and glass. In the second, he was risen, richly robed, with a gold ring encircling his head. Oddly enough, Christ in glory stood shorter of stature than the other ambassadors of heaven and was escorted by a coterie of mere adolescents. One of these, a girl dressed in bell-bottom dungarees and shiny silver tank top, traipsed before the icon with her pinkie finger stuck between her teeth. A boy all in white wagged his head from side to side as if keeping time with a nonexistent band. Another girl in a green shift with a low neckline appeared to be sleepwalking.

The proceedings brought a breath of nostalgia for past Easters Kristina had spent with her family. Like her mother, she was still on speaking terms with the Church but sought her own counsel in many decisive matters. Curious to discover Paul's reaction, she turned toward his backlit visage. No doubt he was impressed with the large turnout, but the prayerful murmur that dominated the march gave him pause. Clear eyes he met and acknowledged from the passing crowd failed to smile back at him.

"You know," she said when, after one such unrequited glance, he bent his furrowed forehead in her direction, "when I was little, I thought it unfair that I wasn't born God. If I were God, I reasoned, I wouldn't have to worry about sin. But he was the Lucky One, and there was no remedy for my inferior predicament. Funny. You're the first person to whom I've confessed blasphemy."

"You can't be God," he answered matter-of-factly. "Because you're real."

"You sound like my father. He's an atheist too."

"I didn't say I was an atheist."

Having intended flippancy, she was surprised at Paul's heavy response. "You implied, at least, that God isn't real."

"Maybe. But being real is not necessarily the best thing."

"Well, it's a pretty good thing."

"Is it? What about the sins you mentioned?"

She didn't get what he meant. "Are you moralizing?"

"Not intentionally. I mean you have to be real to commit sin. In fact, I'd go so far to say that if you're real, you can't help but commit sin."

"What about Christ? According to what I've been taught, he remained pure his entire life. Because he was God."

"Immaculately conceived too."

"Yeah, so?"

"Had to be immaculately conceived, otherwise he'd have ended up a sinner like the rest of us."

"You saying to be real you have to be conceived in the regular way."

"Yep."

"Well, he died in the regular way."

"Did he? The people here believe he resurrected himself. That's what this procession is about, if I'm not mistaken."

"You think they're right."

"I don't know if they're right. I do know their faith doesn't square with my perception of reality."

"That everyone who is born and who dies is a sinner."

"Doesn't that jive with your experience?"

"Certainly. And that's why I find solace in the idea of a resurrection."

"Me too. I don't want to be God. I just want to be resurrected."

His conclusion made perfect sense. The shadow of absence Paul cast about himself coincided with darkness that engulfed Good Friday in Santa Cruz. Dour faces all around bore subdued reverence for doom. Effigies were raised to celebrated self-inflicted torment. No music at this hour; no joy allowed. Amazement only at the weight of past transgressions. Good Christ, it was high time to bring on a resurrection.

"Let's go have another glass of wine," Kristina said. Again she wanted to be away from the sober teachings of her Church.

"Took the words right out of my mouth," Paul answered and again contrived an occasion for her to be grateful for his reassuring ignorance.

The restaurant was near, but upon reaching the doors of the establishment, they found them shut up tight for the night. Paul suggested they search for a *tienda* that sold wine, and she agreed. After passing by several more locked doors and dark windows though, it didn't seem likely their efforts would be rewarded. Then, along one walk within a tunnel of matted tiles and square columns, they chanced upon a shop where a middle-aged woman in funeral garb accepted their commerce. Kristina's companion bought a bottle of *tinto*, and they returned to the hotel.

Paul detoured to his room to retrieve a corkscrew and a pair of plastic tumblers. He rejoined her on the concrete bench located nearest the door to her quarters. They were alone in the garden and no sound reached them from beyond stucco walls that framed a sparsely starred sky overhead. In stillness, the fragrances of hedge and flower were especially strong. The wine gurgled as he filled their glasses. When he handed over hers, their hands made contact, and she thought he might scoot over closer, but he disappointed her. She could have moved toward him if she wanted to feel the warmth of his body and impart her own warmth to his skin, but she wasn't sure what she wanted. Let him initiate the touch of hip and shoulder, and then she would decide whether to accept his overture. But he remained at arm's length and, in the gap that loomed between them, caution set like a curtain of foggy gelatin.

"What should we toast?" he asked with raised glass and with the wine bottle clasped jauntily between his knees. His features had become obscure, his demeanor inscrutable.

"What else besides friendship?" she answered.

"What else indeed," he said and drank.

Kristina listened for what he would say next and then realized he was listening too. Understandable. What do you say in a place where embrace is no more than a fantasy like the fiction of the Easter Bunny?

"It surprises me you're not Catholic," she told him because he had given her no reason to think of him as other than chaste.

"Do I act like a Catholic?"

"You do have a thing about guilt."

"My best friend in high school was Catholic, so maybe he's responsible." Paul laughed softly. "George went through a tough time when he met Emily. She was, shall we say, a vivacious young lady. While dating her, he stood in line to the confessional at least once a week. I used to jab him mercilessly. 'It's Friday,' I'd say, 'have you said your ten Our Fathers and ten Hail Marys yet? Maybe you ought to pray twenty each before you take the girl out, to be proactive.'"

Ornery edge to Paul, wasn't there. "How long did you remain friends?"

"We're still friends. One thing I've noticed about Catholics is, they take a different perspective when they're out among the heathens. Why not? They can always be officially forgiven for laughing at wicked jokes."

"Don't you think it advantageous to wipe the slate clean once in a while?"

"Too easy," Paul answered, "and dangerous too. Looked to me like confession obsessed my friend. I always wondered what the priest advised him."

"Go and sin no more," Kristina said, speaking from experience.

"With a straight face, you think?"

"Your poor friend. He must have suffered mightily."

"Could be," Paul admitted and laughed. "But when he broke up with Emily and got him a new girlfriend, he quit going to the dark little room altogether."

"As a result of your ribbing, I'll bet."

"Doubt it. I think he just wore himself out. There comes a time when guilt becomes more torment than it's worth."

Kristina dared to hope that by his last statement, Paul made reference to himself. Maybe her friend supposed that someday he too would get shed of guilt and regret and thereby break free of his own chastisement. She wondered what event would tip the balance. Would the woman with whom he now drank wine under a starry sky occasion renewal? Go ahead and take a chance, she silently urged

Paul. What the heck, reach out and caress your friend. She might not be unreceptive.

But Paul, even if he sensed her willingness to participate in his renewal, let the moment pass. "What you want to do now?" he asked as if they might go to a movie or have a game of cards.

After pretending to consider choices, she said, "I think I'll go to bed."

"You can't," he protested. "The bottle's still half full."

"Go ahead and finish the wine. I have to get up early tomorrow to catch a bus."

"You're not staying for Resurrection Sunday?"

"There won't be much to see on Sunday. Tonight was the big splash."

"I wish I'd known."

He sounded so disappointed that Kristina thought there might still be hope for them. "Why don't you come with me to the village?" she asked gently. (Or why don't you follow me into my room?)

"That's an idea," he responded and weighed her invitation. "What's to do there?"

He had to be kidding—but no, he wasn't. Kristina expelled a tiny huff of breath through her nostrils. Thus our meeting ends, she concluded, and was tempted to pity the two of them. Looking back, it seemed like the day they'd spent together was over in the blink of an eye.

Paul took her sigh for a parting gesture. "I'm sure glad I met . you," he said and offered his hand. "Damn, I had a good time."

"Me too," she said, clasping his fingers limply. She unlocked the door to her room, reached in to switch on the light, craned her head over her shoulder, and smiled at him. He smiled back. They'd completed a circle.

Inside her rented *quarto*, she sat down on the bed and thought about Paul. Someday he would be resurrected from the tomb he'd buried himself in, and then he might remember his day with the cellist and regret a missed opportunity. Too bad for him because by then she'd be long gone, and by then she'd be through missing what could have happened, and by then she'd be done worrying whether it mattered all that much. While stripping to her underwear, she hummed "El Condor Pasa" to herself.

Alone on the bench, Paul refilled his glass and looked up at the stars. The wine had put him in a tender frame of mind. What a decent woman, he declared Kristina, and not bad looking either. He wished she had signaled him an opening, but she wasn't like that. She saw him as a friend was all. There might be other women down the road with whom things would turn out differently. Someday maybe, if his patience held out.

He'd like to have taken Kristina in his arms though; Lord, she was a cello player—how had he let a cello player slip away? Well, like he had, was how, without even trying. Did that mean the kindly cellist exemplified what it'd be like for him from now on with women? Man, he hoped not, but that was something beyond his current provenance. How does a person change really?

Maybe if he called himself something different he'd have better luck. Change his name, change his life. What a ridiculous idea, the sort of idea that came to a man sitting alone under the stars with a bottle of wine beside him and nobody to drink it with. But maybe if he changed his name. His wife had changed her name after the divorce and become somebody else. Could be she'd known what she was doing all along.

No significa nada

(Don't Mean Nuthin')

Inside the premier executive car, there was a Jackie Chan video showing, which Paul forbade himself to watch. Images and sound emanating from the ten-inch monitor threatened to dispel his lonely sorrow. He meant to keep the sadness close to protect and nurture the emotion and find contentment in its honest revelations.

Outside the rail car stretched a rock-and-gravel plain, plumbed dead-center bubble. Near the far edge of the tableland rose sand dunes whose smooth sides disclosed the shape of a steady wind. Behind the dunes lay an isolate mountain chain, gingerbread in color, with ravines appearing as slight in the distance as creases formed in the knuckles of a sideways extended finger. Above the chain hung an anvil-headed cloud and a pale blue sky that reached up to where up ended.

Inside, he sat in a shadow flung from outside, or in a kind of daunting loneness achieved not by the afternoon light, but by the reemergent dawn of heedful insistence. When outside silence failed to stay the assault of electronic interference, he bounced previously invented phrases off the window glass beside him.

> The story of a journey
> told ad infinitum.
> Bright the aspect
> of an unpaved road
> making for a barren mountain

and humble village
bedded in the foothills.
Set your foot
upon the track,
light your spirit,
heft your burden,
wander on.
No straight course
guides your step
nor new turn
rounds about,
but another
and another
wind ahead instead.
Soon you lose sight
of where you're bound.
To tramp ahead
is to learn
step by step
over open land
to far horizon
that once embarked
upon the journey
you'll never find your way again.

Subsequent phrasing startled him. Real as the words he had recited, the yet fuller sound originated from a recliner chair across the aisle. A young man sat there, where before the seat had been empty.

"You're the only person here," the young man said, his deep, staccato voice effecting a disturbance that overwhelmed even Jackie Chan's lightning fists and feet. He had a mestizo complexion and must have weighed in at better than two-forty. Smooth arms extended from the sleeves of his red T-shirt, but they were the strong arms of an oversized adolescent. His black hair was cropped close to the scalp; his squint-lidded eyes insinuated aggression. "There are no TVs in the other cars," the kid added, convinced he gave information his listener would find indispensable.

"Two bucks extra for premier executive treatment," Paul said, despite there being no requirement for him to justify his choice of accommodation.

"Other cars are exactly the same. They just don't have TV."

"Then how can they be exactly the same?"

"I mean the only thing you're paying extra for is a movie, which you're not watching."

"Point taken. But up to now, I enjoyed the benefit of privacy as well."

The youth paused thoughtfully then decided to ignore the reproach, if that's what he'd heard. He twisted in his seat, lifting his shoulders off the padding, and extended an incongruously small hand with surprisingly dainty fingers. "I'm Simon. You a poet?"

So much for soulful solitude, Paul inferred, and wished he'd recited his verse at lower volume. "No, I'm a Spanish teacher," he said and then, because he felt put upon, added, "since you asked."

"You in South America on a field trip?"

"That's right. In a party of one."

"Practicing the language?"

"More or less."

"Good idea. You didn't tell me your name."

By now, Paul recognized that his interrogator was a type he'd dealt with many times before. At his teaching job, he'd often discussed with colleagues strategies for keeping Simon's sort in line. Admittedly, he'd often lost patience with the hard cases, which he'd more than once regretted. "My name's Paul," he said. "What can I do for you?"

"Want me to leave?"

Naturally, this sort of miscreant intuited a judgmental attitude as surely as his college-bound peers picked up on salient academic facts.

"You caught me unawares is all."

"People get me wrong all the time."

"Sorry to hear that."

"They take one look and think I'm gonna jump 'em."

"Really."

"Maybe you're pissed because I wrecked the poem. I thought you were done with it."

Paul folded his hands in his lap and sagged his shoulders. He felt ashamed of himself for acting like a snob. All Simon wanted was fair response to his show of interest and attention, clearly a small thing to ask.

"It's a good poem," the boy continued while Paul resolved to provide better company.

"Thanks. But I think you're being much too kind."

"You wanna say the rest?"

Paul couldn't help but laugh. "That's all there is," he assured the semiliterate across the aisle.

"Oh."

He watched Simon square his bulk and lean back against the chair rest. After a moment of silence, the kid thought of a way to keep the conversation going. "You wanna say the poem again?"

"Not ever," Paul answered with another laugh, amused by Simon's attempt to establish rapport.

"Well, you wanna know why I'm here?"

"Sure," Paul shrugged. "Tell me why you're here."

"You first," the boy answered, grinning. A tight-assed teacher had fallen for the oldest trick in the schoolyard book, which he should have seen coming. To save face, Paul pretended not to get the joke.

"Haven't we established that I'm here to learn to speak better Spanish?"

"Oh yeah," Simon said and emitted a belly growl that matched his voice.

"And?" Paul pressed.

"And what?"

"Tell me why you're here."

"You really wanna know?"

Paul took a guess. "I suspect you've become separated from your tour group."

"What tour group?"

"You're not traveling with a group?"

"No. I missed out on the field trip."

"I see," Paul said, though he didn't.

"That's why I'm here," Simon continued. "I didn't get to go on the field trip."

"You've confused me," Paul admitted and, at the risk of being taken for a complete dummy, added, "Maybe you'd like to back up and start over."

"Okay," Simon obliged him, straight-faced. "I was Reynaldo's best friend, you see. He needed a friend because the schoolboys treated him like a dipshit. They were supposed to be looking out for him, but all they did was teach him bad words and laugh their heads off when he repeated them to the popular chicks. And then, when it was time for our side to go on the exchange visit, who you think got picked?"

Paul waited for the punch line.

"Com'on, who do you think?"

"If I have to answer, I'd say the schoolboys."

"No shit."

"You present your case to the travel committee?"

"Hell, no. I couldn't."

"They wouldn't listen?"

"Hell, no. I was in treatment by then."

With a slam and shudder, the train braked to half speed as it ground by a *pueblito* erected upon the crushed-rock flat outside. One squat foothill rose behind clapboard and stucco dwellings that stood bunched together with no human being in sight. Doors and windows accessed only darkness, stark in the late afternoon. "MIR 97" had been painted in white figures six-feet-tall on the wall of a near shack. Paul wondered briefly what the sign meant.

"You on meds?" he asked as the train picked up speed again. Increased engine rumble sounded like protest. He turned back toward Simon with the concerned look one expected from a member of school staff.

"I'm prescribed for six hundred megs of Seroquel a day," Simon said, proud of his medical need. "Popped half the pills in Santiago. After I found out Santiago's not in Peru."

"You thought Santiago was the capitol of Peru?" Paul asked incredulously.

"Didn't pay much attention in social studies class," the boy informed him without shame. He had no use for geography instruction, nor books and maps in general probably.

"Ever heard of Lima?" Paul questioned, presuming that sarcasm, in this case, was justified.

"That's where Reynaldo's from."

"Right. You know where you are now?"

"Hey, I'm no moron."

"I didn't say you were. I do wonder, however, if you're aware that you needn't have entered Bolivia to reach Peru by way of Chile."

"Sure. But I figured as long as I'm in South America, I might as well check out the sights."

In other words, the boy was traveling alone with no idea how far off track he'd wandered. For the first time since their meeting, Paul worried that he might become responsible for the kid's welfare. "How you fixed for money?" he heard himself say and dreaded what he might hear in response.

Simon surprised him again. "No problem. I've got plenty of cash, thanks to the ice cream van I robbed. Got away clean, but my partner took a hit. He ended up paralyzed from the waist down."

Paul wished then he'd bought a regular ticket and ridden with the twenty or so other mature adults who had boarded the train when he did. Chances are Simon hardly would have noticed him in the crowd.

"Ice cream business must be good where you're from," he commented dryly as if he were used to keeping company with a stick-up man.

"Don't know. The ice-cream guy sold more than ice cream."

In a regular car, Paul would have been just one traveler among many, and he'd have had the law of averages on his side.

"You on the run?"

"No one stopped me at the airport," Simon answered and graced Paul with a sly grin.

"They check your passport?"

"My counselor helped me apply for one before I discharged."

"Sounds like a real caregiver." Gullible too, Paul might have added.

"Yeah. She kept asking me about my long-term goals. I told her I wanted to graduate high school, but there was that field trip I got rooked out of. Dierdra understood where I was coming from."

"And where you were going to, as the case may be?"

"You got it, Teach. Nobody can stop what's supposed to happen."

Take a trip, Paul thought, lose your way, and you still end up where you're headed. Who needs a map?

"Let's suppose you make it to Peru, then what will you do?"

"I don't know. Hang out, I guess."

"Do you have Reynaldo's address?"

"No, but so what? I'm already where I'm supposed to be."

Simon's laughter confirmed that he saw no reason to worry about what was in store for him.

The train pulled into Tupiza around 10:00 p.m., and as passengers stepped onto the station platform, they were swamped by street kids passing out hostel flyers. With Simon tagging along, Paul hired a taxi and asked to be taken to an economical hotel. The cabby's choice was the Hotel Anexo Mitru at forty Bs a night, but when Paul told the skinny, middle-aged *velador* he'd be staying a week, he was granted a five-B discount. Simon suggested they share a room.

"I'd rather not," Paul answered firmly.

"You don't want to work on your vacation," the kid observed with unmistakable irony.

"Couldn't have said it better."

Simon dropped his duffel next the registration counter. "*Hasta luego*, Teach," he said.

"*Qué le vaya bien*, Bruiser," Paul answered and hurried to his room.

*　　*　　*

Along one of the streets off the square, an ordinary-looking Bolivian man, standing on beat-up wood scaffolding that had been erected before the light blue wall of a two-story government building, sketched a mural. He wore a long-sleeved, black-and-white striped shirt with tails tucked into tight-fitting, dark dungarees. Three women in brown bowler hats and bibbed skirts that flounced to their knees passed at ground level beneath the artist.

Simon watched the women walk by and then tilted back his head to study the mural drawing. At roughly top-center of the picture hovered that eye-and-triangle design you saw printed on the back of US dollar bills. He hadn't thought much about the symbol before, but now figured it for the eye of God, especially since below the delta on the wall extended a hand with splayed fingers whereupon knelt Adam and Eve. First man and first woman were naked; Eve had pointed breasts and big hair.

If the man dressed like a referee intended to do his take on world creation, Simon could get behind him. It was right that his work portrayed not only God but the devil too. Below and cattycorner to the Eden dwellers, the ref had drawn a monster head covered by an executioner's hood with one wicked cat's eye exposed. Somewhat confusing was the paintbrush in Satan's hand—you'd have thought a battle-ax or pike would serve better to bring about death and destruction. But Simon judged the effect totally sick anyway and imagined taggers from back in the hood, if they ever took a trip to Tupiza, Bolivia, would agree.

While examining the unfinished artwork, he sensed eyes other than God's or the devil's upon him. They belong instead to a white guy standing about ten feet up the sidewalk. Simon didn't have to look directly at the man to get the feeling Curious George expected him to make the first move.

The onlooker waited for about a minute before resigning the standoff. "*Película bueno,*" he said, which was wild, because obviously he saw brown, Chicano skin and concluded native.

"*Película* means movie, not picture," Simon answered, turning nonchalantly toward the speaker.

After a pause, the guy asked, "So what's the word for *picture?*"

"Fuck if I know."

The dude laughed. He sounded like a mouse somebody had stepped on. He was older than Teach—a shorter, thinner version of adulthood with washed-out ginger hair receding up his blotchy scalp. Paper-thin white lids shielded faded gray eyes. There were wrinkles at the corners of his sockets and sunken hollows under his cheekbones. The guy wore a button-up, tan cotton shirt with long sleeves rolled to sturdy biceps. His undershirt hung loosely beneath a wattle on his neck.

"You faked me out."

"Faked yourself out," Simon returned.

"Either way, good job." The guy stepped forward and offered his hand. "Jake."

Simon said his name while giving those bony fingers a firm squeeze.

"Pleased, I'm sure," Jake said in a voice that had a rasp to it. "You been in Bolivia long?"

"'Bout a week, give or take. Came on the train from Chile. First to Uyuni and then on another one to Tupiza."

"I'm down from the north myself, by way of La Paz and Sucre. La Paz is an ugly city, but Sucre's beautiful. Buildings there are white as alabaster."

Not to be out-bragged, Simon told about his trip. "Well, the Uyuni train is old as when people down here got around on horses. The seats are so tiny you have to fight for room whenever you want to stretch out."

"Everything's old and backward in Bolivia," Jake agreed. "Me included," he added with a grimace. "I've been in country for about a month and seen only one paved road. Hasn't changed much since Butch Cassidy roamed the territory. There's a tour you can take to Salo where Butch holed up between mine payroll jobs."

"Those jungle boots?" Simon asked, referring to the guy's worn footwear. He found Jake's appearance more interesting than his jive about an outlaw tour.

"Good eye. These boots are more than thirty years old."

"Where'd ya get 'em?"

"Da Nang." Ominous answer, slung at him with a steady, piercing look.

"Vietnam vet, huh."

"'67 and '68, my friend. During the Tet offensive, if you know your history."

What Simon knew about the Vietnam War he'd learned from TV documentaries and hadn't watched them much.

"How many men you kill?"

"Kind of a rude question, don't you think?"

"Maybe. You gonna answer it?"

"When you're lighting up a tree line from the perimeter of a fire base, there's no time to stop and count."

"So you probably capped a few. When I get back to the States I'm gonna join the marines."

Jake reached up, caught hold of a tarnished silver chain that hung from his wrinkled neck, and yanked a medallion from beneath his undershirt. The eagle, globe, and anchor he displayed were famous. "Semper fi," Jake said and waited for Simon to get a good look at the emblem before tucking it back under his dingy collar.

"Right on, bro," Simon said, recognizing at last that he was in the presence of a badass. Funny thing about first impressions. The guy had mistaken him for a Bolivian, and he'd taken Jake for a loser.

"What makes you think you've got what it takes?"

"For what?"

"To be a US Marine."

"You wanna try me?"

Took the jarhead about two seconds to figure out Simon was ready to back up what he said. "Let's take a walk," he suggested in lieu of trading blows.

Simon fell in behind the vet as he led out on a narrow sidewalk. Buildings butted one to another across the dirt street cast dark shadows with edges sharp as knife blades. Rough-set, red brick walls, jutting concrete windowsills, power poles planted at twenty-yard intervals made for a tight course. Half a block down, Simon stepped into the middle of the street to give himself room to maneuver.

Jake pushed on ahead, acting like he owned the street. To show he was with the program, Simon rushed ahead, lifted his arms to simulate a raised rifle, and sighted down an intersection.

"Clear," he called back.

"You're making a fool of yourself," the vet commented dryly as he marched on, and Simon dropped his arms, feeling like a nitwit.

At the end of a street that ran perpendicular to their initial course, they came upon a steep hill, spotted here and there with scrub brush. A well-worn footpath meandered up a rise to a tall white cross that overlooked town. Spaced about fifty yards apart all the way up the path were stone grottos the height of a man's head. Simon had no trouble identifying the structures as Stations of the Cross.

Before setting foot upon the dirt and gravel trail, Jake bent at the waist and picked up a large stone with both hands.

"What's the rock for?"

The ex-marine fastened small dry eyes on the cross at the top of the hill. "Guide on the Salo tour told about lugging heavy stones to the highest point in the territory. Said it was the Indian way of atoning for sin."

"You got sins, huh?"

"War's a sin, my young friend."

"You going to tell me about war?"

"I'll tell you there's no excuse and no good reason for what I did."

Simon tried to keep pace, but the old guy had outdistanced him by several yards before they reached the second Station of the Cross.

He was breathing so hard by the third grotto he had to slack off. Jake humped on as steadily as if he were hiking across flat ground.

By the time Simon made it to the top of the hill, Jake had deposited his rock atop a heap next to the cross and stood by with veined hands resting on his hips.

"You been forgiven?" Simon joked as he approached.

The two of them had a view of the wide flatland upon which Tupiza was built. From below, the town buildings had seemed crowded together, but from above, they looked spread out. A dry riverbed, three times as broad as a highway, divided the berg roughly in half. Wrenched spines of mountains rose one behind the other beyond the city. Patches of greenery clung to lower crags, but the subtle reds and grays of the bare, taller cliffs predominated. It was the kind of country where luck didn't make up for error.

"I'm working up the nerve to head for Colombia," Jake said instead of answering Simon's question.

"Yeah, where's Colombia?"

"Thousand miles north."

"Said you came down from the north?"

"I did. And I also said I'm working up my nerve."

"Ah, com'on. What's a Vietnam vet got to be scared of?"

"Only a civil war that's been going on for forty years."

Simon nodded. "Guess you're kinda old to go into battle. No offense."

"None taken. It's taken me years to figure out armed conflict is the only scenario I'm fit for."

"That mean you're a mercenary?" Simon gushed in a sudden well of excitement.

"Not up till now."

"I wanna go to war." Man, a solemn moment was about to transpire between him and the ex-marine. In the next second, they'd swear oaths and become brothers forever.

But Jake only laughed in a sad way. "Won't be any fun. Like you said, I'm getting old."

"That's why you need me," Simon suggested hopefully.

*   *   *

Considering the harebrain's proposal, Jake allowed that in his youth, he'd been about as witless as Simon. He pondered for a moment on what it was about the corps that attracted defective types like the two of them. "You think war's glorious, doncha?" he said.

"Marines get respect," the kid shot back.

Jake should have held his tongue then but didn't. "Well, let me tell ya. There are no good guys once mayhem commences. Then again, there are no bad guys either. So for a while, everything's copacetic. Then you get back to the world, and the rules change."

The harebrain scoffed, which reaction Jake might have expected. He wouldn't have got the point of his little speech either before he'd walked the walk. To get the point, you had to have wicked memories. Jake had more than a few.

There was the memory of one old man in particular that followed him around like bad karma. He'd run grandpa down on a dusty road outside Da Nang. At the time, it hadn't seemed such a big deal. Cold-blooded murder happened all the time in a war zone. Body count was a matter of prestige in Da Nang of '68. His buddies sat up and took notice when that raggedy skeleton spun around just before the front end of the truck mowed him over. "Uh-oh," said the look on the slope's face. Then he went thump, bump beneath the tires like in a cartoon so twisted they couldn't have shown it on TV. "You think we oughta stop and see if that dink's okay?" Jake quipped from behind the wheel, and hilarity erupted as though it were the funniest thing in the world to be raving insane. "There it is, Jake," the jungle bunny riding shotgun other side of the cab hollered back with his arms clutching his guts. "You're a fuckin' savage." But Jake grew quiet for a second as if one dead gook mattered one way or the other. Then he caught himself well before remorse could set in. "Hey, dipshit, you gonna bogart that joint all day or what?"

A funnier thing happened after he got back to the world and started seeing the old man spin around and around in his daydreams. Guilt he'd managed to blow off in Vietnam came circling back and struck with a vengeance. Shame drove him to meet with other "traumatized veterans," whereby he was afforded the opportunity to share his personal experiences of atrocity. Unfortunately, public confession failed to live up to its billing, and Prozac didn't break the film loop either. Sometime amid hours of dialogue with other baffled sinners, it dawned on him that the theatrics of atonement doled out only temporary relief. He couldn't speak the truth at the meetings, not because he didn't aspire to honesty, but because sincerity itself was a lie. So he gave up trying to atone for his sins and became resigned instead to recurring bouts with despair. What choice did he have?

That is, until he'd spotted an in-depth article on Colombia in the Sunday edition of the *Los Angeles Times.* He'd heard already about drug cartels and various bandit factions that plundered the Latin countryside, but for some reason, descriptions given in this particular insert riveted his attention. Reexposure to chaos and carnage without end made him realize there were still places left on the planet where an old man plowed under a deuce-and-a-half didn't mean squat.

"You wanna come with me, huh?" Jake said, turning in the kid's direction.

"Yessir, I wanna join up," Simon answered, snapping to attention.

Jake straightened, humoring the duffus. "You're gonna need training."

"I'm ready to run till I puke."

"The physical part ain't nuthin' compared to the mental part."

"They say I'm already mental," the boy joked.

"You think that's funny?" Jake barked at him, drawn into the fool's silly game.

"Nosir."

"Nosir, drill sergeant, sir," Jake screamed, amazed at himself.

"Nosir, drill sergeant, sir."

"Nosir, drill sergeant, sir, I'm a fucking worm not worth shit. My mama wasn't worthy of giving birth to worm shit like me."

"I'd just as soon leave my mother out of this," Simon objected.

With one step, he was in the kid's face. Had to hoist himself onto his toes to meet the puke eye to eye. "You don't have an opinion, dickwad. Your mind's soft as hangover shit, and hangover shit don't hold opinions."

The dip actually paused to mull over what he'd heard. "Yeah," he concluded, "that makes sense."

Ah, hell, Jake thought, as he heaved a sigh and stepped back. He didn't have the spunk anymore to lay a power trip on a green kid. "Forget it," he said. "I'm not up for making a man out of you."

"Ah, com'on. I wanna start my training."

"Nah, let's drop it. You're okay, son. Go on back home and join up. Career sadists will kick your ass up one side and down the other. They'll make you a member of the beloved corps. I'm too washed out to be your hero."

"But I can't wait, don't you see?" The poor sap looked like he was going to cry. "I want you to sign me up right now."

"Don't work like that, and you know it."

Simon's shoulders slumped as he shuffled toward the edge of the hilltop. Jake tried to catch his eye, but the kid had focused on faraway mountains.

"Okay, poof. I'm making you an honorary member of the US Marine Corps. Semper fi. Do or die."

But that failed to satisfy aspirations of the would-be devil dog. Simon stuck out his lower lip and jerked his bowling ball-sized head up and down. "How far away are those mountains?" he queried, expecting Jake to give a measurement to the exact meter.

"Who knows? They're a ways."

"How long it take to reach 'em, you think?"

"On foot?"

"Yeah."

"Couple hours maybe."

"Let's go."

"You're out of your mind."

Rather than answer, the goofball spun on his heel and marched off.

Jake hesitated and then figured, what the hell other plans he have till sundown? He'd made a pact with himself to stay sober while it was light out.

With gravity's help, they made it back to Tupiza's side streets in record time. The kid retraced the route they'd followed before at a pace that had them both sweating when they pulled up alongside the mural where they'd first met. Two additional artists standing on the scaffolding were busy adding color to the drawing.

"Holy crap," Simon exclaimed as he eyed details. "You see what I see? The devil's a tagger."

"And I always thought the devil was a government man."

"No! That's his brush making a swoop across the world."

"Okay, yeah, I see what you're getting at. Looks like an upside-down rainbow."

"Not a rainbow. A comet. God created the universe, and Satan painted it."

"Looks like a rainbow to me."

"Goes to show I was wrong about the monster head."

"What the hell you talking about?"

"Com'on. You're the one who said there are no good guys or bad guys."

"Meant it too. We're all the same basic brand of fucked-up individual."

"Know what, man?" Simon said with disgust stamped on his brown features. "You're totally negative."

At the center of town, a concrete border wall ran around a grassy park across the street from a stucco church with a pair of domed towers. Schoolchildren dressed in white shirts and blouses, dark trousers, and skirts had assembled with their instructor under a roofed patio just inside the park's spread of trees. Simon slowed when he spotted another foreigner seated on one of the benches along a walk that bisected the square.

"Hey, Teach, we're on a training mission, wanna come?" he called to the man.

The gent looked up from the Bolivian party he was conversing with. He seemed little surprised to see Simon.

"You go ahead, I'll catch up," the man called back distractedly and then resumed talk with his bench mate.

"His loss," Simon muttered as he picked up the pace.

Outside town, they took to a road littered with shards of rock Jake reckoned would be hell on truck tires. Prickly brush and cacti grew on the nearly treeless terrain; one species of the vegetation looked like saguaros without arms. Another with needle spines protruding from puffy down stood no higher than a man's shinbone. Clumps of green and yellow succulents colonized open spaces, their leaves curved inward like clustered claws.

"We should go back for headgear and water," Jake told the boy, regretting he hadn't considered fully before they left town the labor of a hike undertaken beneath a bright sun.

Simon, however, had his sights set on a line of hills to their front and wasn't about to backtrack.

"You'll be thirsty soon enough," Jake drawled as they continued the hump.

"I'm already thirsty."

"Well then, what's the rush?"

"You see him carrying water?"

He referred to a peasant who approached from the direction of the hills. The man's head was bare, and it was true he carried no water bottle that Jake could see. The man nodded to them without alteration in his dour expression as he passed.

"That guy has lived here all his life. He's used to going without water."

"If he can, so can we."

"No doubt. But what's dehydration prove?"

"Proves we're learning from the natives."

"They should be learning from us," Jake grumbled because Simon's impulsiveness annoyed him. Worse yet, the recruit was fixin' to take over the mission. Mission? Christ, what was Jake doing playing a goofball's game?

"Main mistake you guys made in Nam."

"Gimme a break. What could you possibly know about the war in Southeast Asia?"

"Thought you knew better than the VC. That's why you lost."

What a simpleton, Jake decided, and was tempted to give free rein to ire. But anger admitted weakness, and weakness resulted in loss of command. Who was in charge of the mission anyway? A harebrain who hadn't been born until the Vietnam War ended? That was the trouble with television; every jerkoff with a remote control considered himself an expert.

"We didn't lose the war," he answered, tight-jawed. "During Tet, we destroyed the enemy."

"So how come Saigon isn't called Saigon anymore?"

Luckily, they had come abreast of a lone shade tree that grew beside the road.

"Let's take five while we discuss the issue."

"Okay," Simon immediately agreed. "You gonna be okay?"

"I'm fine. I need to procure a piece of equipment is all."

"Sure. Lots of equipment around here."

"Watch and learn from a native."

"You're about as native as Donald Duck."

"From an ex-jungle-rat then."

Jake poked around the trunk of the tree until he singled out a branch that suited his purpose. While retrieving a folding knife from his pocket, he noticed red peppercorns grew among overhanging leaves. They reminded him of peppercorns that hung from trees in a certain shady, upscale neighborhood in the San Fernando Valley, near the downscale apartment complex where he'd met his first wife. Made him wonder what had happened to good ol' Donna.

She'd worked in a computer factory back then; he drove freight long distance. After they married came the Nixon and Ford recession, and trucking jobs grew scarce. Donna survived a layoff at the factory, which induced acrimony between them. Wasn't long before she resented his idle habits. Pretty soon, she got to bitching at him about his drinking, deriding his war stories, and belittling his fits of temper. Donna finally concluded she was married to a worthless bum. So she stayed in California, and he moved on.

After that, the pattern repeated itself. New starts with two other wives: Carrie the harlot, and after her, Mary the Christian who birthed them a daughter. Heaven help the child, and yet somehow she managed to attend college despite being fathered by a no-account. Through it all, Jake continued making cross-country hauls, and miles of open highway gave him ample opportunity to ponder his screwed-up life. The peppercorns made him remember what a mess he'd made of things. Not only his own life, but he recollected too the trauma he'd caused in other people's lives. Hard to be upbeat when he considered past fuck-ups. Simon was right; ol' Jake had become negative over the years. Less than totaled out though; he still had enough drive left to make a final haul.

As he set to cutting loose the branch, the boy stepped up behind him. With a single tug, he snapped the branch free of the tree trunk.

"There," the smartass said, handing him the length of wood.

Without comment, Jake lowered himself to the ground and began fashioning a staff. Simon stepped from under the tree and scouted toward high ground. Lightning flashed beneath an iron-colored cloud moving toward them. A clap of thunder startled the boy.

"Think you should be sitting under that tree?"

It was what they called a passive-aggressive question in therapy.

"Scared of lightning?" Jake answered in kind.

"It's headed this way."

"So what. You afraid to die?"

"Nope. But I'm not stupid either."

Did he imply that the only other person in the vicinity lacked good sense? If so, it was time to impart a lesson.

"Anybody afraid of being struck by lightning sure as hell's not ready for combat."

"I'm not afraid of you."

"You should be."

"Why's that? Because you got a knife?"

"Not even." Jake set the stick down at his feet and jabbed the knifepoint into packed earth beside it.

"I suppose you know hand-to-hand combat?" the kid said.

Resting forearms on upturned knees, Jake relished the calmness befallen him. He hadn't felt so sure of himself for quite some time. "True, there's my training," he said, "but more importantly, I'm really not afraid to die."

"Me neither."

"Oh, I think you are."

"You're wrong."

For its melodrama, the exchange tickled Jake. "Watch out for lightning," he said.

"You're afraid to die, same as everybody else."

"Have you forgotten my big sin already?"

This gave Simon pause. The boy had trouble wrapping his mind around the message.

"I could whip your ass."

Jake rose slowly on account of his creaky knees. Lightning flashed and was followed instantly by a crack of thunder. Perfect, Jake thought, as large, cold drops of rain fell on his shoulders.

Fatso came at him with head lowered and arms outstretched. Jake held steady until Simon's fingers reached his neck, then ducked and sidestepped. He jumped onto the kid's back and, from there, flung a forearm against his throat. Simon thrashed violently from side to side, trying to shake him loose, but by then, Jake had grabbed the crook of his elbow with his right hand and started prying the kid's head forward with his left. Simon threw himself over backward and landed hard on Jake's chest. It knocked the wind out of him, but he wasn't about to let up. The boy was twice as strong as he was, and if he did break free, the ex-marine was sure he'd take a pounding. Only chance he had of winning the tussle was to hang on long enough for Simon to pass out. The kid let out a strangled cry and used up the last of his wind to roll onto his side. Jake rode the boy till he lost consciousness.

When he was sure his adversary was down for the count, he pushed away from the kid's motionless torso and inhaled deeply several times. His arms felt so weak he could hardly pull up to a sitting position. He crawled over to the tree on his hands and knees and retrieved the knife and stick. Soon as his strength returned, he reckoned he'd head back to town and make himself scarce. But Simon revived before Jake was ready to leave.

"Headache," the boy complained after pushing up onto his arms.

Jake pretended to be engrossed in work on his walking stick. "It'll pass," he answered.

Tossing his head skyward, Simon stuck out his tongue and tried to catch raindrops in his mouth. "Plenty of water around here," he goofed.

Jake returned him a wan smile, hoping the boy had had enough combat training. If Simon came at him again, he doubted he'd be able to hold him off without using the stick and the knife. He had no desire to draw blood but was ready to stab and slash if that's what it took to keep the gorilla at bay.

"Good move, drill sergeant, sir."

"I've got more," Jake responded dryly.

"You gonna teach me?"

"Don't wanna ruin the surprise you're in for at boot camp."

"I'll need to know all the moves before I get to Colombia."

Jake decided then the boy was okay after all. After getting his ass kicked, he only wanted to be friends again. No way he'd bring the fool along on his final ride though.

While the two of them took five, the rain cloud drifted by. On its backside appeared a crosshatch of light rays that reached from upward swoop to gunmetal gray underbelly.

Simon stood up. Time to move out, Jake concluded. Good thing he'd stopped to fashion a cane because he was going to need it.

"You know what decadence is?" he uttered as the two of them approached within a hundred yards of the hills they were bound to climb.

"Nope."

"Decadence is all you need to make war. Nothing matters once you start doing a job on real people."

"Matters that you win."

"Nope. Seems so when you start out, but once you get to blowing people's shit away, victory becomes an empty word."

"You guys didn't want to win the war?"

"Hardly ever crossed our minds, once we saw the war was total horseshit."

"That's why you lost."

"Listen, Simon. Didn't matter whether we won or lost 'cause it was all one big cluster fuck."

"I'll bet you cared when your buddies died."

"Yeah," Jake admitted. "We went after paybacks. But the thing about paybacks is, you never know how much is enough."

Simon's silence convinced Jake he ought to shut up. His lies had begun to disgust the recruit.

Brush near the base of the hills ahead grew in clumps ten feet tall. From the desiccated growth protruded cactus columns with spines lined along their flutes. The road from town petered out just before it reached ground where red clay pillars stood like border guards.

Jake pulled up before this startling work of nature. Earthen spires in hundred-fold assemblage thronged the hill. The elongated cones, climbing its steep slant, made him feel puny. At first sight of these pointed towers, he wanted to reach out and take hold of them. Then he wanted to fall back and let them take hold of him. For about a minute, he waited for the rock-studded steeples to smash him senseless.

Water had formed the pillars, he determined, after getting over his initial shock. There were periods on the land when rain fell in torrents. Limestone pieces sticking out the sides of the closest clay projections reminded him of fish scales. In marked contrast to flat black shadows pitched about the desert floor, quartz crystals among the rocks shone bright as light reflected off a river.

It was going to be a bitch of a hump, no doubt about that. Countless spills of scree, settled amid the pillars, formed gullies winding every which way, with no trodden track in sight. Jake reasoned they'd have to choose carefully their route to the summit. Still, he welcomed the challenge. You didn't arrive at a wonder of nature just to turn your back on it.

If not for an enduring view of the sky, he might have thought they negotiated cramped tunnels in a cave. At one tight crease between two steeples, he proposed to back off and try another alley, but Simon insisted they force their way though. The boy shifted sideways, sucked in his gut, and thrust one leg into the pleat.

"Push," he commanded Jake once he'd managed to get himself stuck.

"I think it'd be better to pull you outa there and look for an easier route."

"Push, goddamnit! I can't breathe."

Rising panic in the boy's voice compelled the ex-marine to lower a shoulder to Simon's ribcage and drive forward. The boy cried out as Jake's boot slipped on rubble. Jamming a hand into the boy's armpit, he shoved harder. Simon's upper body broke through. He jerked his belly free of the fold and yanked up his trailing leg.

"Fuck me," he gasped from the far side of the gap and swiped a tear off his cheek.

"A little help," Jake requested placidly as he climbed into the breech. The kid grabbed his outstretched hand and pulled.

On the other side of the crease, they met a greater gathering of sentinels. Here though, the tall pointed obstacles were gapped wide enough for him and the kid to advance up the hill without losing skin. Since they couldn't see beyond the towers directly in front of them, they counted on the upslope to guide them. At the end of one winding groove rose a riprap dam, which Simon proposed to shimmy up by catching finger and toe holds on its swollen chain-link net. Following a prolonged debate that tried the vet's patience, Jake convinced his partner that were the wire to break loose from its anchors they'd both be buried under a hundred tons of rock. It wasn't what the kid wanted to hear, but he was forced to face facts. He had to face facts again at the end of another short lane where they ran into a sheer rock wall. The way things were going, Jake was ready to order a retreat. He was about to deliver the bad news when Simon located a passageway around the wall.

On the right side of the tower convention, they pulled up at the edge of a narrow draw. It was broad enough to walk shoulder to shoulder in, the only problem being its floor was located ten feet below. Undeterred, Simon searched for way down, and Jake encouraged him, reckoning that the alley if nothing else provided egress. A crack in the near rib gave sufficient purchase for them to back off the draw's lip and drop to its base. Before Jake touched down, Simon was off to the upper end of the channel, which opened upon a multipeaked canyon with walls that swept upward better than a hundred feet.

"There's the top," Simon called excitedly.

"Who knows?" Jake answered, stepping out and swinging his staff.

Though no more than an eighth of a mile long, the hike through the canyon had them both panting by the end of it. Brush tore at their pant legs and small stones scattered before their boots. Bearing left, Jake suspected their luck was about to run out, and sure enough, on the far side of the turn, appeared another cluster of rock and clay spires. Sparrow-sized black and yellow birds flitted among the pillars, their chittering song mixing with the buzz of wasps. Dry flora and sun-baked earth smells stirred in the bright air.

"How much farther, you think?" Simon asked, dropping his back against baked clay.

"Coming or going?"

"I mean to the top."

With both hands wrapped around his stick, Jake pondered the heights. It seemed to him their problem was not so much how far, but how hard. The scramble ahead would likely wear their fingertips raw and bloody their knees.

"I figure we're a little over halfway," he said. "I also believe our chances of reaching the summit are slim."

"Why you say that?"

"Honestly?"

Simon nodded.

"Well, I'm kinda old for this foolishness, and you're kinda large."

"Why don't you just say fat?"

"Okay, fat. Point is, it'll be a tight fit in places, and if we fall, it's curtains."

"I can make it."

"Maybe."

"If you can make it, I can make it."

"I'm more concerned with the first if."

"Com'on, we can't give up."

"All the same, I wish we'd brought water."

"You shoulda had a drink when it rained," Simon said, maybe joking, maybe not, which made Jake regret not coming by himself. Alone, he could have turned his back on the hill anytime he wanted.

"Why we standing here?" Simon mouthed impatiently, thus delivering another one of those passive-aggressive questions.

"Sure you're able?" Jake responded.

The boy ignored him. He got through the first wedge they encountered unassisted, but then the marine vet decided he'd better take the lead. His partner lacked imagination when it came to inching up a cliff. Jake guided them though creases between barely separated spires where he could brace against one side of a pleat and scoot on hands and knees up the other. At one such pass, Simon called out for help. The staff provided needed extension, though the weight of Simon's body nearly yanked Jake off the upslope. After that, they fell into a routine. Jake would crawl six or eight yards forward, reach down with the stick, dig in his heels, and wait for the boy to pull himself up. The maneuver worked, though its many repetitions took their toll.

"I'm done," Jake said as Simon drew even with him for the umpteenth time. "*Fin* and the end." The front of his shirt was soaked with sweat, and his arms hung limply at his sides.

Simon flopped over and heaved like a bellows. "Can't stop now," he gasped. With supreme effort, he raised one arm and pointed to higher ground behind Jake's shoulder.

Above and to the left of them rose a saddle formed between two clay peaks. The swayback hump was damn near in spitting range.

"I can make it from here on my own," Simon panted, though he didn't look as if he could.

"Think so, huh?"

"Know so."

Jake dropped his chin and sighed.

"Know so," Simon repeated.

The ex-marine sucked in breath. "Lord help ya, if I die of a heart attack."

Simon wheezed.

"Maybe we're both fixin' to croak," Jake said and tried to laugh.

He rolled onto his stomach, forced his knees under him, and crawled slowly toward the saddle. Simon was good for his word; he managed to follow under his own power.

From higher ground could be seen break after break of mountains ranging across the horizon. At middle distance, one corner of Tupiza jutted from behind a mottled wall. For a moment, nothing stirred—neither bird, insect, nor the slightest breeze. Jake stretched his legs to either side of the saddle back and gave himself over gratefully to the quiet.

"How much farther?" The boy's question interrupted his rest.

"You've got to be kidding."

"No, I'm serious."

"Com'on, man, look where you're at. Relax. Be in the moment."

"We're still not at the top."

Using his staff, Jake levered himself to his feet and winced at a twinge of pain in his right knee. "Look," he urged the boy with a sweep of his arm and in the process nearly fell over. "Where you see a path from here?"

"What about behind us?"

Jake looked left, back the way they'd come, and fluttered his lips in disgust. One glance should have convinced the simpleton that they'd been unbelievably lucky to have come this far without breaking their necks. The path they'd taken between the spires seemed to have disappeared beneath their feet. Across the ten-story canyon they'd somehow negotiated, another climb, likewise clustered with spear points, reached as high as the saddle they were on. True, above the far face a slope of apparent lesser pitch broke free of towers and extended to a rounded summit. But what about the trench that guarded it?

"If you could broad jump a quarter mile from a standing start, you might stand a chance. And you'd still need a fifty-mile-an-hour wind at your back."

"You're saying we made a wrong turn."

"I'm saying even a mountain goat knows when it's licked."

"So we'll have to climb down and start over."

"Oh, my aching ass," Jake groaned and turned away from the boy. He wished he'd come alone. If Simon weren't with him, he wouldn't feel like throttling a certain harebrain who didn't know when to give up.

His heart jumped to his throat when the idiot grabbed him by the shoulder and screamed in his ear, "Look out!" The sudden move nearly toppled him off the saddle.

"Are you completely insane?" he shouted, still struggling to regain his balance.

Between gags of laughter, Simon choked out an answer. "Sir, drill sergeant, sir, I just saved your life."

Without thinking, Jake swung his stick backhanded, striking the boy sharply on his fat thigh. Simon barely winced as he kept on laughing.

Furious, Jake whipped him a good one on the shoulder.

"Afraid to die?" Simon wheezed and pointed at him.

"You don't know who you're dickin' with," Jake yelled and, because the dumb fuck wouldn't stop laughing, whacked him one upside the head. The end of his stick broke off when it struck bone.

Simon fell quiet then.

"You don't go messing with a man who's been to a war zone," Jake sputtered. A sudden change of expression on the boy's face scared him.

Next thing he knew, fatso's thumbs were pressed against his throat. He let go of what was left of the stick and grabbed hold with both hands the vice tightening on his windpipe. The kid's lips parted and spittle shot from between clenched teeth. His eyelids pinched nearly shut and the noise he made sounded half like weeping and half like a whistle. Jake tried to cry out, but only squeaks broke from his throat. In desperation, he flung a boot in the direction of Simon's groin. His toe struck a shinbone, and the boy's fingers clamped tighter. He clawed at Simon's hands as his vision clouded over.

*   *   *

Too late, Simon realized he'd fucked up. He watched dumbfounded as Jake's body plunged a hundred feet in the direction of Tupiza. Jake landed on his spindly neck, his legs flopped over, and his torso followed after them. Then his body rolled sideways and his head whacked against a clay turret, knocking loose dirt and gravel. After that, the body went into a slide, down a steep slant with tiny bits of rock tumbling after it. Dust obscured briefly all sight of Jake. Then the red grit settled and Simon could see the body had come to rest, face down in a clump of brush.

He refused to believe what had just happened. One second he had been jiving with the marine, laughing at the furious expression on his face, at the way he sputtered and waved his cane all over the place, and the next second, Jake was all beat up and twisted. A hand, a leg, a boot stuck out from under the clump of bushes. One moment Jake had been alive and furious; the next, he was nothing.

Simon dropped onto his haunches and, with palms pressed to his eyes, tried to obliterate his last look at Jake. He half believed that when he opened his eyes, the Nam vet would still be standing in front of him. If only the dude hadn't hit him in the head. Anywhere else, but not in the head. One good whack was all it took, because after that, everything went screwy.

Maybe he shouldn't have startled Jake, but how was he supposed to know? Guy seemed like he could stand being teased, made out like nothin' phased him. Stayed calm as you please, under that tree on the road. Whipped his ass like it was nothing and afterward sat whittling a cane, like, "What other game you wanna play, dog?" So why'd he go ballistic over one more little joke? He could have said, "Okay, fool, you scared the crap outa me," and that would have saved him. Instead, he'd cut loose with his stick.

Simon lowered his hands and stared into the distance. Mountains stood out there waiting, as if nothing had happened. What were they waiting for, an earthquake? Seemed like nothing short of an earthquake made any difference around here. A dead body meant squat to dirt and rocks.

It couldn't have been murder. No way. It was an accident. No way would he murder his buddy Jake, so what happened had to have been an accident. All you had to do was take one look to know what had happened was nobody's fault. Jake had hit him in the head with a stick, and—no, forget that part. See, we were standing on this hump and then Jake lost his balance. There, that's better. He'd needed a cane to lean on, but it slipped out of his hands somehow. Happened so quick he couldn't catch him. He didn't know where the cane was, but there's the body. Jake's head hit that tower there, and then he slid into the bushes. You have to look close to see him.

People in the town down there couldn't see him. Simon couldn't see the people in Tupiza either from where he sat. So they didn't know what had happened. If he didn't report the accident, none of the people in town would ever know how Jake ended up dead. Probably he should go get the cops and bring 'em back out here so they'd understand how Jake ended up dead. But that was a problem. Oh yeah, that was a problem all right. He knew from experience that cops were always suspicious. They'd be watching him like hawks while he made his report and they'd be searching for evidence the witness was lying. But the witness wasn't lying, he was simplifying was all, making it easier to comprehend how a dead body ended up in a clump of bushes. Simon could see part of Jake's head though gaps between tiny leaves; he could just make out a tuft of his hair. "Jake, I didn't kill you," he cried, concentrating on where the man's ear must be. Must have hurt like hell though, he admitted, silently. Must have stung when you hit the turret and skidded on your face. No, my bad, it didn't hurt at all, did it, because you were already dead by then. "I'm sorry you're dead, Jake, but I didn't kill you. It was your fault as much as mine."

Tears running down Simon's face mixed with his sweat. He whimpered softly, quieter than the chirp of birds and buzz of wasps. In a stab of remorse, he slapped his thigh hard. Jake, you gotta help me out here, he beseeched the dead man silently. If I killed you, I didn't mean to. You shouldn't have hit me in the head. I shouldn't have laughed at you, but that's what happened. When you think about all of it, you gotta admit we're even. Now you won't have to go to Colombia—I know you said you wanted to go, but it seemed like you really didn't. Look at it this way, I won't be going either. I'd never go to Colombia without you. So it's a deal, right? We'll say we're even. I promise I'll join the marines soon as I get back to Calif. You're okay with that plan, right? Well, that's my plan, and I'm sticking to it.

Why bring cops into the picture? Simon decided. They wouldn't believe him anyway. Cops never believed a word anybody said. Actually, it was pointless to report the accident because this was Bolivia, not the US of A. People weren't so organized down here in Bolivia. The cops wouldn't know what to do even if he did tell them what had happened. Be nothing but trouble dealing with one dead white guy and a Chicano who they thought was lying. When you got down to it, this thing had nothing to do with the Bolivians. This thing was between him and Jake, and they'd work it out. It was nobody else's problem. He would save everybody a whole lot of trouble by keeping his mouth shut.

He'd go back to Tupiza and take the first bus out of town. He'd head directly for Peru. That's where he should have gone in the first place. If he'd stuck with his original plan, or before that, if he'd paid more attention in social studies class, none of this would have happened. But it didn't matter anyway. That's what Jake had taught him. There was nothing scary about dying, and once you're dead, don't mean nuthin'. Something like that anyway. The Nam vet had taught him exactly what he needed to know beforehand.

Simon looked down the way he and Jake had climbed up to the saddle. He couldn't see how to get off the hill. For a second, he was scared because he thought there was no way down. In a panic, he looked around for someone to help him, but there was only a dead man to appeal to. You gotta help me out here, Jake, he pleaded, you led me up here, and now you gotta get me down. Look at it this way, what's fair is fair. I'm not taking any bus to Peru till I get off this cliff. And the only way the accident is going to be trouble is if I don't get on the bus to Peru. So now you gotta help me out, Jake, you gotta show me the way down.

That's when the marine cut him some slack. Turned out they were brothers after all. Jake reminded him they'd made it up the hill, so going down must be the opposite. That's right, Jake, it's simple how to get down, and you don't have to rub it in. Hey man, I can take a joke.

Simon was crying and giggling as he backed off the saddle. He dropped to his belly and reached behind him with his foot. *Hasta luego*, Jake, I'm leaving now. You go ahead and stay on your side of the mountain. I'll be heading down on my side. I won't forget you, don't worry. You taught me everything I needed to know about how to get outa this mess. Don't mean nuthin'. Good one, sir, drill sergeant, sir. I wouldn't have figured out what you were trying to teach me if you hadn't gone ahead and got yourself killed.

When Simon reached for purchase with his other foot, the first one broke loose. He clawed and grabbed at the ground beneath him; his T-shirt hiked up to his tits, and gravel rasped the skin off his belly. Down he slid, more than twenty feet, until his boots smacked up against a lower turret. The sudden stop slammed his head into the dirt. When he pushed back up, it took a moment for his guts to settle. Good one, Jake, he admitted, you just scared the shit outa me. Turnabout's fair play. He pushed himself up onto his hands and knees and peered over his shoulder. Another slide dropped below him, not quite so long as the first. "Okay, Jake," he muttered, "no more screwin' around. Step back outa the way now."

He found that shifting onto his butt gave him better control of the descent; his heels acted as brakes, and he could see where he was going. When his boots slipped past the next turret, he threw his arms and upper body against the abutment to stop from tumbling into free fall. After catching his breath, he braced and set his feet before turning himself into a pinball again. He didn't mind getting his hands scraped up so long as he kept going down. Last stretch off the wall, he let himself go.

After rolling to a stop on level ground, he rose to his feet. The canyon wall now stood between him and Jake, proving their separation had been inevitable. Come to think of it, the accident had been inevitable too. The crowd of turrets strung up the canyon wall gave fair warning. Tight cracks between them, slippery ground underfoot; hell, an accident was bound to happen. It all made sense now. The signs were there, clear as day. Next sign was obvious too. The path away from Jake's body led down the canyon.

A small herd of goats met him at the bottom of the hill. At first he thought the *chivos* were lost but then spotted an Indian woman standing on a rise across the road. She had ratty hair streaked with gray and wore her wrinkled skirt hiked up to her thighs. As Simon pulled up, the goatherd fixed beady eyes on him.

When he stared back, the woman looked away quickly, which made him wary. Had she seen him push Jake off the cliff? Muscles in his neck tensed when she picked up a rock. But the stone wasn't meant for him; the woman yelled at the goats and chucked the rock in their direction. The *chivos* pranced off with the herder hustling after them. Simon envied the way she moved so nimbly over loose rock and gravel.

Then he heard a bleat coming from a nearby bush. Glancing in the direction of the sound, he saw a kid had become entangled among the clump of leggy shoots and was crying for its nanny. One of the big goats stopped, turned back from the pack, and bleated in response. The bush shook as the kid struggled to break free. Simon stepped toward the baby goat, intending to help it get loose. But the kid scampered off before he reached it.

Back in Tupiza, he stopped by three different stores in search of something cold to drink. The clerk in the third store sold him a plastic liter bottle of a carbonated brown liquid. He found an unoccupied bench on the side of the plaza away from the church, sat down, and drank a third of the cloyingly sweet soda at one go. He lowered the bottle, panted, and raised it again.

A pickup truck, loaded with flowers, passed by slowly on the street in front of him. Several people followed on foot behind the truck. Simon thought he was watching a parade, but there was no brass band in sight, no baton twirlers in spangled leotards, no men in uniform, no horses or wagons, just one old truck trailed by a batch of Bolivians who looked glum and confused. Lifting the bottle again to his lips, he let his eye follow their march. He nearly finished the drink and made a deal with himself to get up and go buy another one. Then he spotted a coffin on the bed of the truck and his heart did a double flip.

His arm went limp, and the bottle dropped to his lap. Tears welled in his eyes and he might have wept outright had not a man walked up just then.

"What happened to you?" Teach said.

Simon squared his shoulders quickly and sat up straight.

"Just got back from a hike," he answered, hoping Teach couldn't tell he'd been about to start blubbering.

*   *   *

To Paul, the boy appeared badly damaged. His red T-shirt was torn, the knees of his trousers scraped thin, his palms were bleeding. Grime streaked Simon's face, and a large welt stuck out from the side of his head. "You fall?"

The man-child hesitated before answering. "I went climbing," he finally said.

"Where'd you go?"

"To the sandcastles."

"Right. And where are the sandcastles?"

"Out that way," the boy said and pointed.

"You mean on those cliffs outside of town."

"Yeah, I guess."

Paul was afraid Simon needed medical attention and looked around for a doctor's office. Not a one in sight. He figured he'd have to ask one of the locals for directions to a clinic.

"You even been to the ocean?" the boy asked him.

"Sure. What about the ocean?"

"You ever scoop up wet sand from the beach and dribble it between your fingers?" To demonstrate, Simon pinched inverted fingers together at waist level and rubbed their tips gently against his thumb. "Pretty soon you have a turret like," he went on as if the object he described formed at his feet. "And you make more of them till you have a castle."

"I don't understand."

"Why not?"

"We were talking about the cliffs outside of town, not a beach."

"You were, not me."

"Okay," Paul answered and waited for Simon to explain.

"Only the castles I'm talking about aren't made of sand because there's no ocean around here."

"I see."

"No. You have to go out there to see. Hundreds of towers out there, taller than you think. And they're not made of sand, they're made of clay, with rocks sticking out of 'em."

"If you say so."

The boy shook himself. "Anyway, that's how I got scraped up."

"Climbing castles?"

"No, I climbed a mountain. But to climb the mountain, you have to crawl between the castle turrets. And then you slide down."

"Sounds like quite the adventure."

"You could say that. I'd say it was more like a training mission."

These last words reminded Paul he'd run into Simon earlier in the day.

"That fellow you went on the training mission with. What happened to him?"

"Jake?" the boy returned hastily.

"That his name?"

"Did you know he's a Nam vet?"

"No. But where is he now?"

The boy shrugged. "Can't say. He went on ahead of me."

"Are you sure he's okay?"

Simon answered more confidently, "You don't have to worry about Jake. He can take care of himself."

Paul considered questioning Simon further about his climbing partner but suspected it'd be wasted effort.

"We should go back to the hotel and get you cleaned up," he said. "I have ointment and bandages in my first-aid kit."

Simon looked down at his hands. Then he raised the hem of his T-shirt to expose more scrapes and scratches.

"Jeepers creepers," Paul sympathized. "You're all banged up."

"No big deal."

"You should shower before I apply disinfectant."

"You a nurse too, Teach?"

"Believe it, Bruiser."

On the way to the hotel, the boy diverted to a *tienda*. Paul suggested he buy water instead of soda pop.

Simon whined about the cold water in the shower and winced when Paul dabbed ointment on his cuts. The black sweatshirt he yanked from his duffel bag when he was ready to dress was nearly as filthy as the red T-shirt he'd taken off.

"You want to take a nap?" Paul suggested when Simon stretched out on the double bed. Flower curtains hanging over the room's single window were drawn, and Simon's eyes had begun to droop.

"I hafta buy a bus ticket," he stammered and jerked upright.

"Surely not right now. Rest will do you good."

"Gotta leave soon as I can. I'll sleep on the bus."

"Where you going in such a hurry?"

"I told you before."

"Peru," Paul answered to show he'd been paying attention on the train.

"Yep, that's where."

"Well, I recommend a good night's rest. In fact, you should think about staying in Tupiza for a couple of days. There's a tour you can go on—"

"Butch Cassidy and the Sundance Kid," Simon interrupted as he stepped toward the door. "I heard about the tour."

"But you're not interested."

"Nope, I have to get to Peru."

Paul shook his head doubtfully.

"You don't know, Teach."

"What don't I know?"

"I have a date with destiny," Simon said and giggled.

Down the street from the park, they ran into a crowd. Several ranks of local men had already rounded the corner of an intersection where Paul and Simon were forced to stop. A cluster of women—some with babies slung in shawls on their backs—trailed behind the men. As the assembly passed, bottle rockets exploded intermittently over the marchers' heads.

"What's going on?" Simon asked.

"They call it the Water War."

"There's a war going on here?"

"Not like you think."

"Where's the fighting?"

"That's what I mean. It's not your typical military engagement."

After the crowd passed, they started walking again. A couple more bottle rockets whistled and popped behind them. "I doubt you'd be interested," Paul said.

"You think I'm dense, doncha?"

"How'd you get that idea?"

Simon exhaled impatiently.

"Okay, I'll explain. There have been clashes with police in Potosi and Cochabamba."

"Where's that?"

"Up north."

"How far?"

"No more than a day by bus."

Simon pulled up abruptly and stared at buildings across the street. "I wonder how Jake missed the action?"

"Missed what action?"

"The war. He came from the north but was about to turn around and head for Colombia. On account of he's a mercenary."

"Then this war wouldn't interest him because there's no money to be made from it."

"Maybe that's why he didn't bother. What's this war about?"

"It's about poor people getting the shaft. Same old story, only now they've had enough. Miners have dynamited some of the main roads. Come to think of it, you might not be able to leave for a while."

"You mean I'm stuck here?" Simon sounded anxious.

"Who knows? We'll find out when we get to the bus station."

"But I gotta leave." Simon sounded desperate.

"Easy, *amigo*. Might be the violence is confined to the north."

"Tell me what the war's about," Simon demanded.

"I was trying to."

"Com'on, tell me."

"As you wish," Paul said. A lesson in current events might calm the kid down. "The government contracted a foreign company to manage water distribution in Bolivia. That's how the problem started really, or at least this particular phase of the problem. Officials here seized another opportunity to pad their pockets. In effect, a country as poor as Bolivia can't afford honest leaders, let alone qualified ones."

"You mind, Teach?"

"Sorry. The farmers objected to the idea of a foreign company controlling their water supply. Makes sense, you know—"

"I get it, Teach."

"So they forced their government to resume administration of Bolivian water. But the problem was foreign interests needed to be repaid for cash received in the original transaction. Now where's the money going to come from to pay the debt? Not from public coffers because elected officials have already helped themselves to the loot. Not from banks either because what financial institution would extend credit to a bunch of scoundrels? Only solution is water users now have to pay for their allotments, which they never did before. And being billed suddenly for their life's blood strikes the *campesinos* as an egregious injustice. Miners have also got in the act—they need water too—and common soldiers are joining the disturbance to protest low wages and an officer corps composed exclusively of members of wealthy families. In short, the Water War is an uprising of desperate people who have no choice but to take to the streets."

At the end of the presentation, Simon looked as if he had just heard of a catastrophe. "When will it be over?" he moaned.

"I don't know," Paul answered, though in truth he presumed the disturbance shouldn't last long. There had been no reports in the papers, moreover, of travelers being attacked, so it was just a matter of hunkering down until the protest petered out. "What we have here is a temporary inconvenience."

"Don't mean nuthin'," Simon concluded after hearing his last remark. He about faced and marched up the street.

Paul hurried after him. He worried about how the kid might react if he found out he couldn't buy a ticket at the bus station. But as things turned out, the busses were still running, and at 20:15 hours, Simon would be off his hands.

"Would you like to go back to the hotel and take a nap?" he asked as they left the station.

The boy studied long shadows in the street. "You been to the top of that hill with the cross?" he returned.

"Yes, I have. Went after I saw you in the plaza."

"You wanna go again?"

There was supplication on the kid's compressed lips and in the subdued tone of his voice.

"Sure. I'd love to look down on Tupiza at dusk."

"Let's go then."

At the base of the climb, Simon hefted a large rock and started up the trail with the stone suspended at his midsection. The weight of the rock bowed his meaty shoulders and bent him at the waist.

"Where'd you hear about the penance ritual?" Paul queried from behind.

"Jake told me," Simon answered without turning around.

"He carry a rock up the hill?"

"Yeah."

Paul quickened his pace to catch up with the boy. "Not many gringos believe in the penance ritual."

"Jake probably didn't either."

"How about you?"

"Not really."

"So why go to the trouble?"

"'Cause of my drill sergeant."

They went on for a while listening to each other pant. A nasty idea had begun to worm its way into Paul's head.

"Seems like superstition to me," he said.

"Maybe you don't have any sins."

"Everybody has sins."

"So grab a rock."

Disquieting were the connections he was making, the inferences he drew from the boy's earlier evasions when questioned about Jake.

"Your friend tell you his sins?"

"Not really."

"You want to tell me your sins?"

Simon chuckled.

"What's so funny?"

"I asked Jake about his sins. Now you're asking me."

"But he didn't tell you."

"In a way he did."

"You think he's back in town by now?"

"Probably somewhere close by."

"I'd like to meet your friend."

Simon stopped, turned, and grinned in that sly way he had. "Sorry. I don't think you'll get the chance."

Paul watched him shift ever so minutely the rock in his hands and shuttered inwardly at what the move suggested. Either drop the subject or face the consequences.

"No, I don't suppose so. He's probably on his way to Columbia by now."

"Yeah," the boy agreed, "he's probably on his way to Columbia." After another couple of seconds, Simon rounded back to the trail.

Paul hung back and watched him plod on. The alarm he'd felt when the kid wagged the rock at him weakened as distance grew between them. As the stooped figure moved farther away, he experienced a nudge of sorrow, which morphed into dread. The look on Simon's face, which he glimpsed as the boy trudged into a jog, made him realize he didn't really want to know what had happened on the training mission. Dark portent slithered around Paul's bones. The kid was bound for doom, and there was nothing anybody could do to save him.

Llegamos al principio

(We Arrive at the Beginning)

1 Apr. 00, Calama, Chile. Had the feeling
all day that I was the butt of an amazing
practical joke. Hard to say who exactly had
concocted the howler because everyone around
me seemed to be in on the ruse. During an
hour and a half tour at Chuquicamata, I kept
expecting the company rep (a thirtyish,
debonair, managerial type) to crack up, and
then other members of his audience to bust a
gut too. So I'd be left standing there with a
stupid look on my face trying to figure out
what was so goddamned funny.

Mr. Flack maintained a straight face
as he continued to deliver his spiel, and
his listeners nodded attentively at each
interesting datum he imparted. Below us, the
largest open copper pit in the world: four
kilometers long, three kilometers wide, one
thousand meters deep, and so forth. Monster
dump trucks shrunk to the size of mice as
we watched them descend to the base of the
trench.

I didn't doubt the guide's veracity but
couldn't get over the feeling that he was

putting me on. When he said that the US had owned the resource until one of Chile's past presidents bought up 51 percent of company stock, after which Pinochet came to power and nationalized the operation, I took the hint that nobody around here was immune to bamboozlement. In fact, since the latest election, higher-ups in the company had started to fret over who would remain on the payroll and who would be forced to step aside to make room for the latest president's appointees. Right, but how did that make me a fool? Well, the flack didn't say; instead, he kept reeling me in like a fish.

After our group finished marveling at the big hole in the ground, he ushered us into a building, where plastic shell chairs stood before a TV and VCR, and popped in a video tape. We were shown solid walls of gray earth being dynamited to bits, and then we were given assurances that the company cared a great deal about worker safety and had committed itself to responsible environmental practices. Water used in smelting at Chuquicamata, for instance, was recycled eight times before being sprayed on access roads to keep down dust generated in the mining operation.

When the video ended, so did the tour. Seemed there was no joke after all, but I still didn't get it.

After bussing back to the city, I walked to the train station and bought a reserved seat for the twenty-four-hour ride to Uyuni. Spent the rest of the afternoon in a spacious theater where an American flick entitled *Hurricane* was playing. Leaving the movie house, I felt ridiculously grand, as if I'd participated in a heroic event. Adolescents sauntering along Calama's grubby streets at twilight looked like they felt grand too. Some wore school uniforms (blue sweaters and ties), some were attired in clothing similar to the garb sold at Walmart, and a few sported punk outfits.

The *choperia* where I stopped for beer and *pichanga* and where I write this journal entry comprises a dimly lit midsized room with ceiling fans and four-foot-square floor tiles. Mirrors cover one wall, and two big-screen TVs broadcast simultaneously a Brazilian soccer match and pop-music videos. Fifty customers make a crowd in here though only about half the twenty or so tables are occupied.

The waitresses wear green velour shifts with crossed shoulder straps, and though none is strikingly pretty, all are curvaceous, and I find it sexy the way they keep tugging at the bottom hems of their skirts to keep their rear ends covered.

When Teresa from Conceptión serves me a third beer, we shoot the breeze. I learn that she's cut her finger while hauling out trash. I sympathize with her for the injury she's suffered though the wound is hardly worse than a scratch. While we talk, an old lady enters the bar from the street and, after exchanging enthusiastic greetings with Teresa, puts the bite on me. I fork over one hundred pesos without hesitation. When a flower girl approaches my table, I buy Teresa a carnation to show what a good sport I am.

2 Apr. 00, Desolation Road. Oh man, the point of yesterday's performance was finally revealed. Simple case of misdirection. No fool like an old fool as the saying goes, the truth of which I realized after showing up for the train ride. Had I been more on the

ball, I could have joined the turf scramble earlier, but I wasn't; and due to oversight, complacency, conspiracy, or whatever, by the time I boarded the single antiquated passenger car bound for Uyuni, all choice spots within the wagon had been taken. One member of a Bolivian sister team with three bundled toddlers in her charge glanced up at me as I dragged my *mochila* down the center aisle. She appeared anxious when I checked my ticket stub, afraid that my reserved slot was located in the nook she'd sequestered for her gang between facing benches. Well, I didn't want to make her move the satchels she'd used to form a defensive barricade, and as matters resolve, the good woman needn't have worried. My seat, it turned out, was located up the aisle.

Figuring the space was up for grabs, an Anglo gent had parked one cheek of his ample ass on my bench half. I apologized for the inconvenience I caused, but it was no sweat; he proved a game sort of chap, ready to make the best of an awkward situation. "More the merrier," he quipped in that aloof manner British people have, which conveys their fancy that all life's a hoot. The French, now, have a different way of expressing a superior point of view, as exemplified by the blasé shrug delivered to me by the rigidly entwined couple seated across the fore-gap. They shifted their legs to make room for my knees while I crammed my shoulder against the Englishman's. Then he and I engaged in the usual flippant repartee meant to ease discomfort, which established that we were both amiable blokes, though neither of us any less regretted the physical closeness of our relationship. How our intimacy would be dissolved remained a mystery until about an hour after departure, when my bench mate, with truly admirable aplomb, lurched to his feet, retrieved a sleeping bag from a knot of wool-wrapped satchels and engorged backpacks wedged into the overhead rack, and unrolled his all-weather sack down no-man's-land. Not surprisingly, other discontents among the cram followed suit, so that by midnight on the Calama train, the center aisle filled with reclining bodies, and trips to the toilet at the back of the car became a test of agility and balance for all concerned.

Didn't take long for cramped quarters, bone-chilling cold, and the locomotive's crippled lumber to wear the insulation off my patience. I hid my annoyance by staring out the window Charles, the Brit, had surrendered me. I slouched into various bent postures in an attempt to capture the oblivion of sleep. When the train coasted to a stop on the moonlit *altiplano*, I sat upright and listened to remarkable rumblings coming from the direction of the engine. Sounded as if the locomotive was being uncoupled from the train, and then it sounded as though engineer and crew drove off by themselves. My fellow ticket-holders stirred briefly but didn't seem particularly upset at being stranded.

In the quiet that followed the engineer's maneuver, most passengers settled back into their seats or stretched out again on the floor. I, on the other hand, felt so mistreated I could have staged a hunger strike, that is, if the train afforded access to a dining car.

After what felt like an age, the railroad crew returned from their errand and our slow journey recommenced. Again I sought solace in the view out my window. A smattering of indifferent stars hung above silver tundra, investing me with a profound sense of futility. Beyond the stars hung darkness that never ended, and beneath them, the obsolete wagon to which I was confined staggered across barren waste like an aimless migrant. I felt the joke had gone too far, but somewhere along the line, my discomfort eased and I had the uncanny experience of living in a dream. I even came to appreciate the surreality of my predicament.

I listened to the rattle of the train, the sounds other passengers made in sleep and allowed myself to be mesmerized by the Southern Cross. Then the train came to another standstill, and the engineer uncoupled his motor yet again and headed off once more for parts unknown. I'm not sure how many times our intrepid captain repeated his hilarious routine. Longest period of abandonment occurred in broad daylight at the border crossing, where passengers languished for a six-hour stretch, during which interval, the conductor, whom I couldn't remember having seen since leaving Calama, opened a dining car, which I hadn't been aware accompanied the train. Fried chicken, boiled potatoes, and tomato salad were offered at reasonable cost for lunch, but having some months before contracted dysentery from the bill of fare prepared on a riverboat in Brazil, I reluctantly declined to partake of the meal. Instead, Charles and I played gin rummy, snacked on a bag of cookies he had on hand and a couple of oranges I'd brought along. After a couple of hours, we tired of our card game and parted company. I wandered away from the customs shack onto vacant land that

stretched for miles and, during my solitary
shuffle, ruminated on how disappointed I
was in the choo-choo ride, and how I didn't
care much for bus rides either, and how I
might as well add cheap accommodations and
forced civilities to my list of resentments.
Naturally, I questioned, too, my reason for
coming to South America in the first place.
Something about living in the moment, I
vaguely recalled, which rounded out to the
best April fool's joke ever.

3 Apr. 00, Uyuni, Bolivia. This morning, I
awoke groggy, unmotivated, and disillusioned
with my lot in life. I could only hope that
once I got out of bed, my sorry outlook would
improve. The room I'd slept in was clean and
came equipped with a comfortable bed and a
private shower. What more did a man need to
conjecture that things were looking up?

After shaving and brushing my teeth, I
located a second-story restaurant along
the town's main square and ordered ham and
scrambled eggs. In that Charles and the other
foreigners on the train were nowhere to be
seen, I assumed they had risen at a much
earlier hour. Probably they were out on the
Salar already (Uyuni's main claim to fame),
which I planned to visit too, otherwise what
the hell was I doing in this frontier outpost?
Good question. Maybe if Charles were around,
he could have enlightened me. Or maybe, if
I didn't have such rotten timing, or if I
weren't so self-engrossed, the question never
would have come up.

Over dregs of tea, I opened my guidebook to
the Uyuni section and perused passages that
had piqued my interest formerly. While I read
again about hotels, hostels, and residences

in town that catered to foreigner travelers, agencies offering tours to the area's geological attractions and noted other bits of information that might have proved useful had I been on the ball, a discreet, wavy-haired gent dressed in a smart white-collared shirt and dark trousers emerged from the restaurant kitchen and stepped to my table to clear away my empty plate. The man's reappearance signaled that it was time for me to pay my bill, tuck the guidebook into the rear pouch on my utility vest, and be on my way. Where to was my problem, not the waiter's. Okay, okay, but surely, he wouldn't object if I smoked a cigarette before making an exit.

Unprompted, my eye looped back to the beginning of a paragraph I'd just read, and the words blurred before me. I saw myself wandering among old train engines in whose company I felt strangely at peace. There was no accounting for my transport among the locomotives but no reason given why I should be elsewhere either. For a while, contentment enveloped me like a blanket, and I felt so reassured that when my chin fell to my chest, I deeply regretted waking.

The world I'd just left reminded me of other dreamscapes I'd chanced upon before, other instances of happiness that lasted only so long as I slept. Usually these sorts of dreams involved a woman though, a strange and wonderful lady who lived in a forest cottage, and who admitted me to her cozy dwelling with gladness beyond comprehension. Why hadn't the lady appeared just now? Probably I hadn't slept long enough for her to show up again. Usually in such dreams, I lingered with the lady for a time and then ended up trying to make my way back to the cottage where she lived and to which I'd promised to return. I never did trace my way back to her in those dreams, though I always woke up feeling grateful to have shared her company one more time. On this occasion, however, I didn't get to visit the magical lady at all before returning to the restaurant in Uyuni, whose bank of second-story windows set gentle light on tables draped in burgundy, whose brass lamp fixtures adorned veneer walls, and whose lonely emptiness allowed me to appreciate how great it was to have just been happy nonetheless. As the sensation faded, I looked back at my guidebook and discovered that before nodding off, I'd been reading about a railroad boneyard located west of town.

Now, I'm not a superstitious man, nor the least bit receptive to guidance from other worlds, but as I rose from my chair and slipped payment for breakfast under an ashtray containing a cigarette butt I couldn't remember stubbing out, and made for the top of a staircase I couldn't remember climbing, there swam in my brain half a notion that out west of town lay my destiny.

A wide, unpaved street with grubby buildings squatted to either flank ran parallel to the tracks at the south end of the *pueblo*. Metal lamp poles with bifurcated necks filed down its gritty median. I walked by a "*casa en venta Tf.* 6413" where a prepubescent boy straddling a bicycle with a crossbar too high for his crotch watched a pair of younger girls sift dust between their fingers in a dirt patch sunken among broken sidewalk cobbles. A life-sized statue of a miner with one arm busted off, displayed atop a five-foot-tall pedestal, constituted the main adornment of

269

the avenue. At sight of the heroic worker, I imagined a chorus of burly men dressed in long-sleeved puffy shirts, knee-high boots, and baggy trousers would soon enter the scene and mournfully intone in baritone the melody of a Russian folk refrain.

At the end of the street, fantasy met reality at the entrance to a drab military post. Since no road veered right or left, I assumed passage through the compound was common practice hereabouts. A young man of truculent demeanor, however, bearing a rifle at port arms, blocked my way. I began to explain to the guard why I needed to walk through his fort, but for my trouble received an apoplectic response, which even if unwarranted, put me on the defensive. The swarthy youth ignored subsequent groveling on my part, went on instead with a vexed tirade I could barely follow, until in conclusion, he shot me a look that might have been a holdover from former duty on a firing squad. Needless to say, I mumbled a timorous apology and backed off.

Convinced I was lucky to have escaped arrest (reason for detention not given), I strode briskly past the fort's left-corner sentry tower and scrambled up a rail bank that passed beyond the compound's crenellated wall. I pursued retreating cross ties for several yards with gaze averted until curiosity got the best of me and then dared peek in the direction of a second tower located at the rear corner of the stronghold. The uniformed duo stationed under its flat overhang scouted my approach as if expecting me to mount an assault. Or so it seemed until I got a grip, for shortly thereafter, I realized those elevated faces looked less intimidating than bored to death. "Sorry for you," I mumbled under my breath and waved to the hapless pair. Then, because the guards ignored my greeting, "As you like," I muttered and added for my own amusement, "all said and done, better you than me."

Against low-slung hills about a quarter mile beyond the *ejercito*'s regional defense sprawled a lateral extension of rusted iron. I proceeded at a more relaxed pace toward the wrangle of railroad castoffs and, while gazing about the surrounding terrain, spotted a trio of crane-sized birds that glided across bright sky to the south. Blush of the aviators' pinions and the hooked droop of their beaks made identification of the species a simple academic endeavor. The flamingos flapped their wings a couple of times before drifting on, not so gracefully as herons, but surely earning a nod over geese. When the exotic birds diminished to mere specs, I turned back toward "*Cemeterio de los trenes*."

At first, the area appeared more or less as my dream had portended. Defunct steam locomotives to be sure, but also boxcars and tank cars rested on a quarter-mile length of track disconnected from any route leading to or from the boneyard. The heaps had been dragged onto the high Andes plain and left to oxidize amid wind-swept accumulations of plastic and paper trash. Evidence of disassembly among the behemoths suggested that railroad workers trucked to the site periodically to cannibalize parts. Recalling my recent journey from Calama, I felt less peaceful in the actual boneyard than I had upon the dreamscape and, to be sure, allowed myself a moment of sweet revenge. I could devise an end no more righteous for the mechanical devils and, thus imbued with a sense of poetic justice, took a little quality time to contemplate their reduction to hapless waste. Inadvertently, I also made a discovery that had ramifications I would come to regret.

Apparently, besides being carted off for use as replacement parts, strips of railway metal were commandeered from the yard as well for construction of a fence at the near border of the wreckage. Far as I could tell, the fence had yet to be completed. Four six-foot-long sections of its framework jutted from below the bank upon which I stood, met a right-angle jag, and then ran on for another thirty feet. Unaccountably, the several pipe-supported segments broke off abruptly at the face of a metal plate planted upright in hard-packed earth. While deliberating on the puzzle presented by this barricade, I allowed my eye to drift farther on and thereby sighted several steel shipping crates clustered about with door- and window-sized openings torch-cut in their sides. White paint labeled one rusting mega-box "*PUEBLO INFERNO*" and another bore the slogan "*VIVA CHE.*"

After reading the signs, I concluded that what I had taken for a fence was in truth nothing of the sort, but one of many obstacles set up on a military training course. With the puzzle solved, I surmised that the boys back at the army base were responsible for the layout's existence. I also deduced that it was no wonder they'd developed chips on their shoulders, for being ordered to undertake the rigors of "hell village" would have put me in an equally resentful mood. In addition to physical exhaustion, I could expect to suffer painful bumps and bruises during the exercise and likely end up with lacerations on my arms and legs, if not a compound fracture to mark the occasion too.

"Better you than me," I repeated to myself and gave thanks that as a successful draft evader (three years at the university had done the trick), I'd managed to skirt the breech of common sense that characterizes army boot camp. Some patriots may consider me a wimp or a slacker for having shirked my duty, but those who do should know that not everyone was born to be a hero. No, some sorry cowards such as myself would just as soon forego guts and glory, thanks for the offer just the same.

And yet I paused.

And yet it hardly surprised me that I was tempted to countermand my convictions. Looking back on what happened, I must admit that I am subject now and again to those proverbial impulses visited upon fools south of fifty who bemoan not having made a name for themselves by taking on a worthy challenge. Thankfully, these moments generally pass uneventfully in my case, and afterward, I am pleased to reflect on how ludicrous it is to harbor regrets or backtrack on a life already lived.

On this occasion, higher wisdom failed me. "Hail, good fellows," I remember jesting under my breath, meaning to address all sad, middle-aged pretenders to fame who wait yet for a call to gird their loins and throw themselves upon a magnificent enterprise. "Hale and hearty fellows all," I went on, enamored of my wit. "Be content you've survived thus far by stealth."

And yet I knew I was about to do something stupid. As if to demonstrate that I, for

one, never harbored regrets, I slid down the
bank and stepped up to the bar. The course's
engineer should have included a ramp for
seniors at the start of the run, but due
to oversight, or due to an assumption that
older folk enjoyed better judgment, or due to
whatever, I received immediate verification
that indeed a body's strength and flexibility
deteriorate over time. It took half a dozen
tries for me to fix my waist to the crosspiece,
and it took more than one swing of my leg
to set my boot upon the rail. And then, oh
damnit anyway, I'd forgotten the teary-eyed
distress that infests a man's lower abdomen
when he accidentally racks his balls.

If not a stubborn coward (stubbornness
being one virtue that gains potency with
age), I might have let loose my grip and
dropped off the obstacle. Instead, pissed-off
as well as stubborn, I hissed and cursed
through clenched teeth while the ache in my
groin peaked.

My hands trembled as I centered my hips and
shoulders along the evil metal piece, and my
arm muscles quivered even after I rocked back
on my butt. In that my testicles could not
be situated either side of the rail without
causing further discomfort, I reconsidered
the practicality of discretion. What was I
trying to prove by means of a circus trick?
Despite what I might imagine, there was no
one in the vicinity keeping tabs on my daring.
Screw it, I concluded, smartest decision at
this pass would be to ease into a cautious
retreat. And yet. Oh Christ-bedecked-in-
olive-drab, I felt certain that if I backed
off the apparatus now, I'd never outlive the
shame.

So I bravely forced my boots under my hips, flexed my thigh muscles, and rose to a crouch. Straightening slowly at the waist, I teetered, wagged my arms back and forth to keep from tottering, and managed in the process to look like an ungainly klutz. So what? The point was to complete this farce as quickly as possible and to hell with style points. So I concentrated on the first joint along the bridge and sidestepped in its direction. Miraculously still aloft through a couple more shuffle steps, I dared to believe completion of the high-wire act was within my purview.

Funny how one moment you can be at the top or your game, and the next, fall flat on your face. On the way back to regular life, my inner left thigh whacked against the bar, my right hand jammed up to my shoulder joint, and my skull slammed against unyielding earth. For several seconds, bright glowworms darted before my eyelids, and I thought I was going to throw up.

Served me right to presume that I could match strength and agility with members of the Bolivian Army. As nausea subsided and the world about me stabilized, I propped myself on an elbow and checked for damage. Luckily, though my shoulder throbbed like a bass drum, and my leg felt numb as a frozen beef shank, there'd be no need to dial 911. Good thing, too, because it was doubtful Uyuni's city council funded emergency services.

Much relieved in learning that most my parts still functioned, I sat up and went so far as to commend myself for an honest effort. Wasn't every day I tried to kill myself and lived to tell the tale. Failure, I concluded, had a beneficial aspect. Did it really matter that my foray to glory had come a cropper? Well, sometimes a man needed to take a foolhardy risk to verify that he still had gamble. So what if he falls on his face, the aftershock proves his mettle.

I rose, tenderly massaged my inner thigh, and considered the cost of assault on other hazards. Too bad I'd just jacked myself up, or I would have lost no time rushing upon the barrier at the end of the raised track in *"pueblo inferno."* If not wounded, I would have dived through jagged windows, crawled under low-slung metal planks, and scooted across more narrow bridges.

On the other side of the metal plate, I came upon a mock-up of the entire layout. Amid piles of railroad junk stacked higher than my head, the entire set-up was represented in miniature. Here, no doubt, army captains devised ingenious battle plans. The 3-D map excited recall of an erstwhile fascination I'd had with toy soldiers and the mock campaigns I'd marshaled during formative years. Of course, the boys back at the post took the business of combat training seriously, which was fine for them in that they possessed sufficient vigor to meet its perils. Fine for them to be hard as nails; they were, after all, still capable of astounding acts of valor.

As I widened my tour of the boneyard, misgivings pursued me. The protracted line of defunct hulks stretching northward now appeared encrusted with an unsavory patina of chagrin. Cannibalized locomotives, rotting passenger cars and boxcars, stacked axle-and-wheel assemblies established a metaphor for decrepitude. Hard to believe, but somewhere along life's track, I too had arrived at uselessness. Must I admit now that relegation to the scrap heap loomed in my future too? Loomed, that is, if I hadn't been decommissioned already, if I weren't deemed already a mere curiosity hanging off the tail end of yesteryear? I wondered if anything remained of my formerly immortal self that bespoke the slightest promise.

Damn the irony of my middle age, that notwithstanding a decline in physical capacity, I retained young conceits. When asleep, I dreamed; when awake, I seized the day. But by the look of discarded railcars—heaps that would never return to service—it seemed that once I'd lost my productive edge, there was nothing left for me but banishment to a scrapheap.

Yuck, I was turning maudlin. To avoid tiresome self-pity (an emotion as enervating as it is cloying) I climbed across the couplings of a pair of tank cars situated midway down the rail line. On the other side of the tracks, I gazed upon a less despondent vista. A dozen or so llamas grazed on open flatland that fronted dun-colored hills. As I approached the critters, two of them raised their heads alertly. The pair returned my gaze as though questioning what business I had with them. When the *camelitos* determined I bore them neither benefit nor harm, they went back to foraging for grass.

I rolled a cigarette, lit it up with some difficulty, and watched the llamas munch on untroubled by the lack of grandeur in their pursuit. Excellent approach to life, I thought, and bemoaned for a while my innate disposition to reach beyond equilibrium hard-wired into lesser beasts. Then I field stripped my cigarette and rounded back toward the ghost train.

It was then a sight I had not expected to encounter at the empty southwest corner of Bolivia caught and held my attention. There was a mathematical formula written large along the cylindrical front of one idle engine. "A. Einstein" footnoted the script. Now, here was a fellow who had managed to preserve his utility beyond middle age, I mused, and resolved forthwith to examine his pronouncement.

This particular statement of elemental principle devised by the physicist proclaimed that capital letter R (with Greek subscript), when subtracted from one-half of what looked like cursive letter g (with Greek subscript), times R (standing alone), equaled eight times pi times G over C to the forth power, times T (with Greek subscript). I had no idea what Einstein described by the formula, but given the man's reputation for brilliance, I concluded that I ought to be impressed by it and mind-boggled as well. Actually I was impressed, mind-boggled and, ta-da, inspired to invent my own statement of elemental principle.

The A. Sharp formula went like this: you take the square root of m (signifying any given malcontent) divided by D (for denial), multiply the result by superfluous intent (i, a constant, to be sure), and what you get is the irony of middle age. If there had been a can of white paint handy, I would have recorded my discovery for posterity, but since I lacked the means to publicize my formula, inhabitants of planet Earth were forced to muddle along as usual without benefit of A. Sharp genius.

Soldiers manning sentry towers back at the fort paid me little mind the second time I walked by. No doubt indifference had characterized their previous attitude toward me as well; it had just taken a walk through a boneyard for me to fully recognize my inconsequence. The embarrassing incident at the gate had caused me to presume scrutiny on the part of Bolivia's military arm, though now I understood well enough that any given *m* posed no threat whatsoever to the world at large. No, I provided only an opportunity for a certain gate keeper to assert his authority as righteous defender of a nation's sovereignty. Okay then. A. Sharp might as well grant ambitious heroes the chance to feel indispensable, for all the significance he embodies otherwise.

03 Apr. 00, Uyuni, later. One more episode before I bed down. It happened in the town square at one end of which stands a clock tower, twenty feet high, beige in color with white borders and vaselike embellishments. Four circles of Roman numerals face from the top of the rectilinear spire in the four cardinal directions of the compass. North end of the walk stands a church whose twin belfries broach a wan blue sky. I remember thinking that the scene would make a stirring photograph.

The reason I mused picturesquely upon church and sky was that a little earlier, I had entered a tour agency along the strip and, while booking an excursion to the *Salar* for the next day, noticed a swimsuit calendar hanging on the office wall next to a poster depicting flamingos in flight. The juxtaposition of Miss April's seminude form with the graceful glide of pink birds struck me as goofy, and I was surprised as well that the female agent behind the desk permitted cheesecake on the premises. Turned out my confusion was the result of culture bias, however. While scouting other commercial venues in the center of town (small grocery stores, café bars, and more tour agencies), I spied skin chronograms in abundance, which, as a consequence of their ubiquity, drew no local notice. Nor did the residents of Uyuni find remarkable my appearance among them either. Though courteous and helpful, they declined to single out, with either acclaim or censure, my depiction of foreign-born beefcake, which, at any rate, recurred in Uyuni, in hardly altered guise over and over, one month to the next. Anyway, by the time I settled on a concrete bench at the center of the walk between gray-brick, one- and two-story buildings, my vision had assumed photographic framing.

Nice scene to record, I judged in studying the church, but I also decided that a camera couldn't possibly capture the square's pervasive atmosphere. Stillness of such widespread seepage rendered physical objects hereabouts in a state of suspension as though consigning them to existence in a vacuum. High altitude possibly accounted for the effect; the same thin air that stifled the flame of a butane lighter that a red-headed traveler standing across the way struck and restruck in an attempt to light his cigarette. After a half dozen attempts, the smoker succeeded in firing up his fag, took a puff, and walked off.

Another journeyman strode forward urgently from my right; to my mind, he was in a hurry to fill the space left vacant by the one departed. Emptiness swallowed the clomp of the newcomer's heavy boots; I heard footfall, but the noise lost its resonance before it reached me. It seemed suddenly as if nothing in the square reached me. Such an eerie sense of detachment invested the scene that when I nodded distractedly at the passerby, I was amazed the man proceeded but a couple paces farther on before he stopped, spun about, and started back in my direction. I watched his approach half convinced that one of us wasn't really there.

He wore a red windbreaker zipped halfway up his gray V-neck sweater. Slick black pants with zipper pockets covered his sturdy legs. He had a strong jaw and a weathered complexion, acne scars at his temples. Brown hair an inch or two in length was exposed beneath the narrow brim of his canvas hat. "You surprised to see me?" he called and scrunched his hazel eyes worriedlike. It took me a moment to understand his question, and during my delay in answering it, he chose to elaborate. "The way you were staring, I thought we'd met before."

I apologized then for my spacey gape and mumbled something about being consumed by the quiet in the square. Relaxing his shoulders, he remarked on the uncanny affect *Salar de Uyuni* had on people.

Nathan told me his name as he lowered himself to my bench. He said he'd recently completed a tour of duty as a lieutenant in the Israeli army and was trying to decide, while on holiday, whether to become a career soldier. To help him make up his mind, I could have recommended a visit to the boys at the fort. Or perhaps I might have suggested that he test his fitness for combat on the obstacle course where I had met my comeuppance. Then I figured why dampen a young man's enthusiasm for his many prospects.

At his urging, I told him how, prior to retirement, I had made my living as a mail carrier, and how on one of my routes in a Denver barrio I had picked up some Spanish and developed a lasting interest in Latin culture. He asked if I were married and if I had children and expressed neither approval nor disapproval when I answered no on both accounts. It might have been interesting to discuss my regret for submitting all those years to the tedium of postal work or to lament my lack of emotional stamina when it came to the caring-and-sharing deal. On the other hand, who wants to sound pathetic to a stranger?

"You're right about the quiet," Nathan said as he made to leave.

"Must be the *Salar's* influence," I answered glibly in reference to his earlier mention of the salt pan.

"You must go," he said and stood up. I assured him that I had every intention of doing just that. "Be prepared for an epiphany," he advised.

"Strong word, don't you think?" I demurred.

"Strong place," he answered before walking away.

And so I'm off to bed with something to look forward to in the morning.

4 Apr. 00, Uyuni. The *Salar* is a great white sea that stretches in all directions without break or contour and thus provides all the proof one needs to assert with the utmost

confidence that the world is flat. I took the ninety-kilometer trip to *Isla de pescado* in a four-wheel-drive excursion wagon accompanied by a Swiss couple. We traveled under a clear blue sky. When I asked our helmsman how he navigated the featureless terrain, his wrap-around shades lingered long on my face. I thought he should watch the road, but of course, there was no danger of collision and we weren't following a road in any case. In answer to my question, the bony-faced twenty-some-year-old pointed to the horizon, and for the first time since leaving town, I viewed the tops of blue mountains located at a distance I could not begin to estimate. Patches of snow so tiny that I might have mistaken them for lint motes stuck to my corneas dotted faraway peaks.

"We are driving on ice," the woman in the backseat said, and I cranked around to have a look at her. She was pretty in a petite way: lank dark hair covered her ears and drew attention to her graceful neck. A mauve jacket and brown cuffed trousers hung loosely on her slender frame. Her husband was a fellow of about my age, outfitted in khaki and a warp-brimmed bush hat. He had the reserved, urbane air of either an artist or an academic.

"Let's hope we don't fall through," I answered the woman, and we exchanged friendly smiles.

On the white tract before us appeared a single dark spot, which grew to the size of a one-room hovel so quickly it seemed to materialize out of nothing. Miguel took his foot off the accelerator, and we coasted to a stop before the building. He said we could buy food, water, and sunglasses inside.

Possibly Miguel had a business arrangement with the owner of the store because he seemed a bit disappointed when none of his riders expressed interest in shopping for supplies. We exited the vehicle, nevertheless, to have a look around, and I noticed the building was constructed of salt blocks that had turned greenish-brown since being stacked and mortared. The edifice had a thatch roof and a pair of windows reflecting blue sky either side of its dark entrance. Two small tables standing in the salt yard cast shadows the color and density of black lacquer. A portly man sat on a narrow bench butted to the shack's front wall. He wore a padded red vest over a long-sleeved flannel shirt, and a dark ski mask covered his face. In the sixty-degree weather, his hood struck me as unnecessary until I realized the man wasn't wearing it for warmth but as protection against the fierce solar radiation reflected off the pan. Out here, light assaulted a body from all angles like a billion tiny flecks of shattered glass.

We drove by a mining operation where men in ski masks used scoop shovels to pile salt into several lengthy rows of perfectly symmetrical chest-high cones. A yellow dump truck stood on the far side of the harvest field. There might have been a front-end loader somewhere in the area, but I didn't see it.

Some distance beyond the mine, we pulled up beside a single-story hotel, got out of the tour wagon, and wandered about the premises. Again, salt blocks had been employed as construction material even in the making of the hotel's rectilinear furniture. To me, the chairs did not appear comfortable, nor did the slab beds, though the latter came equipped with foam-pad mattresses. I suppose the novelty of the establishment enticed some tourists to stay the night.

Humming again across the plain at 70K per hour, I finally received full impact of the *Salar*'s striking singularity. My normal sense of sequential motion took a powder. Not so much as a fence post could be seen within a thirty-mile radius, and staring into the pure white emptiness, I had this odd notion of existing before the world began, or of continuing to exist after it ended. No one in the wagon spoke as a single black spot, riding atop a shimmering drop of mercury, cruised into view from our left. The projectile traced a level line in front of us until it reached an unseen limit to its trajectory and abruptly vanished. I turned to the driver and asked what had just happened. He knitted his brow as if addressed by an idiot. When another quarklike particle popped into view, I realized that from its locale, our wagon must have appeared also to ride upon a drop of quicksilver and would soon slip from sight.

At my request, Miguel pulled to a stop. I had remembered Nathan's admonition from the day before and wanted a moment to come to grips with epiphany.

Outside the vehicle, Jean donned a pair of aviator shades, and Carol put on *gafas* with pink plastic frames pointed at the corners. Sun glare stung my bare eyes and began to bake my facial skin crisp. Still, I had half a mind to remove my clothing and expose my entire body to the unremitting splendor of the pan. The soles of my boots scraped grit as I drifted away from the wagon, and looking down, I discerned at my feet wrinkles on the salt table that took the shape of pentagons.

Every which way around me were uncountable five-sided figures, unvarying in size, stretched out endlessly, making it appear as though I'd stumbled upon an endless plane that reached out to no place distinguishable from where I was at already. Laughter broke from my chest. All my life I'd maintained the conviction that beyond every yonder lay another yonder different from the one left behind. But the *Salar* rendered this assumption, which I'd taken for a basic truth about the physical world up till now, ridiculous. Out here on the pan, it seemed just as plausible that I was everywhere at once.

Carol laughed too when she slipped up beside me and took my hand. What's this? I wondered as my quasi-religious Euclidean notions gave way to her solid presence. When I glanced toward Carol's husband who gabbed with Miguel back by the wagon, her lips widened. "I should say something important," she offered. Yes, you probably should, I thought as her fingers stroked my palm. "We're going to be friends," she said. I held steady, pretending to be not the least bit disconcerted by her prophecy. Her other hand touched my arm as she leaned closer. We were definitely sharing an intimate moment, which made no sense whatsoever. Knock it off, I almost said, but before I did, Jean signaled that Miguel was ready to roll. Carol released my hand and led the way back to our transport.

Isla de pescado sprouted on the horizon, initially about the size and shape of a blackened avocado seed. As we drew near, the seed swelled sideways and lifted onto a glutinous indigo mirror. Miguel identified the dark shape as the only fish left in the lake. He went on to explain that following rainstorms, a large sheet of water formed in front of the island and thus occasioned a reflection that completed the bottom half of a giant bass. No rain today though; the blue mirror below the *isla* produced nothing other than an amorphous shimmer.

As we approached, the shiny mirage compressed, and the landmass above it dropped its shroud. I made out patches of vegetation that mottled a quarter-mile-long protrusion of brown rock. Miguel steered around the island's thinner end and parked among other tour wagons. Up close, the island's nut-colored humps resembled large heads of breaded cauliflower. I couldn't get over the contradiction *Isla de pescado* perpetrated, for where there should have been wavelets lapping against its shores, grainy white hardpan crumbled instead. Stepping down from the wagon, I experienced a sensation akin to vertigo. The salt surface of the lake held steady, but I wasn't wholly convinced it'd support my weight.

Miguel lifted our craft's rear hatch and Jean thumbed the strap of a nylon duffel over his shoulder. "Are you hungry?" Carol asked me from across the hood. Sweet music and promise played on her pretty face. Carol's come-hither act reminded me of encounters with my perfect dream girl, but being awake, I could foresee no end of complications were I to accept her invitation. Then Jean chimed in that they'd brought plenty to eat and would not permit me to decline his wife's offer. I felt sorry for the man. Seemed he had no idea of his spouse's penchant for touchy-feely games with chance acquaintances. Guy was paying the price for marrying a knockout fifteen years his junior.

Carol led the way past a gathering of drivers and tourists who had settled upon open ground above shore. She followed a crease between humps of stone to a dilapidated rock shelter whose rigid front wall supported yet a crosspiece over its entrance.

"Not here," Jean objected when she pulled up.

"Where then?" she responded testily.

He pointed right along the ridge we'd mounted. Cactus columns four- to ten-feet tall grew at random interval either side of the rise. Numerous clumps of knee-high bramble poked out from between jumbles of rock. At the top of the hill, the land widened and gave a panoramic view of white and blue emptiness.

Jean walked around me, past Carol, and guided us to his choice of a picnic spot. As his wife came next to him, he slipped the bag he carried off his shoulder and thrust it at her.

"I hope you like what I've packed," she said, ignoring Jean's peevish behavior and addressing her guest.

"I'm sure I will," I answered.

Jean rolled his eyes as he sat down on a nearby rock. There was a sort of surly struggle going on between the two, which I chose to overlook. Their conduct brought to mind bouts I'd engaged in with a female friend some years ago. Our time together had lasted longer than it should have, and since we'd parted, I'd come to hypothesize that most meaningful relationships outlast good intentions.

Seemed to me Jean and Carol weren't so far removed from voicing those usual assurances that transpire at parting of the ways, those mutual assertions that the breakup is no one's fault. I could have been wrong though, for

I know nothing of partnerships that devolve into marriage.

At any rate, Carol spread a green-and-white checkered cloth on sandy ground and arranged upon it sliced ham wrapped in butcher paper, a wedge of yellow cheese, three tomatoes, an onion, and a small can of olives. To her still life, she added hard-crust rolls, yogurt, hard-boiled eggs, a jar of mustard, oranges, sweet bread, bottled water, and a liter of red Chilean wine.

"Did I forget anything?" she chortled at her husband.

"Glasses," he responded dryly.

With a smirk, Carol produced a short sleeve of plastic cups from the bottom of the bag.

"What? No candles?" I quipped, and both of them eyed me as if I were daft.

While Carol made sandwiches, Jean opened the wine with the corkscrew attachment on his Swiss Army knife. When each of us had a glass of *tinto* in hand, he proposed a toast to *alegría*. There was a cynical edge to his pledge, but perhaps he meant to sound more genial than peevish.

Well, I for one was ready to promote geniality, even the conditional kind. In answer to his toast, I proposed that what's done is done, no matter what, so we might as well enjoy ourselves.

Jean asked me then to specify what I had to be glad about.

"Simply a joy to be here," I responded brightly and slipped into a recount of my enthralling experience at our penultimate stop on the pan. Again I envisioned being everywhere at once, or nowhere different from where I'd always been, which presented a likely recipe for contentment, in my opinion.

Jean nodded blandly, and Carol winked at me. Whatever long-term dispute they had going would be set aside, at least during lunch, I hoped.

For a while, Carol and I made blithe talk under a bright sun while Jean sat there like a man with bummer days in mind. After finishing a sandwich, he got to his feet and wandered off toward the far end of the island. "Wasn't I right?" Carol gushed after her husband had slipped from hearing.

"You surely were," I answered, comforted to know that Jean remained in eyesight.

She rose, shuffled to my side, lowered herself against me, and placed a hand on my knee. "He wouldn't mind if we became closer friends," she purred.

My chest constricted. I wasn't about to take the wife's word concerning her husband's sangfroid, and besides, even if she spoke the truth, this was no predicament for a coward to be in. "What's his angle?" I contested.

"He's a complicated person."

"I'm not the one to save you from complications."

"You don't understand," she tittered. "I appreciate complexity in people."

Okay, so why involve this simple soul in your shenanigans?

"Where are you staying in Uyuni?" she prodded.

I eased up to my feet as casually as I could and took a step back.

"Are you going to disappoint me?" she pouted.

"Maybe things will be different in another lifetime," I muttered, for besides lacking guts in dicey social situations, I'm not very suave either.

Jean returned soon after, and there occurred an exchange of looks between husband and wife that unnerved me. In addition to their domestic spat, these two had something shifty going on between them, that was having an effect on me. As they calmly gathered and bagged leftovers from our picnic, damn if I didn't blame myself for the sense of failure that befell our threesome.

Leaving the island, I riveted my gaze to the windshield, preferring a view of supercharged monotony to eye contact with the pair of charmers in the backseat. I guessed they judged me a callow bumpkin but I tried not to care.

"It is very quiet here," Carol said after we'd been rolling for about ten minutes.

What'd she expect, recitation of the Gettysburg Address?

"I have never been anywhere so quiet," she went on, pleading for a response.

Okay, so maybe I was being unfair; she didn't sound vindictive. Whatever crazy game she and her husband were playing was none of my affair. Long as they left me out of it, I would remain civil.

"It's because the *Salar* produces no echo," Jean answered his wife.

"And the air's too thin for sound to carry," I added.

"Good point," Jean opined.

"It is as quiet as a cemetery," Carol appended to the theme she'd initiated.

Since I hadn't thought of that comparison before, her remark set some usually dormant neurons firing in my brain. The *Salar* would make excellent burial ground, I theorized: cadavers entombed in salt might be preserved indefinitely. Furthermore, what better

memorial for the departed than a vast, radiant
plain where time evened out and settled into
a state of utter passivity. Survivors of the
dead might journey to this featureless tract
to remember their loved ones and to reconcile
their own troubled pasts. What's done is done
they might assure themselves on the pan, for
out here, all disturbing echoes of former
transgression dissipate. Just imagine . . .

"What would it be like to live in a world
that's already over?" I proposed aloud.

"Pardon?" Jean called above the drone of
the wagon motor.

"Yeah, what would it be like?" I repeated
for his benefit.

"My English . . ." he began.

"Let's suppose everything in the world
has already happened," I suggested. "What
then?"

"I don't understand."

"Well, it's easy. Forget the future. Think
of all events as having happened already. In
fact, it's not that difficult to imagine such
a world since whatever happens is over as soon
as it happens in this one too. Therefore,
what is there to be upset about?"

"Are you upset?" Carol sounded concerned
for me.

I looked at her. "No, I don't believe I
am."

"I worry about the future," Jean
confessed.

"You shouldn't though. The future's
past."

"Then why do I worry about what will happen,
or more often, what will not happen?"

"Relax, man. Every event you can think of
is based on nothing other than a memory. We

don't remember all that has taken place, but that's no reason to become agitated."

"How droll," Jean said, although I was fairly sure he meant to say that I was off my rocker.

At my invitation, the Swiss joined me for dinner. We had a genial chat in the restaurant off the square where I'd eaten breakfast the previous day. A candle in a green glass bowl glowed at the center of our table, and Carol's face assumed a lovely aspect in the subdued illumination conjured by the candle's flame. She'd given up trying to enchant me, which was good. As I'd noted before, she had the makings of a terrific dream girl if ever she agreed to be a mere figment of my imagination.

During our conversation, Jean mentioned the three dead flamingos Miguel had located on the *Salar* during our return ride to Uyuni. Someone armed with a shotgun had committed a triple murder. I voiced recall of the birds I'd spotted at the boneyard the day before and hypothesized that they might be the same ones that had met their demise this afternoon. If so, given my recent philosophical conclusions, they were already dead when I spotted them in flight, though how could I know they were dead until memory disclosed their tragic end? Even in death, they had spread their blush wings to proclaim an eternal, animate essence. And although Miguel had assured us that the killings would be reported to the appropriate authorities, I was yet saddened by the loss. Memory, I observed for my dinner guests, often occasions sorrow, despite there being nothing anyone can do to revoke what has come to pass.

Jean made no comment following my story, and Carol merely asked if we should order another bottle of wine.

Outside Uyuni—

I write in my notebook alone in my room at the hostel. A metal-framed window next to the small desk where I sit overlooks a concrete courtyard with a sky roof. Night has fallen.
I write:

> pentagonal   enhancements   of
>   salt's molecular scheme
> crease the granular surface of a
>   white inland sea
> creeping eon by eon up the scales
>   of a petrified fish.

A sudden explosion jarred the ballpoint from my hand. It was followed by a second loud blast, which I feared was set off at the military base. My first thought was that an unwary passerby had given the tense young man at the gate sufficient justification to open fire. Then I worried that upheaval had commenced in Uyuni, blood flowed in the streets, and crazed men at arms were soon to discover my hideout.

Stepping outside the door to my room, I placed empty palms atop a waist-high balcony wall that ran along three sides of the hostel's upper floor. I prayed that when the mob rushed in, they would see I was unarmed and accept my surrender.

Silence occupied the dimly lit space below. I wondered if I should venture outside the building to learn more about the disturbance, or if I best keep to cover within its sturdy shell. While I contemplated the mealy sop of my character, unhurried footsteps echoed from the tiled stairwell at the far end of the second-story walk. A man with dark hair and coarse features climbed out of the hollow and sauntered in my direction. He exhibited not the slightest concern when a third explosion went off.

"*¿Qué pasa?*" I demanded anxiously as the fellow removed a key from his trouser pocket.

The man regarded me for a moment and then drifted nearer. He explained that residents of Uyuni were launching rockets to celebrate their soccer team's victory in La Paz.

I breathed a sigh of relief.

"*Nada grave,*" my informant added kindly.

Returning to my room, I took a pull on the bottle of beer left standing next to my open notebook. After a second gulp of lager, my nerves began to settle.

I caught the day's entry up to the present and then decided to scribble a few more lines.

> The fish swims only in a memory
>   of fish,
> and memory dies in a mirror of
>   memory.
> Take heart.
> All dissolve into a blue
>   shimmer
> that sinks beneath uniform
>   ripples of gritty salt.

I released the pen, hesitated, picked it up again.

Nada grave.

I add now and promise to keep close my neighbor's message of assurance no matter what has transpired.

.

Edwards Brothers, Inc.
Thorofare, NJ USA
March 9, 2012